CALCULATED RISKS

An InCryptid Novel

SEANAN McGUIRE

D1012812

DAW BOOKS, INC.

DONALD A. WOLLHEIM, FOUNDER

1745 Broadway, New York, NY 10019

ELIZABETH R. WOLLHEIM
SHEILA E. GILBERT
PUBLISHERS

www.dawbooks.com

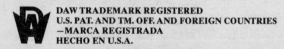

DAW Books presents the finest in urban fantasy from Seanan McGuire:

Coming soon from DAW Books

Praise for the InCryptid novels:

"The only thing more fun than an October Daye book is an InCryptid book. Swift narrative, charm, great world-building . . . all the McGuire trademarks."

—Charlaine Harris, #1 *New York Times* bestselling author

"Seanan McGuire's *Discount Armageddon* is an urban fantasy triple threat—smart and sexy and funny. The Aeslin mice alone are worth the price of the book, so consider a cast of truly original characters, a plot where weird never overwhelms logic, and some serious kickass world-building as a bonus."

—Tanya Huff, bestselling author of *The Wild Ways*

"McGuire's InCryptid series is one of the most reliably imaginative and well-told sci-fi series to be found, and she brings all her considerable talents to bear on [*Tricks for Free*]. . . . McGuire's heroine is a brave, resourceful and sarcastic delight, and her intrepid comrades are just the kind of supportive and snarky sidekicks she needs."

—*RT Book Reviews (top pick)*

"A joyous romp that juggles action, magic, and romance to great effect." —*Publishers Weekly*

"*That Ain't Witchcraft* tells the kind of story that all series should be so lucky to have: one with world-bending ramifications that still feels so deeply personal that you don't question if this could have been someone else's book to narrate. McGuire has honed her craft over a decade-plus of writing, and if you call yourself a sci-fi or fantasy fan, yet haven't picked her work up, you're doing yourself a disservice." —Culturess

"*Discount Armageddon* is a quick-witted, sharp-edged look at what makes a monster monstrous, and at how closely our urban fantasy protagonists walk—or dance—that line. The pacing never lets up, and when the end comes, you're left wanting more. I can't wait for the next book!" —C. E. Murphy, author of *Raven Calls*

For Chris.

Thanks for still tolerating me after all these years.

Price Family Tree

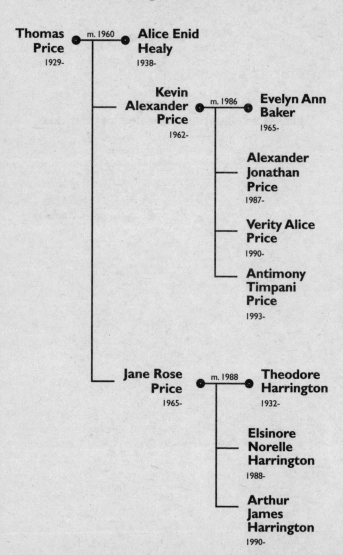

Baker Family Tree

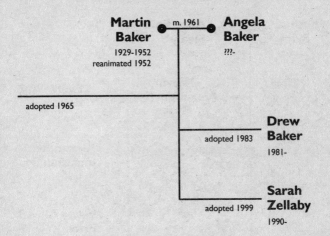

Martin Baker
1929-1952
reanimated 1952

m. 1961

Angela Baker
???-

adopted 1965

Drew Baker
1981-
adopted 1983

Sarah Zellaby
1990-
adopted 1999

Memory, noun:

1. The ability to retain and review facts, events, impressions; to recall or recognize previous experiences.

Delete, noun:

1. To strike out or to remove.

2. Cancel, erase, expunge.

3. See also "lethe." Not to be confused with "lethal."

Prologue

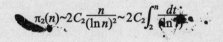

$$\pi_2(n) \sim 2C_2 \frac{n}{(\ln n)^2} \sim 2C_2 \int_2^n \frac{dt}{(\ln t)^2}$$

"As long as you're still breathing, there's a chance. There are surprisingly few things in this world that can't be taken back."
—Mary Dunlavy

A small survivalist compound about an hour's drive east of Portland, Oregon

Nineteen years ago

"NO." THE DARK-HAIRED LITTLE girl clutched her seat-belt like it was a lifeline, shaking her head hard enough that her pigtails bounced wildly, flicking across her eyes and obscuring her expression. That was fine: Angela wouldn't have been able to read the nuances of Sarah's feelings in her face even if she'd been able to see it clearly. Being a non-receptive member of a naturally telepathic species had forced her to get better at reading facial expressions than most cuckoos, who had the neural capability but never developed the skill. Why bother, when it was so much easier to just skim someone's thoughts and know exactly what they were trying to convey?

Why bother, when most cuckoos didn't actually care about the feelings of others in the first place? Being "better" at something didn't mean actually being *good* at it, and since Sarah tended to assume anyone around her could pick up her feelings from broadcast alone,

"What are you feeling?" was a common question in the Baker household. Angela was doing her best to raise Sarah to be a thoughtful, compassionate little girl, and to be fair, Sarah's nature lent itself well to being polite and caring and interested in the people around her, but most of the cuckoo children Angela had encountered had been like that. They were as sweet and sociable and occasionally horrible as human children. Something changed in them around puberty, turning them into monsters.

Whatever it was, she was determined that it wasn't going to happen to Sarah. Not to *her* little girl. She hadn't been intending to be a mother again after Evelyn and Drew were grown and happy in their adult lives, but when the world had dropped a cuckoo child in her lap, she'd found herself both unwilling and unable to refuse. Sarah needed a family who could understand her and give her the best chance at a good life, and at the end of the day, Angela and Martin were in a position to be that family. That was the only thing that mattered.

That, and finding a way to avoid Sarah growing into the homicidal impulses their species seemed heir to. Angela assumed those impulses were somehow tied to their telepathy. She was the only cuckoo she knew of who was non-receptive to the thoughts of others; she could project, but she couldn't receive. She was also the only adult cuckoo she knew of who had never tried to kill anyone. Being able to view the minds around them as if they were open books had to make it very difficult for cuckoo children to make friends, and without friends to keep them anchored to society, maybe they were just having a normal teenage response to raging hormones and changing bodies.

Not that she thought most teenagers were secretly yearning to kill everyone around them and salt the ashes, but it was a theory, if nothing else.

Evelyn wasn't biologically a cuckoo—she was as human as the day is long. But she'd been adopted by a cuckoo, and raised in a house with a cuckoo, and in the process, she had developed a certain bright resistance to the constant aura of "you know me, you love me, you would die to make me smile" projected by most cuckoos. Even her learned resistance wouldn't have been enough to make it safe to bring Sarah around Evie's children, but Evelyn had married a man named Kevin Price.

Kevin was kind, friendly, a little distractable, and most importantly of all, a descendant of Frances Brown, the woman who had been the personal nightmare of every cuckoo in North America from the moment she'd first crossed paths with them back in 1931 until her death in 1945. For some reason, Frances Brown had been resistant—although not quite immune—to cuckoo influence. She could fight off their memory alterations. She could hear their telepathic commands without feeling any need to obey them.

And her descendants had inherited her resistance. When Kevin had met Evelyn, it had been because he'd been investigating reports of a cuckoo in the area who was suspected of preying on local families. Instead, he'd stumbled onto the Bakers, a stable, nuclear family that just happened to be made up of members of four entirely different species. He'd been surprised but pleasant about it, and once he'd established to his own satisfaction that Angela wasn't telepathically holding her family prisoner, he'd run off with her daughter, taking her to Portland to settle down and have two daughters—and a son—of her own, all of whom were better equipped to shrug off cuckoo influence than the human norm.

If Sarah was going to make friends without manipulating their minds, she was going to do it here. Now it was just a matter of convincing her to get out of the car.

Sarah had been excited about the trip while they were still in Ohio, talking animatedly about seeing the three cousins she'd already met and meeting the other two. She'd chattered about how wonderful it was going to be to see Verity again the whole time she was packing, and how she was going to be best friends with all five of her cousins. She'd been excited enough that she'd even left room for clothing between her math workbooks and the various field guides to bugs and birds and reptiles that were native to Oregon but not found in Ohio.

Her excitement had started to fade at the airport, where she was had been bombarded from all sides with strange minds, some of them thinking things she wasn't equipped to deal with. She'd gone from bouncing along at Angela's side to clinging tightly to her hand and refusing to be parted from her for more than a few seconds, flinching away from the thoughts of the people around them.

If she hadn't looked so incredibly much like Angela— all cuckoos were virtually identical, which made it easy for them to pass as mother and daughter—Sarah's growing distress might have made it difficult to get through security. Angela couldn't deflect negative attention as easily as Sarah would eventually be able to, couldn't take the temperature of a room and know when she needed to step in. But they'd reached their gate with plenty of time to buy Sarah a bottle of V8 and some cheese crisps before their flight, and she had almost calmed down by the time they boarded.

The flight itself had been peaceful. Sarah had settled quietly in her window seat, filling out a math workbook and munching cheese crisps. One of the flight attendants had come back to give her a pair of honorary pilot's wings, but as she'd been doing that for all the children, Angela hadn't become overly concerned that Sarah was being shown favoritism because she was changing the minds around her. Angela had actually started to think this would be okay.

And then the plane had touched down, and the thought of seeing her cousins had become abruptly very real in Sarah's mind, and all hell had broken loose. She'd been sobbing and promising to be good by the time Angela had carried her off the plane into the terminal, struggling a little under the combined weight of a child, her own carry-on bag, and Sarah's heavily laden back-pack.

Fortunately, the flight crew was used to children having meltdowns, and given that Sarah was sobbing about being scared to see her cousins because they weren't going to like her, no one had called security. Angela had calmed her as best she could, then led her to the baggage claim and the car rental desk so they could continue their journey.

It would have been better for her to use cash and buy a beater car from the local personal ads, something she could leave behind for Kevin and Ted to strip for parts when she took Sarah back to Ohio. But "better" wasn't always the same thing as "practical," and much as she knew her son-in-law would hate having a traceable rental car parked on his property for a week, it would be worse trying to go through the delicate dance of under-the-table vehicle acquisition while shepherding a crying child. Sarah had been all cried out by the time she'd been strapped into the car, and had ridden quietly for the roughly two hours it took Angela to navigate out of the airport, across the city, and onto the optimistically-named "roads" leading to the family compound.

And all that had stopped now that they were at their destination. "I *won't*," she said, voice peaking just below a wail. Something pushed against Angela's temples, an almost physical pressure. She sighed.

"You know you can't manipulate me that way, Sarah, and it's rude to even try when someone is your friend," she said, and leaned over to unbuckle Sarah's belt. "We came all this way so you could see your cousins, and meet the two you haven't met yet." Arthur and Elsinore were Kevin's sister's children, half-human and half-Lilu. They were still descended from Frances Healy. Whatever protected her descendants would protect them, too.

Sarah sniffled, but she didn't push again, just balled herself tight against the car door, making it impossible to open the door without sending her tumbling onto the gravel driveway.

Angela stifled another sigh. She'd thought she was past these times and tantrums when Drew graduated from high school and went into the world to seek his fortune, whatever that meant. Now she was right back at the beginning, or close enough as to make no difference.

"They know we're here, Sarah. We have to get out of the car."

"How?"

"Kevin has cameras everywhere on the property. He knew as soon as we turned down the road that brought us here."

Sarah sniffled and lifted her head. "That was a mile ago."

"Everything inside the ring of 'no trespassing' signs belongs to your sister and her family," said Angela. "They like their privacy because they have some pretty special people living with them," although "living" was a generous way to describe Mary and Rose, both of whom were definitely dead, "and they don't want anyone finding out or getting into trouble."

Sarah sat up a bit more. "Special like us?"

"Not exactly like us. There aren't any other cuckoos here. But your Uncle Theodore is a Lilu, and his children are half-Lilu, so they're a little bit like us. They're empaths. Do you know what that means?"

Sarah gave her a withering look that even an ordinary cuckoo would have been able to interpret as scorn. Angela swallowed her smile. "Of *course*. I'm not a *baby*. They feel other people's feelings."

"And their own, and they can influence what other people are feeling, just by thinking about it. They don't hear words the way you do, but feelings can be just as powerful if you know how to interpret them." Something Sarah would get better at doing if she spent time with people she couldn't influence, like her cousins.

"Oh." Sarah wiped her eyes with the back of her hand, keeping a death grip on the seatbelt with her other hand. "I still don't want to go inside."

"Why not?"

"I'm tired. I want to go home and sleep."

"We'd have to take another plane to get home. We don't have a hotel room. We're supposed to sleep here tonight."

"In a house with other people?" Sarah's alarm grew again. "What if I hurt them?"

"They have special rooms warded against all sorts of things, like telepathy. If you sleep in one of them, you won't be able to hurt anyone." Angela unfastened her own seatbelt. "Come on, Sarah. Be my brave girl. Let's go inside."

Sarah looked uncertain. Angela opened her car door. Maybe she'd have to dump the girl out on the driveway after all.

As if they'd been waiting for someone in the car to move first, the door of the house burst open and a swarm of children came pouring out. The one in the lead was very blonde, very fast, and roughly Sarah's age, followed by an older girl with hair a few shades paler, who somehow managed to make a flat-out run look like a saunter. Verity and Elsinore. Alex was close on their heels, and Antimony was barreling along behind him, her eagerness not quite compensating for her shorter legs. At the rear of the pack was a smaller dark-haired boy who looked almost as if he was there under duress. Arthur.

"Grandma! Grandma!" howled Verity as she approached, her voice carrying farther than any of the others. "You came to see us! Mom says you're not supposed to spoil us, but I think it's okay if you want to spoil us a little!"

"Of course it is, I'm your grandmother!" Angela slid out of the car and caught Verity as she barreled up, swinging her into an embrace. "Oh, you are the spitting image of your mother at your age. She was a little hellcat, too. I can't believe she has to contend with three of you."

Elsinore stepped around Angela's legs and peered into the car, eyes fixing on Sarah. She raised one hand in a wave.

"Hi," she said. "I'm Elsie. You're Sarah. Ms. Angela says you're a cuckoo like her. I'm a succubus like my grandma. That means I feel your feelings, and you feel real scared right now. Why? We're your cousins. We're not anything to be scared of."

Sarah blinked slowly at her. "Why do you call Mom 'Ms. Angela' instead of 'Grandma'?" she finally asked.

"She's not my grandma, even though I wish she were," said Elsie. "My mom is Verity's dad's sister, so we're cousins, but we don't all have the same grandparents. We both have Grandma Alice, though. She's the best. She makes cookies and lets us sharpen her knives."

"Oh." Sarah bit her lip. "I don't have any grandmas. Just Mom."

"Oh. That must be hard. I bet you can share Grandma Alice. She likes grandkids." Alex and Antimony had joined Verity in flocking around Angela's legs, pulling on her shirt and yelling at her at the same time. Elsie beckoned for Artie to come closer. "I have a brother. Do you want to meet him?"

"Do I have a choice?"

"I didn't get a choice about having a brother, so nope." Elsie grinned. "Artie, this is Sarah. She's our new cousin."

"Oh," said Artie. "Um. Hi."

"Um, hi," said Sarah. She smiled shyly, and the world was different, in the way it only ever can be for children meeting the people who will be important for the rest of their lives.

One

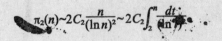

$$\pi_2(n) \sim 2C_2\frac{n}{(\ln n)^2} \sim 2C_2\int_2^n \frac{dt}{(\ln n)^2}$$

"I never felt like my biological parents didn't want me just because they made sure I'd have a family who could take the best care of me. I always felt like that proved they loved me."

—Evelyn Baker

Somewhere else, outside the realm of known experience, facing a new equation

Five minutes ago

WE'RE ENCOURAGED TO CHRONICLE our experiences, both by family tradition, carried over from our time as members of the Covenant of St. George, and by the mice, who would rather witness events with their own eyes, but are willing to concede that sometimes they'll have to be content with written accounts. So:

My name is Sarah Zellaby. I'm an adopted member of the Price family, a mathematician, a cryptozoologist, and a Priestess of the Aeslin mice.

I am not human.

My biological parents were members of a species known as the Johrlac, colloquially referred to as "cuckoos" by people unlucky enough to be aware of their existence. So far as anyone has been able to determine, cuckoos are invaders from another dimension, one where bipedal humanoid life evolved from parasitic wasps instead of from monkeys. Yeah. You know that thing where people make fun of furry artists for slapping tits on a lizard? Well, I'm basically a giant bug with what the people around me frequently think of as "nice boobs." So that's fun. I'm also telepathic, as are all members of my species, which makes it difficult to tune out all those random contemplations of my breasts and what they might look like without my clothes getting in the way.

Being a telepath in a non-telepathic society is a *great* way to learn how much you don't like people or ever want to be around them if you have any choice in the matter, FYI. I don't recommend it. Zero stars, would not buy again. Because people who live in a non-telepathic society don't have any qualms about thinking any dirty, nasty little thing that pops into their heads, and asking them not to is like asking them to stop touching their faces. The very idea that the thing is forbidden makes it impossible to resist. So no, I don't get out much, and when I *do* go out, I try to stay around people with experience dealing with telepaths.

Since the majority of cuckoos are evil assholes, this mostly means my family.

The Prices are ex-Covenant, meaning they're former monster hunters who learned how to take that skill set and apply it to the goal of being monster *saviors*. They believe the world belongs to all the sentient species that live in it, not only to the apex predators, and they do their best to preserve life where they find it, or at least long enough to understand it.

(No, they are not a family of vegans. No, I have never asked them how they reconcile a collective goal of preserving life and a willingness to eat its byproducts. But they do buy local and organic whenever possible, and I once saw Verity break a man's nose for kicking a dog.)

Remember that thing about cuckoos coming from another dimension? We're an invasive species that doesn't belong in Earth's biosphere, and that combined with being really shitty neighbors has made us one of the only things the Prices are willing to write off as monsters without trying to understand us first, which I guess made it inevitable that they'd wind up with two cuckoos actually in the family. My mother, Angela Baker, is a non-receptive telepath, and since it turns out cuckoos are evil fuckers mostly because we're born with a huge telepathic time bomb already implanted in our brains, she's also the first good cuckoo to be born in generations. No telepathy, no bomb.

Fortunately for me, she *is* a projective telepath, meaning she was able to hold me down and dig the telepathic nightmare out of my head before I was old enough for it to detonate—something which it apparently does right around the onset of puberty. It's like becoming an X-Man, only in a really universally lousy way. No chance you're going to get cool powers. Nope. Just telepathy in a world of non-telepaths, and the understandable but unforgivable urge to commit mass murder.

So I dodged that bullet, which spared me from any future bullets my family might have flung my way, and went about the business of being a pseudo-shut-in who just wanted to do math, read comic books, and flirt abstractly with my cousin Artie, who—as you may remember from the convoluted family history I've already provided—isn't *actually* my cousin, because none of the members of my family are biologically related to me. Not even Mom, although at least we're the same species.

My Aunt Mary always says the family you build matters more than the one you're born to, and since she's been with us for three generations and counting, I guess she'd know. My family is my family, biology be damned. I just refuse to consider my cross-species attraction to Artie inappropriate because my mother adopted the woman who married the brother of his mother. That's taking avoiding even the appearance of impropriety to an extreme that I simply don't have the time for.

Lots of things happened after Mom defused me. I grew up; we all did, really. We found and followed our personal passions, whatever those happened to be, and for my cousin Verity, that meant ballroom dance, taken to the point of going on a competitive dance reality show. Yeah, I don't see the appeal either. But she wore sequins and lipstick and a red wig that helped to distract people from the actual color of her eyes, and when she didn't win, she moved to New York City to do a journey-man year working with the urban cryptids while she made one last stab at having a dance career. And like the fool I am, I followed her.

I wanted to put some distance between myself and the rest of the family. I wanted to figure out whether I was doing what *I* wanted to do with my life, or whether I was living up (down?) to their unspoken expectations of me, the ones that said a natural ambush predator would want nothing more than to blend into the background and be forgotten. Most of all, though, I wanted the time to think about my situation with Artie, and decide whether I was really enough in love with him to make it worth risking the relationship we already had by pursuing something more.

It was a reasonable set of desires. Nothing too big, nothing that could hurt anyone else, except I guess maybe Artie. And somehow it still backfired on me, when Verity's cousin Margaret showed up as part of a Covenant strike team, putting the entire family at risk. Most of how the Prices can operate in relative safety in North America is by keeping the Covenant convinced that they're all dead, killed off over a generation ago in a frontal assault on the home of Alice and Thomas Price-Healy. Once Margaret knew Verity was not only alive, but was a living descendant of the Covenant's greatest modern traitor, we were all, in the vernacular, fucked.

Unless we stopped her, she would have gone back to England, and told the Covenant we existed, before returning with a force large enough to shut us all down. Verity was injured and incapacitated. I wasn't.

So I stopped her.

Killing her would have just created more problems. It was a human solution, and I wasn't human. Instead, I reached into her head, and into the heads of the men who were working with her, and I rewrote everything they remembered about their time in New York. I changed their minds against their will, permanently. It was a massive violation of their consent. It was the moment I proved I was a cuckoo, no matter how hard I tried not to be. Nature would always win out over nurture, and it had always been inevitable that I was going to hurt people. It didn't matter why I did it. It was done.

In a very real way, the people I hurt started with myself. The act of telepathically manipulating the minds of three unwilling strangers triggered a biological process called an "instar," a form of metamorphosis inherited from my insect ancestors. It scrambled my mind and left me incapacitated for years. I could perform simple tasks and feed myself, but that was where my competency stopped. I had to relearn everything else, including my own name, as control and memory slowly returned. But they *did* return, and eventually I felt well enough to make the trip from Ohio, where I'd been convalescing, to Oregon, to see the rest of my family again. To see Artie again. To find out whether he had been willing to wait for me.

Good news: he was. Better news: he loved me as much as I loved him. Best news: he was finally ready to accept that I felt the same way, something which should have been impossible to hide from an empath. After years of dancing around each other, divided by the dual barriers of biology and fear, we were finally figuring things out.

Which, naturally, is when my birth family decided it was time to snatch me and trigger my final instar, something they said would elevate me to the position of cuckoo queen. Remember that whole "actually a giant wasp" thing I mentioned? Turns out we're hive insects, and our origins have more bearing on our modern biology than I had ever guessed. Certain things need a queen, and thanks to events beyond my control, I was primed to take the crown.

They wired me up like an explosive charge made of telepathic power and psychic potential, then pointed me at the foundations of the world and set the timer. And that would have been the end of it—where, by "it," I mean "reality as humanity fundamentally understands it"—if not for my cousins. Artie and Antimony managed to follow me to the place where the cuckoos planned to blast their way out of our universe and into the next one, bringing a half-trained sorcerer and a surprisingly helpful cuckoo in their wake. Working with James and Mark—one of the cuckoos who'd originally abducted me, who had changed sides for reasons no one had bothered explaining—they were able to disrupt the cuckoos long enough for me to seize control of the monster equation that was trying to use me to come into the world.

It was math. I can do math. Math and I are good buddies. It was *evil* math, which was a bit more of a concern, and it was math that needed a *lot* of processing space to complete safely. More importantly in the moment, it was math that wanted to devour my mind and would have happily done so if I hadn't found a way to offload some of it to the brains around me, using their physical structures like data storage banks to give me the extra space I needed.

It was a pragmatic decision, made in the heat of the moment, and without it, I wouldn't have survived. There's a solid chance the world wouldn't have survived either. But nothing comes without cost. I learned that a long time ago. And right now, the cost was waking up tied to a chair while my allies surrounded me and radiated distrust.

Annie, my cousin, who had been the youngest when I joined the family and had thus accepted me with the least amount of fuss, never batting an eye at my biological differences or deviations from anything resembling "the norm," glared at me. Her expression was a mystery. Her emotions were not. She was hating me so hard that it was like a floodlight, painting the room in shades of hostility.

"What did you do, cuckoo?" she demanded. "Where are we?"

And that, in a very concrete way, is where our story begins.

٭

Whoever had tied me to the chair had done it very considerately. The ropes were tight enough to hold me upright while I was unconscious, and they would have been cutting off the circulation to my hands if I'd been a mammal with a circulatory system. That probably meant either Annie or Mark had done it. Annie had experience with field dressing a cuckoo, thanks to time spent training with both me and Grandma, while Mark *was* a cuckoo, and although I couldn't be sure he knew how to tie a knot, the chances were good he'd know how tight to tie himself if he wanted to be secure but uninjured.

My mouth was dry. I swallowed hard, trying to tell myself this was just disorientation brought on by what seemed to be a shift to a parallel universe. My chair was positioned to give me an excellent view of the window, and the ripe cantaloupe-colored sky outside. Creatures that looked like centipedes, if centipedes could fly and had absolutely no respect for the square-cube law, undulated through the air, their segmented bodies blending with the clouds. Wherever we were now, we weren't in Iowa anymore.

Iowa was very, very far away.

Annie held up her hand, a ball of lambent orange flame flickering into existence above her palm and hanging there like a child's magic trick. I squirmed against the ropes that held me. Cuckoos don't have heartbeats, and we don't have blood the way mammals do, but we can feel pain, and fire *hurts*.

"You don't want to do that," I said.

"Oh, I'm pretty sure I do," she said. "Everyone, please take note of the fact that I absolutely do want to do this, and if I suddenly start trying to say I don't, it's because the cuckoo has been messing with my mind." She took a menacing step toward me, looming. I had always known my cousins could be terrifying when they wanted to be. It had never been aimed in my direction before, and so somehow I had never really cared.

I may not be human, but I'm still a people, and people can be remarkably good at tuning out things that don't immediately affect them. It's a basic failing of the "being a people" state of being. I can't call it "the human condition" because personhood has never been a human monopoly. Life might be slightly easier if it were.

"Cuckoos can burn," said Mark. He sounded bored. He reinforced that impression by studying his fingernails, looking at them like they were the most important things in the world, and by implication ranking me somewhere well below his manicure. "In case you were wondering, we're as flammable as anybody else. Maybe more flammable. Hemolymph has a lower ignition point than blood."

Was he lying? I didn't know, and I didn't want to push into his mind to find out. My head didn't hurt, but it felt hollowed-out, like someone had taken a melon baller to essential parts of my brain without cracking my skull in the process.

Annie, though . . . Annie was *broadcasting*, and what she was broadcasting was fear and loathing and frustration, a toxic stew of impressions and emotions that was probably giving Artie a headache. Lilu are empaths. All they get is feelings. When we were kids, we argued about whether that made me a better psychic, which came down on the side of "no, just less specialized." While I could detect anger, he could read the nuances of that anger, the other emotions behind or coexisting with it, and the ways it could be unraveled. I just got to know that someone was mad, a superpower shared by anyone with the ability to understand human facial expressions.

Artie was hanging farther back in the room, with James, both of them watching the scene warily, with no mental signs that they had any idea who I was.

"Annie, stop!" I cried, trying not to stare at the ball of fire in her hand. "It's me, Sarah! Your cousin!"

"Oh, my fucking God," said Annie. "James, give Mark a dollar. He warned us she'd start claiming to be family as soon as she woke up. Well, here's news for you, cuckoo. You *can't* put the whammy on me, or Artie. We're resistant to your bullshit."

"I'm not," said James.

"You don't have to volunteer that information," said Annie.

"I know, but . . . I'm not, and I've still never seen this woman in my life." He shrugged. "I just thought that might be relevant."

I would have been tempted to kiss him if I'd been able to get out of the chair, and if it wouldn't have seemed like an assault by a stranger. Because that was absolutely what I was to all four of the people sharing this room with me: a stranger. None of them had ever seen me before, not Annie or Artie, who grew up with me, and not Mark, who helped to abduct me when my biological mother decided it was time for me to do my duty by the family that abandoned me. All three of their minds were open books as soon as I turned my thoughts in their direction, thanks to previous skin-to-skin contact, which had created an attunement that hadn't been erased along with everything else, but even glancing at their surface thoughts was repulsive and enlightening in equal measure.

They were reacting to me the way they would have reacted to any strange cuckoo in a situation like this one—with fear and apprehension and—in Annie's case—the option of violence. They were protecting themselves against an existential threat. I didn't have the same surface-level access to James' mind, but I could tell without pushing that I was just as much of a stranger to him.

Oh, God, what had I done?

It was a simple question, and—like any other simple question—it had a deceptively simple answer: I'd deleted myself. They had given me permission to use their brains for extra space while I tried to tame the equation the cuckoos used to move between dimensions, and I had bundled their core selves safely off to the side where I wouldn't hurt them, but I'd done it believing I was going to die. That there was absolutely no way we could come out the other side of the equation with all of us still breathing. And while I hadn't done so intentionally, it was clear the "do as little harm as possible, and mitigate the harm you can't avoid" ethics that had been drilled into me for my entire life had flared up in the way guaranteed to do me, *personally*, the most harm possible.

I had been convinced I was going to die. I had been struggling to keep the equation from swallowing their identities and experiences whole. And in an effort to spare them future harm and give the equation what it was baying for, I had fed it their memories of me.

I had deleted myself from their minds.

If I'd done it by surgically excising those memories and tucking them into myself, I might have been able to put them back, but I hadn't; I'd been wrestling with a math problem so large that it had achieved both sapience and malevolence, becoming a living thing in its own right, and it had gulped those memories into the endless void of its hunger. There was no getting them back. What we'd been to each other was gone. My side of that equation still existed, but their whiteboards had been wiped clean. And, potentially worse, since their core personalities had been wrapped up so carefully, even without those memories, the places where my presence had pressed against them and changed the people they became—those places were still *there*. I had taken myself away, but I hadn't turned them into new people in the process.

That might make things a little easier for me, since I'd still know basically who they were. It was going to make things a lot harder for them as they reached for foundations that didn't exist . . . and might as well never have existed to begin with.

I'd fucked everything up. I closed my eyes, shutting out the sight of my cousin standing menacingly over me, and said dully, "Mark can tell you I'm not lying. Mark can tell you I believe everything I say. My name is Sarah Zellaby. My mother is Angela Baker. Antimony, Artie, and I grew up together, which is why you hear that humming in the air—we're telepathically attuned to each other. I can't shut you out without an anti-telepathy charm, and you all took those off to let me *in*, so we could stop the cuckoos from destroying the world. I'm assuming you've lost them since none of us are wearing them now."

I felt them staring at me. Finally, in a bemused voice, James said, "That's ridiculous. Everything she's just said is completely ridiculous."

"That's why I believe her," said Artie.

My eyes snapped open. I stared at him. He felt calm, frightened, resolute . . . and unrecognizing. He wasn't miraculously recovering memories that weren't there to reclaim. He was just choosing to believe me.

Even without me, he still knew Mom. He clearly knew Mark. He knew cuckoos weren't always bad people, and he was choosing to believe me. If I'd had a heart, it would have grown two sizes in that moment. He didn't love me anymore, because I'd taken that love away, but he believed me.

"Well, I don't," snapped Annie. "She's the reason we're here, remember? She was at the center of their little circle, and Mark says she's the one who was doing the math that opened the rift in the universe. That means she's the one who has to put us *back*. She's making up stories so that we'll let her go."

She moved toward me again, burning hand raised. "Wait!" I yelped. She stopped, raising one eyebrow as a silent question radiated off of her. It wasn't formed enough to organize itself into words, but I could tell her patience was wearing thin.

"We're not the only ones here," I said. "You have to ask the mice."

Two

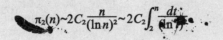

$$\pi_2(n) \sim 2C_2 \frac{n}{(\ln n)^2} \sim 2C_2 \int_2^n \frac{dt}{(\ln t)^2}$$

"Every time I think the world's growing short on wonders, it goes and shows me another one. Nice trick, world. I appreciate it."
— Frances Brown

Still in the same situation, mostly trying not to get set on fire (not as fun as it sounds, and it sounds pretty awful)

"THE WHAT?" ASKED MARK, with unfeigned confusion. "I think the process of transporting us all to a new dimension scrambled her brain if she wants us to start talking to rodents."

James radiated discomfort. Artie and Annie, on the other hand, stared at me.

"How do you know about the mice?" asked Annie, voice gone low and even more dangerous than before. "They're not something we discuss with outsiders."

"Uh, what?" asked Mark.

"I'm not an outsider!" I snapped. "I have my own clergy! Ask the mice, and they'll tell you I'm telling the truth! And don't try to tell me they're not here, I can pick up on three of them clearly and two more vaguely, so there's probably five of them. Ask the damn mice."

I didn't want to dwell on how easily I could detect the minds of the mice, which had always been too small for me to spot without making an actual effort. I wanted to fold my arms and sulk. My arms were tied. I settled for sulking, pushing my lower lip out into an exaggerated pout. Being unable to properly see facial expressions means I'm not always good at making them on purpose. Spending time around other cuckoos had been enough to confirm that I'm abnormally expressive for my species, sort of like a Muppet in cuckoo's clothing. I guess that's what happens when you grow up knowing you're not human but hoping desperately that if you try hard enough, the Blue Fairy from *Pinocchio* will show up one night and turn you into a real girl.

(No, fairies don't actually work that way, and all the fairies I know of are a lot more likely to take things *away* than they are to grant someone a working circulatory system and functioning human brain. But I was a kid at the time, and kids want stupid things.)

Annie gave me one last look, still radiating caution, before she retreated to where James and Artie waited, the three of them beginning to talk in hushed voices. I turned my eyes away, forcing myself not to mentally reach out and listen in. Mark wasn't included in their little circle. Interesting. He hadn't telepathically ingratiated himself with them; he was just here, somehow along for the ride. Given that they'd met him when he kidnapped me from the family compound, I had to wonder what story they were telling themselves to make his presence make sense. I looked straight at him, allowing my expression to fall into its natural neutrality.

Come here, I commanded.

Mark jerked a little, startled, before rubbing the back of his neck with one hand and walking in my direction. Interesting. I couldn't tell whether he was coming because he wanted to, or because I'd somehow left him no choice. My first instar had come with an increase in power level that took years for me to master and control. Who knew what this latest instar had come with?

When he was close enough, I lowered my voice and demanded, "What are you doing here?"

"Trying to get home," he said. "Cici needs me. I'm not going to disappear from her life just because you decided to help Ingrid destroy the world." He radiated discomfort, clearly skipping his thoughts from place to place to keep himself from dwelling. It was an interesting technique, and almost certainly one he'd learned in order to make it safer for him to spend time around other telepaths. I blinked.

"You're afraid the world and this Cici person aren't there anymore," I said. He jerked more sharply upright, staring at me. "You *are*. You think the equation—what—ate it alive? Dissolved it?"

"I think that even if we disrupted the ritual the way we were trying to, we somehow wound up here, along with a college campus, a whole bunch of unconscious cuckoos, and a bunch of dirt, meaning we took a chunk of the Earth's crust with us when we went. Did we destabilize the continental plate? Is Iowa one big volcano now? How deep does the exclusion go? I don't know. And I don't think you do either. But I know one thing." He leaned closer to me, voice suddenly pitched low. "If you've killed my sister, there is nothing anyone can do to keep me from taking you to pieces, *my queen*." The mocking lilt on his last two words sent a shiver along my spine.

He'd do it. He would absolutely do it. He wouldn't even hesitate.

But there was something wrong with his story. Maybe I'd scrambled his brain even harder than I'd thought. "Cuckoos don't have sisters."

"This one does," snapped Mark. "Her name is Cici, she's human, she's twelve, she's a holy terror, but in the normal twelve-year-old girl kind of way, not the evil telepathic wasp kind of way, and the only reason I got involved in this whole mess is because she deserves a planet to live on and not to get murdered by assholes like our family."

I frowned. "How do you think you got involved? Because the way I remember it, you abducted me from my home and family and took me to the hive my biological mother had assembled in order to get me back. I wouldn't be here if it weren't for you."

"I—" He stopped, an odd look crossing his face. "I don't know. I just know these people, and they know me, and they're willing to trust me for however long it takes for all of us to get home. Even though I'm a cuckoo. I don't understand how they can know that and trust me anyway. Even Cici doesn't know everything about what I actually am."

"They know what a cuckoo is and that it's possible to trust a cuckoo because they grew up with *me*," I said. "I was their test case for cuckoo trustworthiness. We also had my mom, who's a cuckoo, but she was an adult when we were children, she was another species altogether, and we learned to trust each other. Only now they trust you because of trusting me, and they don't trust me because of stupid cuckoo magic."

"We're not *magic*," said Mark scornfully. "Magic doesn't exist."

I raised an eyebrow. "Says the man keeping company with two literal sorcerers."

"Sorcery is just physics gone feral. We're psionic. It's not the same thing."

"If you want to debate dictionary definitions, maybe you should untie me first," I suggested. "There's a name for the kind of man who keeps a woman tied to a chair while he monologues at her, and it's not 'hero.'"

Mark scoffed. "I never said I was the hero of this story. That's probably Annie, unless this is secretly a modern update of *Firestarter*, and then I'd put James as slightly more likely to shoot her than the other one. I'm the comic relief who stays out of the line of fire and makes it home to his little sister alive. That's good enough for me."

I wanted to know more about his sister, but it was clear he didn't plan to tell me, and he'd know if I went into his mind and took the knowledge without his consent. What's more, my allies—my *family*—had already decided I was a monster. The last thing I needed to do right now was start giving them reasons to think they were right. So I just looked at him, unblinking, and waited for the moment when he inevitably broke eye contact.

As soon as he did, I said calmly, "If you betray them, if you hurt them in any way, you're never going to see that sister of yours again, because you will be dead, and she will never know what happened to you, or why you failed to come back to her."

To my surprise, he laughed. "You think I don't know that? Annie made it very, *very* clear that I'd have a life expectancy measured in seconds if I tried to double-cross them, and as two of the three carry the blood of Kairos, I know she can do it. There's no way I can seize her mind before she pulls the trigger. You might be able to, *queen*. No one really knows what a fully metamorphosized queen is capable of."

He looked at me then, anxiety and apprehension boiling off of him like steam off of a wet sidewalk on a hot summer day. I could practically see it.

"Yeah, well, I don't know either. I just know I have pretty decent ethical standards, thanks to being raised by a woman who thought being able to read minds was no excuse for me to go around doing it, and that's why you're not my marionette right now." I glared at him. "But I also think I'm getting pretty damn tired of being tied to this chair, so you all had better settle on something to do with me sooner rather than later."

Mark took a step backward, anxiety suddenly tinged with much sweeter nervousness. He was worried that my control would start slipping as my patience came to an end. It was a valid concern. I shared it. I took a deep breath, instead focusing on something that was always relevant: information.

"That's the second time you've mentioned 'the blood of Kairos' in the context of my family," I said. The first had been during my abduction. "What does that mean? Do *you* know why the Prices are resistant to telepathic influence?"

Mark hesitated. Then he sighed, and said, "Knowing won't change anything, so I guess it doesn't matter. Yes, we know. The cuckoos have always known. We're the reason Frances Brown was an orphan."

I blinked slowly, then leaned forward as far as the ropes allowed.

"Tell me what the cuckoos did," I said.

It wasn't a request.

Every inch of Mark radiated discomfort as he glanced at the circle at the back of the room, Artie and Annie engaged in quiet debate while James listened silently. I couldn't hear what they were saying. I wasn't willing to violate their privacy by pushing against their mental boundaries. Not yet, at least. If this went on for long enough, I knew my self-control would fail, and I'd push through any boundaries they wanted to put in my way.

Mark took a deep breath. "You know by now that we're not from around here," he said.

"Yeah, yeah, extra-dimensional ambush predators, I got the history lesson," I said impatiently.

"So you've had it explained, but you don't *understand*, not the way you would have if the woman who raised you hadn't taken the histories away." Mark shook his head. "You should have gotten it all as soon as you reached your first instar. The whole history of our kind, delivered directly into your mind, as evolution intended it to be."

"And driving me into a violent psychotic break at the same time," I snapped. "I think I like the version of my life where I *don't* kill everyone I love as soon as I get my first training bra."

"I can't really argue with that," said Mark, making me wonder again how he could be a cuckoo with a sister when he should have killed his entire family as soon as he reached that fateful, fatal instar. "If you'd received the history, though, you would have a better understanding of what it means to have come here—or I guess, to have come to Earth—from outside. We were refugees, and we needed a safe place to hide while we recovered from the injuries we suffered in the last world we called home.

"It wasn't Johrlar—our world of origin is a dozen dimensions behind us by now, and good riddance—but it was a dangerous world, and humanoid life was rare there, so we stood out more than we're comfortable with. By the time we found the dimension where you and I were born, our numbers were low and our wounds were deep. We needed time to recover. And we might have found it, if not for the creatures that were already living there."

The only "creatures" I've ever heard of posing a threat to a cuckoo hive are ones made entirely of hunger, like lindworms and werewolves, or ones that are also derived from insect stock somewhere along their evolutionary history. Madhura are functionally invisible to us, which can make them dangerous, and Apraxis actively compete with us for resources. "You mean the Apraxis wasps," I guessed.

"No, those came through the rift with us," he said. "They've been pursuing us for dimensions without end, almost as long as we've been exiles. Earth was the first world we found where there was enough food suitable for their needs for them to leave us in peace and let us start rebuilding our own population. There's always a die-off when we move between worlds, although I think you may be personally responsible for the largest one we've ever experienced."

"You'll forgive me if I'm not exactly upset about that," I said flatly. "I may have deleted parts of *your* memory, but mine is fully intact, and I know that everyone who died in the crossing did it because they were trying to hurt me and my family." I paused. "Every cuckoo, at least. I don't know whether there were any humans caught in the blast radius." It was an alarming thought, and one I didn't want to dwell on. I'd spent so much of my life trying to minimize the harm I did, especially when compared to the rest of my species. If I'd just killed the population of Ames, Iowa, then I was the greatest monster the cuckoos had ever produced. Not exactly a superlative I'd been working to achieve.

"Forgiven," said Mark without hesitation. "They were no friends of mine. Cuckoos don't get along with other cuckoos unless it's mating season, and I'll be perfectly happy never to experience the joys of fatherhood for myself, not knowing what any children of mine would grow up to become."

I wanted to ask him how *he'd* managed to avoid that fate, but I also didn't want to distract him from the history lesson he was delivering while my cousins settled on what to do with me. So I sat in silence, and I waited.

"We came to Earth through the rift opened by our last queen, and we settled into the population, breeding and feeding and staying out of sight. Ambush predators. And there were little glitches—the wasps had survived to follow us through, the bee-people who might have become us if they'd evolved in a less crowded ecosystem, but here served only to thwart our designs—but on the whole, Earth was a good and fertile land. Until we met the luck-benders." Mark's thoughts darkened, tainted by a memory not entirely his own. "They divided themselves into three types, depending on what they could do. The jinks saw luck, could borrow and bend it to their own desires. The Fortuna made luck, weaving it out of the walls of the world. And the Kairos were the worst of all, for us, because they were always where they needed to be when they most needed to be there."

I blinked. "How does that . . . ?"

"Their luck was internal, and it drove them through the world primed to do the most harm or the most good. They lived in a haze of coincidence."

Dimly, I remembered Grandma Alice talking about how she'd inherited the "Healy family luck" from her mother. Sometimes it was good. Sometimes it was bad. It was never boring.

"And somehow that haze of coincidence made them immune to us. Our nature was counter to their own, and so our tricks didn't work on them. They always saw us, always knew where we were, could identify our babies as outsiders and as dangers. I'm sure there was some biological reason for it, but they didn't know it, and we were more interested in killing them than we were in sitting down and having a long talk about their specific capabilities. We began hunting them. They weren't blank spots like the Madhura. More . . . blurry, places where the things we could perceive with our minds and the things we could see with our eyes began to disagree. They had to go. They were willing to hunt us when they saw us, and they presented a danger. So we hunted them."

My throat was dry. "What do you mean?"

"I mean we killed them. For someone who claims to come from a family of homicidal lunatics, you're surprisingly sheltered. We followed them to the ends of the world and we killed them where we could; where we couldn't, we found the people you call Covenant and we made sure they saw the impossible coincidences that unfurled around the Kairos. They burned them as witches, they stoned them in the streets, and with every one of them who died, the world became safer for us."

I wanted to throw up. He was talking about the elimination of a sapient species as casually as he'd talk about going to the grocery store to pick up a couple of apples, and while I could feel a lot of things coming off of him—boredom, oddly enough, like he couldn't believe he had to explain all this to me, not when I should have already known it—I couldn't feel a single speck of guilt or regret.

"You weren't there," I said. "This happened a long time ago."

"Yes, it did," he said, sounding faintly amused. "Do you need me to reassure you that there isn't blood on my hands, princess? I'm sorry—your majesty? The only person I've ever killed was a cuckoo who was hunting in the mall near my home. He tried to hurt Cici. I explained why that wasn't a good idea. And then I burned his body, so the human authorities wouldn't find it and figure out something that they shouldn't. I'm not a murderer. I didn't kill the Kairos. I'd never met anyone even connected to them until I met the monsters you call family. The Prices stink of coincidence. They should never have existed. But the memories of the Kairos were deemed essential enough to be added to the lessons we receive from our parents, and so I remember the hunts and the killings and the danger they presented as if I *had* been there. When you find the blood of Kairos, you eliminate it. And because of that command, I remember Frances Brown.

"She was half-human—the Kairos could interbreed with humans, just like the jinks and the Fortuna can, close enough to the same species as to blend and blur their genetics without penalty to the offspring. Her father died when we caught up with him just outside of Sacramento, and her mother ran, a single woman with no preternatural abilities, no experience at making her own way in the world, no money—nothing but the ring on her finger and the baby in her arms. She made it as far as Tempe, Arizona, before she dropped the baby in a box where she thought someone kind might find it and disappeared into the desert. We found her before anyone else could. We would have had the babe as well, but that damned Kairos luck had already found a home for her, in a collection of carnival fools whose ranks were too closed for us to penetrate safely. The blood of Kairos gets thinner with every passing generation, but it's still *there*. They bend the world to suit themselves."

I blinked. Then I blinked again, leaning back in my chair, no longer fighting against the ropes. "The cuckoos came from another dimension and orchestrated the functional extinction of at least one of the species that actually evolved on Earth."

"Yes. We did."

"And you have *got* to stop putting it that way. This isn't some human church, accusing everyone who walks through the door of bearing the burden of original sin.

We didn't do anything. *You* didn't do anything, even if you got the ancestral memories to tell you you did. You may remember it, but you weren't there. You didn't make the choices that led us here. You didn't hold the guns. *I* didn't do anything. I was raised to think intelligent life is valuable and deserves to be protected, and that means all intelligent life, even the lives I don't like very much. We weren't there. Whatever our ancestors did isn't on us. Only what we do of our own free will."

"I wish I believed you," said Mark.

Then he turned away from me and walked to the others, and I was left alone.

Three

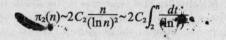

$$\pi_2(n) \sim 2C_2 \frac{n}{(\ln n)^2} \sim 2C_2 \int_2^n \frac{dt}{(\ln t)^2}$$

"Some people like to say that to live is to suffer. They have a very narrow view of existence. To live is to change. Everything else is negotiable."

—Enid Healy

Still tied to a chair in a room full of enemies who used to be allies before everything went catastrophically wrong, hating it here

I STARED AT MARK'S back, trying not to will him to turn around and come back to me. If I wanted it badly enough, he'd probably do it, or maybe not—and honestly, I wasn't sure which would be worse. I had passed the final instar. I had reached a level of cuckoo development that allowed me to wipe out memories and handle world-breaking equations, and I had no idea what that meant or how to control whatever it came with. Worse yet, if I had any new capabilities, I couldn't identify them without actually *using* them. They were buried somewhere inside me, waiting for me to push the right lever and make them happen.

When we were kids, Annie, Verity, and Alex began training for combat while Artie, Elsie, and I sat more on the sidelines, kept out of the field by the essential facts of our natures. I was an ambush hunter, while they were Lilu enough to have evolved to enchant and befriend everyone around them, not to fight. We all learned to shoot and how to field-dress a wound, but the three of us were spared the most intensive physical conditioning, the games of tag that turned serious, the games of Red Rover that left bruises. There was about a two-year period where Annie insisted the distance she could walk without getting bored or winded was a mile because that was where she'd started. But she was walking every day, tackling steeper and steeper inclines, more and more treacherous paths, and by the end of it, she was doing five-mile hikes while insisting, firmly, that she couldn't walk more than a mile without needing to sit and rest.

I felt like Annie's thoughts had felt during that period, carbonated and on edge, unsure of my capabilities, knowing only that they were too big for me. I couldn't call for Mark to come back, no matter how much I didn't want to be alone. The chances were too high that I'd be able to change his mind the way normal cuckoos changed human minds, and I didn't want a pet.

I slumped against the ropes, closing my eyes. This was hopeless. Whatever they'd decided, it clearly didn't involve revealing the mice to Mark or letting me go, possibly ever. Among the three of them, Annie, Artie, and James had to have at least one working firearm. They could put a stop to this whenever they decided to. Cuckoos are dangerous as hell when we're actually willing to fight back, and while I wanted to live badly enough that I couldn't trust myself not to do it, my cousins were some of the only people in the world I loved enough to let one of them put a bullet between my eyes. If they came for me, I'd let them. I was tired and beaten-down and done. I couldn't do this alone. If that was what had to happen from here, I was finished, thank you very much.

My eyes were still closed when I heard footsteps approaching, accompanied by the static hum of Antimony's mental presence. I wasn't reaching for her thoughts, but I could feel her wariness and lingering disbelief without exerting myself in the slightest.

"Tell her what you just told me," she said, voice low,

and from her palm came the welcome, familiar, often frustrating sound of salvation:

"HAIL!" squeaked the unmistakable voice of an Aeslin mouse. "HAIL THE CALCULATING PRIEST-ESS!"

I exhaled heavily as I opened my eyes. "So you believe me now."

"I believe something hinky is going on, and whatever it is, the mice seem to be on your side." Her hand was positioned such that I couldn't see the mouse in her hand, couldn't see what it was wearing or which liturgical branch of the church it represented. None of my mice had been with me when I'd woken from my final instar and made the trip downstairs to rip a hole in reality—a process that had seemed suddenly, ridiculously simplistic, distance becoming just a matter of convincing the numbers underlying it to bend and twist at my command. So the odds were good that I had no theological representation in whatever dimension we now occupied. But that left Annie and Artie, the Precise Priestess and the God of Chosen Isolation, and I was on good terms with both their clergies.

People like to think Aeslin mice are a monolith. Wait, no, that's wrong. People like to think Aeslin mice are extinct, victims of a world too big and too dangerous for their tiny selves. That's if people think about Aeslin mice at all, which most of them don't. But Aeslin are individuals, and every branch of the colony has its own character. I don't get along very well with the mice dedicated to preserving the mysteries of Great-Grandma Fran because they remember all the times she encountered the cuckoos—and all the bad blood between them. That was fine. It was unlikely that any of her mice had accompanied us.

"Hail and well met," I said politely, ignoring the mental daggers Annie was chucking in my direction. "Can you tell me of the liturgy you uphold?"

Proud, chest audibly puffed out, the mouse said, "I preserve the Mysteries of the Precise Priestess!"

That was good. A member of Annie's clergy would know more of the rituals relating to me than a member of Aunt Jane's clergy, or even a member of Evie's. Since she was enough older than me to have always felt more like an aunt than a sister, it wasn't like we'd ever spent a lot of time together socially. I fumbled for the exact title of the recitation I wanted. The Aeslin have so many rites and rituals that some of them, unavoidably, have similar names, and the last thing I wanted to do right now was accidentally trigger a recitation that would make my situation even worse.

Ah: there it was. I turned my gaze on Annie, reading the confusion and apprehension in her thoughts rather than her expression, and asked, "Do you believe that Aeslin mice never forget anything and will always, *always* tell the truth?"

"I do," she said, voice soft. "It's always been true."

"Good." I turned my attention back to her cupped hand. "Can you please recite the Holy Catechism of Coming Home From Lowryland?"

There was a stirring as the mouse pulled itself from her palm and ran up to balance on the tips of her fingers, ears up, whiskers forward, clearly honored by this opportunity to share the sacred mysteries with someone outside the clergy. Aeslin mice don't view their religious rites as secret—far from it. They want the world to know. They just don't get the chance very often.

"It was a Summer Vacation," declaimed the mouse. "Long and long had the Heartless One and her mate driven their Holy Burden across the countryside, returning from the Land of Lowry, where all good things had been accomplished!"

What the fuck is this? asked Mark silently, his mental question utterly bewildered.

I had to swallow my smile, lest it cause Antimony to think I was up to something. *This is an Aeslin mouse going into full recitation of a holy event. You get used to it. I promise.*

Artie and James were drifting toward us, Artie with

two more mice riding on his shoulders, James with an aura of resigned acceptance permeating the air around him. Sort of the "this is so damn weird, it might as well just happen" of emotional responses. Under the circumstances, it wasn't the worst option he had open to him.

The mouse was really getting into the recitation of that long-ago drive from Lowryland back to Ohio, and was lovingly detailing all the snacks Mom and Dad had purchased for their much-indulged grandchildren at the truck stop. Antimony looked at me like she couldn't decide between amusement and blazing fury. I cleared my throat.

"Forgive me if this treads near to the fields of blasphemy," I said delicately, "but if you could skip ahead to the Great Event, that would be very welcome."

The mouse looked flustered, running paws over its whiskers. "To skip a piece of rarely recited catechism is to insult the Priestesses to whom it applies," it said pitifully.

"I'm not insulted," said Annie, as fast as she could.

"And neither am I," I said,

She *was* insulted by that, shooting a quick needle of fury at me for daring to speak to *her* clergy in such a permissive way. I ignored her. This was the only proof I had that I was who I said I was, and proof was what got me out of this chair without dying. I might have done irreparable damage to my relationships with the people who mattered most in all the world, and I was going to have to live with that, but the key word there was *live*. Before the ritual, I had come to terms with the fact that I wasn't going to survive. The cuckoos' big math problem was the last one I was ever going to solve, and I would never see my parents or my home or my newly-minted clergy again. And in the moment, with the fate of the world in the balance, I'd been fine with it. Well, I wasn't fine with it anymore. I wanted to live. I wanted to go home. So I was going to sit here and listen to the mouse and do my best to make sure everyone else did the same.

"Very well," said the mouse. "The road was Clear

and Open and Long when the Heartless One cried, suddenly, a command to stop the car, and threw herself bodily from the vehicle. We did not see what followed, for we had remained with our Charges, but when she returned, she was carrying a child—the Calculating Priestess, who had been found Weeping in the Mud . . ."

"That didn't happen," said Annie.

"But it did, Priestess," said the mouse. "I was not there. I am not among the first generation in your service. My father, though, was with you, and rode with you on the rides of thrilling and of charming through the Land of Lowry. He feasted on your Road Snacks, and even did he steal a slice of apple from the clergy of the Arboreal Priestess."

"I . . . I remember that," said Annie slowly. "Verity was *so* pissed when my mice started taking food from hers."

"This is Holy Writ," said the mouse. "This is As It Was. The Heartless One found the Calculating Priestess weeping, and brought her from the ground into the family's embrace, where she has been ever since."

"Then there must be lots of rituals she's in," said Artie abruptly.

"Oh, so very many!" said the mouse with pride. "She has Always Been There. Your clergy can recite you many rites and catechisms of where her life has touched on yours, for is it not said by the Silent Priestess, Dammit, Arthur, I Love You, But You're Thick As A Plank Where That Girl Is Concerned, and also, Just Tell Her How You Feel Already, She's Psychic But She's Not *Rude*, She'll Never Figure It Out On Her Own. And then did the God of Careful Chances not reply—"

"Um, I think we're done here," said Artie, before the mouse could explain exactly what Uncle Ted said in reply to Aunt Jane. "Thank you."

"You are very welcome," said the mouse proudly, little chest puffed out so far that it was hard to believe it was still breathing. It turned expectantly to Annie. "May I Resume?"

"Maybe later," said Annie, glancing anxiously at me. "I, uh. We needed you to resolve a disagreement between Priestesses," she said the word like it physically pained her, "and now we must discuss it among ourselves. You have my apologies, and my thanks, and I promise to listen to the rest of the catechism later, when the time is more convenient."

In addition to not lying themselves, the Aeslin mice are very bad at hearing lies when they come from a beloved Priestess. The mouse radiated satisfaction as it jumped back into Antimony's palm and raced up her arm to burrow into her hair. She looked back at me. Artie and James did the same.

"What the *actual* fuck was that?" asked Mark.

"Aeslin mouse," I said. "Hyper-religious sapient rodents who worship the Price family as gods."

"Oh, is that all?" He sounded utterly disgusted. "No wonder you people are such assholes. If people treated me like a damn god all the time, I'd be an asshole, too."

"You're a cuckoo," said Artie. "That makes you an asshole by default."

Annie didn't say anything, just continued to look at me like I'd reveal all the answers she was missing if she waited long enough. I squirmed.

"These ropes are getting pretty uncomfortable," I said. "It would be nice if someone could untie me."

None of them moved. After a long beat, James said cautiously, "If she were doing that cuckoo whammy thing, wouldn't we be untying her already?"

"She's not," said Mark. He sounded perplexed rather than cautious, like he couldn't understand what was going on. "Whatever game she's playing, she isn't trying to influence any of us. Not even me, and she's a queen. She could turn my thoughts inside out without breaking a sweat."

"Do cuckoos sweat?" asked James.

"Yes," I said wearily. "We also lactate, probably due to whatever quirk of evolution caused us to wind up looking like mammals instead of giant bugs."

"More attractive that way," said Artie.

"Only to the other mammals," I countered. "Can someone please untie me?"

"I don't like this," said Annie. "If this is some kind of a trick, we'll catch on, and we will kill you."

"I wouldn't expect anything less," I said. "I know you don't remember this, but I was there while you were being trained, and I know what you've been told to do in a situation like this one. I also know that when we get back to Portland, everyone who's there will know exactly who I am, and my clergy will be happy to recite any liturgical truths you need to hear."

"How do I know you didn't mess with the minds of the mice?" she asked.

"It's a valid question, but I can't mess with the minds of the mice. They're too small. They're smart, due to an incredible density of neurons, but they don't have as much empty space as a human mind. I didn't mean to wipe your memories. I did it because the equation the cuckoos were trying to force me to complete—the one that would have destroyed the Earth if it had gone the way it was intended to—was massive. It needed additional processing capacity. And Artie—" I cut myself off guiltily before I could get too close to blaming him for my own actions.

He might have been the one to suggest that I needed more processing space, but he hadn't been the one to make the choice that deleted their memories. That was all on me.

I looked down at my knees, as if being unable to see their faces would render me unable to hear their puzzled thoughts. I couldn't be sure without pushing, but it felt like the channels between us were cleaner and wider than ever, as if the instar or the equation had propped certain doors open in a way that couldn't be closed. The only question was whether it was only the people who'd been my storage buffers during the ritual, or whether it was everyone, and this was just how I experienced the world now.

I was going to be one giant raw nerve and wind up living in a cave in the mountains somewhere like a modern telepathic prioress if this was the way everyone's mind interacted with mine from now on. It was too much, like trying to drink from a fire hose. And that's an excellent way to get flung across the room.

"Talking mice," said Mark, who felt as puzzled as he sounded. "You're worshipped by talking mice. Jesus, you people are like a fucked-up Disney movie in more ways than one."

"Is she telling the truth?" asked Artie. "About how big their brains are?"

"I'd have to push to find out," said Mark. "I'm not a queen. Are you going to freak out and shoot me if I break your mouse?"

There was a soft whooshing sound that I recognized as the air above Annie's palm igniting. I spared a moment to be glad the mouse had already run for Annie's hair and was no longer at risk. She'd never forgive herself if she accidentally Kentucky fried a member of her own clergy.

Or anyone else's, really. The family is very protective of the mice, for good reason. We're all they have in the world.

"Okay, I won't break the mouse," said Mark hurriedly. "Do you still want me to try?"

"Only if Laverne is all right with it," said Annie. "All right, Laverne, you willing to let Mark go digging around in your brain?"

I glanced up. The mouse had emerged from her hair and was sitting on her shoulder, clutching its tail like a security blanket. The Aeslin mice have names, complicated things made of sound and gesture and scent. I can pick them up sometimes, when the mice are thinking of themselves or others as individuals and not part of the greater colony—something that happens more rarely with them than it does with most larger people. Their identities are so wrapped up in the colony and its religious practices that they have trouble thinking of themselves in isolation. It's a strange evolutionary quirk, but it's theirs, and it isn't my place to judge.

Because Aeslin names aren't translatable into human speech, Annie developed the habit of giving them nicknames. Always with their permission and agreement. A surprising number of those nicknames can be traced back to her childhood fondness for old sitcoms on Nick at Nite. Just one more danger of allowing television to handle babysitting duties.

"I . . . for the sake of the Calculating Priestess, I will agree," said Laverne, clutching her tail more tightly as she glanced at me. "I have heard your Discussions, and I know you have somehow been forced to Forget her, although I could not say exactly How or Why. She needs her Family about her, even as I need my Colony about me, and so I will allow this thing to happen, much as I do not Wish it."

She was absolutely feeling unsure for her audible capital letters to be that infrequent. Aeslin mice emphasize their speech in a way that sounds unnatural to the modern human ear, but which is clearly comfortable for them, and anyone who spends a lot of time with them learns to hear the capitals. It's strange, but it works, like so much else about our weird little family.

"All right," said Mark. He held his hand out toward the mouse, palm facing up. "This will be easier if I'm touching you," he said, clearly trying to sound soothing. From the way the mouse was shaking, he was failing. She was terrified.

She still stepped onto his palm. There is virtually nothing the Aeslin mice won't do for the sake of their Priestesses. The Gods are also venerated, but not as seriously. When we were kids, Annie would rant and rave about how even the mice were determined to reinforce human gender roles. She stopped when Elsie asked the mice what they'd do if she told them there had been an error and she was actually a boy. The mice had begun planning a ritual to transition her catechisms on the spot, and it had taken most of the evening and Elsie asserting multiple times that she was definitely a girl to derail them from their plans to celebrate her ascension to Godhood. They had some antiquated and rigid ideas about how humans worked, but they were doing their best.

Mark raised her slowly to the level of his face, eyes flashing white as he focused on her. No one knows exactly what the chemical reaction is that causes that to happen when we use our psychic powers. I'm glad it does. It means there's *something* to betray the fact that we're pushing against the world, and we're dangerous enough without being entirely undetectable. Maybe it's unkind of me to wish detection on the species that made me. I don't care. Nothing says I have to be kind all the time.

The mouse froze, staring into Mark's white-out eyes, trembling whiskers betraying her anxiety. Her hind paws were touching his skin, which would make this infinitely easier for him. It was still almost a surprise when only a few seconds passed before he blinked, the blue coming back into his eyes, and said, "She's telling the truth," jerking his chin toward me to make it clear which "she" he was talking about.

"What?" asked James.

"*What*?" demanded Artie, with far more vehemence.

"The mouse—thank you, mouse, for letting me into your head—has a very complex mind, but a very small one; it's doing more with fewer neurons than a human would be. Structurally, I'm not entirely sure it's possible, but since it clearly is, I'm not going to think about it any harder than I have to. Any changes made by someone my size would be like trying to touch up the paint on a Barbie Doll using a housepainter's brush. They'd be massive and very obvious. There's none of that here. Also, the mouse remembers all sorts of things involving a female cuckoo it truly believes was this one," he jerked his chin toward me again, "and that's without any alterations. I think she was really there."

"Because I *was*," I said. "I've been there since we

were kids. I'm your family, and you're mine." To my surprise and shame, tears sprang to my eyes—one of the many places where I'm biologically indistinguishable from human. I couldn't wipe them away, and so they broke free as I blinked, making their slow way down my cheeks. "I didn't mean to hurt you, and I swear I had permission before I went into your heads, but I had to do *something*, or the equation would have ended everything. And no, before you ask, I don't know what I did. I offloaded as much of it as I could into the minds around me, and then I forced it not to kill us all even though it wanted to. It was supposed to kill me, or at least to wipe my mind clean, but it didn't, and I don't know why!" My voice peaked at the end, becoming a wail shrill enough to hurt my own ears.

"Again, I think she's telling the truth," said Mark. "Ingrid—that was the leader of the hive I was with when we met—said the equation, once it was placed in the queen's mind, would hatch and flower and devour her whole, but in the process, it would open the way for us to find a new world for the harvesting. She implied that the queen's body might come with us into the new world, but not her mind."

"Why did she feel the need to tell you that?" I didn't actually want to know, but I had to ask.

Strictly biologically speaking, Ingrid had been my mother. She was the one who'd given birth to me and abandoned me with the McNallys, the human couple who were the first parents I could remember. And when they'd died, she hadn't come to take me back, leaving me free to find Angela and Martin Baker—Mom and Dad. But Ingrid had tried to claim motherhood once it suited her, saying that because she was my biological mother, I owed her, and by extension our shared species, my service and loyalty. Bullshit. If I owed anyone, it was my *actual* family, and all they'd ever asked me to do was try not to die.

Well, I could probably add "and don't wipe our minds if you have any choice in the matter" to that list, but since they were still fundamentally themselves, they were probably going to forgive me eventually.

Mark looked at me, radiating discomfort and mild disgust. "Because all three of the male cuckoos who'd already been in the swarm when Ingrid picked up on my mind and decided I was going to help them were your brothers," he said. "We're not very nice people by human standards, and our biology is weird as hell by Earth standards, but we don't mate with full siblings. And if your body had survived the transition, they wanted to breed you, to preserve the genes that could create a successful queen. We've done it before, apparently, multiple times, and it's considered a massive honor. She thought she was offering me something worth having."

"Ew," said Annie.

"Double-ew," said James.

"As the presumptive recipient of this honor, I'm going to go ahead, endorse both those 'ews,' and add a nice fresh 'over my dead body,'" I said. I paused. "Ingrid. I remember shoving part of the equation into her before it completed, and she went down hard. She was pregnant. Did anyone see her? Or the baby?" I'm not very good with pregnant people. They're two or more minds in one body, and that's disconcerting, and until Alex's fiancée got pregnant, I never had cause to spend a lot of time around somebody who was in the process of growing another person. And even if I had been around more pregnant people, they would mostly have been humans. So I couldn't be sure of how pregnant Ingrid had been when I'd blasted a thousand years of hostile Johrlac math into her head and shredded her psyche past repairing. If it was possible for the baby to be saved, though, it was worth making the attempt.

"There were cuckoos everywhere when we came to," said Annie, moving around behind me. "Most of them weren't moving. Mark was already awake, standing guard over our bodies to keep anything from coming out of the wreckage of the campus to hurt us, and he realized you were breathing and said you were the one who'd been doing the math and told us to bring you along. So we did." There was a whispering scrape as she pulled a knife out of her clothing, no doubt one of many—out of everyone in our family, Annie was the one who had most passionately embraced the idea that to be unarmed was to be the next best thing to being stark-ass naked in the middle of Lowryland—and then I felt her tugging at the ropes that bound my wrists.

They gave way easily, yielding before the edge of her blade. I sat up straighter, pulling my arms around in front of myself as soon as the motion became possible. My hands felt fine—my circulation is weird enough that they hadn't suffered as a human's hands would have—but my wrists ached. I rubbed them and waited for her to finish cutting me free.

The mouse on Mark's palm took a few steps back, enough to get a running start, and launched itself into the air with surprising strength, sailing across the distance between us while he was still looking on in shock. It landed on my knee and ran up the length of my body to perch on my collarbone, where it began groveling.

Watching an Aeslin mouse grovel is an experience. They don't have a defined human waist, so it's not kneeling and prostrating themselves repeatedly, more a sort of full-body lift and drop that would be guaranteed to attract any local cats.

"We have Failed You!" it wailed. "We have Allowed Doubt of your Divinity to infest the other members of the Pantheon!"

"Shh, shh," I said, letting go of my wrist in order to touch the mouse between the ears with one finger, trying to soothe it. "You haven't failed me. I did this to myself."

Annie was still cutting away the ropes holding me to the chair. There were more of them than I'd realized, a sign of how competently I'd been tied down, as well as how distressed I'd been when I woke and realized what I'd done. There was a final snapping sound and the ropes holding my feet fell away, leaving me free to stand if I wanted to.

I didn't want to just yet. Standing would have meant looking where I was going, and that would have meant really *looking* at Artie. I was aware of him—I was always aware of him, have been aware of him pretty much since I was twelve years old and realized the things I felt when I was with him were the same as the things my mother felt when she was with my father; less sexual, certainly, but equally strong. I'd been in love with him for almost my entire life, and while he'd only recently said he loved me back, his friendship and care had been my bedrock.

And now it was gone, and I was the reason. I'd destroyed the thing I loved most in the entire world. It didn't really matter whether I'd done it on purpose or not; what's done is done, and this was done.

The mouse eventually calmed and tilted its head up to look at me, whiskers trembling in the mouse equivalent of a sniffle. I could pick easily up on its thoughts with it this close to me. It was worried I would blame my clergy for not being present, and the rest of the colony by extension. As with all the Aeslin mice, it was difficult to tell solely from its thoughts what pronouns I ought to be using; Annie had given it a female name, but it didn't think of itself as particularly "male" or "female" in any way I could recognize.

Sometimes I wonder whether telepaths who weren't raised to be polite and considerate of the customs and cultural standards of others have this many headaches. I doubt it.

"Are you truly not Angry?" it asked.

I gave up my attempt to puzzle out the appropriate pronouns and nodded, saying, "I'm angry at myself, a little, for creating this situation in the first place, and I'm worried about where we are and what happened to all those other cuckoos, but I'm not mad at you, or at anyone in this room. It's not your fault I ran into something too big for me to handle without hurting anyone. I'm so sorry." I finally looked up, glancing at Mark and James before allowing myself to meet Artie's eyes. "I didn't mean for any of this to happen, and I'm genuinely sorry it has."

"Yeah, well, that and five dollars won't quite buy you a cup of coffee at Starbucks," said Annie, straightening up behind me and dropping her hand onto my chest for the mouse to step onto. She looked at me defiantly as she pulled her hand away again, and it took me an embarrassingly long time, given that I could literally read her mind, to realize she'd been daring me to try and influence her thoughts.

I was so unaccustomed to being on Annie's list of enemies that I couldn't fully recognize her hostility, and that was going to be a problem.

"We have five mice with us," I said. "Which clergies do they represent?"

"Two are mine, two are Artie's, and one's Mom's," said Annie. "Mom's fine, by the way." She paused. "I'm not sure why I felt like I needed to tell you that."

"Your mother is technically my sister, since we have the same adoptive mom," I said. "We were just never comfortable calling me your aunt. I'm the same age as Verity. It would have been too weird."

Mark made a snorting noise. I looked curiously over at him.

"*That's* what's weird?" he asked. "You're like a kitten raised by gorillas. You don't know how to be a monkey. You don't know how to be a cat. Your biological mother set up a situation that was supposed to end with you functionally brain-dead and being bred to a stranger who doesn't want to be here, and you're worried that calling someone your own age 'niece' would have somehow been past the horizon of weird. I don't understand you at all."

I smiled at him. I may not know what that expression is supposed to look like, but I know what it feels like. I've had plenty of time to practice. "That's good, since you're a cuckoo," I said. "I don't feel that compelled to convince you to comprehend me. I'm happier knowing you don't."

Mark nodded and turned away, leaving me to face my cousins. I wasn't good at thinking of James that way yet, but since Annie had adopted him and considered him her brother, he fit the bill, and it was easier to have one label I could apply to the three of them. "Humans" didn't work, since Artie wasn't fully—and apparently neither was Annie. The answer to the vaunted Healy family luck had been out there this whole time, and only the fact that it was being kept by the cuckoos had kept us from discovering it.

The world is funny sometimes.

"I know what I can see through the window, but I don't want to make any assumptions right now," I said. "Where are we?"

Annie looked me dead in the eye. "Funny," she said. "We were hoping you'd know."

Four

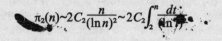

$$\pi_2(n) \sim 2C_2 \frac{n}{(\ln n)^2} \sim 2C_2 \int_2^n \frac{dt}{(\ln t)^2}$$

"The question isn't whether our children are going to surprise us. Children will always surprise their parents. The question is whether they're going to surpass us, and I have the sincere hope that the answer will always, always be 'yes.'"

—Jane Harrington-Price

No longer tied to the chair, but as that is really the only improvement, the situation is pretty much as established

I WAS UNCONSCIOUS WHEN you brought me here and tied me to this chair," I said. "If I'd been asleep, I would have been broadcasting my dreams, and Mark would have yelled at me by now. So I know I was out hard. I also know I was outside when I was doing the big math because it was raining." It had been raining, and I'd thrown up a force bubble to stop us all from getting wet. I remembered making the conscious choice to extend the bubble enough to cover Mark rather than letting him stand outside in the rain—because if I *could* be the kind of person who kept my allies safe and dry, I *should* be that kind of person. Even if I still wasn't entirely sure why he was one of our allies.

Being surrounded by people whose minds were effectively open books didn't actually mean I knew everything they were thinking. Artie and Annie's minds had been like that for years, due to repeated and protracted skin-on-skin contact while we were growing up. Serving as my off-site processing backups had yanked James and Mark into the same level of attunement faster than I would have thought possible, but that didn't mean I heard everything. I would have broken if I had.

The best comparison I've ever found is to think of a sapient's mind as if it were a pond. Most ponds are dark and murky, choked with water weeds and mud. Maybe you can see a few frogs, or even a turtle if they're at the surface, but you can't see the bottom unless you're willing to make an effort. Telepathy is making the effort. Once I'm attuned to someone, their pond is clear. I can see through the water all the way to the bottom, and I literally can't miss something big when it's right in front of my face—if there's an alligator in there, I'll see it. Ditto with a sunken shopping cart. But the little things, fish and tadpoles and mosquito larva, I still have to focus for. I still have to *look*.

I always know when I'm near a pond, or a mind. But I won't get the details unless I go digging. And because I have manners, I usually won't unless I feel like I have to. So why Mark had gone from abductor to ally was still a mystery to me, but I trusted Annie's judgment enough not to view it as a threat. It could wait.

"It stopped raining when you *tore a hole in the world* and we all got sucked through, so thanks for that," said Artie. The distrust and mulish dislike radiating off of him were painful if I focused on them, and so I didn't. I couldn't put his memories back. They were gone. The closest I could come was sharing my memories with him, and if I did that without his permission, I'd just make things worse for myself.

"I was trying to save the world," I said. "I don't think anyone has ever actually finished that equation and survived with their mind intact before, so there was no way to know what it was going to do."

"Well, what it did was pick up the entire campus and drop it into a new dimension," said Mark. "You know about as much as we do. The sky is orange, there are giant flying bugs everywhere, and there are three suns."

"And we can breathe and we didn't all die of anaphylactic shock as soon as we got here," said Annie. "So we're playing more by *Doctor Who* rules than anything more hard science-y."

"The equation was supposed to enable the cuckoos to move on to a new dimension," I said. "It brain-blasts the one who does the math, and it destroys the world they're leaving behind, probably by destabilizing the crust of the planet so severely that the chain reaction is like something out of a bad science fiction movie, but the surviving cuckoos get a safe place to land. Biologically, we're similar enough to humans that it makes sense we'd need a world with compatible biology if we were going to survive on the other side of the rift."

"So you think this equation you keep talking about just went shopping for the best possible world to hand over to a bunch of murderous assholes?" asked James.

"I think it's math complicated enough to have become vaguely sentient in its own right; it's a complex organism and a living thing, even if it doesn't have a physical existence." Ghosts are real. Artificial intelligence is a major goal for the computer programmers of the world. Math advanced enough to have made the leap on its own isn't that big of a stretch. "Unfortunately, it's so big that most of the time it can only exist properly when distributed across all the cuckoos in the world. They bring it together when they want it to wake up and make a queen, and then they let *her* carry the full weight of it. Whatever that means for her psyche, or for her survival."

"How do they get it back when she's finished?" asked Artie.

"I don't know. If they wanted Mark to save my brainless body as a sex doll, presumably they also had a method of harvesting the pieces of the equation from whatever would be left of my mind." It felt right as I said it. They would dig the equation back out of its hole and slice it into pieces they could survive carrying, bundling each one with the history packet that was passed from parent to child, preserving the exit code in the ancestral memory shared among my entire species. Until they needed to do it all again.

Preserving the broken queen wasn't just a matter of keeping her genes. Sure, they might be strong, but with no mind, she wouldn't be able to pass the memories, meaning any children they incubated inside her would be incomplete by cuckoo standards. But they'd have the equation, and that would preserve it to be redistributed among the population. It was a disturbing, disgusting thought, made all the more so because they'd been planning to do it to me. Things always feel worse when they're personal.

"Where is the equation now?" asked Mark, eyes widening and fear rolling off of him as he looked at me. I looked calmly back.

I suppose it wasn't such a reach to assume the strange queen you couldn't remember seeing before might actually be the incarnate world-busting equation your species used to devastate dimensions, but it was still faintly insulting. If the equation had cored me out and taken my body as its new home, I hoped it wouldn't be able to pass for normal quite so easily.

"I have no idea," I said. "I blacked out when I finished solving it, and when I woke up, I was here. Maybe it's loose. Maybe it died when it completed. Can you kill an equation? I guess if it lived in the incomplete pause, then yeah, you can." A solved problem isn't living in the same way an unsolved one is. "Anyway, the point remains, the thing was big enough to have opinions. It wanted to live, which means it wanted the *cuckoos* to live, which means it was motivated to find a world where survival was possible, and if cuckoos can survive somewhere, so can we."

"There's no 'we,'" said Annie. "You *are* a cuckoo. Even if the mice agree that you're secretly family, you're still a cuckoo."

"Okay, fair," I said. "I don't get to change my species,

no matter how much I wish I could." And there was that Blue Fairy impulse again. If I'd been able to hold and work an equation complex enough to bridge the gap between worlds, why hadn't I been able to use that power to turn myself human?

Math defines and underpins the universe. Without it, nothing would make sense. Nothing would hold together. Physics can't exist without math. Biology can't exist without math. Math can do anything. I had had my hands on what was very probably the biggest piece of math in existence, and I'd only used it to do harm.

The thought was sobering. I stood, finally, and looked down at myself, unsurprised to see that I was wearing nothing but a thin white nightgown. This was already such a nightmare, why shouldn't it be a nightmare where I didn't even get to wear a bra? Or shoes?

"Long story short, math gone, and we are somewhere new. Did any of the other cuckoos survive?"

"Some of them were already moving when we came to," said Annie. "They seemed confused, and Mark said he was pretty sure you were the one who'd been doing the ritual, so we grabbed you and skedaddled. If you don't remember the equation, are you going to be able to get us home?"

"I think that's something we work on once we have a slightly better idea of what's going on here." The urge to panic was strong, and strangely comforting. For most of my life, I'd been the one who was allowed the luxury of losing my shit completely whenever something threatened me. I'd always had a bigger, tougher cousin nearby to kick the danger in the teeth. Well, for once, I couldn't count on that. For one thing, here, the biggest danger was either flying bugs that might or might not be friendly, or stray cuckoos. Neither of those was easy to kick in the teeth. For another, they didn't believe I was theirs to protect anymore.

Everything about this sucked. "We know there are ways to safely move between dimensions. Grandma Alice does it all the time."

"Grandma's nuts," said Annie bluntly. "We don't know whether she was nuts before she started hunting for Grandpa in every dimension she could reach, or whether whatever mechanism she's using for travel has *made* her nuts."

"She's not, um, 'nuts,'" I said uncomfortably. "She doesn't have any brain damage or mental illness that I've ever picked up on. She's just very badly hurt and very, very sad. She's been sad and hurt for so long that the way she thinks has changed to make more room for those feelings, and so she doesn't always seem completely rational to people who don't think the same way, but she's not 'nuts.'"

"Okay, fine," said Annie. "Potato, mashed potato. I don't think we can call her means of travel 'safe' is what I'm getting at here."

"Fair enough," I said. "Have you tried to call Rose or Mary since we got here?"

Rose Marshall and Mary Dunlavy are two of my adopted aunts. They're both dead. . . and have been since long before any modern member of the family was born. Mary was Grandma Alice's babysitter, and her versions of some of the stories the mice tell about Grandma as a little girl are filthy and hilarious. Because they're ghosts, they can usually find us anywhere we go, and I've never encountered anything that would keep them away, short of a ghost cage or other ward specifically designed to keep them from reaching their family.

Annie radiated discomfort. "I drew the runes Aunt Rose taught us to use after shouting for Mary didn't work," she said.

"And wasn't that fun to listen to," muttered Mark.

"I have so many knives," said Annie. "I am the Costco of having knives. You really want to provoke me right now, cuckoo-boy?"

"I am not a good place to store your knives," he said. "I don't know how many times I need to tell you this, but sticking knives in living people just because they say something you don't like is the reason no one likes you *or* the rest of your fucked-up family."

Annie growled.

Before she could do anything we'd all regret—but especially Mark, since he was the current target of her ire—James jumped in and said, "Neither of the ghosts came when called. I don't think they can find us here."

"Okay, so we're genuinely cut off," I said. Somehow, that wasn't as frightening as I would have expected it to be. One more thing to worry about later, when we weren't worried about giant flying insects crashing through the window and eating us all alive. "Annie, you're the sorceress. Do you know any spells for moving between dimensions?"

"Okay, one, it's always 'sorcerer;' there's no gender tag for what James and I both are, just elemental tags; I'm a pyrokinetic, he's a cryokinetic, which sort of like being a hydrokinetic, except he doesn't do water."

"I freeze the water that's already in the air," he said, sounding uncomfortable with his sudden inclusion in this conversation.

"So if you never call me a 'sorceress' again, that would be cool, and second, we're both still in training. We don't have a grown sorcerer around to help us learn what we can do without hurting ourselves, which is why we're still so deep in the elemental weeds. Mary does what she can with Grandpa Thomas' notebooks, but until we have a few more years of hard study under our belts, we're not going to be good for much of anything that doesn't involve setting something on fire or deciding to build a snowman."

"Got it." I did, sadly. They were still learning elementary math, addition and subtraction from and to the laws of physics. In a few more years, when they had transcended arithmetic, they'd be a lot more useful in situations like this one. Not that there'd ever been a situation like this one before. Not that there was—hopefully—ever going to be a situation like this one again.

I finally turned my attention to the window. The sky was still profoundly orange, and had grown a few shades darker while we were talking. A millipede the size of a blimp was undulating gently by, not visibly held up by anything. "Does gravity work the same way here that it did back on Earth, or can we all fly now?"

"It feels like it matches Earth gravity," said Artie slowly.

I hopped in place. It wasn't a hearty jump, maybe eight inches or so all told, and as soon as I reached the apex, I fell right back down again, at the speed I would have expected if I'd been playing hopscotch in the driveway.

"I think you're right," I said. "Those things up there don't have wings, but they're flying anyway. What do you think, gas bladders?"

"I think that if there are flying bugs that big, I don't want to see what eats them," said Annie. "What happens when the suns go down?"

"With three suns, it's possible that it's never going to be what we think of as true night," said Artie. "One of them may always be in the sky, or there could even be a fourth sun that's currently behind the planet that's going to rise while the others are setting."

"This dimension is really stupid," said Annie. "I do not like it here."

"No one's asking you to," I said, and moved cautiously toward the window. The millipede was gliding toward the horizon, and was enough bigger than anything else we'd seen so far that I supposed the centipede things were giving it a wide berth. Maybe it was their version of an apex predator, although the mental images that called to mind were uniformly unpleasant and nothing I really wanted to contemplate.

The glass was intact, which was all the more impressive because some of the masonry around the window *wasn't*. I leaned forward until my forehead touched the middle pane of the window, studying the university grounds outside. They were a uniform stretch of green, already starting to brown in places, although I couldn't tell whether it was because this universe was antithetical to Earth life or just because grass didn't enjoy the shock of being transported between dimensions.

If we couldn't survive here—or if my mammalian relations couldn't survive, while Mark and I were going to be just fine—we'd know soon enough. Until we had signs that that was the case, we needed to carry on like everything was normal. Or as normal as everything could be when we were in a whole new dimension.

There were a few cuckoos motionless in the grass outside, sprawled where they'd fallen. Some of them looked charred, and one that I could see looked like poorly-defrosted steak. Annie and James at work. Artie's work would be harder to see from this distance. Cuckoos don't have blood the way true mammals do; we have a clear fluid that's closer in nature to insect hemolymph but serves the same purpose as hemoglobin. Biology is confusing. Anyway, without red stains to mark the bullet holes, I'd have to get right up on top of the bodies to know which ones were down there because my cousin had pulled a gun on them.

The number of bodies I could see scattered around the lawn made me obscurely proud of my family. None of them was obviously pregnant, however, meaning none of them was Ingrid. I clearly remembered holding her close in the white void of my own mind, shoving the equation into her like a knife. All I'd done to her was what she'd been intending to do to me. All I had become in that moment was my mother's daughter, and there was no way she could have survived the experience. I knew that, as surely as I knew that I had ten toes and blue eyes and no heartbeat.

So where was she?

"That's not enough bodies," I said.

Annie bristled. "So *sorry*, princess. We would have been more effective murderers if we hadn't been fighting for our lives at the same time."

"No, that's not what I meant," I said. I was unaccustomed to Annie interpreting my words in the least charitable way possible. I'd seen her do it to other people—her unfriendliness toward outsiders was legendary within the family—but never to me. "I mean, I know how good you are at killing things when you don't have any other choice, and a whole swarm of cuckoos trying to end the world is sort of the definition of not having any other choice. There should be more corpses down there."

"She's right," said Artie. I managed to resist the urge to whip around and thank him for agreeing with me. It wasn't easy. "I saw you set like a dozen of them on fire, and I shot at least six. The numbers don't add up."

"Maybe something down there has been scavenging the bodies," said Mark anxiously.

"Or maybe some of them weren't as dead as we thought they were," said James. When everyone turned to look at him, he shrugged. "It could happen. Cuckoos aren't strictly mammals the way we understand the term. Maybe freezing them won't kill them the way it would a human."

"We've never really had a chance to test that theory," said Annie.

"I don't feel cold the way the rest of you do," I said slowly. "Mom says it's because hemolymph serves as a sort of biological antifreeze. She used to have to remind me to put on shoes when I went outside to get the mail in December."

"I thought you said you grew up with us," said Artie sharply. "It doesn't get that cold in December."

"Maybe not in Portland, but I was in Columbus with Mom and Dad for most of the year," I shot back. "It snows in Ohio."

"And you just didn't notice?" asked James.

"Don't look at me," said Mark. "I grew up in California."

I had to fight the urge to scream. My family was always inclined to argue and talk things to death, but normally, they restrained that urge around me, in part because they knew we were all on the same side and wanted to take care of business as efficiently as possible. Now I was part of the business that might need taking care of. Without the mice to vouch for me, I would still have been tied to the chair, and they'd probably still be arguing about what they were supposed to do with me.

It was a sobering thought. That didn't make it a helpful one. "While we stand up here and argue about my childhood, which I didn't mean to delete from your minds in the first place, we're still missing a bunch of cuckoos," I said, as calmly as I could. "Whether they got up and walked away on their own or something took them doesn't really matter because, either way, they're a problem we need to be dealing with. I need to see how far my scan range currently extends. Is one of you going to shoot me if my eyes go white?"

"Not unless we feel you pushing on our heads." Annie narrowed her eyes. "So don't try it."

"Wasn't planning to," I said. "I need to know if we're alone." And how far my scan could go. Part of me was almost excited by the idea of finding out the limits of this new instar.

My natural telepathic abilities had been present since birth, although they didn't manifest truly until the McNallys died, and for most of my life, they had continued to grow at a slow, reasonable rate. The instar I had accidentally triggered in New York had been followed by a massive increase in my capabilities, and just from the way my head felt already, I could say with some assurance that this latest instar—this *final* instar—had done something similar. It wasn't unreasonable of me to believe that I might be able to scan the whole campus from here.

It was still probably going to give me a headache, which was going to leave me vulnerable around people who weren't exactly allies right now. Sometimes doing the right thing sucks.

I glanced around the room, aware that I was stalling, unable to quite stop myself. "Who found this place?"

"I did," said Artie, putting up one hand in a hesitant wave. He was putting off pulses of anxiety—he didn't like the idea of me using my telepathy around him, even if I wasn't targeting him specifically. "We needed shelter, and the building looked stable."

"Good," I said. "Then you know where we are. The grass looks too far away for this to be the first floor. How many stairs did you carry me up?"

"Just one flight," said Annie. "We would have left you if there had been more."

"No, you wouldn't. Evie and Uncle Kevin trained you too well to leave a potential source of information behind just because you didn't want to keep carrying me, and you have three boys with you. You would have forced Mark and James to carry me."

"Not Artie?"

"Artie probably already noticed that the hum of my presence got louder inside his head when he touched me." Artie looked away, discomfort rolling off him in a wave. "That's normal when you're telepathically attuned to someone. You probably get it around Mom, too, just at a lower volume."

"She's our grandmother," said Annie. "Why would it be a lower volume?"

"She was never one of your best friends," I countered, and turned away from the window, walking toward the closed classroom door.

As I had hoped, Annie followed, too annoyed to do anything else. "Where the hell do you think you're going?"

"The hall," I snapped. "You're the only one who said you wouldn't freak out if my eyes went white, and I don't actually trust you around me while I'm going into a deep scan state, and we need to know where the rest of the cuckoos went." And maybe it was cruel of me, but I hoped—I really, truly hoped—the answer was "into the belly of one of those terrible flying things." I also hoped that if any of them had still been alive, it had been quick.

The period surrounding the equation was blurry. I'd spent most of it in a state of what could only be called altered consciousness, not quite drugged or high, but absolutely intoxicated by the hormones produced by my final instar and entangled in the threads of the equation itself, which Ingrid had been feeding into my mind one piece at a time as she'd received it from the cuckoos who were coming to begin the ritual to carry us into a new world. It seemed difficult to believe that every cuckoo on Earth had been on the campus when this began, and maybe they hadn't been; if every cuckoo normally carried a different component of the equation, passed along maternal lines, then any cuckoo who had multiple children would have passed their piece multiple times. So we might have left some of them behind. That shouldn't have felt like a good thing, and probably wouldn't once we made it back to Earth and still had cuckoos to deal with, but right here and now, with our reduced numbers and total lack of tactical knowledge, it was better if we weren't dealing with the largest number of enemies possible.

But there had been kids. I distinctly remembered children too young to have reached their first instar, little kids in cotton pajamas and frilly fairy dresses and all the other things children would be wearing when they didn't expect to leave their homes. Those children were alien invaders in the homes of their parents, dropped off without question or consent, destined to eventually destroy everything they loved, but they were also *kids*. They liked cartoons and sugary cereal. They loved their moms and dads. And Mark and I were enough of an illustration that sometimes nurture could win out over nature for me to want to help them in any way I could.

Especially if I could find a way to help them and save the families that had raised them at the same time.

Annie dogged my heels all the way to the door, glaring at me both mentally and—I had no doubt—physically. The three boys stayed clustered near the window, not following us. That was fine. Annie alone was enough of a weapon of mass destruction that if she came with me, I'd be perfectly safe.

"Planning to follow me into the hall?" I asked.

"You didn't think we'd let you go off *alone*, did you?" she asked, sounding almost offended by the very idea.

I hadn't, actually, but I couldn't say I minded the chance to get away from the rest of them for a few minutes, either, especially not when Artie looked at me in borderline accusatory silence. I couldn't help myself: I dipped below the surface of his thoughts, into the cool, clear water of his private pond, and immediately wished I hadn't. He believed me—like the rest of us, he'd been raised never to question the mice. They didn't lie, and if they said I was a Price, then I was a Price. I was also, according to both myself and the mice, one of the most important relationships in his life, and I'd taken myself away from him without asking whether he'd agree to that, or whether it would hurt him. He was methodically examining all the memories he could call up from early childhood, looking for the holes.

And he was finding them. My excisions had been clean and thorough; he wasn't going to find traces of me lurking under an unturned stone. But he was finding the places where it didn't make sense that he'd been left alone, or that he'd gotten his way over his sister without someone else to take his side. I'd stolen myself from him.

I was already being punished for that, because I'd stolen him from me at the same time, and I didn't even get the luxury of having someone to be angry with. And that didn't matter, because his anger was completely justified, as much as I didn't want it to be. I withdrew my mind from his as quickly as I could, leaving him to hate me in peace.

One more downside of being a telepath in a largely non-telepathic society: when I allow myself to feel my feelings without examining them first, I can push them onto other people without meaning to, and I can do a hell of a lot of harm in the process. Not hurting anyone around me requires more conscious effort than I like to think about. It's way too easy for me to convince literally everyone to agree with me, all the time, whether I'm right or not.

Artie's anger was honest and pure and, most importantly, his own. He didn't deserve mine piled on top of it, or the disappointment in myself and his reaction that would come bundled with the feeling. I finished pulling back my mind and suited the motion to the thought, turning and yanking the door open.

Antimony followed out into the hall, holding to her refusal to let me out of her sight, even for the duration of a simple scan. I would have been able to pick up on that even if she hadn't said it, and even if I hadn't been reading her mind.

Just what I always wanted: a suicidal cuckoo to babysit, she thought sourly.

I didn't take the bait. When we were kids, my cousins used to think things they knew would upset me, just to see whether my manners were actually as good as Mom and I said they were. Annie was still the same person she'd always been, just missing the experiences we'd shared with one another. It made sense that she'd go back to older methods of getting a rise out of me. I knew these people, but from their perspective, I was a stranger, and they were naturally going to test what kind of a person I was.

"You can stay in the classroom with the boys," I said. "I'll come back in as soon as I finish my scan."

"I'll stay right here and watch you do it," she countered.

"And you won't stab me, shoot me, or set me on fire?"

Annie scoffed, the sound carrying almost as much annoyance as her thoughts. "I already told you: unless it feels like you're trying to enter my mind, I'll stay over here and keep my fireballs and weapons to myself."

"I guess that has to be good enough," I said, and forced myself to relax, chin dipping toward my chest as I focused on reaching outward, beyond the limits of my own mind, and into the world around me.

Five

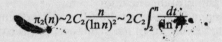

$$\pi_2(n) \sim 2C_2 \frac{n}{(\ln n)^2} \sim 2C_2 \int_2^n \frac{dt}{(\ln t)^2}$$

"I don't want to be a monster. I refuse to be a monster. I am a person, and people get to make our own choices about whether or not we bare our claws."

—Angela Baker

Standing in the hall of what is probably a technically stolen university building, preparing for one hell of a headache

THERE'S ALWAYS BEEN SOMETHING a little strange and dreamlike about performing a telepathic scan. I'm aware of my body and my own existence as a physical being with a physical location to monitor and defend, but it's . . . remote, almost, less important than whatever it is I'm reaching for on a psychic plane. So it wasn't all that strange when my body immediately faded into something inessential, the frustration of being barefoot and vague stirrings of hunger blunting.

What *was* strange was the scope of the feeling. My body dropped away and kept dropping, taking the campus with it. I might have lost track of myself if not for Annie standing nearby, the bright flame of her annoyance burning like a beacon I could follow all the way home.

The boys were the next thing to appear: the boys, and the mice, whose tiny minds were like sparkling candles, pinpoints of thought that I could, I knew, zoom in on and examine if I wanted to. There should have been some distortion or difficulty from being this far away. Even twenty feet had always been enough to make things blurry before, like being shortsighted and trying to read a sign without my glasses. Now everything was crisp, pristine, and perfect.

It was almost disorienting. Of course, even more disorienting was the first mind I found that didn't belong to one of us. It felt like my mind was a mile or more above the ground—high enough that it was like I was trying to signal *space*—when it brushed against the thoughts of a vast flying herbivore. It was about as intelligent as a cow, a true cow, not a minotaur or an Apis. It was on its way to a wide place filled with delicious decay, the thought of which consumed almost its entire mind. It thought of that rotting vegetation and fruit with such swelling joy and hunger that my own stomach growled in sympathetic hunger. Pulling back a little bit gave me enough context to recognize it as the millipede I'd seen from the window.

If the millipedes were herbivores, it wasn't going to eat us, and that was a good thing. Flight took effort, and while it might eat meat by mistake when feeding, it wasn't interested enough in meat as an end goal to hunt.

I pulled back again, this time all the way to the outline of my own body, and was relieved when I was able to separate myself cleanly from the flying herbivore. Learning my new limits was about more than just figuring out how far I could go. It was about avoiding some sort of messed up permanent mind link just because I pushed a little too hard. My body felt odd, too small and limited by gravity, and what was this nonsense about only having four limbs? I needed at least forty if I was going to get a proper grip on the prevailing winds!

"Ugh," I said, rubbing my forehead with one hand and preparing to reach out again. A hand grabbed my wrist before I could finish lowering my arm back to my side. The mental hum of Annie's presence became a roar. I slowly raised my head, blinking at her.

"Yes?"

"Your *hair* was *floating*," she informed me, as if this were a great and profound offense. "Please don't do that again."

"Sorry, but it's not voluntary." I shook my head. "When Artie and I were in a crash set up by my biological mother, I stopped the flying glass from slicing us to ribbons—"

"You hurt Artie's car? Oh, he's going to kill you," she said.

"—and I stopped the rain from falling on all of us during the ritual. So I guess maybe things work a little differently when I really exert myself now that I'm through these most recent instars. I can't really help it. Or control it yet, either." I looked down at my feet, suddenly abashed. "I'm sorry."

"It's fine. It was just a bit of a shock." Annie let go of my wrist, backing off again. "I'm sorry I grabbed you."

"Just please try to remember how much I didn't melt your brain when you did it, okay? Here I go again." I ducked my head and felt the tingle of my eyes going white, trying to spread my mind across the entire campus, searching for signs that we were not alone.

There were a few smaller millipedes nosing around the grass. I made note of them, dismissed them, and moved on. I didn't know the layout of the campus: I had no way of knowing *where* they were, only that they existed. I kept my thoughts low, searching, and suddenly, there they were: human minds, people from our dimension who'd been transported here without their knowledge or consent.

There was a cluster of eight in one location, their minds a welter of confused disorientation and fear. There were other minds with them, one I recognized as a bogeyman like my brother Drew and three smaller, sharper minds that I recognized as cuckoo children only a beat before a childish voice shouted "GO AWAY" in the space between my ears. I pulled back into my own body so fast and hard it was like a rubber band snapping home, gasping.

Annie gave me a sideways look. "Everything all right?"

"I found some students," I said. "And some of the cuckoo children who survived the ritual. They didn't want me thinking at them."

"No adult cuckoos?"

"Not yet." I worried my bottom lip between my teeth. "I know you don't . . . remember . . . much about the way this is supposed to work, but telepathy isn't a magic wand. I can miss things, especially if they're shielded against me. I don't know if the adult cuckoos are hiding themselves somehow, or if they've moved outside of my functional range." Even expanded as it was, my range only seemed to extend a little beyond the edge of campus, or maybe that was just the space I could comprehend. Either way, if there were adult cuckoos awake and thinking in that space, I wasn't finding them.

Annie nodded slowly. "All right. Is that everyone?"

"I don't think so. Hang on." I was getting used to the routine. Look down, reach out, lose all sense of my body, keep searching. I found more students; not many of them, maybe thirty all told, and all but three, including the bogeyman from the first group, were human. The other two cryptids were a chupacabra, and a cornwife. The cornwife made sense, since we were in Iowa, but it took me a moment to recognize him; I didn't encounter them often, not even in Ohio. They're remarkably rare for a country where fully half the industrial farming seems to depend on corn.

There were two more bogeymen *under* the campus, in a slice of steam tunnel that we had apparently taken with us when we made the jump, and there was some other kind of giant insect flying far overhead, just at the very outside edge of what I could reach. It was higher than the millipede had been, which made me suspect that it was something with actual wings, not undulating cilia. Whatever it was didn't seem to have a rider, or if it did, the rider's mind was too distant for me to fully grasp it.

I pulled back into myself with a small gasp, opening my eyes to find Annie watching me. " . . . was my hair floating again?" I asked warily. Speaking aloud felt clumsy and alien, with my mind still halfway-unmoored from my body. Anything else might have been enough to get me stabbed. I'd go for clumsiness any day.

"No," said Annie. "It's not that. It's—did you find anything else?"

I nodded, filling her quickly in. When I was done, she sighed, and said, "I'll go get the boys."

"Um, why?" Her thoughts were still hostile enough. I could happily go a little longer without adding the chaos of Artie's mind to the scene.

"Because we have two clusters of mostly human students out there, and we need a way to keep them inside as long as we possibly can," said Annie. "That means we need to go find them."

"There's two of us," I said, a little desperately. There it was. I shrugged. "At least you're admitting you don't trust me," I said. "Fine. Let's go get them."

It only took a few steps to get back to the classroom. Annie stuck her head inside and snapped, "Get off your dicks and come on, you three."

"Where are we going?" asked James, already in motion. Mark and Artie hung back.

"Come *on*," said Annie. "We're going walkies."

"I'm good here," said Artie.

Annie turned her full attention on him. "Are you?" she asked. "And I'm telling your parents exactly what when they ask why I walked away and left you alone in the horror movie we're currently trapped in? Move it, Harrington. We're all going."

"Going where?" asked Mark.

"Sarah found some students," she said. "On the campus. They're in two clusters, so we need two groups to go and fetch them. Or, you know, make sure they're in defensible locations and convince them to stay put until we find a way back to Earth, whichever seems less annoying. Now come *on*."

Artie and Mark followed James to the door.

The five of us stood in the hallway for a long, silent moment before Annie pointed and said, "This way." She started walking. We all followed.

Whatever the equation had done to transport us here, it had done so with relatively little structural damage to the building itself. The hallway was long, straight, and lined with doors identical to the one we'd just come out of, all of them closed. I paused, reaching out, but found no minds lurking behind them, either human or cuckoo.

James gave me a sidelong look. "What did you just do?"

"I'm sorry?" I blinked, focusing on him. "What do you mean?"

"Your eyes went white for a second there. What did you do? Cuckoos' eyes only go white when they're doing something. Did you do something to one of us?"

"If I were going to 'do something,' as you so charmingly put it, don't you think I would have done it to Annie while I had her alone out here?" Annie was leading us down the hall, a little line of miserable, hostile ducklings. I kept my attention on James. "I know you don't have that much practice trusting the mice yet, but I grew up knowing that they were meant to be trusted no matter what."

"HAIL," shouted a tiny chorus of surprisingly welcome voices.

"So if you can't trust *me*, try trusting *them*."

James sighed. "I'll try," he said.

"That's all I'm asking for," The door at the end of the hall led into a stairwell, dark and echoing and filled with too many shadows. There were no windows here; the only light that reached the interior was thin and watery, filtered through cracks in the masonry and a single skylight high overhead. The whole thing made me anxious. This wasn't a good place for lingering in the shadows.

Annie snapped her fingers and another ball of flame

appeared, hovering above her hand. I wondered if she'd noticed how casually she was summoning and dismissing her little bonfires. I wondered if she'd take it well if I pointed it out, then decided that it wasn't worth the possible conflict. She led us down to the ground floor without a word, glancing back once as if to make sure we were all behaving ourselves before she pushed the door open with her hip.

The outside air had a strange tang to it, almost citrusy, like walking into an airport terminal right after the cleaning crews had been through to disinfect everything. It wasn't unpleasant, but it coated the back of my throat and the inside of my nostrils, covering everything in the faint, distant scent of Lemon Pledge.

Antimony made a gagging sound. I whirled, sticking out one foot to keep the door from slamming shut. I didn't need to. James gave me a startled look, radiating surprise, and caught the door himself. Somewhat shamefacedly, I turned my attention back to Annie.

"Are you all right?" I asked. "Can you breathe?"

"Yeah, I just hate that smell," she said, and sneezed. "It wasn't here when we went inside."

"If you carted me into the classroom as soon as you all woke up, the atmosphere of campus and the surrounding area probably hadn't had time to finish blending." I didn't know whether or not that was bullshit, and as long as Annie wasn't having an allergic reaction to our surroundings, I didn't entirely care. Physics may depend on math to work. That doesn't make it my subject of primary study. "Do the rest of you need to stay inside while Mark and I go and look for the missing students?"

"Leave me out of this," said Mark, sounding alarmed.

"And let the two cuckoos wander off alone? I thought we already established that that wasn't happening."

"Actually, you just established that I wasn't allowed to go off without supervision, but have it your way," I said, and stepped outside, into the light of that strange orange sky.

It was even more jarring up close. Something about the quality of the light itself was wrong, as if it wasn't refracting the way I expected it to. Two suns were currently visible overhead, each about two-thirds the size of the sun at home, surrounded by prismatic coronas of glittering radiance. They looked more like the sun from the Teletubbies than a real celestial body had any right to look, although they didn't have the cherubic faces of smiling human infants. And thank Galileo for that. I don't think I could have coped.

One of those vast flying millipedes was undulating through the sky almost directly above us, as high up as a private plane heading into a municipal airport. I squinted up at it, reaching out mentally to confirm that it was unaware of our presence. I knew they weren't predatory, but it still seemed better to make the effort than to count on the creature—whatever it actually was—being disinterested in us.

"What are you doing?" demanded Antimony. "Why are your eyes white?"

"Shh." I kept reaching up, trying to find the place where the creature in the sky began. When I did make contact, it felt just like the one I'd reached before, placid, content, and disinterested in anything but getting to the feeding grounds. I shook the contact away, settling back into the space of my own skin, and looked at Antimony. "I was making sure our big friend up there," I pointed into the sky, in the vague direction of the flying millipede, "wasn't going to swoop down and swallow us whole, and also checking to see whether she was a member of this planet's dominant species."

"She?" asked Antimony, sounding amused.

"She's an egg layer, and hopes she'll find someone to fertilize her eggs while she's at the feeding place, so yes, 'she' seems like the appropriate pronoun, and you're the one who always says people are kinder to things when they don't think of them as 'it,'" I said. Her lectures about the family tendency to refer to the mice as "it" unless they were found actively giving birth had started when she was in kindergarten, and showed no real signs of stopping.

According to her, the reason so many languages gendered things like furniture, and the reason some people still struggled with the singular "they," all came down to humans seeing an intrinsic gender as part of the human experience. So something that was an "it" was lesser and, as such, could be more easily discarded or ignored.

"Gender is stupid," scoffed Annie. "We don't *need* to know what someone's gender is; we need to know what kind of a person they are. And that goes double for tables and flying millipedes and shit. 'They' is gender-neutral. 'It' is person-neutral. If we want people who don't look like humans to be taken seriously, we have to let them have pronouns, at least until humans get a little bit more enlightened."

"Mean girl from the murder family has a point," said Mark. "Also, now that I have spoken those words aloud, please kill me."

Annie rolled her eyes before focusing back on me. "All right, Sarah, you're the one who found the survivors. Which way are we going?"

"Are we all going together?"

Artie was still thinking sour, unfriendly thoughts in my direction, and for the first time in my life I wanted to get away from him if at all possible. I was enormously relieved when Annie shook her head.

"No, you and I are going to one of the locations, and the boys are going to the other. Divide and conquer, like an episode of *Scooby-Doo*."

"Because splitting the party always works out *so* well for the Mystery Gang," snarked James.

He was probably right. I still didn't want to argue. I dropped briefly back into scan, eyes tingling, and finally pointed in two opposing directions. "The smaller group is this way," I said. "The group with the chupacabra is in the other direction."

"We'll take the big one," said Artie.

"Why the hell not?" asked Mark. "Our horrible deaths wouldn't be complete without a chupacabra in the mix."

"Thank you," said Annie, ignoring the sarcasm. "If you run into any trouble, just run and scream. We'll follow the sound."

She started walking. She had shoes and didn't seem to notice the bits of fallen masonry on the path. I grimaced and followed her as quickly as I dared in bare feet, leaving the boys behind.

She waited until we had a little distance between us before saying, quietly, "You seemed to want to get out of there."

"And you cared about what I wanted? What, have you decided we're friends again and we should sit and braid each other's hair?"

"If I suddenly felt like we were friends, I'd know you were messing with my mind."

I shook my head. It was difficult to reconcile the brilliant if annoying cousin I loved with this mulish, irritating woman. "If I were going to mess with your mind, I would have put myself back where I belonged as soon as I woke up, and you'd have no idea it had happened. We've known each other since we were kids. I remember your first training bra, and how pissed Very was when it was bigger than hers."

"Heh," said Antimony, with a bit of a genuine chuckle under the word. "She was so mad when the Boob Fairy came for me and skipped over her. I thought she was going to set up a deer blind in the backyard and start taking potshots."

"She's never been the most rational."

"No, she hasn't. I mean, she—" Annie caught herself midsentence. "I don't want to talk about my sister with you. It's not appropriate."

I knew why she was saying that. I still felt a pang, even as I nodded and said, "That's your choice. I know you don't remember, but I was there, and we talked about your sister plenty." Verity had been furious when it became obvious her baby sister was going to be both taller and more physically developed than she was, and even pointing out that it was probably better for her dancing if her breasts stayed a little smaller hadn't done anything to allay her anger. Those had been a tense few years within the family, as all the girls had hit puberty one after another—and puberty had hit us all back.

(Pseudo-mammalian means I got most of the obvious physical variances. From a different dimension and having different responses to Earth-native bacteria and the like meant my complexion had stayed clearer than my cousins' throughout the whole process. Verity had also taken this personally. Taking things personally had sort of been Verity's hobby when we were teenagers.)

We had walked far enough from the boys for them to be almost out of sight when I glanced over my shoulder. "Last chance to go back," I said. "If you stick with me, we're on our own."

"I'm not scared of being away from backup," said Annie. "I'm already alone with a cuckoo. I think I'm plenty brave."

"I spend a lot of time alone with a cuckoo," I said. "If that's a sign of bravery, then I guess I'm the bravest girl I know."

Annie sighed and kept walking. Good. For all my bravado, I didn't actually want to be wandering around in a new dimension alone. There was no telling what mindless dangers might be lurking, and Annie represented a lot of firepower. Some of it literal, some of it not.

I glanced at her. Humans seem to find comfort in eye contact. It's never made sense to me, since it's not like their voices carry any better when I can see their mouths move, but if it made her more comfortable being alone with me, I was willing to do it. "Do you have any bullets left?"

"I have enough." She shrugged. "Also plenty of knives, and as much fire as I can pull out of the air. I probably shouldn't burn more than I have to."

"Why not?"

Annie raised an eyebrow. "I thought you knew everything about us, since we grew up together." There was a jeering note in her voice, like she was trying to catch me in the lie she so clearly *knew* existed.

"Okay, one, you remember my mother because she's your grandmother, and you know any cuckoo she raised would have manners too developed to allow them to just rummage around your head without permission. So no, I don't know *everything* about you. I didn't even know for sure that you liked boys until you got with Sam."

Annie snorted. "No one knew that for sure, me included."

"Elsie always assumed you liked girls but hadn't quite gotten around to figuring out how you were going to tell anyone."

"She's not *wrong*," said Annie, with a broad shrug. "I just didn't think I'd ever like *anyone* enough to actually, you know, date them or get physical with them or make deals with the crossroads to save them from drowning or any of the other things I've done with Sam."

I stopped, turning to fully face her. If I'd tried to keep moving, I would probably have tripped over my own feet, and even a cuckoo can be stopped by a broken neck. "Say that last part again."

Annie looked at me coolly, radiating the satisfaction of a younger sibling who had just managed to shock an older relation. "We get physical. We have sex. You know what that is, right? You don't reproduce by laying eggs under the bark of a tree for the males to come along and fertilize later?"

"Oh, God, I didn't even think about the part where deleting all your memories meant taking out playing cryptozoologist when we were eleven and you wanted answers about cuckoo biology," I said in a rush. "Mom and Evie were *so pissed* when they found us naked in the barn. Yes, I know what sex is. No, I haven't had sex. Cuckoo boys are horrifying nightmare factories that I don't want anywhere near me, and dating human boys always seemed a little bit deceptive. And yes, I do prefer boys. Even though their minds are pretty gross."

Annie wrinkled her nose. "I can't even imagine being able to read Sam's mind. It seems like it would be nice to know what he was thinking, but then I think about it and realize I don't want to know most of those things."

"That's what it's always been like for me," I agreed. "But yeah, Sam was a surprise."

"To you and me both," she said. "I think the only person who wasn't surprised was Sam, and that's just because he didn't know me well enough to realize my entire family had already filed me under 'too misanthropic to date.' I always assumed if I wound up with anyone, it would be another derby g—" She cut herself off mid-word, suddenly radiating distrust. "Are you making me talk to you?"

"Oh, for fuck's sake." I started walking again. Maybe I could find something to kick. Kicking something would make me feel so much better right now. "Only if you consider the ancient art of 'making polite conversation with the woman who can set you on fire with her mind' to be some form of devious cuckoo manipulation. I'm not telepathically influencing you, if that's what you mean, and I assume it is. *Assume*, because I'm not reading your mind. It would be rude as hell for me to do that, and you don't know me anymore because I messed up, and while right now I can't imagine why this is the case, I want you to like me again. You're my cousin and I remember you loving me. I want us to make it home. I want you to love me like you used to. I know that may not be possible, but I'm not going to make choices that make that less likely when I don't have to."

"You sure made the choice to mess with my mind in the first place," she countered hotly.

"I was under considerable duress at the time," I shot back. "What with the whole 'trying not to destroy the world as we know it' thing I had going on. I can't promise I wouldn't do the same thing again if it was that or let everything I'd ever loved be destroyed. You said you made a crossroads deal for Sam. You *know* what the crossroads have done to our family. Why would you do that, if not under extreme duress and trying to protect what you loved?"

Annie didn't answer. I sniffed. "Thought so," I said.

"People have a right to think of their own minds as sacrosanct," she said. "Our thoughts are meant to be *private*."

"See, this was a side effect of wiping your memories of me that I didn't anticipate and should have considered," I said. "You get to give me all your favorite lectures again for the first time. That has to be *so* intellectually satisfying. You tested them out on me while you were still workshopping them, and now you get to deliver them to me in their refined form like I'm a fresh audience."

Annie wrinkled her nose. "You don't have to be an asshole about it."

"Why not? You're having a great time being an asshole to me."

Annie has always been the most judgmental of my cousins. Maybe it's because she was the baby of the family until Mom pulled me out of a storm drain, but she's always seen the world in very black-and-white terms. A thing is right or it's wrong. A thing that's wrong is either forgivable or it isn't. And once a thing is unforgivable, that's it, game over. If I could convince her I meant no harm, Artie and James would be a walk in the park.

Of course, there was the terrifying possibility, reinforced by my increased range in the aftermath of the equation, that when I'd actually *held* the equation, when I'd had all of its power and potency to put behind my wishes, I had been able to reach all the way from Iowa to Portland. I'd already demonstrated that while in the grips of the equation, I could convince space to bend enough to make transit between the two as simple as adding two and two together and throwing down the resulting number like a challenge.

What if I had actually wiped myself from the memories of not just the people who were with me in this strange, lovely, potentially terrible new world, but also from the memories of everyone who'd ever loved me? What if we made it home and my mother looked at me the way she would have looked at any other cuckoo, unwanted and untrustworthy and terrible? It was a bit of a reach to jump from "I used the local minds as distributed computing space" to "and now my life doesn't get to exist anymore," but after the last few . . . days? Weeks? Time sort of loses all meaning when you're plugged into the world-ending history of your species. Anyway, it was a reach, but that didn't make it impossible. Not for me, not anymore.

If I could convince Annie to love me again, *without* using telepathy to change her mind, maybe I could get my family back. Even if I'd wiped myself out of their memories and couldn't possibly put myself back in. There was a still a chance all this could end with me going home. Maybe. If I did things the right way.

Annie's cheeks flushed red, a human biological response I've always sort of envied, and she turned her face away. "Whatever," she mumbled.

"My eyes are probably going to go white a lot while we're out here," I warned her. "We know where the human survivors are, but I didn't pick up on any adult cuckoos, and that doesn't make any sense to me. An entire species doesn't just *disappear.*"

"I know," she said.

"So maybe don't point it out every time it happens? You're just going to make me self-conscious, and then I won't be able to focus on what we came out here to do." Maybe this was going to work out after all. We could find the missing cuckoos, who were probably maintaining strong mental shields while they were trying to avoid being devoured by whatever had evolved to eat giant flying millipedes, and then we could join up with the boys and all go back to the classroom and start doing the math we needed to get the hell out of here. We could make it home in one piece, with the beginnings of a new trust between us. We could—

And naturally, that was when the cuckoo came lurching around the side of the building, walking in the uncoordinated herky-jerky way popularized by zombie movies, head lolling to the left and arms stretched out in front of them, heading directly for Annie. Their eyes were blazing white, but I couldn't pick up on any broadcasting thoughts or emotions from them. I shrieked and stumbled backward, out of the cuckoo's reach, grabbing Annie and dragging her with me. She didn't fight. The emotional wave washing off of her actually felt a spark of gratitude.

"You were supposed to *warn* me!" she snapped, producing a knife from somewhere inside her shirt.

"I didn't hear them coming! I can't find their thoughts!"

"Please, please tell me that's a singular 'they.'" She pulled her arm back, preparing to throw the knife if the cuckoo didn't stop coming.

The cuckoo didn't stop. I gathered my mind and shoved it forward as hard as I could, not making any effort to be gentle. The cuckoo still wasn't broadcasting anything I could detect, not even as I reached the surface of what should have been its thoughts, the place where everything it was and knew and wanted began. I realized I was thinking of it as exactly that—an it—in the absence of any opinions or instincts about identity. I couldn't say whether it considered itself male, female, or neither. I couldn't say whether it considered itself anything at all.

And then I broke the surface of its mind, and had my answer: it didn't. All it contained was a whirling maelstrom of hurt and hunger, with no traces of identity or self-awareness anywhere in the black storm that was its psyche. If it had ever been a person, that had been washed away, destroyed by something so much larger than itself that it had had no chance of standing up against the storm, no prayer of survival.

I pulled back to keep from getting sucked under, and

a fragment of a function floated by me on the whirlwind of the cuckoo's mind, numbers glittering like broken glass in the darkness. I gasped and pulled myself completely free just as Annie threw her knife.

It caught the cuckoo in the throat. The cuckoo stopped advancing, made a choking noise, and fell. One thing I have to give my cousin, even when we're technically at odds: she is a very, very good at killing things.

"I know what did this," I said, grabbing her shoulder again, this time to keep myself from falling over. My knees were weak, and my legs felt like they were on the verge of giving out. "It was the equation!"

"What?" She pulled away from me, moving to retrieve her knife. The cuckoo, which was still gasping for breath as it bled out, clawed at her. She kicked its hands away.

"The equation, the one that dumped us here and wiped out your memories of me," I said. "I wasn't just pushing it onto you, I was pushing it onto all of them. All the cuckoos who were in the ritual circle. When I finished the equation, I shattered it back into its component parts and distributed it between them. But I didn't . . . I didn't protect them from it the way I did you. Whoever this was before the equation, it was still aware when I forced it into them, and it *ate* them when it couldn't find a way out of their mind."

"Huh," she said. The cuckoo wasn't gasping anymore. "Is it dead?"

"The cuckoo or the equation?"

"The cuckoo's kind of the problem right now."

I barely had to extend myself mentally before I said, "Yes." The storm wasn't whirling anymore.

"Cool." She turned to me, eyes hard and expression as unreadable as ever. "I guess this is where I'm supposed to thank you for protecting me from a threat *you* created. I wouldn't even be here if you hadn't let the cuckoos use you as their super-battery or whatever the hell it is they were trying to do."

No, you'd be clinging to the remains of your planet as

it shook itself into splinters, I thought, and didn't say anything.

Annie bent to wipe her knife on the grass before giving me an assessing look—the intent was clear in the ribbon of thought that accompanied the expression, if not in the expression itself—and asking, "Are there more of those around here?"

"I don't know."

"You could tell where the survivors are, and those flying things, but you can't hear other cuckoos when they're practically on top of us? Because that isn't at all suspicious."

"Okay, first of all, adult cuckoos can shield their thoughts"—although I wasn't actually sure how well they could shield themselves from my new abilities if they were close by, I didn't think pointing that out right now would help allay Annie's suspicion—"but it wasn't . . . look, I can tell when someone has an Aeslin mouse in their pocket, because mice *think*. I can pick up on dogs, cats, squirrels—even head lice. They have brains. Not big brains. Not complex brains. But brains. There's something for me to latch onto." Most smaller insects had neurons more than they had brains, simple nerves firing off basic instructions for the body to follow, or I would never have been able to sleep when I was within a mile of an ant hill. I was simplifying for Antimony's sake.

And judging by the mixture of boredom and dread she was projecting in my direction, it was a largely wasted effort. I could say virtually anything I wanted and she'd keep viewing me as a threat to her health, safety, and ability to eventually go home to her family.

A family that no longer included me.

I took a deep breath, the scent of disinfectant filling my nose, and said, "I couldn't hear that cuckoo coming for the same reason I can't tell you whether you're about to come down with a cold. Viruses don't have minds. They do what they need to do in order to survive, but it's entirely driven by biological impulses too primitive to even qualify as instincts. They don't think about anything. They don't plan for anything. The equation is like a virus that way—after the equation ate what was left of its mind, the cuckoo didn't have any capacity for thought left. So there was nothing left for it to broadcast. The equation took it all."

The equation in its completed form was big enough, powerful enough, to shatter worlds. What could it do when unleashed on something as small and fragile as a *mind*?

"So you're saying you can't hear these brain-wiped cuckoos coming because there's nothing left for you to hear?"

I nodded.

"Well, isn't that just fucking awesome? And we don't know how many of them are still running around here, and we don't know what happens if they catch us—did you get *anything* before we went and killed the asshole?"

"Hunger," I said slowly. "But not . . . not physical hunger, exactly. It wasn't going to *eat* us. But it was going to devour us, because that was all it knew how to do."

Annie turned to stare flatly at me. "You do realize you're contradicting yourself, right?"

"I do." I shook my head, too frustrated to do anything else. "The words I need to explain this don't really exist. I don't know exactly what would have happened if that cuckoo had managed to get hold of us. But I don't . . . I don't think it would have been good, and I don't think you should let Mark go anywhere alone if you want to keep him."

"Just Mark? Really?"

"You and James are sorcerers. You can take care of yourselves. Artie's a Price. He's armed and he's annoyed enough right now that he wouldn't have any issues shooting someone who was trying to hurt him. Mark is a cuckoo. He's never needed to learn how to defend himself. He just doesn't want people to hurt him, so they don't."

"You say that like you *do* know how to defend yourself."

I rolled my shoulders back in what I hoped would look like a defiant shrug. I didn't feel defiant anymore. I mostly felt defeated. "I keep trying to tell you, I was raised a Price. Evie and Uncle Kevin took me most summers, and they made sure I learned the basics. I'm not as good with a knife as you or Very, but I can shoot, and I can lay a basic snare, and I know how to crush a trachea if I have to. I also don't think a brain-blasted cuckoo will be enough to really hurt me at this point."

"Because you're so much more evolved than they are."

"Because I've reached the final known instar and survived, and no cuckoo has managed to do that since they were banished from Johrlar. It's not supposed to be possible." Probably because surviving the equation required the willing cooperation and support of the people who loved me, and now they didn't love me anymore. It was a sacrifice I didn't know whether I would have been able to make on purpose, or if I'd known that it would be the cost. And how many cuckoos even had people who genuinely loved them in the first place?

No, my family had turned me into something unique long before the cuckoos had come along and tried to turn me into a weapon, and I wasn't going to belittle what they'd done for me by spending too much time dwelling on all the ways it could have gone wrong.

"Great," said Annie, a feral hint of joy creeping into her thoughts. "You go first, then."

"Sure." It was easier to assign pronouns to the cuckoo's corpse, since it wasn't going to care. This one had been male, meaning its shoes were too big for me. Damn. I could really have used something to cover my feet. I started walking, leaving the body behind, glad to be moving again. If I tuned out the mistrust and discomfort coming off my cousin and focused on scanning the area around us, I could almost pretend this was a normal patrol, just two cryptozoologists going for a walk and looking for things that might be dangerous.

Because Mom isn't a receptive telepath—so far as I'm aware, the only thoughts she's ever picked up on were mine, when my adoptive parents died and I panicked, realizing for the first time that I might not be as human as everyone around me; cuckoo children in distress are like human children in that they can scream incredibly loudly, more loudly than they could do consciously, sometimes loudly enough to hurt themselves. When the McNallys died and the policeman who'd come to tell me about my loss had tried to take me home, claiming to be my father, I had screamed myself mentally hoarse, and that had been enough to rip through Angela's natural shields and let her hear me. That didn't magically transform her into a receptive telepath. I don't think anything could. And because she's *not* a receptive telepath, she was never able to teach me how to manage my own telepathy.

I'd been twelve when the lack of lessons on what seemed like it was going to be the most essential skill in my life had started to feel like a real problem. The walls between me and the minds around me were too fragile, and I might force people to do things they didn't want to do. That wasn't fair, or right, or human. And when I was twelve, my response to all problems had been the same: complain to my cousins. Annie, Artie, and I had put together a telepathic training program, with input from Elsie, who was better about going out in public than Artie was, and thus had experience with navigating her empathy in large groups of people.

Sure, it was a curriculum mostly cribbed from *Babylon 5* and old X-Men comics, but it had been enough to get me started and help me figure out what didn't work. All my principles were self-designed, all my techniques were self-taught, and maybe it wasn't going to be enough, but it was what we had. I released my hold on my natural desire to keep my own mind to myself, sending questing tendrils of thought into the area around us, looking for anything that felt like life.

Through it all, Annie's thoughts were a stable, disapproving constant, easy to find and follow, and that was enough to keep me from losing track of where my body was or what it was doing. I didn't find any of the brain-wiped cuckoos, but that didn't mean anything; they could have been absolutely everywhere around us, and without actively reaching out and making contact with the hunger that was all they had left to them—something I couldn't do on purpose, since I didn't know where they were—there was no way for me to detect them. Actions have consequences. Whether I'd meant to or not, this was a threat I had created.

Annie knew it, too. This was maybe the first thing she'd believed since I woke up. Oh, she believed the mice; the habit of believing the mice had been ingrained in her since birth, and she could no more call a member of her own clergy a liar than she could accept that I was a cuckoo she'd called "family" of her own free will. Somehow, Mom's existence only worked for her if she was an extreme outlier, the only good person our species had ever been capable of creating.

Not to get all *It's a Wonderful Life* about my own situation, but removing myself from Annie's memories had definitely kicked the support out from some of her ideas about the world. It wasn't as bad for her as it was for Artie, but it was bad enough that she was feeling shaky.

I was still trying to focus on the question and ignore Antimony's disdain when my thoughts brushed against something and I stumbled to a halt, staring at the building in front of us. It looked like every other university cafeteria I'd ever seen, with tall glass windows and shallow stone steps, flanked by a winding ramp for use by wheelchair users. A coffee cart had fallen over in front, probably during the transition between dimensions, and coffee and creamer were drying slowly on the sidewalk.

"What is it?" demanded Annie impatiently.

My mouth worked without a sound. This would have been so much easier if I'd felt comfortable speaking to her telepathically, and if I hadn't been concerned that she'd put a bullet into my brain for even trying.

Finally, I managed to squeak, "This is where we were going. The first group of students is holed up here."

"These are the ones you said have some of the cuckoo children with them?" She pulled a gun from inside her shirt. "Did you find the rest of the cuckoos?"

"No." My throat was dry, and it was difficult to swallow. "I still don't know where they are. These are the students the cuckoos didn't get rid of before the ritual began."

Annie turned, slowly, to stare at me. I stared back. Neither of us said a word.

Technically, I was there when the cuckoos took the campus. I say "technically" because while I was physically present while it was happening, I was less a person and more a vehicle for the living equation. It had ridden me from Oregon to Iowa and begun the setting up of the ritual that was part of its function, that would allow it to blossom and truly live for the duration of its operation. I hadn't been making choices. I hadn't been truly aware of my surroundings, not in any meaningful way or on any conscious level. But I'd been there.

And while I remembered the cuckoos taking the city, freezing the population in the middle of whatever they'd been doing at the time, leaving them suspended in a weird sort of half-life that had probably claimed a lot of *full* lives—you can't stand in the shower forever without developing trench foot and possibly boiling yourself alive, you can't stay in a tanning bed for more than a few hours, and there are probably a hundred other common, everyday situations that could end in death if extended indefinitely—I hadn't been a part of it so much as I'd been a conduit, a way for them to move the power they had inside themselves into new configurations.

If there was any mercy to the way the cuckoos took Ames, Iowa, it was that they hadn't been malicious when they did it. They wanted to survive. They wanted to get away from the bomb they were priming to blow. They were planning to destroy the planet, and that had been damage enough for them, leaving them with no real desire to torture or humiliate the individual people who happened to get in their way. I couldn't come up with a single instance of them targeting individuals.

Which meant they'd frozen the campus as it was when we'd arrived, and only moved the people who were actively blocking the resources we needed for the ritual.

Why Iowa, I still had no idea. Something about the location had been numerically perfect, and as that had mattered very deeply when I was standing in the middle of the equation, I had allowed it to dictate its own needs. The campus hadn't been crowded, exactly, when we arrived, but it had been occupied, and the cuckoos had taken care of it.

Some of the students and faculty were probably dead now, their bodies dropped into basements or culverts as unpleasant surprises for the authorities to find. The rest might be back in the remains of Ames, wondering where their campus had gone. And of the remainder, a little less than half of them were, apparently, in front of us.

I focused briefly on the building, feeling my eyes light up as I reached out to get a more accurate count. I'd taken one when I did my initial scan, but after meeting the hollowed-out cuckoo, I didn't trust myself anymore.

"We still have eight inside, plus the three cuckoo children, minds intact," I said, relieved to confirm that even when fully sunk in the grips of the equation, I hadn't been feeding it kids too young to know what they were or think that they were better than every other form of intelligent life. A baby viper is still a viper. That doesn't mean it needs to die for having the potential to bite someone.

"And the students are human?" asked Annie.

"Seven of them are," I said. "The eighth is a bogey-man trying to figure out how she's going to explain her light sensitivity to the others when they decide it's time to go outside. She's also the only one who hasn't already manufactured a familial connection to the cuckoo kids."

"I saw more than three kids when we charged into the ritual circles," said Annie.

"So the others are either dead or elsewhere," I said. "I could easily have missed some when I was trying to process the information from scanning the whole campus at once. Just because I *can* do that now, doesn't mean I'm good at it yet. I'm not picking up any faculty. Not even any cafeteria employees. One of the engineering students is upset because he can't get the microwave to work."

"Of course not," scoffed Annie. "We left the power lines behind on Earth."

"I somehow doubt these kids have jumped to 'we're in a whole new dimension,'" I said dryly. "They still think this is business as usual, within the limits of 'everything outside the campus is missing and the sky is the wrong color' and—oh, fuck—they probably think we're in the middle of a nuclear war or something."

"Nukes don't turn the sky orange."

"They do in bad science fiction movies."

Annie paused. "Okay, fair point. Are they hostile?"

"Not right now. Mostly, they're freaked out and upset and trying to figure out if this is really happening. Three of them think this is a really vivid dream. Three of them think it's the rapture. None of the others are projecting hard enough for me to read them without pushing, and I'm not willing to do that."

Annie laughed a little. "Of course I get the only telepath in the world who's not willing to be a tactical advantage if it would mean violating someone's boundaries."

"You're part of what made me this way."

"Whatever." She made her gun disappear again, back into her clothing where it wouldn't risk upsetting the locals—although this *was* Iowa. Odds were decent that at least a couple of them were as heavily armed as she was. "Let's go meet the locals."

"Sure," I said, and together, we walked into the building.

Six

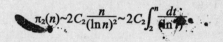

$$\pi_2(n) \sim 2C_2 \frac{n}{(\ln n)^2} \sim 2C_2 \int_2^n \frac{dt}{(\ln t)}$$

"It's never fun to be the stranger. It's never fun to be the one who's out of place and doesn't know what's happening. But it happens to everyone eventually, and maybe that's a good thing. Maybe it teaches us something."

—Alice Healy

Entering a university cafeteria full of potentially hostile strangers because that's the smart choice

THE CAFETERIA HAD CLEARLY not been designed for extended use during a power outage; walking through the doors was like stepping into the antechamber of a haunted house, minus the theatrically groaning high school drama students and the polyester cobwebs. Shadows clung to every surface, some thick enough to make me question once again whether light worked differently in this dimension. The floor was white industrial linoleum that reflected as much of the outside light as it could, but it was a losing battle; nothing short of a full bank of overhead fluorescents was going to make this room anything other than direly gloomy.

Coat hooks hung on the walls near the window, about half still holding various pieces of outerwear. The cuckoos probably hadn't allowed anyone to stop and grab their coats before banishing them from campus. I paused, holding a finger to my lips, and pointed silently down the hall toward the main room. The people were in there.

Annie nodded and started forward, trusting me to follow her. Since it was the first time she'd trusted me to do literally anything, I fell in step behind her.

She pushed open the door to the dining room and stepped through, me on her heels. We were immediately hit by the beams of no fewer than four flashlights. Any element of surprise hopelessly lost, Annie made a noise of protest and threw up her arm to shield her eyes.

"You want to point those somewhere else?" she demanded.

"Are you with the police?" asked a voice.

"She's not with the damn police, she's wearing a hoodie," said another voice. I put a hand over my mouth to smother my smile.

"The other one's wearing a nightgown," said a third voice. "And she's *barefoot.*"

"How about you stop lighting us up and tell us what's been going on in here?" said Annie. "This is not helping my temper, and I've had a long, long day already. You do *not* want to piss me off."

"We've been in here since the earthquake," said a fourth voice. There were eight people in here, not counting the cuckoo children. I hoped they weren't going to sound off one by one like some sort of rogue's gallery. I was sure they were all lovely people with complex inner lives, but, honestly, I didn't have the patience. Or the time, because Annie's patience was even thinner than my own, we had no working cellphones, and none of the people currently looking for the other group of survivors on campus were going to welcome a message from Radio Cuckoo right now.

"Earthquake?" asked Annie.

"You know, when the whole campus shook and the power cut out?" This voice, thankfully, belonged to the first speaker, the—I sent out a quick tendril of thought— boy who'd asked if we were with the police. He stepped forward, flashlight no longer aimed at our faces, becoming more visible as he put the other flashlights at his back. "We lost Internet at the same time. We're cut off, and we're not sure it's safe to go outside when the gas isn't working."

"You *tested* it?" I asked, horrified. We don't get a lot of earthquakes in either Portland or Columbus, but Oregon is technically inside what geologists call "the Ring of Fire," meaning there's always the possibility of a chain of earthquakes setting off a series of massive volcanic eruptions.

Maybe it's not kind to Iowa, but I was suddenly very glad the equation had felt the need to be completed so far away from both my homes. And all my family members, save for the ones who'd gone there knowing what they were getting themselves into.

"Some of the ovens were on when the shake happened," he said. "We were a little worried about exploding in a ball of fiery death, so when we realized we couldn't smell gas, we turned them off. If the gas main broke, I think it happened far enough away from here that we're in the clear."

I wasn't sure that was how gas mains normally worked, but since in this case, the gas main was literally in a different dimension, that was probably fine. "How many of you are in here?" I asked, as if I didn't already know.

"Eight adults, and three kids; no faculty," he said. "Miranda brought her little sisters to school with her today for some ridiculous reason."

So all three juvenile cuckoos had latched onto the same person? That was an interesting development. It might make them easier to get away from the humans. It also might do permanent damage to poor Miranda's brain, which would be rewiring itself constantly to try and accommodate for her being responsible for three sudden sisters.

"Okay," I said. "Is it safe for you to stay in here? I mean for right now, if there's no gas smell."

"It's going to get dark soon," said the boy who had elected himself the speaker for the group. "We don't have candles, and without electricity, we're just going to be sitting like rats in a cage waiting for the firefighters to show up or the Internet to come back on."

"My phone doesn't work," said a new voice petulantly, setting off a chorus of complaints: phones didn't work, the Internet was down, they had celiac disease and without lights they couldn't find anything gluten free, did we know what was happening, did we know why the police weren't here yet, did we know *anything*? I knew it was strange how none of them asked why the sky was orange, but maybe they hadn't been outside to look yet.

Then again, the cuckoo children had been outside when the ritual happened. I squinted into the darkness behind the boy with the flashlight, looking for hints of the bioluminescent glow that would mean they were actively influencing the human minds around them. Normal cuckoos can't consciously use their abilities prior to their first instar. Early trauma can sometimes snap them into a more advanced state, almost like they're borrowing from their future potential. It had been the trauma of losing the McNallys that enabled me to broadcast loudly enough for Angela to hear me in the first place.

These kids had been kidnapped, presumably against their will, from the human families they'd considered their own, and then dropped into the middle of a world-shattering ritual that had gone so comprehensively wrong that they'd seen people die in a variety of deeply unpleasant ways. That had to count as trauma. And if it had been traumatic enough, they might already be well on their way to conscious use of their abilities.

And if it hadn't been, they might not need to reach their first instar to start hurting the people around them.

I didn't see any unexpected glimmers of light in the darkness. I reached out cautiously, scanning the minds around us for ill intent or further comprehension of our situation. I found it, but not where I expected; the kids were all terrified and clinging to the friendly biochemistry major who had somehow become their honorary big sister. One of the men in the back of the room, on the other hand, was thinking about how with the cell network down, he could do anything he wanted and no one would be able to call the police.

His thoughts were like pond scum, polluting and coating everything they touched. I disengaged from his mind as quickly as I could and sent a thin arrow of thought toward Annie.

Antimony, we might have a problem.

She jerked around, spinning to face me. "What was that?"

"I didn't say anything." *I know you're not used to this anymore, but I need you to listen. There's a man in the back of the cafeteria. He told the others he's a student, but he's not, and he doesn't belong here. His name is Terrence. He's planning to clean out the registers and then break into the student health center. He has a gun. I don't think he intends to hurt anyone if he doesn't have to, but he will if they get in his way.*

People are terrible, Annie thought blankly. Aloud, she said, "Hey, did I see Terrence come in here? I was hoping to find him before I go back to our friends."

The man I knew was in the back of the room didn't reply. Only silence answered her question. But his thoughts began to race, tinged with hectic borderline panic.

Not sure what you were hoping to achieve with that, but he's freaking out, I informed her.

Good. "We're going to move along," she said. "We have people waiting in the classroom where we took shelter. If we see the authorities, we'll send them your way." We weren't going to see any authorities, but these people didn't know that, and maybe this would help them stay calm and inside for a little bit longer. Inside, whatever hunted the flying sky bugs wouldn't be able to get them, unless those hypothetical hunters could chew through walls, and if they could do that, we were all screwed anyway.

Annie started to turn away. Lacking any better ideas, I followed her.

Cuckoo kids are never raised by their biological parents. The girls currently attached to Miranda—whose mind felt reasonably intact, around the vague confusion that came from trying to retroactively incorporate three younger sisters into her childhood experiences, some of which didn't make any sense in a world where she would have been expected to babysit—didn't recognize me as anyone they would be inclined to trust or follow. The only adult cuckoos they'd ever seen had been the ones to kidnap them, leaving them with no reason to want anything to do with me.

No one spoke as we walked away. Annie led me to the door and out onto the dying grass, the luridly orange sky casting strange shadows on her face. She motioned for me to be quiet and follow her as she started around the building. I blinked and followed, resisting the urge to reach out mentally and find out what she was up to.

And she was definitely up to *something*. Her thoughts were tightly controlled, reined in to a degree that she had learned in self-defense when we were kids and she wanted to think about naughty things without me asking questions about what she meant. She probably didn't even realize she was doing it, and why would she have? She had no reason to have developed those skills, since as far as she was concerned, we hadn't grown up together. She was Miranda in reverse, like her in silently justifying things that didn't make sense, because acknowledging them would do even more damage than setting them aside.

Despite the level of control she was demonstrating, I could feel the fizzing pop of her excitement, like her emotions had been carbonated, as she led me around the side of the building to a plain metal door, painted brown to blend with the brick around it. She positioned herself to one side, waving for me to get out of the way. I did, plastering myself to the wall like I was afraid the sky was going to fall at any moment. I thought Annie rolled her eyes. It was fine if she did; it was better than any of the things she could have thought about my over-reaction.

Treating her like she was made of glass—fragile, but incredibly dangerous if dropped and reduced to a hand-ful of razored shards—was going to get old, fast. We needed to find a new equilibrium between us, even if it wasn't going to be her trusting me any time soon, or we were going to be in deep, deep trouble.

I was contemplating ways to broach the subject when the door banged open so hard that it slammed against the wall on the opposite side, where neither of us was hiding, and Terrence rushed out.

He was an unremarkable looking man, as I measured such things, pale-skinned and brown-haired, wearing a T-shirt and blue jeans. Not faculty. Not a student, either, for all that he'd been on campus when it was taken. I'd need more time to dig in and find out what he'd been doing there. It looked like I might have the chance, since he had barely crossed the threshold when Annie grabbed him by the back of the head, locked her arms around his neck in a chokehold, and spun him around to slam face-first against the wall.

"Hi," she purred, voice poisonously sweet. "Going somewhere, good friend Terrence?"

"He was getting out of here before we could tell any-one he didn't belong," I reported helpfully, stepping up to catch the door swinging and ease it shut before it slammed. I couldn't feel anyone coming after the unfor-tunate Terrence—not unfortunate because he was a bad person; unfortunate because he was a bad person who'd been caught by my cousin—but I didn't want to make it easier for anything to get inside and eat the other survivors.

"Let me go, you crazy bitch!" he snarled, struggling against her grasp.

It wasn't going to do him any good. Once Annie gets hold of somebody, she keeps it. I've only seen someone break one of her holds twice, and both times, it was

Alex, after they'd been sparring for an hour and she was getting tired. Here and now, she was both fresh and pissed-off, and he'd just made the massive mistake of making himself a target.

Not the best choice anyone had ever made, to be fair. Even if he hadn't known he was making it.

"Sexist *and* ableist," said Annie, grinding his face harder into the brick. "Try again, and maybe I step away before I break your bones."

"He has a gun," I said, keeping my tone as bored as possible. "Thought you should remember me telling you that if you're planning to release him."

"Where?" she asked.

"Not sure," I said, and was rewarded with Terrence immediately thinking of the gun's location, tucked into his left sock. "Left sock," I said.

Terrence shot me as much of a glare as his current position allowed, which, to be fair, wasn't much; it was more of an aggravated side-eye that would have been difficult to read without telepathy even if I'd been able to recognize the subtleties of his expression. It didn't matter. I was already going for the gun, a crappy little thing that no member of my family would have been willing to carry. I popped the chamber and dumped the bullets into the grass before Annie could object to my being armed. Then I held it up for her inspection.

"Classy," she said, shoving his face even harder into the wall. He was going to need some serious exfoliation when she was done with him, assuming he was still among the living.

I glanced around. With no way—and no one—to call the police, there was no real reason for Annie to hesitate if she'd decided this man was a threat. I wasn't entirely comfortable with this level of aggression in response to what had honestly been some vague comments on my part. He was a bad man. Even bad men don't deserve to have their faces scraped off on brick walls.

"I have his weapon," I said. "He's not going to overpower anyone else, and this door doesn't look like it

opens from this direction. There's no way he's getting
back in the cafeteria without someone noticing he was
gone."

"What are you saying?"

"I'm saying we can probably let him go."

"Is she right, *Terry*?" Annie tightened her grip on his
throat for a moment, grinding his cheek into the brick
until there was no way it didn't hurt. He was starting to
turn an unattractive shade of plum.

"Humans need oxygen," I said mildly.

"I hate liars," she replied, and pushed him away from
her as she let go, a motion that had the end result of
slamming him even harder against the wall. She snorted
and stepped back, giving him room to move.

It was a maneuver I'd seen before, usually when one
of our more physical fighters was trying to subdue a
semi-intelligent cryptid or beast, like a bear. Show them
you were bigger, and give them the space to react. If they
responded by running away, the problem was solved. If
they tried to attack, they needed to be put down.

The thoughts rolling off of her were annoyed, but I
wasn't picking up on any murderous intent. Whatever
was happening here, it was better just to let it play out.

Terry pushed himself away from the wall and whirled
around, unable to quite settle on which of the two of us
he should be glaring at. His thoughts were a ceaseless
roiling, loud enough that I could pick up on their edges
without trying. They weren't as clear as Annie's because
I wasn't attuned to him the way I was attuned to her, but
they were clearer than I expected from a total stranger.

Adjusting to the changes in the way my brain worked
was going to take time that we didn't currently have.

He lunged abruptly forward, not for Annie, but for
the grass at our feet. Grabbing several bullets off the
ground, he scrambled back to an upright position and
ran, legs churning as fast as they could go. He didn't say
anything. I frowned, touching my temple with one hand.
It didn't help. He wasn't acting on logic, he was running
on wild panic, and that never gets more comprehensible.

"Why did he do that?" demanded Annie.

"I don't know," I said. "I guess he didn't want us to have his stupid bullets. Like we'd use a gun this crappy? It'd probably blow up in your hand if you tried."

"Probably," she agreed, and stuck her hand out. "Give it."

I blinked. "But it's a lousy gun, and—"

"And while I'm starting to believe *you* believe what you've been saying, that doesn't mean I actually believe it's the truth, and it doesn't mean I'm willing to go walking around with an armed cuckoo. If you're who you claim to be, you would have been taught how to use even an empty gun as a weapon." She waggled her fingers. "Hand it over and we can get moving."

I wanted to argue. I wanted to scoff and tell her she was being ridiculous.

I dropped the gun into her palm and watched her make it disappear. Then she bent and picked the rest of the bullets out of the grass, dropping those into her pocket.

"Let's go," she said.

It would have been easy to get angry at her or act like she was treating me unfairly. It would have been even easier to take this personally, like she was trying to hurt me with her behavior or like I was being punished. Sometimes "easy" isn't the same thing as "right."

Everyone in my family knows cuckoos are bad news. It's one of the first things we learn, irrespective of species. Cuckoos distort the world. They break things because they can, because it's fun . . . because they can't help themselves. When given a choice between the right thing and the thing that will benefit them the most, they take the second option before they even finish registering that they *had* a choice, because they carry the weight of their entire species in their minds, and it says to survive at all costs. The only thing that inspires a cuckoo to self-sacrifice is the survival of the species as a whole. It doesn't even extend to protecting their young.

We'd learned a lot about cuckoos since all this started. Where they really came from, why they were the way they were . . . what Mom had done to save me, even though she hadn't fully understood what she was doing, or that she was doing it at all. She'd been following an instinct deeper than consciousness, clearing out my mind to make room for the equation that was going to do its best to hollow me out and ride me into a new dimension. But she'd done it because she loved me, and I couldn't be mad. Thanks to her, I was a cuckoo who knew how to love and be loved. I was an aberration by the standards of my species, and there was absolutely no reason for Annie to believe I could even exist.

The fact that she hadn't tried to shoot me or set me on fire yet was more than enough to make me forgive her for being a little standoffish and suspicious. I would have been, too, in her place. The fact that she seemed more willing to trust Mark was a bit more of a problem for me—but then again, Mark hadn't started what she knew of their acquaintance by admitting to wiping her mind. She had good reason to like him better and trust him more.

People are complicated. I tried to keep that in mind as I led Annie across campus toward the distant hum of unfamiliar human minds. A large building came into view. The library.

"The rest of the people sheltering on campus seem to be in there," I said, pointing.

Annie nodded. "Makes sense. I know I'd take refuge in a library."

"With no lights or Internet?"

"Yeah. It would be instinctive. You don't think 'at least I'll have something to read,' you think 'the books will keep me safe.'"

I considered this as we walked. "Fair enough." We were getting close enough to see details, like the cracked windows on the third floor, and the uprooted shrubs near the door, and the ring of pale, dark-haired people clustered around the outside of the building, trying to bang their way in. I stopped walking and reached for them mentally.

There was nothing there.

"Um, Annie? We have a problem."

"What's that?" she asked, looking back at me.

I raised a shaking hand and pointed at the people assaulting the library. "I don't know whether we can get to the survivors, but we've definitely found more of the missing cuckoos," I said. "And the boys aren't anywhere nearby." I could spread out my scan to check the full campus for them, but if I did that, I would lose track of my immediate surroundings, and that suddenly struck me as a very, very bad idea.

She followed my finger, displeasure rolling off of her in a wave. "Oh," she said. "Empties?"

"Like the first one," I said. "They're not really there anymore. They're just . . . bodies, acting on instinct, looking for something to devour."

Annie smirked "You know, Sarah, maybe you're a member of this family after all," she said, pulling her gun from somewhere inside her clothing. "I mean, you started a zombie apocalypse on an alien world *by mistake*. That's almost as good as killing the crossroads, or summoning a snake god live on national television." She flipped off the safety. "Alex really needs to up his game. Seriously, he's barely caused *any* world-changing disasters."

"What are you going to do? Aren't we going to go looking for the boys?" I asked. Maybe they were stupid questions, but at least asking them aloud would help to convince her that I wasn't reading her mind.

She rolled her eyes before turning away from me, back to the crowd around the library. "The boys are *fine*. They saw a zombie apocalypse getting underway and they ran like sensible people. Fortunately, no one has ever accused me of being sensible. As for what I'm going to do, I'm going to shoot a bunch of people, *duh*. You said they weren't people anymore, and even if they were, they'd still be cuckoos. We can't afford to let them live. This way at least it's quick, and they don't have time to suffer. Much."

I wanted to argue. I didn't feel any kinship with these cuckoos, but they were damaged because of me—because when I'd used them to help me contain the equation, I hadn't done it gently enough. And even so, I didn't see a good way to make the argument. If we could fix them, they'd still be cuckoos, and they'd be justifiably pissed. If we couldn't fix them, they'd be exactly what Annie was saying they were: the beginning of a zombie apocalypse. No ability to infect, thankfully, but they ticked all the other boxes. This was the only answer.

"At least let me check them individually, to make sure they're like that first one," I said. Annie's thoughts turned dubious. I managed, barely, not to grab her arm. "Please. If any of them have higher cognition left, they might be able to tell us what happened after I collapsed, or how to get home from here."

I was grasping at straws, and they were breaking in my hands. I knew it, and so did she. But she still lowered the gun and sighed.

"The mice know you," she said. "You know too much. Being a telepath explains part of that, but being a telepath doesn't tell you how to talk to someone, or how to argue with them reasonably. So yeah, I guess maybe you are my cousin, and if you *are* my cousin, you're going to be okay with me being very, very angry with you."

"Because I messed with your mind without permission?"

"Exactly." Antimony sounded pleased. "Consent always matters. If it mattered less, Artie would leave his damn basement more often—he was a shut-in *before* you deleted yourself from his memories, right?"

I nodded. She radiated satisfaction.

"Good. We've made it far enough at this point that I didn't really want to shoot you for breaking the cousin I can actually remember. Now check those cuckoos and see how many of them I can kill."

Had my family always been this bloodthirsty? Tempting as it was to give myself the credit—and the blame—for throwing things askew when I went poking around in her head, I had to admit they'd always been like this. We had a very black-and-white way of thinking, collectively, and once something had been filed under "enemy," it was all too easy to pull the trigger.

We probably needed to work on that. "I'll have to get a little closer," I said.

"Do you think they'll attack us if you do?" she asked.

"Only if they notice us," I said. "They're just . . . hungry. They want because they don't have anything else left to them but wanting, and they still have bodies, and those bodies need to be fed. So that becomes the only thing there is, and they follow it, and try to make it matter. If they caught us, they'd rip us to pieces and swallow what they could and probably choke to death on our bones."

"Sounds fun." Annie started walking toward them, slow and easy, a hunter's prowl. It had been so long since I'd stepped back and looked at my family from the outside that it was a little jarring, just like everything else about this damn day.

But then, if you can't be jarred when you're walking under an orange sky filled with flying millipedes, when *can* you? I hurried after her, my bare feet slapping against the grass and my nightgown swaying around my legs. I'd been appalled by Terrence's half-baked plan to loot the student health center, since medication and first-aid supplies were going to be limited as long as we were all stranded in this dimension, but I was considering the virtues of finding and looting the school shop myself. They'd have mascot-branded sweatpants and wooly socks if nothing else, and I really wanted to feel a little bit less naked.

And if not the student store, at least some of these cuckoos looked like they'd been female before I melted their brains. Maybe I'd be able to steal their shoes, even if I wasn't willing to take the bra off a corpse.

Annie slowed as we got closer to the library and we got our first really close look at the mob of cuckoos. There were about fifteen of them, none younger than their late teens, all clawing and banging at the front of the building with single-minded determination. Their faces were slack and expressionless, enough so that even I could see that the lights weren't on and nobody was home. Some of them were drooling. At least one had ripped out all of her own fingernails trying to claw through the brick; her fingertips were shredded ruins, leaking viscous fluid onto the stone as she continued to claw, not appearing to notice the pain, much less care about it.

They were dressed in a variety of styles, from "girl's night out" to "ready for bed," and I realized with some horror that I was assessing their clothes based on whether or not they would fit me after Annie put their original owners down. Probably—cuckoos have very little physical dimorphism across the species, and most of us look enough like all the rest that we can share everything. Shoes, makeup colors, photo IDs . . . everything. But we didn't have access to a laundry service, and at the end of the day, I'd rather find the student store and steal some sweatpants than strip a corpse.

Quiet, I whispered in Annie's head, and ducked my chin toward my chest, focusing on the swarm in front of us. My eyes tingled as they made the chemical shift to bioluminescent brightness and I began skipping myself across the surface of their minds. *Only* the surface; the depths were as horrifyingly chaotic as the first one we'd encountered, filled with howling winds and endless voids.

I could get trapped there if I wasn't careful. I could get ensnared and dragged down into those infinite depths, to drown or starve in the emptiness they had become. They weren't lost to madness; madness would have required that they have the capacity for anything else. These weren't broken people. They weren't people at all. They were things. Terrible, shattered, starving *things*.

And I had done this to them. All the "I didn't mean to" and "it was an accident" in the world wouldn't change

the fact that I'd done something a lot worse than anything Annie was planning, and it couldn't be taken
back. They were never going to be the people they'd
been before. Maybe that was a good thing, since it was
likely the people they'd been were monsters, but I wasn't
judge and jury, I was just a math nerd who'd been sucked
into something much too big for her and now couldn't
find any way out.

I pulled myself loose from their minds, which felt
sticky somehow, like they were trying to grab hold of me
and pull me into the abyss of their empty yearning.
"They're gone," I said aloud.

Annie nodded, grim determination rolling off her as
she raised her gun. Fifteen of them meant that even if
every shot was true, she'd have to pause and reload before she took them all down.

And even so, we would probably have been fine if not
for the glass beer bottle that soared by overhead, smashing onto the stone walkway in front of us. The sound it
made when it shattered seemed impossibly loud, almost
like a gunshot in its own right.

The cuckoos weren't intelligent anymore, but they
knew they were hungry, and had been targeting the people holed up inside the library. They turned toward the
sound, still drooling, and one of them actually snarled
before the whole swarm began to shamble in our direction, attracted by the promise of easier prey.

"Whoa, Sarah, what the *fuck*?" demanded Annie,
backpedaling.

I matched her step for step, turning to look behind us
as I did, and caught sight of a man running around the
corner of the nearest building, arms pumping. I sent out
a tendril of thought, barely brushing against the edges
of his mind. "Terrence."

"From the *cafeteria*?" She was paying more attention
to the cuckoos now coming after us, probably because
she wanted to live long enough to get back to the others.

"Yes!"

"And this is why it's never a good idea to be merciful," she muttered, and began to fire. Her gun spoke twice in quick succession, followed by the soft sound of bodies hitting the ground before she fired again. "Is he still there?"

So she was running backward. That made sense under the circumstances. She knew I could see where we were going, while she stayed focused on the danger that was bearing down on us. Speaking of which . . .

"Sarah, *answer me!*" she shrieked.

"No, he's gone," I said, and kept running. The ground was starting to hurt my feet, little rocks buried in the grass digging into my skin. "How many did you get?"

"Three," she said, with some satisfaction. There was a whooshing sound, and the brief sensation of intense heat. "Four—no, five, that one tripped and now two of them are on fire. Take that, you zombie assholes!"

She sounded so pleased with herself that I hated to say anything. I hated being on fire even more. "Annie, are they still running?"

"Um."

"Are we being chased by *zombie cuckoos on fire*?"

"A little bit! But they're slowing down!"

"Yes, *being on fire* will do that to you!" Or at least I assumed it would. I had never actually *been* on fire, which was a situation I wanted to preserve for as long as possible. "Run faster!"

"We can make it back to the cafeteria!" A gunshot followed her words, before Annie pulled up next to me, now facing in the same direction as I was. That was an improvement, although it meant that in remarkably short order, she was the one leading, while I had to struggle to keep up.

I glanced over my shoulder at the remaining cuckoos. We had started with fifteen; four of them had fallen, victims of gunshots through the forehead or throat, their empty eyes fixed on the orange sky. Of the remaining eleven, three were on fire, the two she had hit originally and then another that had been running too close to them. That's the trouble with fire. Unlike bullets, it's a renewable resource—and under the right circumstances, it can be really, *really* renewable.

"We can't lead a bunch of burning zombies back to the cafeteria!" I snapped. "They'll set the building on fire, and there are *children* in there!"

"There's a whole campus here!"

"Do you really want to set *kids* on fire?"

"No," said Annie sullenly, and stopped dead, turning to face the cuckoos as she lifted her hands.

Oh, this was going to be really stupid.

Seven

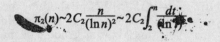

$$\pi_2(n) \sim 2C_2 \frac{n}{(\ln n)^2} \sim 2C_2 \int_2^n \frac{dt}{(\ln t)^2}$$

"This is all temporary. That's part of what makes it amazing. Even the longest lived of us is only planting seeds in a garden they won't see finish growing, and that's what gives us the luxury of making mistakes. It's easier to take chances when you know you may not have to carry the consequences."

—Mary Dunlavy

Standing in the middle of the campus green, probably about to be on fire (which is really going to suck)

THE CUCKOOS KEPT COMING as Annie raised her hands, not quite running, but definitely moving at the sort of determined, unvarying shamble that explained why we hadn't been able to leave them behind. There was nothing physically wrong with their legs, nothing stopping them from continuing to advance.

Annie spread her fingers wide before snapping them shut and jerking her hands briskly downward. The flames that writhed around the three cuckoos guttered out, leaving not even an ember behind. One of the cuckoos collapsed. The other two kept coming, not seeming to realize how badly blistered they were.

I reached for their minds to reassure myself, and found no pain, no discomfort . . . no real awareness of their situation. The howling void of their hunger was too vast to allow for anything as small as suffering. I appreciated that, even as I didn't appreciate the fact that we still had eleven zombie cuckoos coming after us.

"Annie . . ."

"I know, I know. But bullets run out, and I don't have infinite knives." She still took aim and fired twice more, downing two more cuckoos, before shooting me a hopeful glance. "I don't suppose you've been hiding a gun from me this whole time? I promise not to be mad at you if you hand it over right now."

"No weapons. I'm in my *nightgown*. I don't have any shoes. And I'm not you or Grandma. I don't sleep with a machete."

"It was worth trying." She fired again, and tried to fire a second time, only for the chamber to click empty. She made a face before making the gun vanish and producing the one she'd taken from Terrence, loading it with his discarded bullets as fast as she could manage.

"Couldn't you have done this before?"

"I didn't expect our new playmate to come right back and start breaking things to get us swarmed," she snapped.

I turned to make sure Terrence wasn't sneaking up on us again. There was no sign of motion, and I didn't detect anything close by when I lowered my mental shields and stretched myself out to scan. I still couldn't detect the empty cuckoos, so I wasn't sure what I was hoping to find. There were a few more human survivors huddled in the buildings around us—and at least one of them was watching us, had seen Annie's little trick with the fire, and was cursing his inability to livestream whatever weird-ass reality show we were clearly filming—but Terrence wasn't close enough to detect easily, which meant he wasn't currently a threat.

Unlike the cuckoos. And unlike everything else about this situation, which seemed determined to go from awful to truly terrible without taking any of the steps in between. The only silver lining I could currently see was that if I couldn't pick up on Terrence without pushing to find him, my new range wasn't perfect, and when we got home, I might still be able to go out in public without losing my mind from the noise.

Range . . . I stopped and looked up, scanning the sky, and there, near the edge of the campus, was one of the flying millipede things, cilia waving as it undulated through the air.

You want to come down here, I thought, as hard as I could.

It continued to undulate smoothly forward, giving no sign that it had heard me on any level.

You want *to come down here,* I thought again, and accompanied the words with a picture of the millipede thing coming to rest on the ground, preferably atop the attacking cuckoos.

They weren't carnivores, and the cuckoos weren't decaying plant matter, but maybe if I pushed the idea hard enough, this would work. I pressed my hands against the sides of my head the way people always did in the comics, and thought for a third time, *YOU WANT TO COME DOWN HERE.*

And the millipede came.

It descended as slowly and ponderously as a hot air balloon being reeled to the ground, only there were no ropes, no ground crew pulling it safely to port; there was just the millipede itself, undulating through the air with legs and cilia waving, growing larger with every second. *All the bad CGI was better than it looked,* I thought, almost dizzily, because this was happening, this was real, I could feel the creature's small, malleable mind pressing against the edges of my own, unable to comprehend its sudden urge to come to a landing, but unable to muster up the coherent thought necessary to resist me. The closer it got, the more details I could make out, the little dents and scratches in its chitin, the way the fronds of its antennae weren't quite even, but were jagged and missing tiny spiky quills.

The thing that didn't quite fit any cultural design or pattern I knew, but was something like a braided sling and something like a very ornate piece of macramé, tied tight across the narrow dip that distinguished head from body. There was no rider. It was still very clearly a saddle. This was someone's mount.

From the size of the saddle, our missing "someone" was roughly bipedal and about the same size as Annie and me, which made sense. According to my grandmother, who spent most of her time swinging wildly across convergent dimensions looking for my missing grandfather, reality is sort of like a casserole. You can cook different things on different levels, as long as you separate them with a lot of cheese, but every time you push a knife through, you're going to drag little bits of the other layers through, which means you want complimentary flavors. So while there are absolutely dimensions full of lava, or plague, or howling voids, the ones we can reach easily are mostly suitable for humanoid life.

"You can find dimensions with people who *look* like us, even if science says they probably shouldn't, or dimensions with people who *think* like us, and they're not always the same place," she'd said to me one day, while she was frosting my birthday cake. (Lemon with tomato icing. Birthday girl picks the cake, everyone else either eats it or makes do with sad box-mix brownies.) "Don't assume everyone who looks human is a friend, sweet girl, and don't assume everyone who *doesn't* is an enemy."

"Cuckoos look human, Grandma," I'd replied. "I would never think looking human was enough."

And she'd laughed and gone back to plastering frosting over cake, and the day had been beautiful, unflinchingly so, and now there was a millipede wearing a saddle Antimony could have used skating through the sky toward us, and sometimes the lessons that matter the most are the ones we learn in family kitchens when we're eleven years old.

Annie had finished getting the bullets into Terrence's gun. She fired twice before it jammed and she swore, turning to face me. "We have to run," she said. "Us versus seven cuckoos who don't feel pain or understand logic anymore? That's bad math. That's math we lose. So we have to— Sarah, that's a giant fucking millipede."

"Yes, it is," I said, continuing to beckon the millipede toward us. Part of me felt a little guilty; what if these things couldn't get back into the sky after they landed? The rest of me was too focused on survival to worry about ecological damage.

The buildings were close enough together to make for a tight squeeze for the millipede, even as they provided plenty of open space for us. Differences of scale. *Follow me!* I thought to Antimony as I spun and bolted for the nearest cover, infusing the thought with as much urgency as I dared project her way—too much and she wouldn't have a choice, and all the ground I'd gained during this little bonding exercise would be wiped away—and at the same time, projected the idea that the cuckoos shambling after us were made of delicious rotting vegetation to the millipede. I didn't really know what a millipede would find delicious, and so I thought about the way I felt when I bit into a really ripe heirloom tomato, all filled with complex sugars and flavors that had developed in a thousand generations of fertile soil.

Thinking about how delicious that would be made me hungry, which I hoped meant it would also make the millipede hungry. I threw that flavor all over my mental map of the cuckoos, and when the millipede landed with a soft thump, its heavily-armored body barely missed us. I could have reached out and touched its side if I'd wanted to, brushing my fingertips across plating that had touched the clouds.

It was an oddly tempting idea. I've never wanted to be a pilot, but the idea of being that close to infinity was amazing. Annie apparently had the same thought, or else I was broadcasting more loudly than I meant to be—she stuck her arm out as we ran, letting her fingers run across the plating closest to us.

"It's warm!" she shouted. "Why is it so warm?"

"Absorbing the sunlight," I said. This close, it smelled

spicy, like the formic acid put down by ants when they wanted to lay a trail for the rest of the colony to follow. That explained the strange odor in the air, a bit; given the size of the bugs, it was like we'd been shrunk down to their scale, and so all the side effects of their presence were hitting us harder.

"Why did it land?"

"I asked it to."

"Just that?"

The millipede was swinging its head from side to side, like it was looking for something. The cuckoos didn't seem to have noticed it, which was ridiculous, since it was easily the size of a train, and were still shambling briskly forward, heading for the two of us as quickly as their unvarying pace allowed. The millipede stopped swinging its head, seeming to focus on them for the first time. I couldn't see its eyes, but it clearly knew where they were. Its antennae trembled. The cuckoos shambled. Annie and I kept running.

Then the millipede's head opened like some sort of terrible flower made of jagged edges and sharp angles. Each petal was a knife, each knife was wedded to two more, and it was almost an infinity of cutting surfaces. Annie stumbled and stopped, leaving momentum to carry me easily five or so feet beyond her.

" . . . whoa," she breathed. "Holy *shit*."

The millipede didn't strike so much as simply lowered itself over the first cuckoo in line. The flower closed again, and when the millipede reared back, the cuckoo was gone. There was no visible swallowing motion. It was like a magic trick, there one second and gone the next—a magic trick which the millipede repeated six more times, until all seven cuckoos had disappeared, down into the depths of its digestive system.

I mentally reached for it, and winced as I found their minds traveling through its gullet, moving toward whatever horrifying system of biological processes it had to serve as a stomach. They still felt no pain, and no confusion; they were still hungry, and from what I could pick up, some of them were scrabbling at the walls of the millipede's esophagus, trying to consume it even as it swallowed them.

"Good luck with that," I said dryly.

Annie turned to look at me, one eyebrow lifted in silent query. I shook my head.

"I'll tell you later," I said. "For right now, let's get out of here before the big fellow decides it has a taste for flesh now."

The millipede didn't feel like it had a taste for flesh. If anything, it felt disappointed; its mind was slow and simple, but it had been promised a feast by its own standards, and instead it had found a few flavorless, squirming mouthfuls. It hadn't worked its way around to anger yet, if it even had the capacity, but I didn't want to linger too close in case it made the leap.

"Yeah, okay," said Annie, and put her hand on my arm, staying close as we first backed away and then, when the millipede failed to turn and take notice of us, ran.

We ran until we reached the cafeteria and plastered ourselves against the wall, both of us breathing hard. It was a little reassuring that I wasn't the only one out of breath, but only a little. I wanted Annie to be invincible, because I wanted the luxury of breaking down when we made it back to the others, and I couldn't do that if she was breaking down, too. She looked at me.

"What the *fuck* did you do?" she asked.

"I sort of told the big flying thing that if it came down to where we were, it would get a snack," I said. "They're not natural meat-eaters, but I told it they were plants. And even herbivores eat smaller animals sometimes when they get mixed in the leaves! If it's really an insect, it shouldn't have any trouble digesting them. It's not like I fed the poor thing a bunch of mammals."

We could see the curve of the millipede's body through the break in the buildings, even from as far away as we are. Annie turned and gave me a flat look, disbelief rolling off her in a wave.

"Are you seriously telling me you telepathically compelled Mothra's leg-day obsessed little brother to swoop down out of the sky and *eat your enemies*?" she asked.

"Um, yeah," I said. "Although mentioning Mothra makes me wonder if the square-cube law doesn't work differently in this dimension. If not, the giant flying insects probably have lungs of some sort."

"Ew."

"I have lungs," I objected. "I'm a giant insect with lungs."

"And I really try not to think about that when I have to interact with cuckoos because you have to admit that it's gross as all hell, and it leads to some nasty questions about evolution in the dimension that your people originally came from."

"I think the telepathy raises more, personally," I said. Earth had started out with at least two species of cryptid that had naturally-occurring psychic powers of one kind or another; I say "at least two" because there's some evidence to support the idea that Lilu, like cuckoos, originally came from somewhere else.

Earth has been studded with invasive species since long before humans opened shipping routes and started moving interesting plants and animals around the planet.

"Whatever." Annie let go of my arm as the millipede lifted off the ground and began to undulate back into the sky. "How the hell does that thing even fly?"

"There are a bunch of possible answers," I said. "Air bladders. Different atmospheric density than what we have back at home. Or maybe they're density-manipulators like the sylphs. However it does it, I want to go and find the boys before it comes back looking for another meal."

"Picking up on anything dangerous around here?"

I paused to check the surrounding area before shaking my head. "No, nothing, not even Terrence. I'd need to scan a much bigger area than the immediate threat to find him. All the other people who were in the library before the fight are still there. Most of them don't even realize they were in danger."

The millipede was well on its way back to its original

elevation, ascending much faster than it had come down, which made sense; it hadn't come down because it wanted to, it had come down because I'd been compelling it. Now it was following its own instincts and desires again, and those instincts told it to get as far away from the confusing thing as possible.

"Good," said Annie. "We'll just have to keep our eyes open. Do you think the suns are setting yet?"

It seemed like a non sequitur, but with no way of knowing what threats this dimension might produce once the sun was down, it was a valid question. I looked up at the sky, squinting as I tried to decide whether it was a darker shade of orange than it had been earlier. Insect eyes are structurally different than mammalian eyes, and my vision trends more toward the "wasp" side of the spectrum than "woman," which can make gradations of the color red difficult for me to see clearly.

"I don't know," I said finally. "It . . . looks like it might be a little darker? Maybe? It might never be night here the way we think about it."

"Yeah, maybe," she said, giving the horizon a mistrustful glance. It felt like she was concerned the sky was about to fall. I didn't like it.

Out of all my cousins, Antimony is supposed to be the rock. She's the one who doesn't get flapped, because she does the flapping. She's never been worried about bad things happening to her; she's the bad thing that happens to other people.

"Let's go," she said. "We can talk to the people in the library later, now that the apocalypse isn't trying to break down the door."

I nodded gratefully. "Cool."

As soon as I lowered my shields for a broader scan, I found the boys. As Annie had predicted, they had returned to the classroom where we'd started, viewing retreat from an overwhelming enemy as the greater part of valor. Smart boys. I told Annie where they were, and we started making what would turn out to be a gloriously uneventful trip back across campus to join them. No zombie cuckoos or giant millipedes showed up to make things worse or slow us down, and neither did any additional survivors. That was a good thing. I didn't want to talk to anyone else until I'd had an opportunity to steal or scavenge some real clothes, or at least slippers and sweatpants. A bra was absolutely too much to ask.

The concept of an underwire that fit was alluring enough to distract me from the discomfort of walking in my bare feet, and soon enough, the familiar hum of Artie's thoughts reappeared, bright as a neon sign reflecting light across the landscape. "Love of your life who thinks he just met you and you might be the enemy, this way." The lack of concern for me in those thoughts was depressing, but I kept going, focusing on the classroom window until James and Mark joined him, their own minds less familiar but no less worried. All three of them were focused on Annie and the threat posed by the zombie cuckoos, with only Mark sparing more than a flicker of worry for my well-being.

"I hate everything about this," I muttered.

Annie, who had been opening the door back into the building, looked over her shoulder. "What was that?" she asked.

"Nothing," I said. She raised an eyebrow, her surface thoughts making it clear she didn't believe me. I sighed. Watching myself around my cousins wasn't habitual, hadn't been for a very long time, and it was clear that if I didn't get back into the habit quickly, I wasn't going to be forming any more habits in the future. "Seriously, nothing. My feet hurt and I'm exhausted, that's all."

Annie's eyes flicked downward, to my feet, and widened. "Holy sh—have you been barefoot this *entire* time?"

"Um, yeah?" She finally stepped through the doorway and into the darkened stairwell on the other side. I followed, grateful to no longer be exposed to the whole of the outside.

In the dimness, she could no more read my face than I could read hers. That evened the playing field a little bit, while also tilting it unfairly in my direction, since my telepathy wasn't light-based. I blinked.

"Oh, hey, that answers your question from before," I said. "It's definitely moving toward whatever the local equivalent of sunset is, because it wasn't this dark in here when we left." I paused, sending out a reaching tendril of thought. "And there's no one else in here."

"I thought you already checked the building," said Annie dubiously.

"The zombie cuckoos aren't broadcasting any sort of thoughts or emotions, because they essentially don't have them anymore," I said. "I wouldn't be able to tell you even if there was one in the room with the boys," I admitted. "But if there was one in the room with the boys, they'd be freaking out right now, and they're feeling pretty calm. Worked-up and freaked-out, but calm. Artie's halfway convinced that I'm going to come back alone, because cuckoos can't be trusted, Mark is wondering whether he picked the wrong side, and James is keeping the air around him as cold as possible to counteract Artie's pheromones, but they'd all be a lot more upset if there was a zombie in the room with them."

"That's really what we're going with, huh?" Annie began climbing the stairs, summoning a ball of flame and holding it suspended over her palm as she did. It provided a measure of uneven, flickering light, which didn't help me as much as I wanted it to. It definitely reassured her, however, calming the surface of her thoughts with its mere presence. It was weapon and light source at the same time, so that effect made a certain amount of sense. "Zombie?"

"They're mindless shambling husks that used to be people, can't be people anymore, and just want to consume," I said. "Do you have a better idea?"

"I don't know. 'Husks'? Has a nicely insectile feel, isn't vaguely culturally appropriative and arguably racist, which is funny in its own way, since you come from a whole species of white serial killers. Whoever decided to call you 'cuckoos'—"

"Pretty sure that was Great-Grandma Fran." I was eventually going to have to tell her what Mark had told me, about how the Healy family luck came from their connection to a presumably extinct species of cryptid . . . how the Healys had not been, after Fran married in, entirely human, meaning Annie herself was not entirely human, meaning Artie and Elsie were even more of a genetic patchwork than we'd always assumed. Some of the implications were staggering.

The Covenant of St. George really believed they had a divine right to "cleanse" the planet in the name of humanity's dominion. But if we'd been underestimating the number of cryptid species closely related enough to humans to interbreed—and not only interbreed but have fertile offspring, as Fran had had two children, and her daughter had done the same—then even they might have to do some rethinking.

"Whatever," said Annie dismissively. "Whoever decided to call you 'cuckoos' should probably have taken a little more time to think before just spitting out a sobriquet they thought fit in the moment. I'd rename you all to 'locusts' or something else suitably bug-based if I could. So I don't think 'zombies' is the right word."

"Cool. We can put it to a vote when we get back to the boys."

Had the stairs been this long before we'd gone traipsing all over campus and bruised the hell out of my poor feet? I knew they must have been, since the architecture seemed to be sticking with the normal laws of physics, but this staircase felt like it was a thousand miles long, like I was making the unending march across the floor at San Diego Comic-Con. I'd only been twice, and only once with a badge, but the distances involved had been more than enough to make an impression.

Then the stairs were over, finally, and we were stepping into the long dark hall between us and the classroom. I froze, skin humping up into knots, suddenly convinced that all my assurances had been lies; I wasn't picking up distress from the boys because the zombies weren't in the classroom, but they were in the building. They were clustered in the corners, just out of the range that worked for detecting them, watching us with silent, starving eyes.

Logic said I was wrong. Logic said they no longer had the ability to make even rudimentary plans, and setting an ambush qualified as a plan; they were like kittens, pouncing on anything that caught their eyes, incapable of hesitation or restraint. The hall was safe.

Logic could go stuff itself. I knew what I felt, and what I felt was creeping terror.

"Are you coming or what?" Annie looked over her shoulder at me, still holding the ball of flame in her hand. "You're so weird. I always assumed a cuckoo my own age would be more like Very. All pushy and aggressive. You're an apex predator. Act like it."

"I don't think you really want me to do that," I said, and forced myself to take another step into the hall. The next one was easier, as was the one after that, and the one after that, and nothing came out of the shadows to attack us, until we were standing in front of the classroom door, still safe, still together, and Annie blew her ball of flame carelessly out, like it was nothing of consequence.

"Come on," she said, and opened the door. "Let's tell the boys what we've been up to and figure out what we're going to do next."

She stepped inside. I followed.

Eight

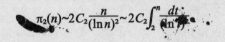

$$\pi_2(n) \sim 2C_2\frac{n}{(\ln n)^2} \sim 2C_2\int_2^n \frac{dt}{(\ln t)^2}$$

"No sane man would want this life for his children. I certainly don't. Sadly, the universe seems determined not to give me a choice."

—Jonathan Healy

Back in the classroom where this terrible, awful, no-good, seemingly endless day began

THE BOYS HAD BEEN busy since their return to the classroom. Mark and Artie had dragged chairs over to the window, where they could watch the lawn outside warily. James was at the front of the room, working on what I would have called a sandcastle if it hadn't been sculpted out of tiny sheets of ice. A snowcastle, maybe, if that's a word. The mice who hadn't accompanied Annie and me were with him, moving ice sheets into place, using the heat of their paws to melt fine details into the structure.

Everyone looked over when Annie opened the door, the air growing suddenly thick with tension and several degrees colder. The tension faded when they saw who it was. The cold didn't. Annie made an exasperated huffing noise.

"Sorry," said James sheepishly. The air warmed back up.

I frowned. I hadn't been around much for the last few years—when I'd injured myself, Annie had still been hiding her sorcery from the rest of the family, and I'd been allowing her the polite fiction of fooling the telepath, and James and I had been strangers until my arrival in Portland had kicked this whole mess off. Still, we had a family history of sorcery, and both Grandma and Mary were happy to talk about the way Grandpa Thomas used to change the world with a few clever hand gestures and a thought. It had never been this extreme in their stories, and I didn't remember it being this extreme in Portland, either.

Maybe that meant I wasn't going to have to live with quite as many long-term consequences as I'd feared. Keeping my tone light, I asked, "Has either of you been noticing that sorcery is easier for you here?"

Annie and James exchanged a look. Her thoughts filled with the way she'd pulled the fire off those burning cuckoos, how quickly she'd called up her fireball in the stairwell. James, who had not just done a bunch of recreational murder, was a little more measured, pondering the ice castle and the speed with which the temperature had dropped. He was the first of them to speak, saying in a subdued tone, "Maybe. Why do you ask?"

"Because I'm starting to think that some of the rules governing this universe are different. I thought the square-cube law might be suspended here, but since Annie hasn't burnt us all to a smoldering crisp by mistake quite yet, we can probably assume that we still *have* a square-cube law. We just also have giant insects."

"They could have lungs," said Artie. "You're a giant insect, you have lungs."

"It's nice how you remember dissecting cuckoos without remembering me," I said mildly. "It makes me feel very special and not at all like you're going to slit my throat as soon as I fall asleep. We already discussed the possibility of lungs, and to be fair to you and your ideas, I think lungs are very likely, given that these things have gone a step past arboreal and into aerial. I'd assume air bladders at the very least, and adapting those into rudimentary lungs wouldn't have been much work at all."

Evolution is a crapshoot under the best of circumstances. People like to pretend "survival of the fittest" means "survival of the best," the biggest, strongest, cleverest, most attractive examples of the species. What it really means is "survival of whatever fit into its ecological niche the most efficiently, without getting eaten by something else before it could make more of itself." The first Johrlac to develop telepathy probably looked a lot more like a yellowjacket than a YouTube influencer, and it almost certainly hadn't been an X-Men style leap forward, going from non-telepathic parents to the level of mental dexterity that Mark and I possessed. Maybe it had been an empath like Artie, or able to push compulsions out but not receive them, like Mom. There was no way of knowing. Trying to guess now wouldn't change anything. How did the flying bugs get so big in the first place? If whatever had made the saddle kept histories, maybe we'd have the chance to find out. If we didn't, then we had to admit that it didn't matter as much as we wanted it to.

Humans like things to make sense. It's a failing of the species, and part of why they're so bad at overall risk assessment. And I, lucky me, may not be human, but I was raised by humans, and that means a lot of their thought patterns encoded themselves into me. I want the world to be as logical and rational as a well-honed equation. It's never going to give in to my desires, but that doesn't make them go away.

Annie snapped her fingers. "Okay, Nerd Herd, focus. What the hell do lungs and the square-cube law have to do with me and James going up ten levels in Sorcerer from one monster encounter? Do we need to worry about Wild Magic surges all of a sudden?"

James' thoughts turned baffled. "Did you just start speaking Greek?"

"Oh, God, Jimmy, how have I not pinned you down and forced you to learn the beautiful intricacies of Dungeons and Dragons?" asked Annie without any real heat.

"We've been a little busy, what with the cross-country move and the change of identity and your cousin forcing through an adoption posthumously but not literally approved by my long-dead mother to keep my father from having any legal right to come after me, even though I've been an adult for years now," said James mildly.

Annie responded with a wave of smugness so heavy that even the non-psychics in the room should have been able to feel it. "Oh, yeah," she said. "I guess we have been getting some shit done. Anyway, when we get home, we're grabbing Elsie and Artie and putting together a new family D&D campaign. I don't . . ." She faltered. "I don't remember why the last one ended."

"And then did the God of Chosen Isolation state with Firmness that as Abelard the Artificer could not continue his good and necessary work without the aid of Ashfire the Cleric, the Campaign must be Suspended," squeaked a tiny voice from Annie's hair. "And all were direly disappointed by the Pausing of the Game, but as the Calculating Priestess was unavailable, it was agreed that this was indeed fair."

"Oh," said Annie. "I guess that explains why my plans for the campaign don't make sense to me now. I forgot we were supposed to have a cleric." She shot me a look that even I could interpret as murderous, underscored by the fury now roiling in her mind. "You messed with D&D."

"I'm sorry," I said. "I didn't mean to. You should know by now that I didn't mean to do *any* of this. Everything is terrible and strange, and I think we're in a dimension that amplifies sorcery, which probably means the people who ride the giant bugs can throw fireballs at us if we upset them, and there are zombie cuckoos everywhere, and I don't even have a *bra*!" I didn't expect to start yelling, but somewhere in the middle of all that I did, my voice peaking on a wail.

Annie took a step toward me, holding one hand out and open in a calming gesture. "Hey," she said. "Hey, it's going to be okay."

"Zombie cuckoos?" asked Mark, who had been staying quiet while we dealt with one more piece of nonsensical family drama. As much as I didn't like the situation, he had to find it even more frustrating. He was watching a bunch of semi-strangers scream out their problems, while all he wanted to do was go home. "What do you mean, zombie cuckoos?"

"She means that while she was surgically jumbling our memories, princess here," Annie hooked a thumb toward me, "also wiped the minds of all the cuckoos she was psychically connected to. They're not really people anymore. They're shambling husks and they're neither dead nor infectious, so we're *not* calling them zombies, got it?"

Mark blinked. "Got it," he said, in a tone that implied he absolutely did not "got it." For someone who could literally read minds, he was incredibly confused.

It's okay, I know we're a lot, I said quietly in his mind. He jerked upright like he'd been poked with a pin, looking wildly around for a moment before focusing on me and narrowing his eyes.

"What?" I asked aloud.

Annie and James both turned toward me. Artie, who seemed to be making a game of not looking at me, turned back to the window. "Something on your mind?" asked Annie.

"Mark was being weird," I said.

"I'm not being weird," he snapped. "You talked inside my head!"

"Um." I blinked very slowly. "That's pretty normal for cuckoos? We did it before, while you had me tied to the chair, remember? And we've had skin contact, and you were part of the ritual circle, so you're attuned to me; I don't think you could keep me out if you were trying. Which you weren't just now." Running up against another cuckoo's shields—or a non-cuckoo who knows how to protect their thoughts against psychic intrusion—is like hitting a flimsy but locked door. Sure, you could bang it

down if you felt like you had no choice in the matter, but
you'd make a bunch of noise and attract a lot of attention
in the process.

Someone who was shielding themselves would know
if you broke into their mind. They'd feel it happen, and
they'd be able to take steps to make it stop. None of that
had happened just now with Mark, I was sure of it.

"Yes, I was," he said.

"No, you weren't." There had been a bit of resistance,
but only for an instant, less of a door and more of a soap
bubble, thin and incidental and easily popped.

Mark pushed away from the window and strode toward me, chin down and brow furrowed, clearly spoiling
for a fight. "Yes, I *was*," he snarled, biting off every
word. "I wake up with a bunch of people I know I know,
who know about Cici, but who I can't remember meeting or why I would voluntarily spend any time around
them, and there's an unconscious *queen* on the ground
in front of us—something that isn't supposed to be possible, by the way, you should either be dead or blasted so
far out the other side of yourself that you're a gibbering,
pissing wreck. Not a *person*. Queens aren't *people*."

From the way he was describing things, the fate Ingrid
and the other cuckoos had intended for me was basically
the one that had been wrought on the cuckoos from the
ritual: hollowed out of everything but the barest instincts
necessary for survival, eternally hungry, unable to put
anything resembling a self back together in the face of
the howling internal void. I shook my head.

"If there's never been a queen who was still herself
after the ritual finished, why are you surprised that I can
apparently do things you don't expect?" I asked. "I'm
sorry to have violated your privacy. I legitimately didn't
feel your shields. I will be more careful in the future.
Every instar is triggered by something, and every instar
leaves a cuckoo stronger. Well, I've survived the instar
that was supposed to end me. I think it's pretty obvious
that it comes with a power boost, at least in this dimen-

sion. Maybe we'll all get lucky and it'll be like the increase to Annie and James' sorcery, and it'll go away when we make it home."

"You mean 'if' we make it home," grumbled Mark.

"No, I mean when. We've broken the rules already, just to get here." I spread my arms, indicating the room around me. "Everything about this is supposed to be impossible. I can't say for sure that we'll be able to take the whole school with us, but we're going to get home, and we're going to take all the people who are still alive and capable of being people with us."

"Even the larvae?" asked Annie.

I turned my attention back to her. "Okay, one, I'm pretty sure calling cuckoo kids 'larvae' is racist as hell. If you're going to say that we can't use the word 'zombie' because it's cultural appropriation, we're not going to start calling *kids* a word that means *worms*. The hollowed-out cuckoos will kill us if we let them. I've looked inside them and there's nothing there to stop them from taking us apart. But the kids are still just that: kids."

"Wait." Mark straightened. "The children survived?"

"Yes." I looked at him. "Why do you sound so surprised?"

"Because your—because Ingrid said they wouldn't. She said there wouldn't be room inside them for the ritual we were going to perform and all the pieces of our heritage that they carried with them, and they'd short out like lightbulbs plugged into a current that was too strong." He shook his head, thoughts turning baffled. "There's no way those kids are still alive."

"Well, they are, at least some of them, and since the three we found have managed to convince one of the human survivors she's their sister, their pre-instar abilities still function; there might be some time bombs buried in there, but I doubt it. I wouldn't do that to kids."

Annie snapped her fingers. I jumped. She pointed at me.

"That's it," she said.

"You want to explain for the non-psychics in the room?" asked James.

"If everything she's been saying is true, and she's part of our family but managed to remove herself from our memories by mistake, she grew up with *our family*." She shook her head, responding to the blank looks I assumed they were directing her way. "We don't hurt kids. Species doesn't matter. Unless we're culling a nest of something where the young ones literally won't survive without the adults, we don't hurt kids. That's how Alex wound up with a damn Church Griffin for a pet. No one does that on purpose, but if he hadn't taken the kitten, it would have died before it fledged. If she could protect us from the ritual the cuckoos were trying to perform—"

"I was the only one actually performing anything," I said.

Annie ignored me. "—then of course she also protected the kids."

"That assumes she didn't hurt them at the same time," said Mark. He narrowed his eyes as he looked at me. "Ingrid said the issue was storage. Their brains aren't big enough to take both themselves and the ritual, and one of them would have to go. How do we know she didn't wipe out the part of them that was going to tell them their own history?"

"You mean the big time bomb of murder that they were born with?" asked Artie. "If she deleted *that*, more power to her."

"No, *not* more power to her!" snapped Mark. "That's our history, our culture, everything we have left from Johrlar. Without it, we're just a bunch of confused bipedal wasps trying to figure out what to do with ourselves. No killer instinct—no instincts at all!"

"I did okay for myself," I said quietly.

"Yeah, because you fell in with a family of murderous assholes who thought keeping you was the same as keeping a baby Church Griffin, whatever the fuck *that* is! What's going to happen to these kids? How are they going to survive if you've stripped out everything that makes them cuckoos?"

"They're going to survive the same way anyone does!" I glared at him, prying my own shields open as far as they would go in the hopes that he'd register and understand my displeasure. Artie winced, caught in the unfiltered rush of my emotions. "They have families right now, families who are probably at home in a panic because their children have been abducted, families who will be delighted to have them back! They'll still be cuckoos, whether or not they remember Johrlar—and I don't think remembering Johrlar has done us any fucking favors, if it turns us all into serial killers as soon as we get old enough to hit that instar! They'll grow up and go to college and they'll figure out they aren't human and maybe they'll find each other and maybe they won't, but either way, they'll get to stay *themselves*! They won't get some bullshit about instincts and instars plastered over the people they want to be!"

"Their heritage—"

"Don't try to make this about heritage, like you give a fuck about heritage." The urge to march across the room and slap him was almost overwhelming. "This isn't about heritage because we're all adoptees with unwilling adoptive parents, people who didn't know what they were being tricked into taking, people who never chose to take us in but still wound up responsible for us! It's not our responsibility to carry the sins of our ancestors forever, not when it turns us into family destroyers the second it gets dropped onto our shoulders. If I deleted that bullshit from their heads, *good for me*. I've freed them. They can *learn* it if they want to. You still remember every horrifying scrap, I'm sure. You can be the one to educate our people, and I can be their great destroyer, but if you want to act like preserving their minds was less important than preserving a history book, then *fuck you*."

The sound of James' palm striking Mark's face was very loud and somehow underwhelming at the same time, like it should have been a bigger deal when one of my allies struck another. Mark raised his hand to cover the stinging spot on his cheek, eyes going white as he focused on James, who was radiating confusion.

Oh, fuck me—James wasn't a Price by blood, and didn't have Frances Healy's protection from my telepathy. I had accidentally turned him into a puppet by dropping my own shielding. I pulled back, so hard and firmly that the effort made me slightly dizzy, like I'd stood up too fast after riding a roller coaster or something.

"I'm sorry, James," I said, rushing to put myself between him and Mark, in case the compulsion hadn't fully faded. "Annie thinks of you as her brother, and I forgot you weren't a Price by blood for a second there. I didn't mean to."

"Oh, so you're the reason ice boy went and whacked me?" asked Mark, in a dangerous tone. "Not cool."

"No, and it was an accident, and it *won't* happen again."

"Everything seems to be an accident with you," snarled Artie, turning away from the window so fast he knocked over a chair. It fell to the linoleum with a clatter. No one said anything, all of us just staring at him in stunned silence. "Wiped our minds? Accident! Deleted our memories? Accident! Became a cuckoo queen? Accident! Made James hit Mark? Accident! This is all bullshit. It's the way you people hunt, taken to eleven. You think we don't know cuckoo tactics? My *grandmother* is a cuckoo. I know exactly what you're trying to do, and you can go get fucked if you think I'm going to let you get away with it."

He stalked toward me, and I shrank back, until my shoulders bumped against Mark's chest, stopping me from going any farther. I didn't think Artie was going to hit me, and based on his surface thoughts, he wasn't planning to, but that's where the most danger can sometimes lie; in the space between the intention and the action, where people do things without thinking about them. I didn't know this version of Artie, the man I'd grown up with, the man I loved, the man who had—until I found myself in the position of needing to set everything I loved on fire to save the world—loved me. He was a stranger.

"I'm not trying to do anything," I said, in a small voice. "I just want to figure out how to get us all home, and do it, before anyone else gets hurt." We had so many obstacles between us and that goal. We didn't need to be fighting among ourselves.

Artie made a scoffing noise and started to pull his arm back. I cringed. It was automatic. I don't enjoy getting hit. I'm not like Verity, who seems to take a twisted sort of pleasure out of seeing how much pain she can put her body through, like she's going to pop down to the store and get herself a new one if this one wears out.

"*Arthur James Harrington-Price.*" Annie's voice was the snapping of a whip, striking each syllable of Artie's name with the precision of a sharpshooter. He froze, arm still cocked, and turned to look at her. She advanced across the room like she was on her way to war, eyes narrowed in a fury I had rarely seen from her when her siblings weren't involved.

"I don't care if she's playing us or if she's telling us the truth," she said, voice going low and tight and terribly dangerous. It was a voice that demanded to be listened to—because refusal would have repercussions. Mark took a step back, getting away from that voice, and I moved with him, letting his shirt and my nightgown protect us from skin contact. "*I* think she's telling the truth. *I* think the mice are telling the truth. We believe the mice. Isn't that what we were raised to do? She doesn't act like a normal cuckoo. She has regrets. She's afraid. And even if she's lying, we're in a bad situation here, we can't afford to be alienating potential allies because we think they *might* be less than honest with us. Do I make myself clear?"

"She's a cuckoo!" Artie objected. "Cuckoos can't be trusted, we know—"

"Your own grandmother is a cuckoo!"

"Who do you think taught me not to trust them?" he demanded. "*Both* our grandmothers taught me that if you trust cuckoos, you'll only get hurt. And Grandma Angela is broken, you know that, *she* knows that. This cuckoo," he pointed to me, "isn't broken. She and Mark both say that she's some kind of super-cuckoo. How is that better?"

"But you trust Mark."

"Of course I trust Mark! He helped us . . . helped us . . ." Artie's thoughts turned confused, roiling around a place where his memories had been improperly patched together, where the sequence of events no longer made any sense if I was extracted from it. "I don't—what did you do?" He swung his attention back to me. "What did you *do to me*?"

His wail, while anguished, was more pained than angry, and he didn't lift his hand again, just pushed past me and Mark and rushed for the door, leaving Annie staring after him.

None of us moved. I wasn't even sure that all of us were breathing. I finally straightened, stepping away from Mark with an apologetic glance back over my shoulder.

"I'm going after him," I said. "I'm sorry. This is all my fault."

"Would it still be your fault if we were dead?" asked James.

"Yeah." I shrugged. "Sometimes no matter what you do, you're to blame. I didn't make a lot of the choices that got us where we ended up, and when I finally got to choose, it was Artie who showed me how many options I actually had. I owe him. But this is still on me."

"Sarah, he was going to hit you," said Mark. Mark, who had less power behind his telepathy than I did, but who also had fewer reservations about reading the minds of my family members. "He could *still* decide to hit you."

I shrugged again. "So he hits me. Verity used to make

me spar with her so she didn't slow down while we were in New York, and that girl never learned to pull her punches. Artie hits like I do. He's afraid of damaging his hands. I won't *like* it, but I'll be fine."

Mark blinked. "But he could hit you."

"And thus do we see two people performing an accidental example of why I think you might be telling us the truth," said Annie. "No one who didn't grow up with our ridiculous family is this blasé about getting clocked. Are you sure you don't want one of us to come with you?"

"I'm sure," I said. "This is going to be hard enough. No need to make it harder." I ducked my head and hunched my shoulders, making myself look smaller—a technique I had perfected while fighting my way through an almost all-human high school, one it would have been all too easy for me to silently dominate without even trying—and walked across the room to the classroom door.

This time, they let me go, and I managed not to resent that. I had asked them to, after all.

Nine

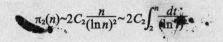

$$\pi_2(n) \sim 2C_2 \frac{n}{(\ln n)^2} \sim 2C_2 \int_2^n \frac{dt}{(\ln t)}$$

"I always knew I was different from my parents. I think every child knows that on some level, although in my case, it was a difference in species, not just ideology."

—Evelyn Baker

Following someone potentially hostile out into a dark hallway, like that's a sensible plan

STEPPING BACK INTO THE dark hall without Annie was no easier than leaving the stairwell had been. It helped a little that Artie's confused, wounded feelings were a beacon, bright and bitter and easy for me to follow. Even if the mindless cuckoos had been swarming, filling the air with their infinite hunger, it would have been easy to follow that beacon, and almost impossible not to, at least for me. He was hurting. He was hurting badly, and there was no way of pretending it wasn't at least a little bit my fault.

Well. If I wasn't pretending, then it was more than a little bit. It was a lot. This was almost entirely on me, and if there's one thing my Grandma Alice taught me, it's that intentions don't matter to the people you hurt. The Covenant of St. George started their campaign of cleansing and terror with the best of intentions; when compared to the rest of the natural world, humans are weak, short-lived, and easy to kill. Only the fact that they demonstrate a near-inherent grasp of pack tactics ever gave them a chance at survival. They started out-numbered and vulnerable, easy prey for dragons and manticores and everything else that wanted a fuller stomach and fewer neighbors. I can't say the Covenant was wrong to feel like they needed to guarantee the survival of their species. Everything that lives wants to survive, even when it hurts everything else around them. Survival is the first impulse we get, along with our first breath of air.

I *can* say they were wrong not to stop and pull back once they'd won. They fought a war and proved themselves the worst kind of victor: the kind who turns a victory into a genocide. I glanced nervously at the shadows and kept walking, following the beacon of Artie's thoughts to another door, identical to the one we'd been sheltering behind. It was closed, but I could feel him on the other side, all but screaming for someone to come and find him.

He wanted Annie, of course, or James if he couldn't have her; even Mark would have been acceptable. Me, he didn't want anywhere near him. Me, he never wanted to see again.

Too bad for both of us that I was what he had.

I opened the door and stepped inside.

This classroom was darker than the one I'd been in before, the window aimed less squarely at the suns. The day cycle of this dimension might be a long one, but they had a nighttime, that much was becoming increasingly clear, and if it was like the nights back home, that was when the *big* predators would come out, the things that fed on the flying millipedes and centipedes and whatever else this biosphere had to offer. It was a chilling thought. Well, maybe they could take care of the remaining cuckoos for us. I normally wouldn't wish death by ravenous predator on anyone, but it wasn't like the cuckoos would hesitate to rip us apart themselves if they got the chance. And we're back to survival again.

At all costs. No matter what.

Artie had either pulled one of the desks over to the

window or found it already there; he was sitting atop it, hands between his knees, legs dangling. He turned as the door swung shut again behind me, and while I couldn't see his face in the gloom, I also couldn't help feeling his sudden, sharp bolt of irritation.

"Go away," he said.

"I can't." I walked toward him. "We're going to have to work together if we want to go home, and that means we're not going to let you run away. Mom would straight-up murder me if I got everyone else home and not you."

Artie made a scoffing noise. "She has other grand-kids."

"So you believe me now?"

"I believe you think my grandma's your mother. Doesn't mean I believe she is. That would mean admit-ting you're telling us the truth, and you're the worst per-son I've ever met." He lifted his chin, the thin light through the window glinting off his glasses. "I'd rather have to work with a liar than a monster. So maybe you're just confused. Maybe you believe what you're saying, but you didn't do any of the things you think you did. Hell, all cuckoos look alike. Maybe you're not this Sarah person after all, but some other cuckoo whose head she messed with the same way she messed with all of ours. Maybe you're a victim, not a monster. Doesn't mean I have to like you." He turned away from me again, back to staring at the outside world.

"Doesn't mean you have to be a dick to me about it."

"I don't see where I have to be nice to you."

"Um, because either I saved your life and your di-mension, or I did nothing wrong and you don't have any good reason to be mean to me?"

"Not being mean to you and being nice to you aren't the same thing."

"Artie—"

"*My life doesn't make any sense!*" He stood so quickly that the desk shook unsteadily, nearly toppling over. "Do you understand what that *feels* like? What it's like to not know your own history?"

"Not exactly," I said nervously, rubbing my left wrist in a self-soothing motion that utterly failed to soothe. "But I broke myself for a little while, and I had to put myself back together one piece at a time, and while that was going on, I didn't know my history, or my future, or my present. So I know what something sort of similar feels like."

"Bully for you," he snapped. "I remember spending most of my life shut in my bedroom because I was scared that if I got close to anyone, they'd have to love me whether they wanted to or not. Is that true? Did I really grow up without any friends, without anyone who wasn't related to me who gave a damn if I lived or died, or did you *do that* to me?"

I blinked slowly. I'd been in so much pain over my own losses that I hadn't considered whether deleting myself would leave the people I cared about questioning their entire lives. I knew I'd protected their core identities but not the pieces of them that contained me. James and Mark had few enough blank spaces in their memories that they could be mostly sure they were still the same people, even if recent events were a jumble. But Artie and Annie . . .

"I didn't do anything to you on purpose," I said, forcing my voice not to shake. "And what I *did* do, what I can't walk away from or force you to forgive me for, I did to keep you alive. I'm sorry. I didn't know what was going to happen when I made the choice I did." The urge to tell him that he had been the one to suggest it was strong, but it wouldn't change anything. He probably wouldn't even believe me. He didn't believe me now.

"So why did you do it?" He sounded utterly miserable.

Aw, hell. There was no way out of this. "Because you told me to."

Artie narrowed his eyes, taking a step closer to me. "I *told* you to mess with my memories and delete yourself from my life. I *told* you to do that."

"No, not exactly like that . . ." I could still see Artie the way he'd been in that moment, eyes shining, face an open book, standing in the white room of my mind, the equation howling around us. He'd loved me then. It had been one of the last moments when he'd loved me, and he was never going to love me again, and it broke the heart I didn't have. "The equation the cuckoos use to move between dimensions was too big for me to control. It was going to consume me, and once it did, it was going to complete itself. I was going to go full Dark Phoenix."

He blinked and chuckled, apparently too surprised by the fact that the telepath who grew up in the modern media landscape would have heard of the X-Men to suppress his reaction. "Eat a sun, gotcha."

"Maybe," I said, more solemnly. "I don't think the equation would actually have pushed Earth's sun into supernova, but it would certainly have devastated the planet, not just Iowa. You were the one who reminded me that the planet is where I keep everything I care about. My family and tomatoes and comic book stores and everything. It was very Crowley talking down Aziraphale before the apocalypse, and I was very impressed. Impressed enough to listen when you reminded me that SETI functions due to distributed computing."

"They use other processors to carry part of the load so that they don't need storage facilities the size of New Mexico," he said.

"Exactly. The equation was winning because it was too big to fit inside my brain, but if I put it into all the minds around me and just kept hold of the pieces I needed to modify in order to change its function, I could handle it. I used the cuckoos as hard drives. Just slammed it in there and let it wipe them clean." Except for Ingrid, who I had pumped the equation into like a weapon, and except for the kids, who had been innocent of their elders' crimes and deserved to be protected. "But my brain is structured to hold things like this. I'm a telepath. I'm able to withstand certain strains, and every instar I've gone through has made me better at holding big, complicated equations like that one. I'm literally built for it. You're not. Not even Mark—he's a couple of instars behind me, development-wise. So when I pushed the pieces of the equation I still needed to offload into you, I tried to use the open spaces first, the places where your brain had storage capacity. And then, when that wasn't enough, I wrapped up the core of your personality and moved it to the side where it wouldn't be touched." Saying it like that sounded so easy, like it had been one more thing on a carefully considered checklist, and not an act of desperation, performed in a panic. "And the equation just kept coming and coming and I was so *scared*, I was going to die or I was going to destroy the world, and either way I wasn't going to be there for you anymore, and I didn't . . . I didn't . . ."

I was crying. I wasn't sure when that had started, and I wasn't sure how to make it stop. Cuckoos cry just like humans, tears leaking from our eyes and snot running from our noses. We don't get red eyes or faces, but that's about the only upside I can see to the situation. I swiped ineffectively at my cheek with one hand and forced myself to keep going.

"I didn't want you to be sad that I was gone. If I could work the numbers fast enough to keep you alive, I didn't want you to have to live with the fact that you couldn't save me. And I was still shuffling things around as fast as they would go, I was still trying to run the numbers, and I guess my fear of dying and the fact that I was scared you were going to miss me too much to forgive yourself crashed together and made sure I got the worst parts of both. I didn't die, and you don't have to miss me." One last gift from an equation that had to have felt itself being torn apart, twisted away from its original purpose. It had been made to do something terrible and wrong, but I had still perverted it in the basic sense of the word: I had refused to let it be what it wanted most to be, and it had been aware enough to take its revenge. "It erased me from your minds. I had everything you were in my hands, given willingly, and the equation took me away from you because it was the best way to punish me for killing it."

"Did you kill it?"

"I think so. There are still fragments, trapped in the husked-out cuckoos, but if Mark's right and I wiped the memory packets from the juvenile cuckoos, then it's lost. We'd need . . ." How many cuckoos had been needed to serve as distributed storage for the pieces of the equation without being overwhelmed and dying horribly? How many cuckoos had been required to give me pieces of their minds to make their terrible creation whole and unleash it on the world where we'd all been born? That math was surprisingly easy. "We'd need at least two hundred cuckoos to have chosen staying on a doomed world over joining the ritual that would take them to a new one, and cuckoos are too self-interested to have made the choice to stay if they didn't have to. I'd guess there might be a couple dozen, maybe, who weren't able to get to Iowa fast enough, but that won't be enough to resurrect it, or to fix what I destroyed. It's dead."

"*Good*," he said, with fierce, violent loathing. But for the first time, it wasn't directed at me.

I wiped at my cheeks again. "And back to what you asked me before, whether you really grew up mostly staying in your room or not, you did. Your parents started telling you to be careful around humans before I even met you, and by the time I came around, you knew that people sometimes liked you even when they didn't want to, because of your pheromones. Aunt Jane and Uncle Ted taught you to be careful. They taught you to stay away from people. They taught Elsie, too; she just . . . didn't listen."

"Elsie never listens," said Artie, with a flicker of dark humor. "She likes it when people like her."

"You didn't. Not if they were just liking your pheromones, and not *you*. You hated it when you made people like you—said it was forcing them to do something they didn't want. By the time we were ten, you knew you didn't want that." But when we were ten, he'd been too young for his abilities to have reached their peak; he'd still been able to go out among humans without getting swarmed. Smiled at and occasionally bought ice cream by kindly grandparent types, but not swarmed. Lilu don't have the protection of their pheromonal shields until they reach puberty; prior to that, they have to rely on their empathy, and the fact that most people find baby Lilu damned adorable. Artie hadn't *needed* the lockdown until he was almost sixteen. That should have been plenty of time for him to form normal social bonds that could endure even after he'd been pulled out of public school for "distance learning." Teenagers who want to keep seeing their friends are usually very good at finding ways to do so, even when the adults involved don't want it to happen.

I worried my lip briefly between my teeth. "I think . . . maybe . . . it was partially my fault. Not because it happens differently the way that I remember it, but because I was a factor for you in a way I wasn't for Elsie." He looked at me, thoughts radiating blank confusion. I took a deep breath. "When you were eleven, you got a Pac-Man frog."

"Trashcan, yes," he said, tone dubious.

"And he mostly liked to hang out in the moss in his tank or sleep in his water bowl when no one was handling him." That frog had never really warmed to me because my body temperature was enough lower than a human's to make me uninteresting. It's tough, being a preteen girl with a crush on a boy and having even his pet frog reject your love.

Or maybe the full sentence is "it's tough, being a preteen girl."

"Uh-huh."

"Unless you gave him something to eat. As soon as there was food on offer, everything changed." Artie had fed Trashcan giant Dubia roaches and thawed, previously frozen mice: Alex would never have allowed or tolerated live feeding, even if it had been a good idea with the colony around. No one had wanted him to get a taste for living rodents.

Artie nodded, very slowly. "He would get active, he would strike, he would eat his meal and then be surly for hours, because even if he wasn't hungry, there might be more food around."

"Exactly. Adding something new to the enclosure changed his behavior and changed the situation. I think I was maybe the mouse."

I could feel the confusion rolling off of him. I worried my lip again.

"This might be easier if I just showed you, but I need to ask for your permission first."

"What show me, like, telepathically?" When I nodded, he laughed. It wasn't a pleasant sound. "Yeah, sure, show me. Why the hell not? You've already been rooting around inside my brain, and while you say you had permission then, I don't remember it. May as well go another round."

"Thank you." I let go of my wrist, allowing my arms to fall back to my sides, and ducked my chin, feeling the vitreous humor inside my eyes tingle as they lit up. "This won't hurt," I said, and *reached*.

I was right.

It didn't hurt *him*.

Diving into the changed landscape of Artie's mind was effortless. We'd been attuned to each other since childhood, locked into constant low-grade telepathic contact by handholding and naptimes and all the other little casual contacts inevitably initiated by children who enjoy each other's company. I'd expected a little resistance, but I was still learning my new limits, and I slid into his thoughts as easily as a hot knife slides into butter.

All around me were familiar events and experiences, and I was a gaping hole in every one of them. This close, I couldn't help seeing what had been causing him so much pain, because some of these things *didn't* make sense once you took me away. It wasn't just the D&D

game, although messing with Annie's plans was bad enough, and she was probably going to hold that against me for the rest of time; it was family gatherings where I'd become overwhelmed by too many people thinking too many things and fled to the backyard, only for Artie to follow and comfort me; it was the family trip to Lowryland when we were seventeen, which he'd agreed to only after I promised to go wherever he went the whole time, even if it was back to the hotel. It was the time Annie had taken us all to Emerald City Comic-Con to confront a misbehaving siren, using my natural cuckoo cloaking capabilities to keep my incubus cousin safe in the crowds. It was everything. I'd flavored and informed *everything*.

It would have been a sweet reminder of how much we'd always meant to each other, if not for the situation.

I took another deep breath, centering and stabilizing myself in the shifting firmament of his mindscape, and froze the scene as I pulled his consciousness in my direction. There was a momentary pause, probably no longer than it took to blink, and he appeared beside me, looking exactly as he did in the "real" world, with the fun and recently discovered wrinkle that here, in a wholly mental world, I could read his face without pausing to interpret his thoughts, or questioning whether he was thinking "smile" as he actually frowned.

He looked baffled. Not angry, which was a nice change, but utterly and completely out of his depth. He turned to look at me. "That's my twelfth birthday," he said, in an almost accusing tone. "No one wanted to come. My parents had to bribe my *sister* to get her to agree to sit down with the nerd."

"Elsie was having a phase." Fourteen-year-old girls don't often want to attend their little brothers' birthday parties. They want to hang out with kids their own age, reveling in the assumed maturity of being newly-minted high school students. She and Alex had both been feeling very grown-up and mature that year, and had wanted nothing to do with the "babies" of the family, even though Artie, Verity, and I were all only two years behind.

"It still sucked," he said, sullenly. "No guests. No surprises. Nothing."

"Can I show you how I remember it?" How it had really happened, unless my ability to rewrite memories extended to rewriting reality itself, which it didn't. It couldn't. If the equation had carried that much power, the cuckoos would have been able to move between worlds without destroying everything they left in their wake, and while they were selfish enough to ruin things just because they didn't want them anymore, they were also smart enough to have wanted to preserve familiar worlds for them to plunder.

Also, if I had rewritten reality, I'd have a heartbeat, and I wouldn't be reading anybody's mind. All I'd ever wanted was to be human, and no matter how much I sometimes hated myself, I would still have granted my own wish.

Artie hesitated. The question scared him. So much of who he thought he was in this moment depended on a childhood of unloved isolation, of being the odd man out in a family of people who were addicted to connection— who sought it to such a degree that everyone who left to go out into the world and become an adult came back with new people they called family, new people they were so connected to that they wouldn't dream of letting them go.

"Yes," he said finally.

"Thank you."

I closed my eyes, and when I opened them, everything was different, and everything was the same.

My excision from Artie's memories hadn't been precise, thankfully; if I'd been doing it on purpose, building him a new reality the way I had for the Covenant team that had discovered Dominic and Verity in New York, he wouldn't have been left with a vague, nagging sense of loss, and so wouldn't have been able to believe me when I said there was something missing. He would have been someone new, someone who didn't need me. My own sloppiness was the only reason I might possibly be able to pull this off.

Artie's younger self was sitting at the dining room table, a chipped old oak thing that I was pretty sure Aunt Jane had rescued from the side of the road somewhere. Certainly, no one had ever paid for it. It was old without becoming antique, scarred, and marked up from decades of family dinners with a family that thought knives were tool, weapon, toy, and friendly companion, all at the same time. There was a large sheet cake at one end, next to a plate of cupcakes with surprisingly red frosting, like someone had gotten a little over-enthusiastic with the strawberry flavoring.

They weren't strawberry. They never were at Artie's parties, because he loved chocolate like a normal kid did, and I . . . didn't.

The doorbell rang and he was out of his seat, moving fast. Beside me in the present, in the mist of his own mind, Artie frowned.

"I don't remember any deliveries during the party."

"I know."

"I've got it, Mom!" he yelled, as Aunt Jane appeared in the kitchen doorway, smiling the amused, indulgent smile of a mother watching her son excited about his first love. She was a beautiful woman. I'd only seen her from this angle in other people's memories, as someone with such an expressive face. She looked a lot like her mother, something she probably wouldn't have appreciated hearing. The relationship between Aunt Jane and Grandma Alice is famously strained, and she's thrown Grandma out of the house a few times.

"How are you showing me this? You weren't there."

"Not yet, but this party was such a good time, and it was so nice to spend a day with you, that I got the memories from you and Uncle Ted and Aunt Jane years ago, and used them to build a recreation of what happened. I can't do this with everything. This isn't how I give your

memories back, because I didn't have room in my head
for all of me and all of you. But I got enough to make a
full picture here." I wasn't telling him the full truth. The
party had been fun, but lots of things had been fun, over
the years, and I hadn't collected the memories I'd need
to make them into tableaus I could revisit. This party
had been *important*. Maybe for both of us.

The younger version of Artie reached the door and
yanked it open, revealing me and Mom standing on the
stoop. I was wearing what had been at the time my favorite blue dress, the one that almost matched the color
of my eyes, and had an overstuffed backpack over one
shoulder. Mom was holding a brightly-wrapped box
with an enormous bow on top. She offered it to Artie,
smiling the polite smile she had learned from the maga-
zines, that I had learned from her.

"Happy birthday, Arthur," she said.

"Thank you, Grandma," he said, suddenly shy as he
took the box. He couldn't look directly at me, and
watching him, I felt like my skin was two sizes too tight
and there was no oxygen left in the world.

This was the boy I'd deleted, the boy I'd wiped away
with a careless choice during a crisis. This was the boy
who had grown up to be the man who loved me. And
except in memories like these, which were a little bit
false because they were assembled from so many
sources, I was never going to see him again.

"I remember that box," the real Artie said abruptly.
"Grandma got me a chemistry set."

"And a mix-your-own-perfume kit," I said. "I picked
that out."

"No, I didn't get that for my birthday; that's a girl's
toy, and no one would have brought me that for my
twelfth birthday." He was starting to sound uneasy, like
he wasn't completely sure of what he was saying. "I don't
remember where I got that."

"But you *do* remember having it," I pressed.

"Yes, I used it all through high school. But it's not
because you bought it for me. It was probably something

of Elsie's that she got tired of when she started ordering from those weird little online boutique places." He scrunched his face and shook his head, trying to deny the logic of what I was saying, because for him, it was barely any logic at all. He didn't want it to be.

In the memory, child-Artie grabbed child-me by the hands and hauled her to the table, pointing proudly to the cupcakes with the lemon-tomato frosting and telling her in a bright, fast voice that he'd been waiting all morning for her to get there, since now they could have a *real* party. Mom and Aunt Jane retreated back to the kitchen doorway, watching the children with an indulgent sort of amusement that neither of us had been able to fully recognize at the time. I'd been young enough that my control slipped sometimes, but old enough to have learned it was rude to read other people's minds without their express permission. I certainly hadn't been probing the minds of the adults I trusted to take care of me to see if they were in the early stages of matchmaking.

Oh, Mom was going to be *so mad* at me when she realized her plan had finally come to fruition, only to be undone when I wiped the boy in question's mind. Not exactly the kind of complication you expect in your daughter's dating life, but here we were.

I loosened my grip on the memory, allowing it to skip ahead to our child selves sitting on the couch, Artie with a plate of half-eaten chocolate cake, me with reddish frosting on the tip of my nose, the two leaning toward each other so their shoulders brushed, staring raptly at the television, where *The Mummy* was well underway. Brendan Fraser was threatening a rotting corpse with a cat.

"Weird choice for a birthday movie," said Artie. "I would have preferred *The Matrix*."

"You always did," I said. "This was a compromise. It was either *The Mummy* or we fought for hours over whether we were watching a horror movie or a comedy, and then there was a chance that even though it was your birthday, Elsie might come in and want the TV, or Evie might show up and Annie would demand to watch a cartoon. I can only sit through *Goblin Market* so many times."

Artie shuddered. "Funny thing: that's exactly what I remember happening."

"Yeah," I said glumly. "Funny."

"So how is it your fault I locked myself in my room? Why are you making me watch something that isn't true?"

"Just hang on a second." On the couch, Artie suddenly stiffened and turned to look at the girl next to him, before smiling a small, oddly wistful smile.

"I like you, too," he said.

The child version of me sat bolt upright, eyes wide as she twisted to stare at him. "What?"

"I said I like you, too," he repeated.

"But I didn't *say* anything!" I—she—time travel, even when it isn't real, makes pronouns so *confusing*—blinked, still staring at him as her eyes filled with tears. "I promise I didn't say anything. I was just thinking how nice this was, and how glad I was you didn't decide to have a big party like you wanted, and how much I liked you, and you *heard me*." The child me scrambled to her feet, leaving Artie alone on the couch. "I shouldn't have come, I'm sorry."

"I thought you said you had fun at this party," muttered the adult Artie.

"I did, until this happened." The adults were emerging from the kitchen. Mom gathered the sobbing younger version of me in her arms, while Aunt Jane moved to comfort a confused Artie. The scene accelerated again as Mom bustled me toward the door, shooting an apologetic look over her shoulder at Aunt Jane and Artie, until they were alone.

Artie was also crying by that point, wiping his eyes and trying to make sense of what had just happened. The scene lost some depth, reduced as it was to a construct of Artie's own memory and his mother's experience of the moment. I sighed and released it back into the greater sea of Artie's modified memories, letting what he *knew* overwhelm what actually *was*.

"Aunt Jane said that was when you decided it wasn't safe for you to be out among humans because you could influence and hurt them," I said, voice dull. "They'd been telling you to be careful before that, but you didn't really *understand*, and you didn't like to think about how your abilities were getting stronger, and you couldn't stop that from happening. But I—I already knew I was a monster. Even the people who loved me had made that exquisitely clear. You and Mom were the only people who didn't treat me like I was semi-feral and would start biting as soon as I was given the opportunity. Because I was a monster. And that day, when you realized how much I hated myself for what I was, was the day you started hating yourself, too."

"Bullshit," said Artie, voice gone shaky.

"Really? Don't you wonder why your father is completely comfortable being a Lilu, and your sister found ways to walk in the world despite getting the same warnings from your parents that you did, and you're still sitting in your basement, staring at life through a screen, not willing to risk accidentally making someone think you're a decent person? Your parents may have been a little too careful with you, but they didn't say anything to make you this afraid of yourself, not once you take me away." I was almost proud of myself, in a terrible, inappropriate way. I had shielded their personalities but not their memories, and so when I'd ripped pieces of them away, the cores had remained the same. They had tried to patch the holes themselves, and sometimes it wasn't possible; sometimes, as now, they had effects but no causes, creating a feeling of loss and disorientation.

But if I hadn't shielded their personalities so well, they would have suddenly become the people they would have been if I'd never been a part of their lives in the first place. And it was nice, in a messed-up way, to know that they were still at least partially the people I'd known. There was a chance they could learn to accept me again.

And maybe that thought alone was proof I was the monster Artie was accusing me of being.

"So my whole life I've been lonely and afraid and now you're telling me it's *your fault*?"

"Not entirely. Your parents did more than their share of damage, and so did Elsie, when she started spending more time around humans and telling you how awful it was. They primed you to have these issues, but if they set the charges, I think I lit the match. Not everything we cause is our fault," I said, as carefully as I could. "We change the situation by observing it, and by being present. I never wanted you to hate yourself. I've spent years trying to lure you out." But had I really tried all that hard? Or had I enjoyed being the one girl who wasn't affected by his pheromones too much to make as big a fuss as I should have once I realized what was happening?

Or had I ever even realized what was happening? Artie's withdrawal from most of the world had happened at the same time as my own, two children feeding off of one another's fears, and neither of us had influenced the other any more than friends will always influence each other. My mother had been encouraging me to accept myself, while his had been warning him constantly that none of his friends were really going to be his friends; they were going to be attracted to his chemical signature. In the scope of things, she'd done more damage than I had. I still felt bad about the part I'd played in the situation. I turned away from him, watching as a flickering memory of a family trip to watch the jackalope migration played out in front of me.

"It's like you said," I said quietly. "Things just happen around me, and I didn't mean to do any of it. I did this to you, and neither of us ever noticed, because you loved me enough not to care if I was responsible. But you don't love me anymore, and so now you care, and I guess you get to hate me forever, if that's what you want to do."

"Sarah—"

"I can't change your mind. I mean, I *can*, and that's the problem. You can't trust that I'm not doing *that*, and so I have to stop doing *this*." I released my grip on his mind and memories, letting us return to the reality of the empty classroom and the setting suns. It had gotten even darker outside while we were deep inside the caverns of his mind; I could barely see him at all anymore.

That was probably for the best. My eyes burned as the fizz of actively exercising my abilities faded; the cost of all the crying I'd done without the awareness to wipe them clear. "I'm going back to the others," I said. "You should probably come back as soon as you're up to it. It isn't safe to be out here by yourself."

Then I turned and walked away from him, leaving both of us alone.

Ten

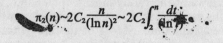

$$\pi_2(n) \sim 2C_2 \frac{n}{(\ln n)^2} \sim 2C_2 \int_2^n \frac{dt}{(\ln t)^2}$$

"Sometimes you gotta stop whining and start shooting, even if you don't feel like you're ready. Even if you don't feel like it's your job."

—Frances Brown

Stepping back into a room full of people who used to be allies but probably aren't anymore, emotionally exhausted

THE AIR IN THE classroom was actually a pleasant temperature when I slipped back inside, and the light was better than I'd expected, almost entirely because Annie and James, working together, had constructed a plinth of ice, topped with a burning ball of fire. The ice wasn't melting, and the fireball wasn't putting off nearly as much heat as it should have been. I stopped in the doorway and blinked.

Mark turned to look at me. "Sorcery does work better here," he said, a vaguely harried note in his voice. "You were right, and it's awful."

"Sarah, you're back!" said Annie, not sounding like she resented my existence, which was a nice change. She waved. "No Artie?"

"He's pretty pissed at me," I said, walking over to drop into one of the open desks and prop myself up on my elbows. "I spent more time with him than I did with you, when we were kids, so more of his life doesn't make sense now. You've been busy."

"The laws of physics in this universe are *fucked*," she said, with far more glee than I felt appropriate under the circumstances.

"The laws of thermodynamics, fortunately seem to be holding steady," said James, in a much more appropriately solemn tone. "Most of the laws that impact people who can't excite particles on a subatomic level have remained functionally the same, and we have neither the time nor the resources to perform more thorough testing, so if the gravity isn't exactly what it should be for an orbital body of this size—"

"Not that we know the size, as both of you have been careful to explicate repeatedly," interjected Mark.

"—we're assuming roughly the same as Earth, since it seems to possess Earth-normal gravity and the curvature of the horizon matches up with standard expectations," said James, not seeming to mind the interruption. "As I was saying, if the gravity isn't exactly what it should be, we can't tell. Things fall as fast as they should fall, and when we jump, we don't wind up leaping for miles like some sort of cartoon superhero."

"Says the man who makes bricks of ice with his hands," said Annie, nudging him with her elbow. "I can pull more fire out of the air than I've ever been able to before, and it's completely obedient! Isn't that awesome?"

"Yeah," I said, not sure what else to do. "Awesome."

She frowned, radiating a spike of sudden discontent. "What's wrong with you?"

I threw my hands up. "So you and James get to be superpowered here in this new dimension full of *giant flying insects* that I accidentally transported us all into! That's fantastic! Bully for you! In the meantime, everyone I think of as an ally hates me, my own abilities are too big for me to use safely, hollowed-out cuckoos are stalking the campus, we haven't found all the survivors yet, at least one of them is hostile, and I have no idea how we're going to explain this to the rest of them!" I put my head in my hands and groaned in frustration. "I hate this, I hate this, I *hate this*."

"Sarah, I'm sorry." Annie's voice came from closer than I expected. I lowered my hands and my shields at the same time. I needed to keep myself reined in enough that I didn't accidentally mind-control the people around me. That didn't mean I needed to let them go sneaking up on me.

I eyed her warily. "For what?"

"The mice are very clear that everything you've been saying is true, and that we came to Iowa not because we were trying to stop the cuckoos, but because we were trying to save you." She paused. "I guess stopping the cuckoos was part of saving you, so I can't actually say whether we succeeded or not, but you're here, and that means we got part of what we wanted. I'm happy for that. I'm sorry we don't know you anymore, but once we get home, the colony can make sure we learn your catechism, and isn't that why we have the mice? So nothing ever gets lost, or left behind, or forgotten?"

"Getting a little *Lilo and Stitch* there," I said, and wiped my eyes with the side of my hand. They were still burning. Too much crying does that to me.

Annie shrugged, radiating amusement. "Got you to stop crying, didn't I? Look, this all sucks, for everybody, but it's nothing we can't handle. We've dealt with worse. James lost his best friend and his mother to the crossroads, and his father's a giant dick."

"Leave me out of this," said James mildly, without rancor.

"Just a giant fucking cock stomping around New Gravesend, Maine, on a pair of dusty, flat old balls," continued Annie, unflapped. "Mark here had a massive psychotic break when the entire history of his horrible species got dumped into his head at once, and the only reason he didn't kill his parents and become a mass murderer like every other normal cuckoo we know is because his little sister is basically the second coming of

Ramona the Brat, and kept him awake playing Keep-Away until he had time to come back to normal."

"That is the most succinct, crassest way you could possibly have chosen to explain my life story," snapped Mark.

"I have a gift," said Annie. "As for me, I threw myself backward through time, sort of metaphorically, sort of literally, and may actually have been the reason the crossroads had such a hate-on for our family that they went and targeted Grandpa Thomas. Hell, for all I know, trying to stop him from spawning me may have been what inspired them to ask Mary to be a crossroads ghost. Shit gets confusing once time travel gets involved."

I blinked slowly. "I was never a big fan of *Doctor Who* for precisely that reason."

"But you get my point. Shit sucks for all of us. My boyfriend is probably climbing the walls right now—literally, since Sam can do that—because I've disappeared without a trace, along with an *entire* university campus, so you know that's made the news, and he's going to be worried sick." She paused, a ribbon of fondness tinting her thoughts. "It's sort of nice to know I have someone who's going to be worried about me. I've never had that before. It's *really* nice to know that I almost certainly just got a bigger slice of the news cycle than Verity did."

Unasked question officially answered: I had done just as good a job of shielding her personality from accidental changes as I had Artie's. It was harder to tell with Mark and James, since I didn't know them as well, but since Annie was behaving as if they were behaving normally, I had to assume they were also intact.

One small concern removed from a pile that seemed to grow every time I paused to take a breath. Which I did now, keeping my eyes on Annie.

"So why are you sorry?" I asked.

"Because we've all been acting like this was somehow something you wanted to have happen, even when you were telling us it absolutely wasn't, even when you were freaking out." She sighed. "I am choosing to believe the mice, which means I am choosing to believe you, which means I have been being a very bad cousin, and should apologize, and try to do better."

I cautiously lowered my shields even further, and detected nothing but honest apology from her. She was really willing to try. She was really ready to make the effort. I slumped, a weight I hadn't even realized I was carrying dropping from my shoulders. "Th-thank you," I said. "That means a lot."

"We should probably go get Artie, though, before something decides he's vulnerable and tries to eat him."

"I guess that's possible, but I think he wants to be alone right now. He's doing some self-examination, because pulling me out of his past left bigger gaps for him than it did for the rest of you."

"I can't imagine you left a very large gap in me. Even if we were instant BFFs, there's no way I met you before I met Annie," said James.

"No, I met you after she decided you were her brother," I said. "She brought you back with her from her trip to Maine."

"He was in the discount bin at a gas station," said Annie, and laughed. James threw a snowball at her.

I rolled my eyes. "Please don't let the fact that sorcery is easier for you here turn you into a five-year-old," I said.

"I never really got to be a five-year-old," said James. "It would be a nice way to pass the time."

"I know I didn't know you long," interjected Mark, before we could get too far off the topic. I looked at him blankly, not shielding my emotional response. He shrugged. "I don't like cuckoos. They pretty much suck, and they're a danger to Cici. She's only twelve. I don't want her spending time around terrible people. There's still a chance she might turn out decent, if I can just get her some good role models. Cuckoos need not apply."

"I still don't understand how a cuckoo has a twelve-year-old sister," I said blankly. "I get why you didn't kill her, but does somebody want to fill me in on how she can exist at some point?"

"As if you couldn't take the answers you want right out of my head," said Mark. His tone and attitude, which filled the air around him like the smell of burnt popcorn, were snide and dismissive. He really didn't want me here. He didn't trust any cuckoo to have good intentions, especially not one who had already, however accidentally, become attuned to his specific mental frequency. Radio Cuckoo was broadcasting in his area, and he didn't like it.

I couldn't blame him.

Annie snapped her fingers, drawing my attention back to her. "Mark told us about his sister right before we all left to do . . . something, I don't remember what, so you must have been a major part of the situation."

"Probably rescuing me from my biological mother and her hive," I said. I'd been unconscious after Ingrid triggered the next instar in the series destined to make me a Queen, but I'd also been in the custody of the cuckoos, and when I'd woken up, disoriented and unable to control my own actions, I'd been in my bedroom in the Portland compound. I had vague memories of speaking to Artie in that gap, meaning he must have entered my mind during the instar, but they were only shadows, light and color splashed across the nothingness. I looked at Annie, and said, "Ingrid took me. Mark helped her, actually, because she forced him."

"It's a thing cuckoos can do," he snarled. "I remember Ingrid. She threatened my family. She was going to hurt Cici. No one hurts Cici. That's the only rule. Anything else, we can possibly discuss, but *no one* hurts Cici."

"So she used the same threats whether I was there or not." I didn't want to poke at this series of events too much. If it all came crashing down, Mark could wind up as shaken as Artie, and that wouldn't do any of us any good. "That's fun to know. So yeah. Ingrid took me, and at some point, you all came and took me back, and I woke up at home. And then I used a smaller equation to open a hole in the world and fold the space on the other side just enough to get us from Oregon to Iowa."

Annie's thoughts brightened with sudden excitement. "You made a tesseract?" she squealed. "Are we going to go all *A Wrinkle in Time*?"

"Not quite a tesseract, and I don't think the math works across dimensions; it's purely a local shortcut," I said. "I'm not sure I could do it again without the equation driving me, and it's not worth the risk. Can we get back to how Mark is a pretty average cuckoo who managed not to start murdering people for fun for some reason, and has a sister he wants to make it home to?"

"I don't want to discuss her with you," said Mark, abruptly standing and moving away from the window where he'd been seated. "This feels too much like the part of the horror movie where one person talks about getting home to their wife and kids, and everyone else says 'oh yeah, you're going to make it, we're going to make sure you make it home,' and then the very next scene there's a giant snake or something, and the person who told the personal story is dead. I don't want to be your cliché."

"That's fine," I said. "I won't make you."

"And we didn't see any signs of giant snakes out there, which is pretty amazing in and of itself," said Annie. Mark radiated blankness. She explained: "According to my grandmother, there are a disturbing number of dimensions out there where the only higher life is snakes."

"Snakes," echoed Mark.

"Yes, snakes. Big snakes, little snakes, fire snakes, ice snakes, snakes that think and snakes with hands—a snake for every day of the year. If the cuckoos were moving randomly, they'd have all been eaten by giant snakes by now. I don't suppose that under normal circumstances, proximity to a cuckoo queen creates another one?"

"No," I said slowly. "I'm not entirely sure how it works—and to be honest, I'm not sure the cuckoos themselves know how it works, because they're working from incomplete information, they're exiles who had to figure this all out from bits and pieces—but a Queen has to be nurtured through multiple instars, and at least one of them is always incapacitating. Trigger it when there aren't people around to take care of her, and she'll be completely helpless if something wants to come along and take her apart."

"So that means the equation has been, what, filtering through the adjacent dimensions to pick out the ones that *aren't* wall-to-wall giant snakes?" Annie was starting to sound frustrated. "I wish you hadn't taken that thing apart. I'd really like a look at it."

"You wouldn't understand it, and it would melt your eyeballs," I said coolly. "I took it apart because it shouldn't exist. It was definitely filtering the available dimensions based on a variety of factors, including whether they had the potential to be healthy environments for cuckoos. I assume anything with too many snakes wouldn't make it into the column for 'healthy.'"

"That makes sense," said Annie. "I prefer my eyeballs unmelted, as it turns out."

The suns were now completely down, casting the sky into relative darkness. Without light pollution to block them, rivers of alien stars created enough brightness that it was still possible to see the shape of the buildings outside, and the long stretch of the grass. Something moved in the shadows, built to scale with the flying millipedes. There were no moons.

"Um, Annie?" said James.

"If we can't tesseract home and we can't reach Mary, I'm not sure how we're getting back," said Annie. "I know there are ways to use sorcery to open doors between dimensions—Grandpa's journals have talked about sorcerers who do that more often than he considered healthy, and who got lost because they *didn't* have an automatic snake-detection protocol to keep them from being eaten—but I don't know what any of them are. I'm not far enough along in my studies. James is even farther back."

"Yes, speaking of James," said James. "*Annie*."

"We'll get you caught up soon enough, you're a quick study," said Annie. "I just don't know how we're going to get home from here."

"That millipede before was wearing a saddle," I said. "Something humanoid has used it as a mount, often enough for it to be reasonable to keep the thing saddled up and ready to go. Maybe they know how to move between dimensions."

"I don't know that we want to involve the locals if we can get out of here before that happens," said Annie. "They might not be friendly. Or maybe we accidentally pulled a Dorothy and dropped a university campus on somebody's sister."

"As long as we don't steal anyone's magic shoes, we're fine," said Mark.

"*Antimony!*" snapped James.

She whipped around. "*What*?"

"Gosh I'm glad they told me he was adopted," said Mark. "If I didn't know, I'd swear they were blood relations."

"I think we're about to meet the neighbors," said James. He raised one arm, hand shaking as he pointed at the window.

I followed the line of his finger, and swallowed a small, unproductive shriek when I saw what he was pointing at.

What looked like nothing so much as a praying mantis the size of a firetruck was looking in the window. It cocked its head from side to side, getting a better sense of what was inside, but seemed to be most focused on the fire. As I watched, it raised one long, serrated arm—also looking just like part of a praying mantis, so at least it was consistent—and tapped the glass with incredible, surprising delicacy. The sound rang through the room, soft but undeniable.

The glass cracked, but didn't break.

Yet.

"Maybe this is no longer a good place for us to be," said Mark.

"Agreed," said Annie. "I could probably set the giant bug on fire, but who wants to spend the time? Or burn down the entire school when it thrashes around and bumps into things?"

I didn't say anything at all, and neither did James. Both of us were too busy backing away, moving slowly but steadily toward the door.

"Sarah?" said Antimony. "Is it intelligent?"

"I don't know!" I replied. "Maybe." I reached out.

The mind I encountered was much like the millipede's in terms of complexity, although it was sharper, structured for a predator's needs. The mantis had seen us, that much was sure, but it was far more interested in the impossible light than it was in the small moving things. "Annie," I hissed. "Put out the fire."

"What—oh!" She snapped her fingers. The fireball went out.

The mantis hit the window as fast as a bullet being fired, sending shards of glass flying through the room. Someone screamed. I think it was James. We all scattered for the door, moving as fast as we could.

Mark got there first. "Great idea, *Sarah*," he said snidely, as he wrenched it open. "Got any more awesome plans?"

"Shut up and run!" I shouted, accompanying the command with enough of a mental push to get him moving through the door and out into the hall.

More smashing sounds came from behind us as the mantis punched through the other windows. James spun around, and the air became suddenly very cold.

"Nice ice wall!" yelled Annie. "Keep moving!"

We kept moving, all four of us piling into the darkened hall. Then I froze, stumbling, and nearly collided with Artie, who had come out to see what all the noise was about.

The mantis wasn't alone. There was another mind with it, behind it, guiding it. A smaller, quicker, warmer mind, belonging to an intelligent creature. More—belonging to an intelligent creature that, when I brushed against the edges of it, knew I was there, recognized me as another being, and pulled the mantis back.

We were not alone.

"What are you doing out here?" asked Artie, automatically moving to steady me before he realized what he was doing and pulled his hands away as if he'd been burned by almost brushing against my skin.

"Giant praying mantis broke the window," said Annie breathlessly.

"Uh, *what*?"

"Giant praying mantis broke the window, so I put up an ice wall to stop it from reaching across the room with its giant murder arms and doing the same thing to our skulls, but I don't know if it's going to hold," said James. He and Annie moved to either side of Artie, each taking an arm and hauling him along with them as they rushed down the hall. Mark and I followed.

"No, seriously, *what*?"

"Giant praying mantis broke the window, Jimmy did his ice thing, we ran," said Mark, picking up the thread.

Not wanting to be left out when I actually had information to share, I added, "And it had a rider."

Annie stopped, dragging James and hence Artie to a halt as she turned to look at me. "What?"

"A rider. Remember, the millipede had a saddle? Well, one of the people who uses the giant insects as carousel horses was on the back of the mantis." I paused. "Move faster, they're in the building now."

The thoughts of the rider were getting closer. I couldn't understand the language they were thinking in, but their feelings were reassuringly comprehensible, curiosity and caution and mild annoyance, probably directed at James' wall of ice. They couldn't get past it easily. We might be safe—

Oh. Crap. "Move *much* faster." I shoved Artie in the

back, starting him walking again. James and Annie moved with him. I couldn't shove Mark at the same time, but I could direct a needle of urgency at him, urging him to move faster without forcing him. If he wanted to linger and get caught, that was his choice, but I'd be happier if he didn't. "Come *on*."

"What? Why?" asked James.

"The person in the classroom we just left is calling fire to melt your ice."

Annie got the point first. "They're a sorcerer."

"Yes, apparently. Keep going!"

"But if we can talk to a sorcerer who knows how this reality's magic works, maybe they can help us figure out how to use *our* magic to open a doorway back home!" She started to turn, intending to go back to the classroom.

The needle of urgency I slammed into *her* was larger, sharper, and verged more closely on compulsion. "Not until we know more about these people. It isn't safe right now," I said. "Keep moving."

We made it to the door to the stairs and through to the safety of the stairwell just as the classroom door swung wide and a figure stepped into the hall. There was enough starlight coming in through the classroom behind them to give us the broadest of details: they were humanoid, bipedal with two arms and a head that clearly had something close to either feathers or hair crowning it and blurring their silhouette. They held a spear with a curving blade at the end in one hand, some sort of fancy polearm that Annie could probably identify by name—and actively desired to get a closer look at, given the new tenor of her surface thoughts—and which would pierce our flesh easily if thrown. No wings, no tail, nothing outside that basic human body plan.

The light was too low and the distance too great for us to make out any details about clothing, features, or coloration, and as the figure moved cautiously farther into the hall, spear at the ready, I pulled deeper into the shadows.

Not necessarily friendly, I thought to Annie. *Not necessarily hostile, either. Confused. There's a language barrier I can get over with a few hours, but right now, all I'm getting are feelings and impressions.*

Okay, she thought back. *All I'm getting is the need for a closer look at that sweet fauchard.*

Presumably, that was the weird polearm. I patted her arm and pulled her with me as I inched deeper into the stairwell. Artie and James were still directly behind the door, keeping it from swinging shut. That was tactically a good thing, even if it kept them somewhat exposed; the sound of the door closing would attract attention if the figure in the shadows had ears, which wasn't guaranteed—I was still trying to filter through their thoughts enough to figure out what senses they were using to navigate the hall. Sight was clearly involved. They, like the mantis, had seen the light from our fire, and had come to investigate, since this was a strange new place that shouldn't have existed, much less been setting beacons.

But could they hear us? Could they feel the tiny vibrations of my companions' heartbeats traveling through the air? Did they have the ability to see us through the shadows, or to smell us? The possibilities weren't endless, but in that long and frozen moment while I waited to see what they were going to do, they might as well have been.

Finally, the figure turned and walked back into the classroom, but didn't close the door. We stayed where we were, barely daring to breathe. There was a soft scuff and a clatter, as of broken glass hitting the floor, followed by the whirr of insectile wings. The feeling of the unfamiliar mind receded, growing steadily more distant, until I couldn't pick it up anymore.

"All right." I straightened. "They're gone."

"They were shaped like a person," said Annie. "I know that's humanocentric—a wadjet is a person whether they're shaped like a human or a snake—but they had hands and legs, they understand how to use tools, we probably have some things in common."

"Everything you just said is true of cuckoos, too," I said. "We're shaped like people by even the most human-focused standard. That doesn't make us friendly."

"That's for sure," muttered Artie.

I pretended not to hear him. "So now we know we're not alone, and we know there are still human survivors on campus."

"Which means we need to get out there and find the rest of them before something else does," said Annie. "Everyone ready to move? And yes, boys, this time I mean *everyone*. We're not splitting the party again."

Her hair—or rather, the mouse concealed in her hair—cheered. "And then it was said and Stated, as it always shall be, Never Split the Party!" shouted a tiny voice.

Annie laughed. "That's right. Never split the party. And you did very well keeping quiet before; I'm proud of you."

Out of all the cousins, Annie is the only one I know of who's been able to successfully train her mice to the habit of silence. It's a big accomplishment, and no one's really sure how she managed it. Elsie even tried to bribe me once to uncover the exact method, so it could be emulated. She was deeply annoyed when I said ethics didn't count if they could be abandoned the second someone needed me to go against them.

The mouse made a happy sound and was quiet again, still concealed by the mass of Antimony's hair. She looked over at me. "I know you can't feel the husked-out cuckoos coming, but we can watch for them visually, and just not let you go first into any enclosed spaces."

"Why, because the rest of us are more worthy of being devoured by starving cuckoos?" asked Artie.

She scoffed. "No. Because she doesn't have any weapons, and neither does Mark, and I don't think you want me to give them weapons, do you?" She managed to make the question sound almost sweet, and not as pointed as the feeling behind it. Being the youngest child has left her with a terrifying arsenal of manipulation tactics.

Artie's spike of confused fear was less pleasant. He wasn't radiating hatred and mistrust in my direction anymore, and his emotions were a lot more complicated and confused when he thought of me, but he was still afraid of me. That was never going to be okay, and it was always going to be my own fault.

"So we move," said James, sensing another fight brewing and trying to get himself out in front of it. He took a step toward the mouth of the stairs, then paused, frowning. "Annie, I know it's not safe to set up another bonfire, but could you—"

"On it." The silhouette of my cousin lifted one hand, and a ball of light appeared above it, perfectly spherical and glowing a soft, clear white that brought all of us into sudden relief. Annie blinked. "Huh. It's never done *that* before."

"What spell did you cast?" demanded Mark.

"I'm a sorcerer, not a witch. I don't 'cast spells,' I influence the universe to give me what I—oh, never mind." Annie sighed. "We don't have time for a lesson in magical theory right now. I told the universe I wanted a ball of light. Normally that results in a fireball, because I'm fire-attuned. This is the first time I've gotten one of these."

She lowered her hand. The light remained floating serenely in midair, not moving even when she nudged it gently with a finger.

"If it's just going to hang here, it's not going to do us much good when we get to the bottom of the stairs, but it's not going to give our location away either, and it's not hot, so we don't need to worry about burning the place down," she said finally, with a shrug, and started for the stairs.

The ball of light followed her.

"That's new," she said, approvingly. "But fine by me. Come on, guys. Let's go face the terrifying new dimension the cuckoos were planning to call home now that the lights are off."

"Does she make everything sound this appealing?" asked Mark, slanting a glance at me.

I beamed, keeping my shields low enough that he'd be able to translate the expression. "Only when she's having fun," I said. "Let's go."

"Your family are such *assholes*," he grumbled, and followed me, happier to spend time with assholes than to be left alone.

That was a sentiment I understood all too well. Cuckoos are solitary by nature; we don't enjoy one another's company, probably because most of us are monsters, but also because being around another telepath creates an annoying subliminal hum, like standing right under power lines. It's grating and unpleasant, and eventually it makes us squirrelly. On the plus side, I had now been around Mark for long enough that I'd be able to pick his hum out of a crowd the size of the main plaza at Lowryland. If I heard that specific psychic tone, I'd know there was another cuckoo nearby, and that it was, for lack of a better word, harmless.

Annie's ball of light continued to bob at the height it had been initially summoned at as we all walked down the stairs, her in the lead, flanked by James, with Artie close behind them, as Mark and I brought up the rear.

"I don't normally spend this much time around other cuckoos," he said abruptly.

"Could've fooled me," I said.

"I don't remember how we met," he said. "Thanks to your little math trick, the first time I remember seeing you, you were lying in the grass in front of us, and the sky had gone orange."

"Then how did you know you needed to grab me?"

"You were the only body that we could see breathing," he said. "We assumed the rest of them were dead, and we picked you up so you could tell us what the hell had happened. I figured you had to be the queen we'd come to Iowa to stop."

"Had you really been intending to stop me?"

"Whatever I had to do." He looked at me gravely,

dropping his own shields so I could more easily read the depth of his sincerity. "I needed my sister to be safe, and Ingrid wouldn't let me bring her with us. She said Cecilia only made me weak, and she deserved to die with the rest of her stinking mammalian species."

"Why didn't you kill her when she said that? My sister is old enough to be my mother, and I'd still kill anyone who talked about her that way." My brother and I had never shared a house, and he had no kids, so there'd been no reason for me to visit him during the summers, and I'd be happy to kill for him, too. That's not always what family means. Sometimes the people you're related to aren't family at all—witness Ingrid. But it's what the people you choose to call family mean. Or maybe I'm just violent because of the way I was raised. I don't know. I was still horrified.

Mark sighed. "Because all the other cuckoos thought activating a queen and getting the fuck out of that dimension was just the best damn idea they'd ever heard. I could probably have taken Ingrid. She was like, super pregnant, and super pregnant people don't usually fight that well, especially not when you stab them in the back before they have a chance to react. But I couldn't take all the cuckoos who'd decided she was their salvation. They would have swarmed me in a second."

"I had almost finished the equation before I pulled you all in," I protested. "How were you going to stop it?"

"I knew you'd left your tear open too long when you were on your way out of Oregon, and some of them had followed you through. I was waiting for them to finish navigating the break and come take care of you for me. If they hadn't gotten there in time, I had a syringe full of Hershey's Syrup ready to go."

I blinked. "You were going to inject me with *Hershey's Syrup*?"

We had reached the bottom of the stairs. Annie closed her hand, extinguishing the ball of light, before stepping forward and cautiously working the door open. The groundskeepers and maintenance crews of the school deserved some sort of reward for the quality of their work; even moving very slowly, the hinges didn't groan or creak at all, allowing us to spill out into the yard in relative silence.

"It would kill you."

"I think it would kill anybody." I couldn't think of any species with a blood chemistry that would tolerate a sudden injection of literal candy. The fact that cuckoos are allergic to theobromine was secondary to the part where he was talking about shooting someone full of *Hershey's Syrup*.

"We have two telepaths and we're walking into potentially dangerous territory," said Annie, spinning around to face us. Outside, the starlight was sufficient to make her fully visible, if somewhat monochromatic. "Is there a *reason* we're all talking out loud right now?"

"Some of us aren't comfortable having people project voices into our heads," said Artie.

"And some of us aren't comfortable being expected to wear underpants that crawl up our asses when we have to put on a damn dress, but occasionally we have to," snapped Annie. "If I can tolerate a thong, you can tolerate a little telepathy. Got it?"

Artie's eyes crossed with the effort of not picturing his cousin in a thong, an effort that ended with him projecting the image so loudly that I couldn't have missed it if I'd been shielding myself against him. I put a hand over my mouth to hide my smile, but I couldn't hide my amusement. He glared at me, broadcasting the intent to make his annoyance known. My smile only grew.

"Silence from now on," said Annie. "Sarah, Mark, get broadcasting."

"I can't broadcast to all four of you at the same time," said Mark apologetically.

"I can, and I can make sure I broadcast anything one of you thinks to the rest," I said. "That's what we used to do during camping trips when we didn't have cell service." I was a cuckoo queen. I could damn well do whatever my family needed me to do. *Is this what you wanted, Antimony?*

It is—hey, your "voice" has a lot more inflection when I hear it this way, did you know?

I did. Artie always says it's because tone is influenced partially by mouth shape, and half the time I'm just making mouth shapes for the sake of looking like everyone around me. Can we please find the student store before we hole up somewhere else?

Why would we—oh, you want shoes, don't you? The question came from James, who sounded embarrassed not to have guessed sooner that I'd be getting tired of walking around barefoot all the time.

We can do that, said Antimony. *Now everybody move.*

She started walking briskly across the lawn, trusting us to follow, which of course we did. There was no way of training someone for this situation, which was horrifying and unplannable, but out of all of us, she was the one whose training made her the closest to actual preparation. If anyone was going to know how to navigate the dangerous waters ahead, it was her.

Plus she could set things on fire with her mind, and that was potentially awesome, depending on what those things happened to be. Sometimes you just need to know that you have a pyrokinetic on your side.

We made it back to the cafeteria without encountering anything—no humans, no giant insects with unknown riders, and—best of all—no hollowed-out cuckoos looking for something to eat. That was unnerving in and of itself. Ten minutes of peace wasn't something I was accustomed to anymore.

I wish we had some flashlights, said Mark. He had moved a little bit away from the group and was squinting at a map affixed to the front of the cafeteria building, protected by a sheet of slightly scratched-up plastic. *This could tell us where the student store is.*

I have my phone, offered James, moving to stand beside him. He pulled the phone out of his pocket and turned on the flashlight app, holding it up so that it illuminated the map.

It also reflected off the plastic, creating a spot of intense brightness.

You have to turn that off, said Annie, instantly switching to high alert as she spun around and scanned the area for signs of movement. *Sarah?*

Checking, I said. One of the nice things about telepathy is that it's both more and less precise than speech—she didn't need to tell me what she wanted because I was already in her head, and I'd seen the thought as it was forming. Her deeper structures were safe from me prying around in them—I had less than zero interest in learning the sordid details of her sex life, for example. I'd already learned more than I liked from her occasional comments about how every boyfriend should come equipped with a prehensile tail—but the surface thoughts were fair game.

I dropped the running telepathic connection between the members of the group and spread my mind outward instead, searching for signs that we were not alone. I found the seven students and three child cuckoos holed up inside the cafeteria immediately, and kept reaching. We knew they were there; we'd been coming to . . . not collect them, probably, but definitely check on them, and possibly raid their supply of snacks. I didn't know how long it had been since I'd eaten, and my stomach was beginning to grumble. I kept reaching.

The hollowed-out cuckoos could have been advancing on our position, and I would have had literally no way of knowing about it unless they were also close enough to see. They couldn't make complicated plans, so if they *were* advancing on us, the odds were good that they'd be doing it in full view, but that was it.

None of the students I'd detected before had moved from their original boltholes, seeming content to stay safe for the moment. Part of that may have been a residual command from when the cuckoos took the campus: it was possible we were going to be dealing with a bunch of newly-minted agoraphobes when all this was over. I'd have to try to undo the damage if that was the case. But not yet. It wasn't an assault to leave them as they were long enough to get us all back to safety.

Terrence had managed to find the student health center and was sleeping the blissful sleep of the heavily drugged. He was still alive, thankfully—although I wasn't sure how *thankful* I should actually be for having a hostile human we couldn't kill without moral quandary potentially running around the campus again.

I pulled back into myself with a small gasp, opening my eyes to find the rest of my party watching me. " . . . what?" I asked warily, feeling too disconnected from my body to want to risk telepathy. Plus I knew we were alone. There was no point.

"Your hair started floating, and it was very upsetting," said Mark.

I blinked. Then I shook my head. "I already went over this with Annie. It happens when I really push, and since I was just scanning to the edges of my current range, that was enough to qualify as pushing."

"I can't say having another way to detect cuckoos is a bad thing, even if the telekinesis is a little worrisome," said Mark.

"You're fine, Sarah. I should have warned them," said Annie soothingly, and leaned over to put a hand on my shoulder. "You're okay. What did you see?"

"Um. Other than Terrence, none of the people I picked up on before have moved, so that's probably a good thing. The cornwife isn't withering yet, so this dimension probably isn't inherently hostile to Earth vegetation. That's good news for your internal bacteria."

"Dimensional travel requiring probiotics, not something I ever considered," said Artie dryly.

"Wait." James held up his hands. "What the fuck's a cornwife?"

"This one's an agriculture major named Michael," I said. "They're a type of cryptid that's either pseudo-mammalian the same way cuckoos are, just with evolutionary origins in the vegetable kingdom—don't ask me, I didn't do it—or they're primates that have evolved to mimic some attributes of plants. They thrive in agrarian settings, and they can pass for human well enough to get college degrees when they feel the need to contribute to the family farm."

James blinked, very slowly. "That," he said in a portentous tone, "is *ridiculous*."

"If things being ridiculous meant they couldn't be true, we'd never get anything done," said Annie. "I have talking mice hiding in my hair and you give people frostbite with a touch. Now listen to the nice giant wasp girl while she tells you what we might be walking into."

"Thank you."

"Don't mention it."

"I don't know how many of the cuckoo children are still alive," I said. "The three in the cafeteria are reasonably easy to spot, because I know that they're there, but cuckoos that young are still a little fuzzy around the edges, telepathically speaking."

"It's so the adults don't hunt them down and slaughter them," said Mark mildly. We all turned to look at him. He shrugged. "It's instinctive. We don't share territory, not even with kids."

"Must be part of the DLC you got and I didn't." Even if deleting that massive packet of inherited memories was some kind of war crime, I was coming to hope more and more that I had done it. That these kids were free to grow up to be whoever they wanted to be, and not be burdened and broken by the shadows of their past.

Forcing someone to forget where they came from is a crime. There's a reason people say history was written by the winners: once one side claims victory, destroying the history and culture of the losing side is a great way to make sure that victory endures. But these kids weren't choosing to learn their history. It was being forced on them in a way no human mind had ever experienced, meaning it was outside the framework of human morality—and thus outside the framework of my own

morality because all I had to work from was what I'd
been given. If these kids still carried those memories,
I'd have to decide whether or not to take them away,
knowing they were a ticking time bomb that would erad-
icate the lives the children had built for themselves if
they were allowed to go off.

Mark had the history. He could always teach it to
them, in a less invasive way. It didn't have to be lost. But
maybe it didn't have to keep hurting us, either.

"No more dimensional natives with giant predatory
insects?" asked Annie.

"There's something flying so far overhead that I
could barely pick up on it, but I don't think it had a
rider," I said.

"Good. The sky looks more Earth-normal at night,
and none of us are bloody. That's a good thing; we can
talk to the cafeteria people now. Mark, did you and
James find the student store?"

"We did," he said. "It's on the other side of the campus."

"Of course it is. It's not a horrible, life-threatening
situation if we don't have to run back and forth across
an easily drawn space like we're characters on *Scooby-
Doo*." Antimony sighed. "All right. Let's go talk to
these people, and then we'll get Sarah some shoes."

She turned and walked to the cafeteria doors, not
giving anyone time to argue. I admired her certainty.
We followed in a ragged group, less certain but still willing, and under the circumstances, that was the best that
we could hope for. She pushed the door open and we all
stepped inside.

I felt the person moving on the other side of the dining room door just before she pushed it open.

Annie, wait!

She paused with her hand just shy of the door. *What?*

*There's a person on the other side of the door with a
chair. They're planning to hit whatever comes through.*

Oh. The tone of her thoughts turned feral. *Well, I
guess we'll just see about that.*

She kicked the door open so hard it slammed against the far wall. The person with the chair swung for the body they assumed was coming through, unable to see in the darkness, and overbalanced as they encountered no resistance, tripping and falling on the floor, which was when Annie actually stepped through the door, crouched to place one abnormally warm hand on the back of their neck, and said, very mildly, "Hi."

"Holy shit! I think I'm in love," murmured Mark.

"My family is made of assholes, remember?" I asked.

"Yeah, but she's a badass asshole with an amazing rack."

James shot him a look backed by feelings of poisonous menace. "Hands and eyes off my sister."

Annie's new friend wisely didn't attempt to move or get up, but more figures moved in the darkness, shifting positions as they came toward us. Annie sighed and straightened up, another ball of light appearing above her outstretched palm. We were officially giving up on subtlety or secrecy, it seemed. Those were tools for another world, one where the sky wasn't orange or filled with flying bugs and extra suns.

"Hello," she called, more loudly this time, pitching her voice toward the back of the room. "We're the ones who were here earlier, remember? My name is Antimony Price, and I came back to make sure everyone's okay."

Someone in the back of the room dropped the tray they had been holding. That was our bogeyman. She was the only one in the room who knew what the name "Price" meant in this context, and she didn't like being shut in a room with it.

My family has that effect on people. But not, for the most part, human people, who don't have the same relationship with the Covenant that the rest of the world does—funny thing, given that the Covenant is almost certainly a hundred percent human. The evils we create ourselves are always easier to ignore.

The people who'd been approaching us through the

dark were armed with plastic trays and, in one case, a metal ladle. Of the makeshift weapons I'd seen so far, that was the one that seemed the most likely to do something actually *useful*, and not just end with the person who'd been attacked turning the tables on their attacker. But then, most people don't start training with improvised weapons when they're in kindergarten, and I probably shouldn't judge them by our standards.

A man who was still holding a plastic tray stepped forward, clearing his throat. "I'm sorry if we overreacted. Terrence went out after you came by the first time, and he didn't come back. We thought—"

"Terrence is a drug-seeking junkie who followed us out of here because he thought we were going to clean out the cabinets in the first aid office before he could get there," said Annie flatly. We had moved beyond the stage where she was willing to soft-pedal or pretend Terrence's intentions had been good ones, and frankly, I was relieved. I was too tired for lies. "He ran because he thought we knew him, making me think he's not supposed to be on campus at all, and then he attacked us outside. He had a gun."

She didn't mention that we had taken it away. Sometimes people get squirrelly when they hear that somebody has a firearm.

"This is Iowa," said the man. "Most of us have guns. Miranda doesn't, but that's because she brought her little sisters to school with her. You one of the science and technology kids? Is that where you got your little floating light doohickey?"

"No, I'm a sorcerer," said Annie, voice still flat. "I pulled it out of the substance of the universe."

"Oh, they're *LARPers*," said the woman with the ladle, sounding deeply relieved. "That makes so much sense. Did your people rent out the campus for an apocalypse LARP or something?"

James and Artie exchanged a look as Mark stepped forward. I slammed my shields up as fast as I could, but not before I caught the leading edge of the wall of "trust me, you've known me for years, you can always believe me" that he was shoving in their direction. I managed to resist the urge to turn and glare at him. With my shields up, he wouldn't have been able to decode the emotion behind the expression, and if he was already hitting these people, there wasn't anything I could really do to stop him.

"Apocalypse LARP, absolutely," he said, voice smooth and warmer than I'd ever heard it. He wasn't holding back at all. "It's supposed to last all weekend."

"But this is Thursday . . ." said a puzzled voice.

"They brought in all the latest in LARP technology, including screen projectors and hard-light constructs," he continued. "That's why if you look outside, you may notice the sky is orange during the day and the stars are different at night. It's all done with lighting."

"That sounds expensive," said a woman dubiously.

"It was, which is why participants are not supposed to break character whenever we're out in the open," he said. "You may see one of our 'zombie mobs' shambling by, and I don't recommend engaging. We've all signed waivers in case of injury, so they won't be pulling their punches."

I had to admire the dexterity with which he was spinning his cover story, even if anyone who'd ever actually encountered a LARP would know that he was spitting pure bullshit. None of the tech he was talking about existed, and even the most immersive LARP experience didn't come with intentional threats to the safety and well-being of the players.

The man who had appointed himself spokesman blinked slowly, then asked, "Is this what that release form was all about?"

"Right on the money," said Mark. "You would all have been expected to sign one before you were allowed onto campus this morning."

Murmurs of agreement and sudden recollection followed his statement. He didn't have the strength to actually create false memories without hurting himself—that would have meant triggering his next instar and going through the years of mental weakness and recovery that I had already struggled through—but he could suggest things for them to conveniently "remember." It was a fine distinction, and one that was saving us now.

"So while we're sorry for any inconvenience, you did agree to be off campus before this started, and as you're still here, I'll need to ask you to stay inside as much as possible to preserve the experience for our players," he continued. "We're rounding up the other stragglers now, and will probably be bringing many of them here."

"Why here?" asked one of the women. "There's only one couch, and the kids won't get off it, so we have nowhere to sleep."

"There's no place else better on campus, Heidi," snapped another woman. "And we agreed to let the kids use the couch while we waited for the authorities to show up."

I couldn't read either of their faces without lowering my shields, and I wasn't going to do that while Mark was broadcasting to the room. Ironically, right now, Annie and Artie were safer than I was—cuckoos aren't resistant to other cuckoos. I paused, eyes widening.

Neither was James.

I turned, and even with my shields up, my alarm must have been visible enough for Mark to read, because he pointed at James and shook his head before making an exaggerated "okay" gesture with his left hand. Interestingly, he didn't flash the circle and raised fingers the way most people did, but signed an "O" and then a "K" in ASL, flicking the letters together so quickly that they became a single sign. I blinked and returned my attention to the people.

Mark thinking it was okay didn't mean it necessarily was, but it meant he was doing something to make sure he didn't mess with James' mind, and that was more than I'd expected. He was really making an effort, and in a way, that made me more nervous.

Being a Price, even adopted, means growing up with

a lot of lectures about responsibility and conservation and doing as little harm as possible. Even the most dangerous cryptids were to be caught and relocated away from human settlements when possible—something that gets more difficult every year, as people push their way deeper and deeper into the previously untamed regions of the world. Give us another few decades, and we'll be worrying about how to get the deep-sea cryptids under cover before the submarines go by. And for as long as I've been alive, all those lectures have gone right out the window as soon as cuckoos were involved.

Cuckoos are dangerous monsters, say the journals. Cuckoos are always the bad guy, say the field guides. Cuckoos will do their best to destroy anyone who gets in their way, they're incapable of consideration or compassion, they only care about the things that belong to them, or that they can take. That's what I grew up knowing. That's what everyone told me—even my mother, who was a cuckoo herself, albeit a broken one.

Angela Baker was a genetic sport, a glitch in the biological programming that was supposed to make sure we were all essentially the same, good little worker bees ready to protect and bolster the hive. And according to Ingrid, she was also an essential part of the normal cuckoo life cycle: one of a few cuckoos born every generation without the ability to receive the racial memories normally passed down in utero, who would be able to both instigate and see through the process of removing those memories from an otherwise ordinary cuckoo child. She had done that to me, because she had believed, truly and completely, that normal, unaltered cuckoos were irredeemable monsters, incapable of learning or of change.

Mark hadn't had a cuckoo for a mother. He hadn't undergone years of delicate psychic surgery to remove the past of our people from his mind. He'd gone through the instar like any other cuckoo would, cracked open the egg of his memory like it was the right thing to do . . . and then he'd stopped. He hadn't killed anyone, hadn't gone on any monstrous rampages, had just gone home and continued going about his life.

It was Mark, not me or my mother, who proved we'd been wrong this whole time. Cuckoos weren't irredeemable. They weren't beyond saving. And maybe it was harder to scoop the memories out of the children's heads now, while they were young and hadn't gone through that first terrible trauma, but it was easier than putting a bullet between their eyes, which was the solution we'd been pursuing for generations.

It was no wonder the cuckoos wanted out of our dimension. We'd been pursuing them like it was our job to exterminate them, and they had never been the simple, superficial monsters we wanted them to be. Nothing ever was.

Mark was still talking about his imaginary LARP. Antimony nudged me with her elbow, rolling her eyes exaggeratedly. I lowered my shields just far enough to shoot her a quick thought.

I'm going to go check on the kids.

I caught her ribbon of surprise before I slammed my shields shut again, and she nodded. I stepped away, heading for the back of the cafeteria, where I'd picked up on the soft, fuzzy outlines of three cuckoo minds.

I found the girls packed onto the cafeteria's one soft green couch. They weren't all the same age, and their clothing was mismatched; the youngest looked to be about six and was wearing red-and-white polka dot pajamas. The next was probably nine or so, wearing a sundress and ripped yellow tights, her feet confined by scuffed Mary Janes. The third looked to be about thirteen, just about to topple over the edge into that fatal instar, wearing jeans and a faded old My Chemical Romance shirt that she'd probably acquired at a thrift store.

They were with an older girl, early twenties, with walnut-brown skin and curly brown hair. It was only their natural telepathic ability to fit in that would have caused anyone to think she was their sister; they were clearly almost identical to each other, and looked nothing remotely like her. Just one of them and there could have been an adoption involved. Three, and the cover stories necessary to make it work became more and more complicated.

The girl—who had to be Miranda—was sitting backward in her chair, watching Mark with rapt attention. The cuckoos looked at me warily as I approached. The youngest twisted and hid her face against the middle one's shoulder, beginning to make a terrified keening sound. The oldest stood, raising her hands in what was clear emulation of a fighting stance she'd seen on television.

"Stay back," she said, in what was no doubt intended as a threatening tone. "You stay back, or else."

"Or else what?" I cocked my head.

She didn't have an immediate answer for that. She kept her fists up, glancing wildly around as she tried to come up with something suitably dire. In the end, she couldn't find anything, and so she just repeated her warning: "Stay back."

"I'm not one of the people who abducted you," I said, raising my hands defensively, palms toward her. "I'm one of the people who was abducted."

She didn't lower her fists. "You *look* like them," she spat. "You look like him, and he's trying to make us think the way he wants us to, just like the man who hurt my daddy did."

Crap. I'd already known there was no way the cuckoos would have left these children with adoptive families to go back to, but I'd been hoping I might be wrong. They'd been on the cusp of anointing a queen, after all, firmly believing they were on their way out of the dimension where the monsters were. They might have been willing to cut corners.

Expecting an ordinary cuckoo to cut corners when murder was involved was like expecting a cat to sit in the middle of an aviary without killing anything. It was a nice thought, but something being nice didn't make it realistic. Realism and actual reality have never had more than a passing acquaintance anyway.

"I didn't hurt your daddy," I said sincerely. "A bad woman who looked like me hurt my daddy once because that's what bad people do sometimes. I don't know why. It's just the way they're made." I was simplifying, but she was a telepath, or at least she was going to be one when she got a little older and all those noises around the edges of her mind started making sense. She'd learn the truth about people soon enough.

She looked at me with narrow eyes and what I had to assume was suspicion. "You promise that wasn't you?"

"If I was the lady who'd taken you away from home and brought you here, wouldn't I have shoes?" I lifted one bare foot and wiggled my toes at her.

That seemed to get through, at least a little, because she lowered her hands and relaxed her shoulders, something I recognized as giving up readiness to attack. That was a good thing. Miranda was still focused on Mark, and didn't seem to have noticed the interplay.

"Why aren't you listening to the funny man?" I asked. "He's saying what's been going on."

The middle girl scoffed. "He's talking nonsense and he's trying to make us believe it even though it's all just rubbish," she said, Scottish accent thick as heather in every syllable. "I've shut him out."

Nine years old and already shielding herself and the other children against another cuckoo. She was probably the one who'd swatted me away on my initial scan. I paused, looking at her more carefully. "Did a bad woman hurt your parents?" I asked.

"Nah. Haven't had parents since I was five an' their train went off the tracks. I live with my gran. When I saw the magpies in the garden, I went out to them as fast as I could. I'd seen them once before, right before my parents died, and I didn't want them to hurt my gran."

Magpies? "Magpies?" I asked, blankly.

"You know. The black-and-white people. Like you are." She jerked her chin, indicating the length of me.

"Like I am, and my gran is. My mam had hair as red as you've ever seen, and my da was blond as summer, but then they got me, and now all I've got's my gran. So when I saw them there, I knew they were down to no good, and I went fast as a whisper to make sure they didn't do nothing rotten to her."

"La gente de Blancanieves," mumbled the youngest cuckoo, the one in her pajamas, who was still trying to burrow into the middle girl. Some of the red polka dots on her pajamas weren't dye, I realized; they were too dark, the color of dried blood. Cuckoos don't bleed red, but our adoptive parents do. She glanced at me and began keening again, pressing her face back into the middle girl's shoulder.

Great. Three kids, two of them severely traumatized, the third possibly another potential queen, and this was only the beginning. I looked over my shoulder. Mark's eyes weren't glowing anymore, although he was still talking, apparently answering more questions from the crowd without the psychic push. Annie had moved away from him, leaving her ball of light hanging in the air to illuminate the room, and was talking to a tall, thin woman with a grayish cast to her skin—our bogeyman. Cautiously, I lowered my shields, relieved to find out Mark was no longer broadcasting his "believe me, I would never lie to you" field.

It was a useful trick. That didn't mean it was one I wanted to get caught in. Miranda was starting to snap out of her cuckoo-induced fugue, recovering more slowly because the girls had been influencing her all day. She turned toward me, eyes clearing, and offered a small, polite smile that was almost overwhelmed by the feeling of relief that emanated from her when she saw my general coloration.

"Oh, hello," she said. "Are you their mother? I told them I would find you."

"No," I said. There are lies I'm not willing to tell, and with cuckoo kids, claiming a parental connection can very quickly become the equivalent of a binding contract. "I'm their cousin. Sarah."

"Morag," said the middle girl, the Scottish one. She slid her arm around the youngest, holding her protectively. "This is Lupe."

"And I'm Ava," said the oldest. Now that my shields were down, I could feel her wariness like heat from a stovetop. But not as much as I expected to—Morag was still shielding them. "What's going on?"

I glanced at Miranda. "That's hard to explain." We'd abandoned a certain degree of secrecy, but I didn't want to claim responsibility for three kids at the moment, especially not if we were planning to gather the rest of the human and cuckoo survivors here in the cafeteria. Maybe it was unfair to Miranda to expect her to keep providing unpaid babysitting services, but I needed her. "Morag, that little thinking trick you're doing right now? Can you stop for a few minutes? I promise my friend is done telling people what's going on."

I just had to hope she understood when I was asking her to do, and I was rewarded when her eyes flashed white, and the feeling of wariness from Ava suddenly increased, now accompanied by a razor line of terror from poor Lupe.

Cuckoos are an invasive species, and we can be found wherever there are humans. How many cuckoo children were here who didn't speak English as a first language, or didn't speak English at all? They were lost, confused, surrounded by strangers, and they couldn't even ask people what was happening to them. This whole situation just kept getting more and more unfair, and I hated it.

Thank you, I said silently. Ava gasped. Lupe lifted her head and stared at me. Morag smiled, eyes flashing white.

Thought so, said her mental voice, which was just as thickly accented as her normal one. *You're like me, not like Gran.*

So she really was another Queen being prepared to deploy, in the event that I had failed. It would have been at least another decade before they could force her into the final instar, but I guess when you're plotting to destroy a dimension, you're willing to take your time and get it right.

I'm like all three of you. The people who took you did it because they thought they were going to save you that way. They wanted to use me to destroy the world.

Lupe gasped. The language barrier wasn't so strong she couldn't understand at least a little of what I was saying, and translation is always easier when it's happening without words.

Is it gone? asked a new voice, younger and softer and still carrying her Spanish accent, but speaking distinctly in English. That was a relief. I didn't want her to be scared and unable to talk to anyone, and while they might still be too young to initiate telepathic conversation without an adult to guide it, this was at least something.

No, I don't think so. My friends stopped me before I could hurt people, and we stopped the bad cuckoos from doing any more damage. That's what we call the magpies, Morag, cuckoos, because we leave our babies in our people's nurseries the way cuckoos leave their eggs in other people's nests. I paused. *But now we're on another world, and things are scary here, and we're trying to make sure everyone stays safe inside and doesn't get hurt.*

Cuckoos, said Morag, trying the word on for size. *Gran always called us magpies, and it made sense because of the black and white, but cuckoos makes even more sense.*

I needed to be absolutely sure . . . *Your gran, she's like us?*

Yeah. Mam was adopted when she was a babe, and Gran always said I was her little miracle. Doesn't mean she expected to be a mam again when she was meant to be entering her dotage, but she's always looked young enough to be my mother, so that's all right, then.

We live longer than humans do. I'm sorry. I glanced at Ava, who was staring at me, radiating horror and confusion. *You thought you were human, didn't you?*

I am *human! I'm not a thing! You're a thing, you and those cuckoo people who hurt my father, you're all things!*

I sighed. This wasn't my department. This was the sort of thing we called Alex or Elsie to deal with. Verity had always been too self-centered, and Antimony was too focused on finding something she could hit. Alex and Elsie were the sensitive, thoughtful ones who listened and dealt with messy emotions.

You're not a thing, I said, as patiently as I could. *You're just a different kind of person. We're all different kinds of people. My friends—two of them are sorcerers.*

Like Dumbledore? asked Ava dubiously.

Dumbledore was a dick, I responded, before I could think better of it. Then I sighed again. *Sorry. Not quite like Dumbledore, but close enough, I guess. They do magic. And my other friends, one of them's a cuckoo like us, and the other is an incubus. He can feel other people's feelings, and he's really good at computers. But we're all people. Not being human doesn't make someone a thing, it just makes them different.*

Ava continued radiating wariness. Lupe was young enough to be more traumatized than furious, but Ava had seen her father taken to pieces in front of her, and she was on the cusp of her first instar; if I was going to clean out the big memory packet, I'd have to do it soon. She was angry and mistrustful, and I looked just like the people who had made her an orphan.

Miranda's polite curiosity was getting more pointed and concerned as we all stared silently at one another, and I knew her patience had to be running thin by this point. Soon enough, she would demand to know what we were doing, and I would either have to lie to her and claim responsibility for the girls or back off. Not fun. Extra pressure has never been my favorite thing.

I have to go and help my friends find everyone else,

*and I need the three of you to stay here and stay together.
You've done very well so far. Miranda will keep you safe.*

Miss Miranda is taking care of us, said Lupe shyly.

Yes, she is. Very good care. The fact that she didn't
have a choice didn't matter to me as much as it should
have. They were kids. They needed someone looking
after them. And they weren't hurting her, or doing any
lasting damage. That had to be good enough. *When we
get home to Earth, Morag, we'll make sure you get back
to your gran, and Lupe and Ava, we'll find your families.*

All I had was Daddy, said Ava.

Then you'll find my *family.* Mom wouldn't mind me
coming home with one stray, while she might have con-
niptions if I came home with all of them. Then again,
she might not. She'd always been fond of children, and I
knew she'd been considering adopting again before
Shelby informed us that she was pregnant. Two kids in
the house wouldn't be a major change for her. *We'll
make sure you're safe. All of you.*

Promise? asked Morag with the sharpness only a
child can manage. *You swear you'll make sure we're
safe, not go taking people to pieces or anything rotten
like the rest of your lot.*

They're not my lot, they're just our species. I blinked,
breaking the connection. Lupe was still clinging to
Morag, but she felt less terrified now. That was an improvement. "I'm going to go help the others so we can
go and get the rest of the people on campus. I'll check in
with you when we get back."

"You won't," said Ava sullenly, folding her arms as
she dropped onto the couch in a sulk.

"We'll see, won't we?" I knew better than to argue
with a teenager who was determined to be unhappy. It
never ends well, not for the adult *or* for the teen.

Miranda looked at me uncertainly. "So you're leaving them with me?" she asked.

"You're their sister, I'm just a cousin." Their sister
who couldn't speak to one of them at all due to language

barriers. That was fun. But she wasn't hurting them and they weren't hurting her, and this was really the best they were going to get.

"Sarah!" Annie's shout brought me whipping around to face her. She was walking toward me across the cafeteria, the bogeyman woman at her side.

"Yeah?"

"This is Crystal. Crystal, tell her what you told me."

Crystal was nervous. She glanced at Miranda, and then at the three girls, nervousness increasing. I waved at Miranda and stepped away, moving to meet Annie and Crystal, out of easy earshot.

"What's going on?"

"The two bogeymen Annie said you, um, found under the campus?" she said slowly. "That's my fiancée and her father. They're here for a contract negotiation. I'd rather you left them alone, they don't know the campus and they don't want to surface until everything gets back to normal."

"I can agree to that for now," I said slowly. "We're still trying to figure out how we're going to get everyone home. If it means we're opening a door, they'll have to come walk through it like everyone else does. And if it means we're transporting the entire campus, there could be more structural damage. Things could collapse. I'd feel better if everyone was at surface level when that happened, because if they get crushed, you're probably not getting married."

"I'll tell them," she said. "There's an entrance to the access tunnels at the back of the kitchen. I've been using that to move back and forth when no one was looking." Bogeymen are naturally good at moving through shadows, exploiting them in a way that probably strains the bounds of probability, but works for them well enough that no one's ever wanted to question it. She'd be fine.

"I picked up two more cryptid students during my scan. Do you know either of them?"

"Miss Price said there was an ag major who's something I've never heard of before, and um, I'm a comp sci major? We don't really hang out in the ag department. Sorry." Crystal shook her head. "I know the chupacabra, though. She's in physics. Her name's um, Maria, and she's pretty nice, as long as you're not super attached to the bio department lab animals."

"I don't want to know, I'm not going to ask, Sarah, don't go looking in her head for the answers and share them with me later," said Antimony. "Thank you for your help, Crystal. And thank you for staying here while we check the rest of campus."

"I know Mark said this was a LARP, and he made it sound very convincing, but this isn't a LARP, is it?" asked Crystal.

Antimony shook her head. "No, we're really in a new dimension, and we have yet to make contact with the people who actually live here. So it's not safe for you to go outside." She shot me a quick look.

Not planning to tell her the zombie mobs are real? I asked.

Not as yet, no.

It made sense from a standpoint of keeping things reasonably under control. It seemed like a little bit of a dick move, but I was letting her take the lead, and that meant trusting her instincts.

"Are we heading out?" I asked aloud.

Annie nodded. "Mark's done convincing everyone that this is less apocalypse, more Dream Park, so we need to move. James and Artie don't like holding still this long."

Odds were good that neither did she—she's never been the most patient—and I had done what I could do here. I nodded in answer. "So let's go."

"Crystal, we'll see you later," said Annie.

Crystal waved as we walked back across the cafeteria to where the boys were waiting, Annie pausing to pluck her ball of light out of the air as we passed it, and then the five of us left, returning to the lobby, where Annie blew out her light like it was a candle.

"That went well," she said.

Something was nagging at the edges of my awareness. I frowned, not quite sure what it was. Morag trying to make contact, maybe, as she figured out that whatever we were, it was something that came with extra bells and whistles. I reinforced my shields and the nagging feeling faded. Much better.

"Let's go get Sarah some shoes," said Annie, and pushed open the door to the outside.

The cluster of people who had been waiting for us out there pounced.

Eleven

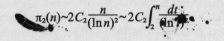

$$\pi_2(n) \sim 2C_2 \frac{n}{(\ln n)^2} \sim 2C_2 \int_2^n \frac{dt}{(\ln t)^2}$$

"There's no shame in being caught flat-footed. Happens to all of us eventually. It's how you react after the surprise that matters."

—Enid Healy

Under arrest? Maybe? Or being abducted, it's hard to say when you don't know the people who are in the process of restraining you

THE STRANGERS WERE BASICALLY human-shaped, the same way aliens on *Star Trek* are basically human-shaped; if not for their outsized eyes and too-sharp cheekbones, they could have been people with elaborate face paint, striped and swirled like ocelots, wearing cat-ear headbands and wigs that made their hair look more like fur. Their clothing was loosely fitted, clearly hand-made from some kind of rough, woven fabric, tied tight around their calves and forearms to keep it from impeding their movements. The starlight was enough to give us the gist, but not the fine details like color, and I was way more focused on the polearm the one in front of me was holding to my throat than the exact shade of her eyes.

None of them were the rider who had almost confronted us before, meaning there was a chance none of them could throw fire. That was nice.

She said something in a language I naturally didn't

know, fluid and staccato at the same time, with liquid syllables melding into sharp clicks. I shook my head.

"I'm sorry," I said. "I don't know what you're saying."

Her emotional state was jumbled, but I could pick out curiosity and concern; she wanted to know what we were more than she wanted to slit our throats. That was good. She was perfectly willing to slit our throats if we presented her with too much of a problem. That was bad. I did not want to have my throat slit. The differences between cuckoo and human anatomy mean I can take a hit to what would normally be my heart and keep going without any major organ damage, but slash the arteries connecting my body to my brain and I'm going to have issues, same as any other biped.

What I could see of her mouth looked very much built to the same blueprint as the rest of us, and her language contained sounds I'd heard in human and cryptid languages back on Earth. Communication should be possible, if our minds were similar enough to make it work. I closed my eyes and lowered my shields.

Without the shielding in the way, her mind was louder, almost as loud as a human I'd already attuned to. Whether that was due to my own increased strength or the magnifying effects of this dimension, there was no way for me to know. Confusion and suspicion were at the forefront of everything: what were we, what were we doing here, how did we bring our entire hive with us?

That was the first word I was really sure of: it was accompanied by a flickering image of something that looked like a giant termite mound, swarming with tiny figures that could have been insects or could have been distant bipeds. We had at least that concept in common, and it explained some of the concern: for her, any strangers were either scouts looking for a hive to raid, or they *were* a new hive springing up in established territory, and needed to be destroyed.

If we had one concept in common, we might have more. I'd encountered Spanish and Spanish speakers before "talking" to Lupe; while this language was completely new to me, the theory was the same. I pushed forward, searching the images and ideas filling her conscious mind for points of connection.

And there they were.

The next time she spoke, for all that her words were still entirely strange to my ear, I knew what she was saying: "Pretending to be stupid isn't going to save you. Tell us why you trespass here, and how you moved your entire hive without workers or beasts of burden, or it will not go well for you."

The translation was clumsy, and might be inexact, but I had enough faith in the basics of it to believe I had the gist of what she was saying correct. I cleared my throat, searching her thoughts for the words I needed, and then said, in her own fluid, click-filled language, "We are strangers from another world. We came here unintentionally. We want nothing more than to depart, back to our own world. The hive came with us, through the same unintentional means. None of the people here intended any offense, or mean you any harm."

That last was a bit of a lie. The hollowed-out cuckoos were nothing but harm. Terrence would also happily do us all harm, but Annie had his gun, and he was still in a drugged stupor in the health center, and we were unlikely to see him again. I hoped. As for the cuckoos, we just had to hope they stayed away, too.

The woman's thoughts turned chaotic with excitement and surprise. Until that moment, she hadn't been sure we were intelligent beings, and not simply very clever mimics. "You speak our language. How is it you can speak our language when you claim to come from another world?"

I opened my eyes, aware that they would be shining white and eerie. She didn't flinch away. That was a pleasant surprise. "I'm what we call a . . ." I couldn't find a word for "telepath" in her mind, and so I continued, somewhat clumsily, " . . . mind-speaker. I am reading your thoughts right now, looking for the words I need, and our mouths share enough of their shape to make it possible for me to form them. You could speak our language as well, if you wanted to do so."

"We have mind-speakers," she said. "They come from the," and she named a local insect that had no English cognate, but which looked in her thoughts like a giant rosy maple moth, "line. They are very gentle and very fragile, and do not mingle often with outsiders."

"My line is not so gentle as a moth," I replied. "We came from wasps. We are still predators. Most of us are dangerous, not to be trusted."

She shifted her grasp on the shaft of her polearm, suddenly nervous. "Why are you the exception?"

"If I were one of the dangerous ones, would I tell you so? Or would I lie to you and pretend to be harmless, risking harm later when you discovered my lies?"

That appeared to work. She relaxed again. "Your friends, they are mind-speakers as well?"

"One, the male who looks like me, is a mind-speaker. The others are not. We come from many different lines, on our world."

"As we do here." Her eyes narrowed. "I don't know if I like you inside my mind."

"If I withdraw, I lose your language, and we cannot communicate."

"Then I will allow it, for now. You will speak to your kind for us." She grabbed my shoulder, her thoughts becoming louder with the skin contact, and turned me to face the rest of our commingled groups.

Annie was staring at the polearms, all but ignoring the people, and the avarice rolling off of her was predictable and familiar and almost enough to make me smile. Girl does love her exotic weaponry. James was silent and resigned as another of the strangers prodded him with a polearm, hands at his sides and shoulders slumped. Mark was standing farther back, jaw clenched; he might be a problem, if he decided we needed to turn this into a brawl.

Artie, on the other hand, looked like he had internally collapsed. He was standing with his head bowed, ignoring the two strangers flanking him, ignoring literally everything. This had all been too much; he was overwhelmed, and he had shut down, maybe entirely. We needed to untangle this before his panic attack got too deep to deal with.

"Speak," commanded the woman who was still holding my shoulder. At least I was sure of her pronouns now. That was something.

"These people own this territory," I said slowly, having to make a conscious effort to speak English. The rest of my people turned toward me, visibly startled, except for Artie, who remained exactly as he was. Oh, this was bad. This was very, very bad.

Normally, I can help when Artie gets overwhelmed. Normally, I can talk him out of a panic attack. But normally, he believes me when I say we've been friends since we were kids, and normally, he's not blaming me for the fact that he's basically lived his whole life as an agoraphobe, leaving him unaccustomed to crowds and too much novel stimulation. He wasn't going to listen until things calmed down.

"They are not our enemies," I continued. "They did not come here because they wished to do us harm, they came because they were curious about the sudden appearance of our hive." The woman hadn't told me half of this—I was picking it up from the surface of her mind, unable to disengage my thoughts from hers while she was touching me. Oh, I wanted so badly for her to stop touching me, but that wasn't going to happen any time soon.

Her fingers tightened as she leaned forward and whispered her commands in my ear. I swallowed hard, nodding.

"We will allow ourselves to be restrained," I said. "They will be gentle, but we must be rendered harmless before they can take us to see their leader."

At the word "leader," Artie finally raised his head. "Like hell we will," he spat, and punched the nearest stranger in the throat, sending her reeling away from him, choking. In a pinch, the throat or the genitals are the best places to strike a biped, and since we had no idea what these people had for reproductive organs, or where they might be kept on the body, only the throat remained as a truly viable target.

The other stranger who had been responsible for keeping an eye on him spun her polearm and shouted something I only half-translated. The woman holding my shoulder caught the full meaning and transmitted it unwittingly to me: "Stop moving, or I will stop you."

"Artie, you have to stop!" I shouted. "She's going to hurt you!"

He responded by grabbing her polearm mid-spin and wrenching it out of her hands, flipping it around so that the pointy end was pointed at her chest. "I don't know what you have in there, but I'm betting I'd pierce something essential if I stabbed you," he snarled.

"You know, if I'd been taking bets on which one of us was going to snap first, I would have said one of the cuckoos, not *Artie*," said James, in a surprisingly mild tone. He sounded like was making observations about a nature documentary, not watching his adoptive cousin set himself up to get annihilated.

The rest of the strangers—the swarm, if I wanted to go by the words forming in the mind of the woman holding me, who had yet to think about anything as useful as her own name—were shifting their attention away from the others and toward the commotion Artie was making. Annie moved her hands subtly toward her sides, where I knew the bulk of the knives would be concealed.

"According to Sarah, worrying about her was one of his main sources of self-control," she said, in the same mild tone as James. "He spent a lot of emotional energy keeping her safe, and he's an incubus. They have a *lot* of emotional energy."

The nearest stranger stopped, turning to look at Annie. "Incubus?" he echoed, the word strangely accented but still recognizable. "Incubus?" he asked with more urgency, this time pointing to Artie.

"Uh." Annie stopped reaching for her sides and let her hands fall back into a neutral position, blinking at the man for a moment. Then she nodded. "Incubus," she confirmed.

"Incubus!" shouted the man joyfully, rushing to put himself between Artie and the others. "*Incubus!*" They all began shouting excitedly.

The thoughts of the woman holding me became a swirling mass of hopeful excitement, as infectious as it was inexplicable. "*Incubus . . .*" she breathed, and let me go, breaking the forced telepathic channel.

I stumbled away from her, taking several deep breaths as I tried to remember the limits of my own psyche. No, that memory of flying above an endless forest on the back of a giant praying mantis wasn't mine, because physics didn't work that way in the dimension I came from. The practice SATs, now, those were mine, and so were all the other standardized tests I could remember taking. I began to settle back into the shape of my own skin.

Artie still had the polearm, but he wasn't threatening anyone with it anymore. Instead, he was watching with uncomfortable bafflement as the strangers embraced and laughed, saying "Incubus" over and over again. The woman who'd been talking to me rushed past, joining the impromptu party. This was getting weird, but it was also getting less hostile, so I should probably be happy about that.

Naturally, that was when the swarm of hollowed-out cuckoos attacked.

They seemed to come from everywhere, flowing around both sides of the cafeteria. It was a pack of at least fifty, which I was afraid was not the majority of the cuckoos left on campus—I had no idea how many we'd actually started with.

(To take a brief digression into the math, Mom always said that for cuckoos, the ideal ratio was about one to every million humans. If that number were strictly maintained, it would put the cuckoo population of Earth at roughly eight thousand, which is more than I had any desire to deal with. Eight thousand is small when you're talking about a population. It's immense when you're talking about an opposing force, especially when your side of the fight consists of five people, one of whom refuses to trust another. We didn't have the numbers to win in even the best-case scenario. And after seeing the number of minds chained into the ritual, I didn't feel like that number had ever really been accurate. It didn't count the kids, for one thing, and it wasn't like any cuckoo who wanted to reproduce was going to wait until they received a death certificate for an older member of the extended hive. "Ideal" does not mean "actual," and never has.)

All of them moved with the same blank-faced shamble, the low roar of their hunger becoming audible long after they shuffled into sight.

One of the strangers barked a command, pointing a polearm at the pack of cuckoos. They ignored the order, whatever it had been, and kept advancing. I rushed after the woman who'd been talking to me before, dispensing with formalities and shoving the words forward, into her mind.

These are not your friends. They are not our friends. They are broken inside, and they will destroy you. Tell your people to fight.

She jerked away from me, radiating confusion, as the cuckoos reached the stranger on the edge of their formation.

His screams as they dragged him down were horrific. They wrenched the polearm from his hands, although not before he had been able to successfully stab two of them. Neither seemed to notice their injuries, which were freely bleeding but non-fatal, as they continued their assault. The rest of his team was starting to react, but not quickly enough; this was a scouting party, armed because they were examining something new, not because they had expected to encounter any actual resistance. They didn't know what to do.

Then the cuckoos ripped him apart. In a matter of seconds, before his thick, red-brown blood began to spurt and cover the field, I learned more about the anatomy of these strangers than I would ever have wanted to know. They had lungs like humans, and what looked like two hearts, one stacked right above the other, both beating frantically as they fought to keep the shrieking stranger alive.

One of the cuckoos ripped the top heart out of his chest and began to eat it like an apple. His screams stopped.

The cuckoos kept coming.

Artie produced a gun from the waistband of his pants, reminding me that my family is always, blessedly, prepared for a fight, and shot the first three cuckoos to approach him before the chamber clicked empty. When he realized he was out of ammo he threw the gun, bouncing it off another cuckoo's forehead, and grabbed a fallen polearm from the ground. He'd be fine, assuming he didn't slip in the gore that was increasingly muddying the field.

Annie, meanwhile, had woven what looked like a burning net out of strands of pure energy. It was definitely on fire: the flames licked at the air, spitting and sparking, as she moved it, spinning it first over her head and then flinging it at a patch of cuckoos. It entangled their heads and shoulders before bursting into taller, brighter flames, consuming them much more quickly than her earlier fireballs had done. Annie whooped.

"I always wanted to do that!" she yelled.

James, meanwhile, was doing . . . nothing. He was standing perfectly still, head cocked to the side, watching the cuckoos advance. He didn't move, but his fingertips were turning blue, and as I watched, the color crept slowly up the length of his hands and began to cover his forearms before disappearing into his sleeves. It was like watching the end of *Frozen* in horrifying real-life slow motion, except that his flesh wasn't actually turning translucent, just a deep, frostbitten blue.

Then the cuckoos approaching him began to fall down.

It was a slow process, although it only took a few seconds; the stress of the attack was making everything slow down, the world stretching like an elastic band. The cuckoos closest to James fell one by one, their expressions never changing, their bodies slowing before the collapse, then bending at the knees and hitting the ground without flinching or reacting in any way.

They landed facedown, and they didn't move. He continued to stare, and the frost on his hands continued to creep upward, until it was tracing the edge of his neck, and the cuckoos continued to fall.

Mark was not quite cowering at the back of the group, but he was definitely shying away, raising his hands to protect his face, avoiding any contact with the attackers.

The strangers snapped out of their shock as their companion stopped screaming. The woman I'd been talking to before began barking orders and they all raised their polearms, surging forward and beginning their attack. It was a thing of beauty, as fluid as one of Verity's dance routines, but involving a lot more flying ichor. They mowed down cuckoos in a steady wave, killing them as effortlessly as swatting a bug. It was beautiful, and it was terrifying.

Someone grabbed my arm. The feeling of ceaseless, all-consuming hunger swept over me, chasing all rational thought away. I did the only thing that made sense. I screamed like a little girl and whipped around, driving my fist into the face of the cuckoo behind me.

It dropped my arm and staggered backward before advancing again, seemingly unbothered by the fact that its nose was broken and clear blood was flowing from it in a thick gout, rapidly covering the lower half of its face. It raised its arms to reach for me.

I punched it again. Again, it fell back a step before

shambling resolutely toward me. I fumbled to get a grip on its mind, only to be buffeted by the howling hunger that had replaced all rational thought. It was like trying to grapple with a windstorm. I backed off a step, increasing the distance between us while putting myself closer than I liked to the main fight, and began attempting something I'd never done before: constructing a shield *inside* someone else's mind.

Normally, throwing up a shield is almost instinctive, something I learned to do more for the protection of everyone around me than myself. If I was shielding, I wouldn't pick up thoughts I wasn't supposed to have, or accidentally influence people. Normally, I can set a sturdy shield in a second, buttressing myself against the rest of the world with little more than an idea. This was different. This was construction, laborious and exhausting. I felt the tingle as the bioluminescent cells in my eyes activated and the vitreous humor lit up like a lightbulb, followed by the sensation of my hair lifting away from my shoulders. If I was going to get telekinetic every time I exerted myself from now on, I was going to need to start putting my hair in a bun.

The cuckoo kept advancing. I kept constructing my shield, angling it against the howling void of the cuckoo's hunger. It felt like an unstoppable wind when felt from the inside. I needed it to stop.

The last imaginary brick of my shield slotted into place, creating an effective windbreak inside the cuckoo's mind. The storm shattered, unable to continue blowing with an obstacle in its way and unable to blow around it. The cuckoo wobbled and stopped advancing, but even feeling around with every scrap of mental strength I had left, I couldn't find anything resembling coherent thought. There was nothing left but the storm. My first impression—that the equation had devoured them after being set free inside them, and they were no longer "people" in any meaningful sense—had been an accurate one. Whether I wanted it to be or not.

"I'm sorry," I said. I didn't have any weapons; the

consequences of being taken in my nightgown and surrounded by people who were still trying to decide
whether or not they were willing to trust me. I looked
around, eyes landing on a brick that had fallen from the
building's façade during the seismic shift between Earth
and whatever this reality was called. I reached my hand
out toward it, and was fundamentally unsurprised when
it lifted off the ground and sailed across the three or so
feet between me and it, slapping into my palm.

Maybe the telekinesis was like the enhanced sorcery
and would go away when we went home. Or maybe this
was one more thing I would have to learn to control as
a consequence of this whole terrible adventure. Either
way, I had a brick now.

I turned back to the silent cuckoo, hefting the brick.
"I'm so, so sorry," I said, and brought it down on their
forehead as hard as I could. Bone cracked. The wind that
had been howling on the other side of my shield died,
and I pulled myself out of the cuckoo's mind before the
synapses could short out and do me a whole new kind of
harm. My hair settled back onto my shoulders as they
collapsed, hitting the ground like a normal corpse, not
like the rigid dolls still toppling over in front of James.

Two more cuckoos immediately appeared in the
space behind where the first had been. One of them
dropped to their knees, beginning to scrabble at the
corpse with hooked, claw-like hands. The hunger had its
own ideas about appropriate disposal for the dead. The
other advanced on me, storm raging in its eyes.

I did the only thing that made sense at this stage in
the fight. I spun on my heel and fled for the dubious
safety of my cousins, weaving between the fallen to tuck
myself in behind Annie. She was radiating heat like a
furnace, starting to pant as she spun another web of fire
to throw at the oncoming cuckoos. She glanced over her
shoulder at me, the barest flicker of frustration rising
through her chaotic emotional state.

"Running away from a fight? And you *really* want me
to believe you're a Price?"

"I'm not, I was adopted by Angela Baker, not Evelyn Price. Your mother's my sister." Explaining that despite my adoption, I had taken the last name "Zellaby" when I turned eighteen, rather than claim a familial relationship that wasn't biologically there, would have been confusing and taken too long for the situation. "I don't have any weapons."

"So brain-blast them." She flung her net, entangling another five cuckoos. They fell, burning. None of them screamed.

"I can't brain-blast people who've already had their minds wiped," I objected. "And I don't want to get into the habit of brain-blasting people in the first place! It's antisocial and probably not a good idea for me to get too comfortable with it."

"Oh. Then I guess when this is over, we should get you a knife or something."

"Yeah, that might be good!" I managed not to yell at her, mostly because her amusement was strong enough to tell me that she wasn't worried.

Seven strangers with polearms, two sorcerers, and one pissed-off Price seemed to be a match for fifty opponents with no sense of strategy or tactics, and no weapons but their hands. After that first stranger had been taken and torn apart, none of the others had been careless enough to let themselves be grabbed, and Mark was staying well clear of the cuckoo swarm. None of them could get near James, who was starting to shake as the lines of frost traveled up his cheeks. I sent a line of thought in his direction, checking for signs of distress, and rather than his mind, I hit what felt like a wall of ice. I grabbed for Annie's arm as she was starting to motion for another web of fire. She turned to look at me, irritation boiling off of her.

"*What*?" she demanded.

I pointed to James.

She followed the line of my finger and swore, pulling away from me. "Dammit, Jimmy. Jimmy! Jimmy, it's your fucking sister." She set two more cuckoos on fire in the process of getting to his side. Unlike the ones she'd netted, they didn't fall right away, but kept shambling forward, burning as they went. Shit. I glanced around, looking for weapons, and spotted a few of her knives, abandoned on the ground.

A thought summoned them into the air, and another sent them speeding into the throats of the two burning cuckoos, piercing them through and sending them toppling.

"I don't think I like this new trick of yours!" called Mark.

"That's okay, I'm not so sure about it either!" I called back, and spun the knives in the air before sending them off after another target.

Keeping things not only off the ground but actively in motion was exhausting, and I could already tell I wasn't going to be able to do it for very long. Ingrid and Mark had both insisted that the instar which carried me to Queen was the last one, but if they'd never been able to keep a Queen alive past the ritual, did they really know for sure? We already knew the final instar wasn't debilitating like the ones before it, since they normally pushed Queens straight from transformation into world-destroying. That didn't mean any future instars would be this kind. I didn't want to find out that they'd been wrong by accidentally triggering a bonus metamorphosis and falling into another week-long coma, or worse, another multi-year period of severe mental instability.

Being a bug isn't all it's cracked up to be. I guess the same could be said of being a true mammal; I could bathe in butter and not need to worry about heart disease since I don't have a heart to compromise, but the grass, as they say, is always greener on the other side of the fence.

Annie had reached James. She grabbed him by the shoulders, casually setting three more cuckoos on fire at the same time—I sent my new knives spinning through their throats, slashing them open and leaving them to bleed out on the grass—and began to shake him, saying something low and urgent that I was too far away to hear. James didn't respond. That wasn't necessarily a good thing. It also wasn't necessarily a bad thing. None of this made any sense.

None of this apart from Artie. He had continued to pummel the cuckoos coming at him with fists and feet, knocking them down and then kicking them until they stopped trying to get up. He wasn't beating them to death: once they were incapacitated, our new friends-slash-captors were stabbing them repeatedly with their fancy polearms, and thus reducing the number of cuckoos left for the rest of us to handle.

The mob had been reduced to less than a quarter of its original size, with maybe ten still standing, but those ten were still coming, as fresh as they'd ever been, while we were running on empty. They didn't seem to notice or care that all their friends were dead, and honestly, I was pretty sure they couldn't: the hunger was too big to allow for self-preservation, much less worrying about other people, which had never been a cuckoo strong suit in the first place.

Even as that thought finished forming, two of them demonstrated that they *did* notice, by dropping to their knees next to a group of charred corpses and beginning to wrench chunks of meat off of the bodies, shoving it into their mouths. The smell of charred cuckoo wasn't quite what the smell of charred human would have been, more like the smell of fire-roasted shrimp. My stomach rumbled, and I realized I didn't know when I had last eaten, even if the realization was coming from something completely disgusting.

Maybe cannibalism was normal on Johrlar. Maybe this would have seemed okay to me if I'd been raised by my own kind. But I wasn't, and it didn't, and I sort of wanted to encourage Annie to start setting them on fire again, just to make it *stop*.

Annie was still talking to James, voice pitched low and tight. I didn't listen in. It wouldn't have been appropriate or kind to do so, not when she was being so careful to keep her voice soft enough that none of us could hear her with our ears. Artie punched another cuckoo in the throat, sending it sprawling, and his new friends stabbed it until it stopped moving. We were winning. I pulled my knives back to me, plucking them out of the air and managing not to grimace at the film of viscous hemolymph covering the handles. Right. When you telekinetically rammed something through a person's body, it didn't come back to you clean. That was something to remember.

James finally blinked and snapped out of his fugue, attention shifting to Annie. Then he wobbled, sagged, and collapsed, in that order, crumpling into her arms. She caught him without hesitation, and his hands—no longer blue, no longer frosted-over—came up to clutch at her forearms, looking for purchase. Annie sank to her knees, carrying him along with her, and held onto him as he shook.

One of the few remaining cuckoos loomed behind them. I flung one of my knives back into the air, sending it flashing toward the cuckoo, embedding it in the center of the thing's throat. The cuckoo tried to look down for a moment, then toppled, taking my knife with it.

Mark grabbed my arm, pulling me around to face him, and nearly got stabbed for his trouble. He must have recognized the impulse as it flashed through my mind, because he let me go and put his hands up defensively, showing me that he wasn't an attacker.

"Whoa, whoa, it's me," he said. "Sarah, it's *me*."

I took a deep breath and released my "grip" on the knife still embedded in the cuckoo, abandoning my silent efforts to pull it free. If he tried to start anything, I still had the other knife, and way more combat training than most people would assume from a quiet, relatively unassertive mathematician.

"I see that," I said. Then, with a tiny bit of humor: "You still have brainwaves. You're not an empty, screaming void."

"Yeah." He shuddered, projecting dismay and disgust

at the same time, like the kissing cousins they were. "I thought you and Annie were exaggerating about them. I won't make that mistake again. I'm sorry I didn't take you more seriously. And that I'm not more use in a fight. Where did you learn to hit like that?"

"Same place he did." I pointed at Artie, who had just swept the legs out from under the last attacking cuckoo. "I keep telling you, we all grew up together. I may have accidentally deleted *their* memories, but I didn't touch *mine*. I know everything my sister and her husband taught their kids, and I know a lot of what Uncle Ted taught *his* children. I don't know everything Aunt Jane had to teach, because she's a little more bloodthirsty than I like to be."

Mark wrinkled his nose. "There's a point past which a Price won't go? I don't think I want to see that."

"Well, you've just seen some of it." I nodded toward Artie, who was panting as he kicked the corpse of the last cuckoo with an intensity that should probably have worried me more than it did. I was exhausted. I needed something to eat—something that wasn't barbequed shrimp, the smell of which was still causing my stomach to roil and grumble. I needed clothes, and a bra, and shoes, and a bed. Not necessarily in that order. I would happily have shanked Mark if a set of fitting undergarments would've magically fallen out of the hole I made.

I took a deep breath and sank to the ground, sagging in place. "Annie?" I called. "Are you and James all right?"

"He's completely drained," she said. She was still holding him, one arm wrapped around his torso, the other resting against the top of his head. "He pulled more sorcery out of himself than he ever has before, and it's going to be a while before he's feeling like himself again. Your little trick with the knives was impressive as hell."

She didn't call it a new trick, because she didn't know. This day was just an unending stream of horrible discoveries that I didn't want to make.

"Thanks," I said, fighting to keep the hurt out of my voice. "I don't think that was the last of them."

"No, we saw hundreds when we got to campus."

"Ingrid sent out the word that we were going to activate you as soon as she confirmed your final instar had been completed," said Mark. "She told everyone where to go. A naturally telepathic species can spread news very quickly when we need to, and a Queen arising is one of the only messages we're all programmed to receive. Not every cuckoo in the world came. Every cuckoo that wanted to live did."

"Can cuckoos be suicidal?" asked Annie.

Mark snorted. "Anyone can be suicidal, and when you spend your days bathing in the thoughts of the people around you—the petty, cruel, small-minded thoughts—suicide and homicide start looking equally appealing. Only the fact that most of us think we're superior to the best the human race has to offer keeps us alive."

Annie frowned, broadcasting confusion and displeasure. The more we learned about the cuckoos, the harder it was not to think of them as people, and if they were people, we'd been behaving like the Covenant for years.

Artie and his new band of admirers were done kicking corpses. He straightened and walked back over to the rest of us, the strangers trailing along behind him, the closest of them occasionally touching his sleeve or arm and whispering "Incubus" in awed voices, like they still couldn't quite believe he existed.

"Can one of you translate?" he demanded, looking at me and Mark. "These people are making me really uncomfortable."

"No," I said. If he wasn't going to ask nicely, I wasn't going to push myself, not when I was already wrung out and exhausted. I stayed where I was, looking placidly back at him.

"I can try," said Mark. He moved toward the group, eyes going white.

Seen from the outside, that really *was* unnerving. If not for the fact that cuckoos were very good at erasing traces of their presence from the minds of the people who witnessed them, they—we—would have been caught a long time before we were.

After a long, silent moment, Mark pressed a hand against his forehead and staggered back, the light flickering out. "I'm sorry," he said. "I can't. Their minds are too strange, and they're all thinking too fast. I'm not strong enough." Then he looked at me.

It was clear what he wanted me to do. I didn't need to be psychic to figure that out. I pushed myself to my feet, my knees wobbling as I tried to get my balance back, turned, and walked away from them.

Behind me, Artie demanded, "Where the hell is she *going*?" Annie shushed him.

"Sarah?" she called, more gently, more like I was a person who could make her own choices, and not a badly-trained dog that needed to be brought to heel. "Are you all right?"

I spun to face her. "No," I snapped. "No, I'm *not* all right. I'm exhausted, I'm starving, we just fought off a fucking zombie mob and I didn't start out with any weapons because none of you want to *trust me* enough to let me protect myself, I don't have any shoes, I don't have a bra, and I want to go home!" I wanted my mother, and my own clothes, and a tomato sandwich, and to sit and watch *Square One* reruns until my head stopped spinning. I wanted not to feel like I was risking an instar no one knew existed just by trying to stay alive.

I wanted Artie to put his arms around me and tell me it was going to be all right, he still loved me, he still believed that I could fix this.

Wanting something doesn't make it possible. It never has, and that's a good thing, since a whole lot of little girls want unicorns every year, and unicorns do not make good pets. But oh, I wanted. I felt like I was going to explode with wanting, and that meant I needed to be somewhere he wasn't, because I was too tired to put up another shield, and what I wanted was going to radiate out of me and become what *he* wanted if I wasn't careful.

I waved a hand, calling the second knife out of the cuckoo's throat. Yanking it free from the cervical spine was harder than I would have guessed, but in the end, my will was stronger than its inertia. The handle slapped into my palm, slick with hemolymph as I closed my fingers around it. I didn't drop it. That would have been embarrassing.

"I just need a minute without any of you standing around and *thinking* things at me, okay? You're giving me a headache. You won't like what happens when I have a headache. I'm going to the student store," I said wearily. "I need shoes."

Then I turned and walked away across the darkened campus, their confusion and displeasure following me into the shadows.

I didn't look back.

Twelve

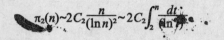

$$\pi_2(n) \sim 2C_2\frac{n}{(\ln n)^2} \sim 2C_2\int_2^n \frac{dt}{(\ln t)^2}$$

"Being the black sheep doesn't mean you're not family anymore. We're not all going to fit together like puzzle pieces. We're not even all going to like each other most of the time. That's all right. Family doesn't have to like each other. We just have to step up."
—Jane Harrington-Price.

Walking alone across the darkened campus, which is maybe not the most mature thing ever, but is vitally necessary for my sanity right now

WALKING AWAY FROM THE others wasn't the smartest thing I've ever done, but the math said it should be safe enough, at least for the moment, and if I had to spend one more second so close to their minds that their thoughts were like steel wool scraping over my sanity, I was going to scream. Also, the mob of husked-out cuckoos that had attacked us had been massive. It would have picked up any smaller groups as it moved toward us. There were unlikely to be stragglers in the immediate vicinity, and even if there were, I had knives now. And yeah, maybe this was an elaborate means of committing suicide—I couldn't take fifty cuckoos by myself on my best day, and this was so far from my best day that I couldn't have found it on a map—but going foolishly up against impossible odds is sort of the Price family motto. And if I stayed around my friends for much longer, I was going to slip and melt their brains trying to turn them back into the people I needed them to be in order to keep myself from breaking.

Even Mark wasn't safe. I had the fewest expectations where he was concerned, but I also had the fewest scruples. I was less likely to hold back where he was concerned, and that wasn't any better in the long run. I needed a few minutes to myself. I had a destination. So I was walking away.

I was too exhausted to shield properly, but not too exhausted to scan; if anything, that was easier without my shields in the way. I didn't try to push myself to "see" the whole campus, just the area close enough to matter. Thanks to my white nightgown, general pallor, and the fact that all the blood I'd been spattered with had been clear, I looked more like an ingénue who'd been slimed than the survivor of a pitched battle, and I was virtually glowing in the starlight. It was almost nice to know I was so visible because I didn't want to be, and if my abilities had been pushing that close to the line of being completely out of control, I would have found a way to distort the light and disappear.

Right. Because an inability to become the Invisible Woman was really proof that I wasn't verging on a post-Queen instar. I scowled at my feet and kept on walking.

A few minds flickered at the edges of my consciousness; the bogeymen in the steam tunnels, the individuals who'd taken up hiding places in various classrooms, either solo or in trios and pairs. None of them were looking out their windows. I was passing unseen, a ghost in the night.

Not quite a ghost. I was too tired to be dead. Cuckoos don't leave ghosts in the version of the afterlife we know exists; Aunt Rose says that may be because it's usually "unfinished business" that keeps people from moving on, beyond the boundaries of the twilight that butts up against the land of the living, and cuckoos live such self-pleasing, hedonistic lives that they rarely leave anything undone while they're alive. It's as good a theory as any, and better than the one the mice proposed when I was a kid, which was that cuckoos didn't leave ghosts because we don't have souls.

I don't know if I believe in souls per se, but I know that when humans die, they sometimes leave something behind for a little while, something that thinks and acts and exists just like they did when they were alive, something that endures. It's hard not to equate that with the idea of the soul, and I refuse to think that cuckoos are so alien, so inhuman, that it can't happen for us.

Not that I'm in any hurry to find out firsthand. I kept walking, watching my feet flash pale against the grass, following the map I'd taken from a glimpse at Mark's mind, until the lawn ended at a wide expanse of brick and concrete. The student quad. I walked faster and more carefully at the same time, since the chances of broken glass and gravel were—or at least seemed—higher here, heading for the tall building looming on the other side. It was free of detectable minds. I was close enough that even cuckoo children would have been detectable. Unless there was another predatory mob waiting to grab and devour me, I was in the clear.

Nothing lunged out of the shadows as I finished crossing the quad and climbed the four shallow brick steps to the front of the store. The campus had been open when the cuckoos seized control, and they didn't give a shit about human ideas of property and possession; no one had bothered to lock the door. A small bell rang overhead as I pushed it open, revealing . . . very little.

The starlight that made navigation possible outside didn't really reach here, and while I could see the counter and the registers in the light that passed through the window, everything else was cast in shadow.

This was Iowa. They had some pretty big storms here. Not as bad as Florida or Alabama, but bad enough to make a dent in the local power grid. I made for the counter and started feeling around below the register, focusing on the shelves low enough to not be visible from the window. Humans like to put their valuables where no one will notice them and try to take them away. There was no chance they didn't use this space for storage, and equally little chance that what I needed would be on the top, where it could be easily spotted.

I was feeling around under the third register when my hand struck the familiar, oddly reassuring shape of a handgun. Normally, I would have grabbed it and shoved it into my waistband. Under the circumstances, all I could do was move it to the counter to serve as a reminder to myself to get it before I left.

A full box of ammo was shoved a little farther back on the shelf. I'd be much better prepared when I left here, whether or not they had sports bras in their gym section. That was a relief, if nothing else was right now.

The next shelf down was where I hit paydirt. A flashlight. Not just a flashlight: a good heavy Maglite, the kind that seems to have been genuinely designed to double as a melee weapon. I pointed it away from me, held my breath, and flipped the switch.

A strong beam of battery-eating light shot out and illuminated the floor. I stopped holding my breath and started laughing instead, giving the Maglite a hug. It was heavy and awkward and fully charged. It was going to save me.

I left the gun on the counter, along with the knives, and made my way deeper into the store. I still wasn't finding any minds in here with me. If I was wrong, I could club anyone who attacked me with my new flashlight, which was now my favorite thing in the whole universe, and would likely stay that way until I got a bra that fit.

The store was large enough to be confusing when seen by a flashlight's beam, with multiple long aisles terminating in end caps and table displays. Almost everything had the school's red cyclone logo on it, and it was all colored red and black. I was going to look like a Carmen Sandiego cosplayer when I finished raiding the place.

And I didn't care. Looking like a cartoon art thief was better than continuing to run around in my nightie. The first section I found was athletic gear: sweatpants, sweatshirts, and best of all possible outcomes, *sports-bras*. They wouldn't be as good as the real thing, but they would take away some of the ache. I grabbed one of each in what I guessed would be my size and kept on moving.

Socks were one aisle over, along with sneakers that apparently retailed for seventy dollars, but felt about as high-quality and worthy of the investment as the canvas shoes at Target. Whatever. Just holding them made me feel better about my chances of surviving this with the remains of my sanity intact.

I wandered deeper into the store, looking for a changing room, and found something better: a rack of chips, candy, and other shelf-stable snacks, next to a small cooler, dark without electricity to power it, filled with bottles of water, soda, and Gatorade. I shoved my ill-gotten gains onto the nearest shelf and grabbed a double-handful of chips and individually packed nuts, ripping the first bag open with such force that potato chips flew everywhere.

In the moment, I honestly didn't care about making a mess. All my focus was on shoving chips into my mouth, enjoying the small luxury of calories. Potato and salt and artificial sour cream flooded my senses, and I kept digging deeper into the bag, until there was nothing left. Only then did I stop and catch my breath, suddenly realizing how exposed I'd been during that little episode.

The bell over the door was still silent. I was alone. I took a deep breath, tucking the rest of my stolen snacks under my arm, and retrieved the clothing I'd gathered from the shelf. I'd have to come back for some beverages before the salt turned my mouth into a desert biome, and it would probably be a good idea to find a backpack and fill it with chocolate for Annie and the others, except for Mark. Not that he didn't deserve snacks: no one should have to "earn" food, and even enemies deserve snacks. But cuckoos are allergic to chocolate, and "here, have something that could kill you if you're not lucky" didn't feel very friendly to me.

I was trying to build new bridges, not tear down the few that remained. I moved still deeper into the store, and was rewarded with changing rooms that reminded me not to go in without an attendant, and not to bring more than five pieces of apparel with me. Well, the rules were suspended for now. I opened a door and stepped into the deeper dark on the other side.

Nothing lunged out of the shadows. I relaxed marginally as I dumped everything I'd gathered so far in a heap before pulling my nightgown over my head and throwing it on the floor. I never wanted to see it again. I honestly didn't know where it had come from in the first place. Ingrid, probably, since I'd been in her custody when my clothes were changed.

It didn't matter now. A lot of things that would have felt very important not all that long ago didn't matter. They were artifacts of another time, another life . . . another world. What we had now was what we had to deal with, and we were going to survive it, or not, based on what we did now.

I was still filthy, but the clothes I put on were clean, baggy in the way of collegiate athletic gear, but close enough to fit correctly. The smaller of the sports bras I'd grabbed was *too* small, but the next size up fit perfectly, and I could grab another on my way out. I stepped into the sneakers and out of the dressing room, Maglite in hand and snacks under my arm, feeling much more prepared for the apocalypse.

Which was naturally when the hollowed-out cuckoo that had followed my light lunged out of the shadows and grabbed for me. The sound of the bell must have been muffled by the dressing room door, allowing it to sneak up on me.

I hit it in the head with my Maglite, and when that wasn't enough to knock it down, I hit it three more times, until I heard the distinctive sound of bone giving way. It was a meaty crunch that was somehow impossible to describe and completely predictable at the same time. My flashlight beam wavered but didn't die. The cuckoo wobbled but didn't fall down. I hit it one more time, and it fell, collapsing motionlessly to the floor.

If one cuckoo had found me, more could be coming. I needed to move. I stepped over the broken cuckoo, playing my flashlight across the shelves, until I found a backpack. Like everything else in the store, it was black and red. I grabbed it anyway, stuffing my snacks inside, then turned to head back toward the snack section and grab several more handfuls, as well as multiple bottles of lukewarm water, Gatorade, and soda. Caffeine would help us all function better, although not as much as calories would.

People need to eat, drink, and sleep to stay alive. Everything else is negotiable. I slung the backpack over my shoulder and hurried to the front of the store, collecting my knives, gun, and box of bullets from where I'd left them. I also grabbed a spare pack of batteries. Keep the Maglite alive at all costs, as it was both guide and weapon, and who doesn't like a multipurpose tool.

That was about as much as I felt comfortable carrying, and so I paused to look out the window for signs of motion, then stepped out the door and back into the world.

The sharp formic-acid scent was still clinging to the wind, although it wasn't as sharp as it had been during the day; heat probably made it rise out of the ground. I glanced around, both visually with my flashlight and mentally, and found no signs that I was being observed, so I set out across the quad, back toward the lawn I'd cut across from the cafeteria.

It felt like I'd been gone for hours. Rationally, I knew it had been less than half an hour, if that; it wasn't like I'd been lingering over my choices as I looted a student store for overpriced school mascot gear. I couldn't even feel bad about the petty theft. We'd already stolen the entire school. What was a sports bra and a pair of sweatpants compared to that? I felt much more mentally centered, and like I might be able to tolerate my own allies without screaming.

I turned off my flashlight to conserve the batteries once the starlight was bright enough to let me see without it. The nice thing about the lawn: it was a wide sweep of open green, and I'd be able to see anyone approaching with relative ease. I relaxed, enjoying the fact that I couldn't feel the grass between my toes, or the gravel and small rocks digging into the soles of my feet. Especially, I enjoyed the fact that I was wearing a damn bra, and could no longer feel the distracting motion of my breasts whenever I moved at any speed higher than a stroll.

I love superhero comics. I've been reading them since I was a kid, and while they have their share of wicked telepaths, they're also the only place where I can consistently see people like me—both psychics and bug-girls with inexplicable mammalian features—presented as "the good guys" in any sense of the phrase. And the only thing I *don't* love about superhero characters is the way all the female characters run around in skin-tight spandex that somehow lacks the compression to act as a decent sports bra, and then go home and lounge around their secret base in a tank top that offers no support at all. I assume every superhero team in existence has an Olympic-level masseuse on staff, because otherwise none of the female characters would be able to stand up straight. Bras are *important*.

And still nothing moved around the corners of my vision, until I reached the cafeteria and the sound of voices from the other side of the building told me I was approaching my destination.

"—run off like that," Annie was saying, a peevish note in her voice. "It's irresponsible."

"She's a cuckoo queen," said Mark. "She can take care of herself."

"You're the one who said you don't know exactly what that means," countered Annie. "Maybe Queens physically explode if they get too far away from their hives! Maybe they drop dead after a certain period of time. We don't *know*."

"It would solve some problems, if we didn't need her to translate," said Mark.

"Which she can't do if she's dead," said Annie. "The mice know her, and she fights like she's one of us. She's telling us the truth. That means she's family, whether we remember her or not. We'll just pretend she's the new James. Everyone handled it fine when I came home and announced I had a new brother and everyone was going to accept him or else."

"Because you were *terrifying*," countered Artie. "You showed up after being missing for *months* with a new boyfriend and a new brother and a wild-ass story about *killing the crossroads* and frankly the new brother was the most believable part of the whole story."

"So let me be terrifying again," said Annie. Her voice dropped. "Sarah is my cousin, because I say so, and I'm the terrifying one. That means you will all treat her with the respect and protection family deserves."

"You can't force us to like her, no matter how loud you yell," said Artie.

"I wouldn't even try," said Annie. "But you can dislike someone and still be polite to them."

"I don't know about that."

"Try." There was a pause, and then she called, "You know how you make a sound in our heads when you get too close? Like someone's playing a theremin right on the edge of my hearing. It's not annoying, I get used to it fast, but I know you're there. You can come out."

If I'd already been caught, there was no point in staying out of sight. I walked around the curve of the building. Annie and the others were still there—*all* the others. Artie's new cheering squad was arrayed behind him, polearms at the ready, looking for all the world like they were prepared to defend his honor against a cold, unfeeling universe. Mark stood off to one side, looking uncomfortable.

Someone had taken my absence as an opportunity to

pile the dead cuckoos into a massive, horrifying heap. Somehow a mountain of corpses with my face didn't make me feel any better about the situation.

Annie nodded when she saw me. "I figured you went to get changed," she said. "Feel better now?"

"I found shoes," I said, as if that were the most important thing that had ever happened in the history of things happening, as if I couldn't have looted a dozen pairs from the mountain of corpses. *And a bra*, I added, on a private, no-boys-allowed line of thought.

I felt her smile, even though I couldn't quite decode the expression on her face. "Good for you," she said. "Are you feeling recovered enough to translate yet?"

"I will be if Mark goes into the cafeteria and sweet-talks them out of a fresh bottle of ketchup," I said. "They should have them in the kitchen." People are incredibly unhygienic where condiments are concerned, and while I can't catch most human diseases, that didn't mean I wanted to put my mouth on something someone else had already licked.

Mark sighed. "On it," he said, before turning and walking into the cafeteria.

"Find anything else good in the student store?" asked Annie.

I held up my Maglite. "*And* I got batteries," I said, before shrugging out of my backpack, unzipping the main flap, and pulling out a handful of Snickers bars. "Chocolate for the mammalian weirdoes."

"Bless you," said James, who had been sitting with his back against the cafeteria wall. He staggered to his feet, looking almost like a zombie himself as he shambled toward me. His brain waves were still smooth and normal, so I didn't flinch away, but held my ground as he swiped three of the five Snickers bars and shambled back to the wall, already beginning to unwrap them.

"He burned a lot of calories while he was *dumping his own core temperature* past all safe limits," said Annie without rancor, strolling over and plucking the remaining candy bars from my hand. She tossed one to

Artie as she passed him, and he snatched it out of the air without a whisper of gratitude. She sighed.

"You know, just because it took more out of us to keep you from dying horribly, that doesn't mean you need to be a butt about it," she said.

"I didn't ask you to fry or freeze yourselves," said Artie. "We were doing just fine."

"Because we were keeping half of them from reaching you," snapped Annie. James didn't say anything, being too busy shoving chocolate into his mouth. "Even Sarah did her part. You would have been swarmed without us."

One of the strangers jabbed their polearm at Annie, saying "Incubus," in a tone that implied she was doing something wrong by speaking harshly to their new hero. Annie responded by rolling her eyes and turning her back on them.

"It's been like this since you left," she said. "Arthur's new cheer squad doesn't like us when we raise our voices to him—even though he's *being an asshole*—and one of them threatened to stab Mark until I took their fauchard away. Which reminds me, I have a fauchard now." The polearm in question was leaning against the wall next to James. Since all the strangers were visibly armed, I had been assuming it belonged to the one who'd died. It was good to know it had already been claimed.

"They're not my cheer squad," said Artie. "They're making me really uncomfortable."

"We can't explain that to them when the word we have in common is 'incubus' and they say it like a creepy snake cult getting ready to reset the altar for the next sacrifice," countered Annie. "Hopefully, Mark gets back soon with the ketchup, so we can get the translation going again."

As if on cue, the cafeteria door opened and Mark emerged, carrying a large squeeze bottle of ketchup.

"They don't know why we needed this for the LARP, but they were happy enough to hand it over," he said. "None of them followed me."

"Cool. Most people don't get excited over a mountain of corpses."

"Eh, they'd believe they were props. I whammied them but good." Mark walked over and passed me the bottle. "I hope this is what you wanted, princess."

"Not my favorite brand, but it'll do," I said, and popped the lid, squirting a stream of thick, over-sweetened ketchup directly into my mouth.

It tasted like Thanksgiving dinner and the hot pretzels from the carts in Lowryland and my mother's pancakes, all at the same time. It was the best thing I'd ever eaten, and as I swallowed, I realized that everyone was watching me. I took my time filling my mouth with ketchup again, swallowing a second time, then pulled a bottle of blue Gatorade out of my backpack.

"Oh, my God—please tell me she's not going to mix those," moaned Artie.

His broadcast disgust took a little of the pleasure out of the first sip of fruity electrolytes, but not enough to keep me from finishing the bottle. I tossed it aside— we'd already covered the lawn in corpses, so what was a little littering?—and turned my attention to the clustered strangers, who were watching me with bemused wariness, untouched by the horror and revulsion coming from my relations. Mark wasn't disgusted. Mark was envious, having forgotten to grab a bottle of ketchup for his own purposes.

No one knows quite what quirk of cuckoo biology makes us like tomatoes so much. Evie thinks it's something to do with the chemicals responsible for their color, but I'm not sure I agree, since the color has never mattered to me. Tomatoes are ambrosia, plain and simple, and having a bottle of ketchup made me feel like I was ready to take on the world.

I dropped the shields I'd reconstructed and reached out, trying not to get distracted by the mental states of my allies. James was exhausted, and his thoughts were worrisomely jagged around the edges, like he'd stuck his finger in a light socket and was trying to shake off the aftereffects. Annie wasn't quite as tired, but was definitely not up for another mob attack. Mark was basically fine, having held himself back from the conflict as much as possible.

Artie . . . looking at Artie was like trying to see my reflection in a broken mirror. He believed me. That should have been a good feeling, but his belief that I was who I claimed to be was entangled with his belief that I was the reason he'd never been able to get out of his room and have a real life. That was partially my fault for showing him the birthday party, but it was also a cruel confirmation that I made the lives of everyone around me worse. Not the sort of thing I wanted to have confirmed, even if I had literally always suspected it. Now he was surrounded by strangers who said "Incubus" like it was a catechism and who wanted to worship him as much as he was willing to allow. They were freaking him out, but they were doing it in a familiar way that made him feel less unmoored—and weirdly, even angrier at me.

But that was a problem for later, when we got home and had time to worry about little things like who approved of who and who wanted who to go away. I steeled myself and plunged into the mind of the stranger I'd been speaking with before. She was as alien as the rest of them, but at least I'd started the process of building a rapport with her. It felt like it would be less traumatic, and while I was definitely recovering, I was still wrung out from the telekinetic tricks with Annie's knives.

The woman—and she was definitely a woman by the standards of her species, and thought of herself accordingly; now that I was attuned enough to her to perceive her pronouns, it seemed ridiculous that I'd ever missed them—was doing her best to suppress her reaction to Artie's pheromones, which had been getting more difficult to resist the longer she spent in his immediate presence. So not only female, but a mammal in the true biological sense, and attracted at least partially to men, since Lilu pheromones aren't powerful enough to completely override biological predispositions or self-determination. Elsie learned that when we were all teenagers and she was still figuring out her lesbianism. She's a succubus whose natural abilities mostly attract men, and she only wanted to attract women.

But she got more than her fair share of those and was able to dodge a few girls in high school and after who thought they "might" be lesbians and wanted her to be their lab partner for any experimentation they were willing to undertake. Two of them she'd turned down politely but firmly when they didn't react at all to her chemical attraction. A third, she'd taken around the block sixteen times before the end of the weekend, and left her swearing off men forever.

For all that I'd been in love with Artie for most of my life, it had never been due to his pheromones. We were too biologically different for them to work on me. It was because he'd been sweet and thoughtful and kind, and he'd shared his crayons when we were little and his colored pencils when we were bigger. He'd cared. That was all I'd ever wanted him—or anyone—to do, was just to . . . just to care about me without it being because I'd forced him or controlled his mind or tricked him into thinking I was someone I wasn't. I'd just wanted him to care. It had been easy enough to tell myself that everyone'd who'd been on that trip to Lowryland, where the deaths of my first family had pushed me into a level of broadcast strength no cuckoo child was supposed to possess, had been somehow whammied by a compulsion I hadn't even known I was projecting. But Artie hadn't been there. Artie hadn't been in the path of any influence I was projecting, not until later; not until I'd been stable enough not to do that to anyone else.

I had loved him for not being influenced by me, and he'd loved me at least partially for the same reason, even if he'd never been able to quite believe his pheromones didn't impact me. That had been one of his greatest fears, and the knowledge that he might be influencing these strangers without their consent was making him uncomfortable enough that it was amplifying his existing discomfort with me.

We'd have to deal with that later. I plunged back into the stranger's mind, digging until I found something that felt like a coherent sentence. Their language was getting easier to understand; the more exposure I had, the more that ease would increase. *We can talk now,* I thought, willing the words to translate themselves for her.

She jerked absolutely upright, eyes going wide as she turned to me. She asked a question in her own language, all clicks and hard stops. I nodded as I repeated her words in English, "Are we able to communicate again? You will translate?"

Yes, I informed her wordlessly.

Her excitement was immediate and obvious. She clapped her hands, managing to make a sound despite the polearm she was still holding, and turned to inform her companions of the situation. Then she looked back to me and spoke again.

"We should call our—the word is complicated, it means 'steeds' and 'friends' and 'vehicles' all at the same time—and go, this place is not safe for much longer," I translated. "The smell of death will attract hunters in the dark." I paused to make it clear I was speaking for myself, and not her, when I continued: "I don't know what 'hunters in the dark' are, but I don't think they're something we want to mess with. She's really worried about them. This sounds like a good time to go."

"Where do they want to take us?" asked Annie analytically. "All the giant bugs we've seen so far could fly, so it could be a long way from here if we're not careful."

"Fair." I turned back to the speaker. *Where? We need to return here. This is a piece of our home. We hope to take it with us when we leave again.*

Her response was quick and prompt. I translated: "This is not a safe place when the night is deep. We live in a safe place. We would take you to see our patriarch. He is very wise and remembers the last time we had an

Incubus grace us with their presence. He will tell us what should be done."

I paused again before saying, "She doesn't feel like she means us any harm. This isn't a trap. She just really, *really* doesn't want to be here when the hunters in the dark show up, and she doesn't want to leave us by ourselves either—partially because her species has encountered Lilu before and apparently they really, *really* like them. I'm not catching any hostility or ill-intent, although I can't be absolutely sure I'd know what that looks like. Her brain is very alien to me. It probably will be for a while."

"Do you know what the deal is with all the creepy 'Incubus' stuff?" asked Annie.

"I'll ask." I focused back on the woman. *Why do you call my cousin 'Incubus' the way you do?*

What is cousin?

There are always concepts that don't translate across cultures. Wadjet have no concept of "divorce." Dragons have no concept of "fidelity." And a surprising number of cryptid species, even after years and years of dealing with the overwhelming cultural dominance of humanity, lack a concept of "personal property." I blinked.

Family—same ancestors—but not as close as brother and sister, I replied finally. It was overly simplified but close enough for my purposes.

Her interest sharpened, and she focused her attention more firmly on me. *You are Incubus also?*

No, only Arthur. The rest of us have different parents. Why do you keep calling him that?

Incubus came here once, long ago. Mated to our queen. Had many, many children, who grew tall and strong and helped us rise to dominance, helped us tame our first, and again that complicated concept that wasn't quite "vehicles" and wasn't entirely "friends." *His children are among us now. Our patriarch is among them.*

Well, that answered some basic questions about their biology in the most blunt way possible. Lilu have incredibly flexible genetics. They're cross-fertile with almost every bipedal species we've discovered. Not the synapsids, and not the reptiles, and not the bugs like me or the Madhura, but if it walks on two legs and has warm blood, the odds are good a Lilu can mate with it. These people were definitely mammals.

And if they didn't have a concept for "cousins," when she said his "children" were still among them, she could be referring to great-great-grandkids. That, or the incubus who'd come long ago had only been gone for a few days. I turned back to Annie.

"They've met an incubus before," I said.

"No big surprise, given their reaction. I take it he was a pretty popular guy?"

"Married their queen, had a bunch of babies—so even if they have a eusocial hive structure, they're not bugs."

"Not like you," said Artie, sharply.

"Yes, Artie, and wow, does knowing that removing myself from your memory turns you into an insensitive jerk make me feel good about how much of my life I've spent hanging out in your room," I snapped. "The point is that they're mammals, and some of them may be distant relatives of yours." It also meant the ones who weren't related to him were definitely vulnerable to his pheromones, but I wasn't feeling quite cruel enough to point that out. Not yet, anyway. Soon, if he kept thinking at me like that.

I don't necessarily know what it's like to be glared at. I can tell when people are looking at me, but my inability to visually read facial cues means I miss the heat they're trying to project, unless I'm also reading their minds. But right now, I was reading everyone's mind, and I could feel his glower. I didn't like it.

"Artie," snapped Annie.

"Whatever," he said, voice turning sullen as he stopped focusing his anger quite so intently.

I returned my attention to the leader of the strangers. *Do the children of the Incubus, any of them, speak our language?*

Some still do. You will have a better time of commu-

nication if you come. There was an air of desperation in her thoughts. *The hunters in the dark will be here soon. We must depart, even if we must leave you behind.*

Dutifully, I relayed this to Annie, who sighed and scrubbed at her face with both hands before she said, "All right. We're going with our new friends before more cuckoos show up, or these 'hunters in the dark,' whatever those are. Sarah, tell them."

"What about the people in the cafeteria? And the library?" asked Mark, sounding alarmed.

"If we stay here and die, we can't help them. If we leave, we won't help them, but we can pick up the pieces in the morning. Protect yourself, then anything innocent, then the rest. That's the rule," said Annie. "Sarah, *tell them.*"

"Yes, ma'am." *We will go with you.*

Wonderful. Do not be afraid.

I hate it when people tell me not to be afraid. They never do that when something awesome is about to happen. No one says "don't be afraid" and then hands you an ice cream cone, or a kitten, or tickets to Comic-Con. I backed away, putting myself next to Annie, as the woman placed her fingers in her mouth and whistled shrilly. The others in her group did the same, each producing a sound any second grader would have been incredibly impressed by, loud and high and intensely carrying.

It was actually surprising that a mammalian throat could produce that sound, and I was starting to wonder about the shape of their larynxes when I heard the buzz of wings growing steadily closer. The strangers stopped whistling, all save their leader, who trilled three short, sharp notes, like she was giving some sort of instruction.

The sound of wings got louder, and three of the massive mantis-things dropped out of the sky, landing in front of us.

Two were the standard green-brown kind that I'd seen in the garden, stalking around and chewing the heads off of smaller bugs. The third was larger and glossy black, like it had been welded out of wrought iron. It had a head like the blade of an ax, sharp and terrifying, and only getting more so as it bent forward to study us with one compound eye. The leader laughed and gestured for us to follow as she started toward the big black one. Naturally. If there were three large, frightening options for us to ride, of course the most frightening one was the one we were going to be using.

But these were still better, at least in the eyes of the locals, than the "hunters in the dark." That thought was enough to get me following the leader. She grabbed a swinging rope studded with fist-sized knots as soon as she got close enough, still gesturing for us to follow her even as she swarmed nimbly upward and swung her leg over the mantis' neck, settling into a saddle very much like the odd macramé one I'd seen on the millipede.

Annie was the next up the rope. I expected her to go up fast and easy, as befit someone who was trained on the flying trapeze, but she took her time about it, helping James along. As for James himself, he struggled despite the knots that gave him the handholds he needed, pulling himself laboriously along. Artie was behind him and pushed him up with one hand. Between the two of them, they were able to get James to the top relatively quickly, although not quickly enough for our new friend, who looked down and shouted something I didn't need to understand to interpret as "hurry it the hell up."

Mark approached the rope, looking at it dubiously. "I don't think I can do this," he said.

"Of course you can do this," I countered. "It's just a rope. Didn't you have to do rope-climbing in high school? It's a standard part of phys ed in Ohio."

"I dropped out halfway through my freshman year," he said. "My parents never noticed. They were busy taking care of Cici, and it wasn't like they saw anything I didn't want them to. I played a lot of video games instead. Not as good for the upper body."

"I don't think the giant mantis can help you up with its big stabby spear arms," I said.

"I know." Mark grasped the rope, looking unhappily upward. "I can do this."

"I hope so." The other strangers had climbed onto their smaller mantises and were looking at us, thoughts judgmentally concerned. The hunters in the dark were coming. Whatever they were, we didn't have much time left before they got here, and if we didn't hurry, we were going to meet them.

Somehow, I didn't think I was going to enjoy that much. I stepped up behind Mark as he started trying to haul himself up the rope, reaching out with both my hands and the newly activated telekinetic part of my abilities to boost him upward.

"Careful there, Handsy," he said, smirk audible in his voice. "Or I'll start to think you want to repopulate the Earth with cuckoos when we get home."

"Ew." I managed not to recoil. It wasn't easy. "Keep your hormones to yourself."

Mark laughed and kept pulling himself upward. I kept pushing as long as I could, until he was outside of my reach, then stuffed my Maglite and ketchup bottle into the backpack and started climbing after him. It didn't take long before my head brushed against the sole of his foot and I had to stop.

"Can you go any faster?" I asked.

"I'm a psychic, not a circus performer," he snapped. His voice was shaking a little; just enough to betray his growing exhaustion. We were less than a third of the way up the rope, and I wasn't certain he was going to be able to hold on long enough to make it to the top.

Which was, naturally, when the mantis leapt into the air. The rope jerked and swayed with the motion, and Mark yelped, nearly falling off. One of his hands actually lost its grip, leaving him dangling. I didn't pause to think before mentally clamping down on his waving hand and using telekinesis to jerk it upward, slapping it back against the rope.

Thankfully, he grabbed on immediately. I let go,

focusing on keeping myself from falling now that he felt stable.

Sarah, what the hell? he demanded wordlessly.

You were going to fall. You're welcome, I countered. *Annie? What's going on up there?*

We've still got a pretty big language barrier to worry about, so I'm not completely sure, but she seemed to see something, and she tapped on the big bug's head. I'm guessing that was the signal to take off.

I looked down. The campus was a starlit sweep below us, dwindling rapidly as our steed gained altitude. I didn't see anything moving, until abruptly I did.

It was like stop motion animation. The thing didn't move so much as it had moved, going from one position to another without any of the natural transition between gestures. The overall effect was jerky and staccato, like I was looking at something that wasn't entirely real.

But then, that's probably the best way to think about looking at a spider easily the size of a city bus.

Form-wise, it was probably closer to a wolf spider than anything else, massive and hairy, lacking the smooth body and elegant legs of a garden weaver. It reared onto its back legs, waving its front legs in the air like it was somehow tasting the vibrations of our departure, and then it leapt, as effortlessly as it had done everything else so far. It simply . . . stopped being on the ground and appeared in the air only about ten feet below our current position.

I'm not proud. I screamed, clutching tighter at the rope. Mark screamed, too, but he couldn't clutch any tighter than he already was. He scrabbled instead, like he thought seeing a really big spider right below us would suddenly given him the upper body strength he lacked. I saw him start to fall and felt it at the same time, as he broadcast his mental panic on all wavelengths. If the spider had been telepathic, it would have fallen away, driven back by his fear. The mantis, which wasn't telepathic, but *was* considerably smarter, lurched as it flapped its wings harder, lifting us into the air, away from the spider.

Mark's panic was infectious, thanks to the way he was screaming it into our minds. I felt the fire gather in Annie's fingers as she prepared herself to attack an enemy she wasn't in any position to fight and felt the ice in James' veins responding to the same urge. I did the only thing my own rising panic and my rational mind could agree might help, gathering my thoughts under Mark and *shoving* upward just as hard as I could.

Cuckoos don't fly. But for the six feet remaining between him and safety, Mark did, soaring upward on a telekinetic wind that dropped him safely onto the webbing of the saddle and left me alone on the dangling rope.

His panic continued, and my grasp was slipping. I barely had time to form the thought that this was all happening much too fast, and I couldn't possibly be expected to deal with it until I'd been given a moment to sit down and process, and then I was losing hold of the rope, and I was falling.

I had nothing to push against—the ground was too far away for me to reach—and even if I had, I'd exhausted myself getting Mark up to the saddle, and there was nothing I could do but watch the others get smaller as I toppled toward the waiting jaws of the giant jumping spider.

Thirteen

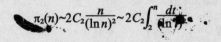

$$\pi_2(n) \sim 2C_2 \frac{n}{(\ln n)^2} \sim 2C_2 \int_2^n \frac{dt}{(\ln t)^2}$$

"There's no such thing as 'getting what you deserve,' because none of us are born deserving anything. We get what we work for, and we don't always get that. The universe is fickle. We just have to keep on going."
— Jane Harrington-Price

Falling. Which is pretty straightforward, as these situational updates go. Just . . . falling

THE WIND WAS COLDER than I expected, cold and aggressively harsh against my skin. I closed my eyes to shut out the sight of the panic above me, and raised my shields to shut out the sound of Annie and the others frantically trying to find a solution. I didn't want to die with Artie thinking "Serves her right" or something equally awful ringing in my ears. So I put it all aside.

Physics seemed to work here mostly the way it did at home. There were clearly a few differences in things like the square-cube law, but since Annie could throw her fireballs without vaporizing us all, it wasn't fully suspended. I spread my arms like I was performing a swan dive, hoping the increased resistance would slow my fall, and spared a moment to be brutally relieved that I wasn't falling to my death wearing nothing but a nightgown.

I fell forever. I fell for seconds. Then I slammed into something huge and hairy, like landing on a Muppet or in a field of fake fur, and my eyes snapped open. I grabbed fistfuls of the shag around me, trying not to wince from the grasshopper-sized lice hopping around my fingers, and stopped myself before I could slide down the slope of my landing place.

I was on the back of another giant spider, smaller than the first by a large measure but still the size of a draft horse, bigger than any spider had any business being. I swallowed my scream, tightening my grip. This was terrible. It was better than falling to the ground, and without a neck, the spider didn't have the flexibility to turn and bite me off of its back.

Spiders may glide, but they can't fly, and as I realized where I was, suddenly neither I nor the spider were there anymore. It had landed atop one of the university buildings, and was bringing up one of its rear legs to scrape the annoying intruder away. I rolled to the side, still trying to catch my breath and process the fact that I wasn't dead.

Overriding another creature's free will is the greatest sin the cuckoos commit. It had been drilled into my head since childhood that it was never okay for me to override someone else's choices. In that moment, I didn't care. The spider tried to scrape me off its back, and I did the only thing I could: I gathered my thoughts into a solid ball and slammed them into the rudimentary bundle of neurons it would have called a mind, if it had been that self-aware.

STOP THAT RIGHT NOW, I commanded.

The spider stopped. It froze with its leg still lifted in the air, posed to rub me off its head as soon as I let go. I took a deep breath and gentled my approach ever so slightly, trying to be less of a sledgehammer and more of a scalpel.

Lower your foot toward the center of your abdomen, I commanded.

The spider did, lowering the foot until it was close enough for me to grab hold of. *Transfer me to the ground*, I thought. The spider did so, moving more slowly and with more deliberate care than I would have thought possible. I clung to its foot until my own feet touched the rooftop. Then I let go and stepped back, putting a few feet between me and it.

Not enough. Given how fast I already knew the thing could move if I loosened my mental grip for even a moment, it would be on me before I could react. Was I too small for it to eat? No, that didn't make sense; I was the same size as the mantis-riders, and they had been afraid of the spiders. So while I might not be a full meal, I was definitely a potato chip, or something else a spider would think was tasty.

At least it wasn't the really big one. That didn't seem like much of an improvement right now, but I was confident that it was.

I am not food, I told it firmly. *I am not prey. I am not for you to harm.* It didn't move, just continued watching me with its many eyes.

I tried to feel what it was thinking, and found only confusion, primitive and incoherent, like the world was good because the world was always the same, and now here I was making things un-same. Different was dangerous and bad, therefore I was dangerous and bad, but I was not food, and for some reason it didn't fear me the way it should have feared a not-food thing. There were only five categories of thing in existence: self, food, mate, enemy, and terrain. I didn't fit into any of those categories.

It did at least recognize that sometimes a thing could be one type of thing, only to become another. A mate, for example, could become food or enemy at a moment's notice, if hunger came to either party. It was a male spider, and it had the vague impression, from the behavior of previous mates that it had failed to eat, that they might have a sixth category, a protect category, because when they went away to lay their eggs, they would drive males from the location they chose with violence that could go as far as killing the intruder. That was unusual. Females who did not wish to mate would generally leap

away and leave, or else attempt to corner and consume,
not fight directly.

I should have found a female spider, I thought grimly,
and dug deeper into its primitive mind, looking for the
switches that could send mother spiders into protective
mode. If they were hormonally-activated, they might
not be present, and then I'd be stuck standing here and
mind-controlling a spider forever. That would suck.

That was the motivation I needed to dig even deeper,
until I found a little complex of instinctive behaviors buried behind one of the few lessons it had absorbed over
the course of its lifetime—run away from things bigger
than you, or you will be consumed, and what was friend
before may not be friend now; the memory was accompanied by the image of another spider so much larger
than the self that I assumed it must have been the spider's mother, on the day her own instincts had stopped
treating the babies as things to be protected and started
treating them as things to be consumed. The memory
had faded. The trauma had survived, and probably survived for every new generation of spiders, all of them
unable to recall or learn from what they'd experienced,
allowing their instincts to play out the same scenario
over and over again.

Until that day, the mother had been dragging prey—
some of which looked dismayingly like the mantis-riders
now disappearing with my family—wrapped in silken
cocoons back to the lair to feed her brood of growing
spiderlings. They had filled their stomachs with flesh,
and spent their time learning how to use their natural
weapons, playing hunting games with one another, and
doing no harm.

That was the part I focused on. Back then, the spider
had been fully equipped to harm its siblings, born with
claws and fangs and venom. But until the day its mother
turned against it, it had believed it was safe, and had
treated the others the same. I gathered up the spider's
own feeling of safety, wadding it into a bundle shot
through with the spider's own perception of me, then fed

it back into the system, trying to build a connection between me and the idea that I was something to be kept
safe, something to be protected.

The spider seemed to relax. It was hard to tell, with
an arachnid the size of a Clydesdale, whether I was getting the effect I wanted or—ironically enough—trying to
judge it by mammalian standards. I stayed inside its
mind for a moment more, using the way the spider itself
saw safety and things-to-protect to connect myself into
instincts it didn't fully understand having, instincts that
would normally only have activated if it had stumbled
across an unhatched clutch of eggs with no matriarch to
provide protection.

When I had done all the work I could do, I pulled
back, still more than halfway convinced the spider
would eat me immediately if I relaxed my grasp on its
mind. Still, I had to take the chance eventually. I
couldn't stay embedded in its thoughts forever, and if I
tried, one of the really big spiders would come along and
eat us both, since my tinkering had the spider effectively
frozen until I let go.

It was time. I pulled back further, detangling myself
strand by strand from its rudimentary thoughts, hoping
the connection between me and protecting its young
would be strong enough to stand, even though this was
a spider too recent to adulthood to have raised spiderlings, or triggered those instincts the natural way. I had
never done anything like this before, and while the theory was similar to the memory manipulation I'd done in
humans, I was risking my life here.

Wincing, I screwed my eyes shut and let the spider go.
It was faster than me. If it wanted to pounce, there was
no way I could get clear before it struck. Maybe this was
where it ended for me. If so, I just had to hope Mark
would be able to attune to the minds of the strangers
enough to translate, learn more about how sorcery
worked in this dimension, and allow Annie and James
to open the gate that would get them all home.

I'm sorry, I thought, to no one. There was no one close enough to hear.

Something touched my hair. It was light, nonaggressive, putting out about as much pressure as a mother cat cleaning her kittens. The touch ran from my scalp to my shoulder before it lifted away and began again at scalp level. Cautiously, unwilling to risk any sudden motions, I cracked open my left eye, keeping the rest screwed tightly shut.

The spider was even closer now, barely a foot away, compound eyes focused on my face and pedipalps moving up and down in a slow staccato motion. It was stroking my hair with a foreleg, combing out the tangles with the hooked claws of its foot. I straightened, opening my other eye, and reached for its mind again, not to reclaim control, but to observe what it was thinking.

Mine, thought the spider. *Protect. Keep. Care for. Mine.*

I laughed out loud before I could catch myself. The spider flinched. I stopped laughing and tensed again, dipping back into its thoughts.

They were still possessive and paternal. I had managed to convince the spider that I was its natural responsibility, and taking care of me was the most important thing in the world, greater even than the pressing, ever-present need to hunt and feed. It would pass up prey if pursuing it would risk me getting hurt. It would set its own interests aside in favor of my own. It was an apex predator—maybe *the* apex predator of this strange world of giant insects and super-powered sorcery—and I had broken it, making it my own.

I couldn't quite find it in me to be proud of that as I took a step toward the spider, raised my hand, and stroked it—him—gently between the two largest clusters of its eyes. He couldn't close them, lacking eyelids, but he radiated pleasure and contentment at my touch, remembering a time when he had stroked his own mother in exactly that spot, reminding her of his scent and reinforcing the protective instincts that would see him through his first and most vulnerable molts into a life stage where he could begin fending for himself.

Great. So now in addition to being an invasive tele-pathic apex predator, I got to be a giant spider. "I'm sorry," I told him gravely. "I'm sorry I had to do this to you, and I'm sorry I probably won't have the opportu-nity to undo it. But we have to go now."

He didn't understand my words. I sent him an image of the flying mantis-things, soaring toward the horizon with my family along with the ride. Then I asked, in as basic of terms as I could manage, whether he knew where they went.

He did. Or at least, he knew where the bounds of their territory was, the point past which no spider re-turned. He didn't understand why I would want to go there. I wasn't controlling him so completely that he couldn't resist me, and I didn't want to; I was looking for a helper, not a slave. If I had to enslave him to get him to cooperate, I might as well let him eat me right now.

I told him, again, that I wanted to go, and he resisted, again, unable to understand why I'd want to go to a deeply dangerous place. Spiders who went there didn't come back.

I stroked his head again. "Yeah, I know. Many Bo-thans died to bring us these plans." He didn't want to go, but he wanted me to be safe, and I needed to go there. I pushed a little harder, asking whether he was willing to take me if I promised we would both be safe.

He didn't understand how something as small and soft as me could even dream of such an impossible promise, which it knew I would never be able to fulfill. But he wanted me to be safe and cared for, and he knew the mantises would eat me if he let me go on my own. The thought was graphic enough to make me cringe away, and included absolutely no acknowledgment of the fact that *he* had been intending to eat me not all that long ago. I was his now. He worried about me and wanted me to be safe.

Grudgingly, the spider agreed to carry me into what

he saw as another predator's territory. I stroked him between the eyes, sending feelings of gratitude and awe that he was such a good and powerful protector. Then I carefully, deliberately walked around him, moving out of what would have been a mammal's field of view.

The spider watched me go, my image simply transferring from one set of eyes to the next. All right, that was unnerving, but it wasn't necessarily a bad thing: I didn't need to disappear, I had just been hoping to confirm that my quick, cheap adjustment to his natural behaviors would hold once he couldn't see me anymore. Well, if I couldn't check my work, I'd just have to trust it.

Can you crouch? I asked, sending an image of a spider with its belly flat to the ground. The spider obliged, and I climbed onto his back, burying my hands to the wrists in the wiry hair of his shoulders. Were they shoulders? I didn't really know the terms for spider anatomy.

It didn't matter. I made sure I was as anchored as I could be, then informed him, *I'm ready.*

The spider leapt.

There was none of the muscular tension I would have experienced from a mammal of this size, no bunching or sudden feeling of impending motion; one second the spider was holding perfectly still on the rooftop, and the next he was soaring through the air, propelled by a powerful leaping motion so fast that it felt almost like I was attached to an out-of-control roller coaster.

They have this one coaster at Lowryland, called the Midsummer Night's Scream, that uses a rocket launch to go from perfect stillness to incredible speed in under a second. This felt like that, but better and worse at the same time, since there was no seatbelt or safety harness keeping me from flying off into the void. The urge to thrust my arms into the air and shout was almost overwhelming. I held out. The urge not to plummet to my death a second time was even stronger than the joy of the moment.

The spider touched down on a clear stretch of campus lawn, turning to orient himself. Two more spiders came around the corner of the building, both larger than the one I was riding, and his alarm resonated through his entire body, almost overwhelming me. These were big enough to hurt my spider, and more, they were big enough to make an easy meal out of me. And they were advancing toward us.

My spider could leap away, but bigger bodies meant more jumping power, and these two would likely follow, responding to the intrusion into their shared territory. How the spiders had already divided the campus into individual territories was a mystery to me, but as it seemed to make sense to my spider, I wasn't going to confuse us both by trying to have a detailed conversation about it. I sat up straighter, gathering the feelings of fear and rejection that I'd been marinating in since waking up tied to a chair and surrounded by people who should have known and loved me, and when I was sure I had created a toxic bludgeon worthy of the swing, I rammed it forward, away from me and my spider, into the two who were even now moving toward us, their appetites radiating outward.

The mental attack slammed into their primitive minds and sent them reeling, knocking the larger of the two off its feet, while the smaller staggered and collapsed, making an improbable mewling noise that reinforced the idea that the size of the local invertebrates was less about suspension of the square-cube law, and more about their development of lungs.

With the spiders distracted, my spider took advantage of the opportunity to leap away, springing into the air even more forcefully than he had before. The leap this time had less height but more distance, and when we landed, we were off campus for the first time.

Everything was gilded in starlight, silvery and unreal, making it difficult to look at the landscape without feeling as if we'd just leapt into Mordor, or someplace equally fictional. Mountains loomed to the left, high and jagged as a crocodile's teeth. Several were smoking, volcanoes preparing for their next great eruption. To the right was a seemingly endless forest, the treetops wreathed in cottony foam that I could recognize even at this distance and in this low light as cobwebbing. More spiders, then, a different type than this one, more ambush predators than active hunters.

That didn't make them any less dangerous. A thing doesn't have to pounce on its prey to be deadly; it only has to have the capacity to kill. The spider turned slightly, almost as if it were trying to get a look at the full landscape, then leapt again, away from the campus, threading the narrow line between mountains and forests. More spiders passed us, heading toward the campus, which must have been dropped right into the middle of their hunting grounds. It was the only way to explain the number headed in that direction, especially since none of the ones we'd seen had figured out how to get *inside* the buildings yet.

When they did, the people who were sheltering there would be easy prey, stars in their own abrupt, unplanned horror movie. I felt bad for them. They hadn't done anything to ask for this; they were just in the wrong place at the wrong time. But then, couldn't I say that about all of us?

I was in the wrong place at the wrong time and wound up adopted by a family of cryptozoologists, rather than going into hiding with an ordinary human family who would have nurtured me to be the perfect little cuckoo. The bomb in my head would have gone off at puberty, the way it was supposed to, and I would have been part of one of those concentric circles forming around the new queen, not the sacrificial lamb standing at the center and waiting to call my own mathematical death down on my own head.

The spider was in the wrong place at the wrong time, just following his instincts toward an easy meal, and instead of plucking a defenseless alien biped out of the air, he had managed to catch a predator even more dangerous than himself, losing control of his own mind and desires as I overwrote his will with mine. That was an uncharitable way of looking at my actions—I'd been doing what every creature does, and fighting to survive. Staying alive is not a crime. I still felt like I'd done something wrong as the spider landed, adjusted direction, and leapt again.

Something new appeared on the horizon. I sat up straighter, squinting. It looked like a skyscraper, almost, but organic, or like a mountain that had been pressed until it became impossibly tall and thin. The spider kept leaping, bringing the structure closer and closer, and casting its details into view. It was pale in color, irregular, reinforcing the idea that it was organic, with small openings in the sides.

We leapt close enough for me to see what looked like one of the giant mantids slip through an opening, tense, and launch itself into the air. I reassessed my idea of its size. It couldn't be that small if the mantids could fit inside.

The spider landed one more time, anxiety growing until it threatened to overwhelm my admittedly flimsy compulsion to take me back to the others. No one who approached the territory of the stabbing ones—the closest I could come to it having a name for anything, since he thought of the mantids by picturing the scything motion of their forearms—came back to known territory, ever. He didn't want to go any closer. He especially didn't want to take me any closer, not when I was so small and soft and had yet to go through the molts that would make me big and strong enough to fight for a territory of my own, to protect myself against a world full of things that would be happy to devour a delicate, underdeveloped spiderling like me—

His anxiety was threatening to become overwhelming. I projected soothing calm, trying to ease his concern. He wasn't going to get hurt while he was with me, I told him; I was going to keep him safe the same way he was keeping me safe. The mantids were my friends the same way he was my friend, and all my friends could be friends together if they would just trust me to make sure it was okay.

The spider wasn't sure, but he didn't have the logic or sense of coherent resistance to argue, and in short order, I had him calmed again, sufficient to take another leap toward the mound. That was what this structure was: a mound, like the termite mounds I'd seen on National Geographic specials, only massive to fit the insects that must have made it. It was made of heaped-up mud and insect feces, which was gross to think about, but probably not as gross as it could have been. True insect poop doesn't smell nearly as bad as mammalian or pseudo-mammalian poop, thanks to their simpler digestive systems. A mound of monkey poop that size would not only have been rotting, we would have smelled it all the way back at the campus.

The closer we got, the stronger the formic acid scent I'd noticed before got. So maybe we had been smelling the mound, it just wasn't as unpleasant of a smell. It didn't matter now. One more leap and the spider was clinging to the outside, trembling with the fear I hadn't been able to entirely smooth away. I leaned forward and stroked his head as soothingly as I could.

Hold still, I instructed it. *I'll find out where we need to go.*

I lowered my shields, extending my thoughts into the mound. Near the top, I found the edges of familiar minds, close enough that I could identify them, too far away for me to transmit anything other than a vague feeling of proximity. I thought I felt a pang of quickly-smothered excitement from Mark, but at this distance, I couldn't be sure.

Can you climb without jumping? I asked the spider. The answer I got was a hesitant, faintly offended affirmative. He knew how to walk. He wasn't a hatchling. If I didn't know that, he wasn't sure I could really be a spider—

I sent more thoughts of reassurance and calm, telling the spider we were safe as long as we were together, and nudged him upward, encouraging him to walk on the surface of the mound. I could stop any mantids I knew were there from attacking us, but if the spider started leaping and one of them struck fast enough to snatch us out of the air, I wouldn't necessarily have a chance to intervene. After everything I'd just been through, that was not how I wanted to die.

I tried projecting a field of "keep away—we are not for you to have" as the spider cautiously crawled up the wall of the mound, keeping the spider and myself sheltered from the feeling in a tight bubble of simple calm. Partitioning what I was projecting seemed to be getting easier. Which meant, apparently, that I was developing a specialization in mind-controlling bugs.

That would be less useful when we got home, but I was still more than fine with it, since "less useful" would still have some applications in my daily life, and it would also be a lot less intrusive than controlling people with fully formed identities and ideas. The spider continued to crawl upward, and whether it was my repelling field or coincidence, nothing attacked us.

The feeling of the minds I was looking for got louder, accompanied by the distant hum that always kicked in when I got close to people I was already attuned to. I started picking up their feelings. Annie was hopeful; James was relatively neutral, and a little more alert than he'd been when I fell; Artie was sullen and annoyed. Mark, unexpectedly, was jubilant. I guess the idea of being the only mature cuckoo who still had a mind hadn't been a very appealing one.

Their thoughts were coming from one of the highest chambers. I leaned forward, urging the spider onward, and it kept walking, freezing only when one of the mantids came idly strolling around the side of the mound.

Being surrounded by things that seemed to think of gravity as something that happened to other people made me appreciate how much Gwen Stacy's supporting cast had to hate her fondness for hanging out on walls. I froze, projecting my "go away and leave us alone" field even more fiercely at the mantid.

It cocked its head, looking at us first out of one eye

and then out of the other, not withdrawing, but not attacking either. I could feel the spider's tension increasing. It would jump soon, and then there would be no way for me to prevent any nearby mantids from getting involved in what would surely be an irresistible hunt.

Go away now, I thought, as firmly and loudly as I could. The mantis crouched lower for a moment, snapping open its wings, and then it was gone, launching itself into the air and flying away, presumably to obey my command. I hoped I hadn't just banished someone's favorite pony from the stable yard, and stroked the top of my spider's head again, whispering soft words of encouragement that he couldn't understand, buttressing them with thoughts of how strong and brave and good he was to have carried me this far, to be continuing on when I knew he was afraid. We were in a new place. This was the territory of the stabbing ones, and he was walking boldly, unharmed and unafraid! How mighty he was, how incredibly powerful!

I kept stroking as the spider resumed walking, holding on as tightly as I could when the slope got steeper, threatening to dislodge me. I've never been a big fan of push-ups, but I was suddenly glad that between Mom and Alex, I had resumed my daily workout long before I'd gotten on that plane to Oregon. My arms were starting to shake, the muscles in my biceps aching with the strain of resisting gravity for such a ridiculously long time.

Someone below us shouted. We'd been seen. The people who lived here had to rely on their mantis-friends to keep hunters like my spider away, letting their instinctive hunting behaviors stand in for most security precautions. It's what I would have done in their position. But now someone had looked out one of the openings, or else returned from a trip on mantis-back, and noticed a spider in their space. It wasn't a large spider as the hunters in the dark went, not based on the other spiders I'd seen. It was still large enough to kill a lot of people before anyone could puncture its exoskeleton and stop it.

I took a deep breath and redoubled my "keep away from us, leave us alone" field, urging the spider to move faster if he could, to get us to that top chamber where I could feel the minds of my friends. The spider was getting tired too, even if sticking to the wall didn't exhaust him the way it did me, and his answering thoughts carried a distinct flavor of weariness.

We're almost there, I informed him.

Sarah? Is that you?

The thought was Mark's, which made sense; he was the most likely to be able to gather and project coherently, since Annie and Artie had forgotten the years they'd spent practicing that exact trick. *It's me,* I replied. *I'm riding a really big spider. Can you please ask everyone to be chill and not attack us when we come in?*

A really . . . big . . . yeah, okay, I can do that. Mark sounded dubious. I couldn't exactly blame him for that.

Then the spider was reaching the opening we'd been crawling toward all this time, and poking the tips of his forelegs into the room. Someone screamed. I thought it was James, but it could also have been one of the locals. The spider froze for a moment, presumably waiting to see if there was about to be an attack before he committed himself to going all the way inside, and then he proceeded, through the opening into a room large enough to have held an entire roller derby practice with room around the edges for spectators.

There was light, provided by massive glowing grubs clustered on the ceiling, placidly munching on some kind of lichen. There was furniture of a type, rough-hewn from the local wood but still recognizably functional for all that it was basic. And there was my family, along with a large cluster of the locals, all still holding their polearms, which they were aiming firmly at me and my spider. It was difficult not to take that personally, even as I understood the reasons for it.

The light cast by the grubs was bright enough to let me see the people in more detail. They looked basically human in form—what Mom always calls "*Star Trek* alien," a morphology that's proven common across dimensions and cryptid species, thanks to the Covenant wiping out anyone who looked different enough to be an easy target—except for the pointed ears and the rosette spots on their cheeks, foreheads, and exposed arms, like the markings of a leopard. Their eyes were slightly too large for the human norm, clearly anchored in outsized orbital sockets, and colored in shockingly feline shades of yellow and green.

A few smaller mantids were with them, young enough to be only about the size of an ordinary human, and I took a moment to be grateful that evolution had decided my molts would be internal, instead of splitting my skin and increasing my size every time I grew.

You can stop now, I said to the spider. *I need to get down.*

He stopped walking and bowed so I could slide off of his back. My legs, which felt like they were made of jelly, protested the motion. I braced myself against the spider's side for balance, looking toward the group.

"Hi," I said. That didn't feel like enough, and so I added, "You dropped something."

Annie laughed, the sound choked-off and dismayed, like she couldn't believe this was happening. "We did," she said. "I'm sorry. We didn't mean to."

"Gravity happens," I said, still leaning against the spider. It was easier to understand what he was thinking when I was in contact with him. He was concerned about our situation, sure that the mantids and the strangers were going to attack at any moment, and he was going to fail in his mission to keep me safe. It was difficult not to feel a little guilty about that. I had subverted his natural instincts, and I'd done a thorough enough job that I wasn't sure what I'd done could be reversed.

"You, uh, seem to have made a friend," said James, somewhat anxiously.

"I did." Humans have an easier time treating creatures as individuals worthy of care and respect when those creatures have names that they can use to refer to them, rather than just "the lion" or "the wolf." The spider didn't think of himself by any specific label; he barely had a concept of "I," although he did understand that if he were to be devoured, he wouldn't exist anymore. I gave his head another pat. "This is Greg."

" . . . Greg," echoed James.

"Yes."

"The giant cannibalistic spider is named Greg," he said.

"I mean, 'cannibalistic' is accurate, since they eat each other, too, but I don't think we can exactly pass moral judgment on it for eating what's available," I said. "I wouldn't be happy if Greg had eaten me, but I wouldn't blame him either."

"Hard to be happy when you're dead," said Artie sullenly.

"Aunt Rose manages it pretty well," I said. "I sometimes wonder if she's discovered the ghost equivalent of heavy uppers. Anyway, I'm fine. Greg's fine. Please don't let your new friends stab my spider."

"I want to hug you and throttle you at the same time," said Annie. "Is that normal?"

"Usually you're directing that particular combination at Verity, but it's not unheard of," I said, and she laughed, and the world felt a little closer to normal.

It wouldn't last, of course. It never did.

Fourteen

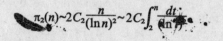

$$\pi_2(n) \sim 2C_2 \frac{n}{(\ln n)^2} \sim 2C_2 \int_2^n \frac{dt}{(\ln t)^2}$$

"Sometimes we have to rise above our natures. Sometimes we have to give in to them. At all times, the most important thing is telling the two apart."

—Angela Baker

Leaning against a giant spider at the most uncomfortable debriefing ever

MARK HAD BEEN ABLE to establish slightly more reliable communication with the strangers while I was away, sitting and staring at their surface thoughts until he could start to organize them into something he could start to understand.

"I still have a headache," he confessed, massaging his temples with his fingers.

"Poor baby." Annie elbowed him lightly. "At least you didn't suffer for nothing. Tell the girl what we've won."

Mark took a deep, long-suffering breath as I tried to quash my jealousy before either he or Artie could pick up on it. They were all so *comfortable* with him. Artie still looked at me like I was a monster half the time, and while she had decided to believe me about who I was, Annie also blamed me for stranding us here in a place we didn't know, where her sorcery threatened to burn out of control and overwhelm her if she loosened her grip for even a moment. I was a stranger and a threat to them, and Mark was the one who'd helped them to defeat the great cuckoo danger, which I at least partially represented.

It was enough to make my head hurt as badly as Mark's did. I let it loll until it hit Greg's side, the impact cushioned by the soft hairs covering his body. I was starting to feel pretty attached to this spider.

Although not to the lice still crawling through his wiry hair. They were too small and brainless for me to order away, although they were avoiding me for the most part. I wasn't a viable food source, but I might be a predator.

We were gathered in the room where I'd first arrived with Greg, the strangers off to one side, while my family and I—and Greg—all sat across from each other. Greg wasn't sitting so much as he was folded up like a complicated origami model of a spider, all his legs tucked underneath his body. The younger mantids had gone shortly after we arrived, too nervous in Greg's presence to remain.

"The people who live here—this is their home, they built it with the help of their cows, which we haven't seen yet, but I get the impression are sort of like termites the size of your spider there, or maybe slightly larger, which gets filed under 'terrifying' along with everything else in this dimension—are partially native to the area, and partially the descendants of the incubus they mentioned earlier," said Mark. "They've sent a group to find the elders who actually knew him, and might understand more English, which is going to be *such* a relief. The way people think is affected by the languages they speak, and their language is weird as hell."

"Weird how?" I asked, suddenly wishing Kevin were with us. Out of everyone in the family, he's probably the closest we have to a cryptosociologist. He likes studying sapient but nonhuman cultures, and handing him a whole language to dig into would have been enough to make up for a decade of missed birthday presents.

Not that I've ever missed a birthday. When you can read peoples' minds, you know exactly how important their birthdays actually are to them, and you never get them the wrong present. I've been helping Annie and her siblings buy gifts for their parents and each other since I was twelve. It's always felt like one of the few truly positive applications of my abilities.

"They don't really seem to have a sense of time as anything immediate," he said. "Everything is happening either now or a long, long time ago. I'm not actually sure how long it's been since they met an incubus. Long enough for him to have grandkids, at the very least, but maybe not any longer than that."

"Huh." I closed my eyes. "Greg's getting hungry. Do you think we could have one of those ceiling grubs?"

Mark's thoughts turned apprehensive. "I can ask," he said.

"Please do."

There was a pause before one of the strangers began speaking, sounding annoyed, if not quite angry. Mark sighed.

"She says the ceiling grubs are vital workers who will grow to be cows, and your hunter in the dark is a dangerous monster that should be destroyed."

I opened my eyes and sat up, putting one hand possessively on Greg's side. "Yeah, well, your giant mantises are scary as fuck and should be destroyed, too. I'd send him out to hunt on his own but I'm afraid they'd eat him before he could get back to me. He's my friend, he got me here when you left me behind, and no one's going to destroy him."

"I always knew that one day someone would temper the hunters," said a new voice, older and deeper than any of our own. The accent was odd as well, probably because the speaker's first language was the clicks and whistles of the locals. I turned.

A tall man stood in the tunnel entrance that would have led us deeper into the mound. He wasn't all that old; based on appearance alone, I would have placed him around Kevin and Evie's age, although that assumed these people aged the same way humans did, which was a big assumption. He was wearing a patchwork robe that appeared to have been stitched together out of the casings of giant beetle wings, and the spots on his face were paler than any of the others had been. His eyes, instead of being bright and feline, were a pale, pleasant orange, almost exactly the color of the daytime sky.

"When our mind-speakers said they were going into seclusion to avoid another seeking mind, I didn't expect it to be one of the heartless ones," he said, tone not wavering as he looked at me. His eyes flicked over each of us in turn, finally settling on Artie. "Two humans, two Johrlac, and an Incubus. That's a story waiting to be told if ever I've seen one. Do you wish to tell it to me?"

"Who are you?" I asked the question almost before I realized I was going to speak, scrambling to my feet. Greg, picking up on my surprise, unfolded himself and stood, looming next to me as six feet of solid, vaguely menacing spider. I patted him on the back, trying to calm him down, but kept my eyes on the newcomer.

"My name is Kenneth," said the man. "My grandfather gave it to me before he left us, saying he had been long enough in this dimension, and had need to continue on his quest. He traveled with others such as you, and with a woman who had no scent—she was the only other I ever saw stand next to a hunter in the dark unscathed and unafraid, for it could not find her—who became a great and glorious beast when she entered her battle rage. They came here by mistake, guided by a predictive ritual the Johrlac had designed which said our dimension would be the next target of their misplaced fugitives."

Mark and I both straightened. I spoke first. "Wait—when you say Johrlac, you mean *actual* Johrlac? Like, from Johrlar?"

"From the cradle of your kind, yes," he said. "They were born to the hive, and the three who traveled with my grandfather did so at great personal cost to themselves, for they knew they would never be able to go back when their quest was done. Their minds would have drifted too far from the harmony of their kind, and they would no longer be welcome, but would be fugitive in their own right, little better than those they came pursuing."

Mark and I exchanged a sharp mental glance. What kind of prison dimension was Johrlar, if falling out of synch with the hive mind was an offense worthy of banishment? Maybe finding a way to get back there wasn't a good idea after all.

"How did he get wrapped up with them?" asked Annie delicately.

"My grandfather was a good man, eager to see the universe made better than it was. He had made the acquaintance of his human companions in their home dimension, and they met the waheela woman who traveled with them as she was fleeing from a place known as the High Arctic. They were a close-knit group, virtually a family, and when they met the Johrlac who claimed our dimension was next to be attacked by the heartless ones who had become such a plague on their shared home dimension, they agreed to aid them."

Kenneth stopped then, saying something in the local language to the others. His grasp of English made the process of translation easier; I could follow his thoughts, which included his statement in both tongues. *Watch them, for we do not know the nature of their heartless ones.* I broadcast his meaning to Mark, who nodded solemnly, but didn't protest. Kenneth had no reason to trust us, and as warnings went, it was a small, simple one, well within the bounds of understandable caution.

It was still enough to make me tense against Greg, not taking my hand off his back. If we needed to fight our way out of here, we were going to want him with us.

"Their equation opened the path to this world, but they had no numbers to take them back to Earth again, and they were dismayed beyond all telling to realize that they were here too early by many, many years. Time is not always aligned between dimensions, it seems, and not enough had passed for us, or perhaps too much had passed for them." Kenneth shook his head. "The heartless ones set themselves to working the equations that would let them travel onward, and my grandfather began preparation for the war to come. He took three mates from among our kind, calling them his wives, and fathered many children, all of whom he taught what was to come, and that preparing our people to resist would be our sacred duty. He taught us how to recognize the people he called 'cuckoos,' who differed from his heartless ones because they had no mercy, no compassion, and no eternity."

Eternity? I asked Mark.

I think he means soul, said Mark.

Ah. Lots of people think cuckoos don't have souls, and they like to share that belief, loudly, because in their eyes, it explains the way some of us behave. Of course, we do terrible, awful, unforgiveable things! We're soulless monsters! Of course, it's fine to kill us when we get in your way! It's not murder if we don't have souls! Never mind that even my dead aunts don't know whether the soul actually exists, or what it would look like if it did; it's a convenient excuse, tied into centuries of religious dogma and self-justifications. And now here it was in a whole new dimension, one that had yet to reveal its religious leanings, if it even had them.

"She," Kenneth pointed to me, "is Johrlac, as they were Johrlac. He," and he pointed to Mark. "is not. You harbor a cuckoo among your kind, and we will do you the great and glorious favor of removing it for you."

He snapped his fingers, and the strangers were suddenly in motion, surrounding Mark in a circle of bristling polearms and visible aggression. Annie leapt to her feet, hands already burning. Kenneth blinked at her, impressed.

"Get the *fuck* away from him, he's ours!" she snarled.

"He may have convinced you of such, sorcerer, but I

assure you, he is no such thing," said Kenneth. "He is a monster walking like a man, a hunter in the night, and he has not been tamed. We will remove him for everyone's benefit."

"You know, where we come from, people call incubi like me, and like your grandfather, and like you probably, if you inherited anything from him beyond a decent grasp of English, monsters," said Artie. "Humans like to dismiss anything that isn't exactly like them as monstrous. It's ridiculous, it's cruel, and it's unfair. Get your people to stand down."

James stood more slowly. I was too far away to tell, but from the way the grubs on the ceiling above him began to shuffle uncomfortably to the sides, I was willing to bet the temperature of the surrounding air had started to drop precipitously.

"Sorcerers," said Kenneth, with thoughtful approval. "We have your kind among us, and one of the humans who traveled here before was a sorcerer."

The fire in Annie's hands went out. "Really?" she asked. "What was his name?"

"It was one of the women," said Kenneth. "She called and twisted the wind like it was a woven thread, and threw it where she so desired. She said the power of our dimension was stronger than her own, because something in her world had been draining their magic for generations."

"The crossroads," said Annie. "They're not a problem anymore." She slumped slightly, wilting.

I could understand why. She'd hoped, for a moment, that we had a new lead on where Grandpa Thomas had gone, a new direction we could tell Grandma Alice to follow. And instead we had one more dead end, one more avenue that had closed itself off before it could properly open.

"Her name was Betsy," continued Kenneth. "She left with the others. All of them left, save the one Johrlac who did not survive the mathematical working to open their new doorway."

I straightened. "What do you mean?"

"Uh, guys? Still being menaced here," said Mark. "If you nice people could all lower your stabbing-sticks, I would really appreciate it."

"Stand them down," said Annie, her hands reigniting. "We're leaving, too, and we'll take him with us when we go."

Kenneth sighed, saying something in his own language. The others stepped back, lowering their pole-arms. They didn't feel happy about it.

Feeling . . . "Incubi are empaths," I said. "They feel the emotions of others. Artie's half-Incubus, and he can feel what other people are feeling."

"Whether I want to or not," muttered Artie.

"Can you feel other people's emotions?" I pressed, eyes on Kenneth.

Kenneth stiffened, looking obscurely as if he'd been caught doing something wrong. "We do not intrude on the minds around us so," he said. "That is the place of mind-speakers, not Incubi."

"Incubi aren't mind-readers," I said. "Neither are Succubi, their female equivalents. But you can't help what you feel. Do you feel other people's feelings?"

Reluctantly, Kenneth nodded. "I do," he admitted. "Not as strongly as my mother did, but I cannot help myself. It has been an endless source of shame for me."

Interesting that empathy, and not sex pheromones, were what he considered shameful. I wondered whether he would have felt that way if his culture hadn't been exposed to Johrlac on a cuckoo-hunting expedition. That's not going to be the sort of first encounter that leaves you with warm feelings toward any psychics you encounter later. Although his people had psychics of their own, which made things more complicated.

It's impossible for cultures to meet without impacting each other. Even if they come at things from a position of perfect equality, there are going to be bits and pieces left behind. In this case, the incubus who'd started this whole thing had left a lot more than a few prejudices and a family recipe: he'd left literal genetic material, tying these people permanently to his mission. And they still hadn't been able to stop the cuckoos from breaking open the walls of the world and coming through when the time arrived, dropping an entire college campus on a world that could never have been properly prepared.

"Then try to feel what Mark is feeling," I said. "See if he's hostile."

"Um, right now, feeling pretty hostile," said Mark. "Just so you know. Not comfortable with any of this, not really in a charitable state of mind."

"Anger and annoyance feel different than malice," I said.

Artie turned to look at me. "That's a pretty narrow distinction for a cuckoo," he said.

"Yeah, well, my cousin the Incubus and I used to spend afternoons indexing feelings so we'd be able to identify them quickly and know if someone posed a potential threat," I said. "It was something we could both do when we were needed in the field, without endangering or overexerting ourselves."

Artie's cheeks flushed red as he turned his face away, resolutely not looking at me.

Kenneth took a step toward Mark. "I will look at your feelings, if you agree I may," he said. "And if I am wrong, and you are not here to harm us, I will release you with your companions when they are allowed to go."

"Wait, we're prisoners?" asked James.

"You may," said Mark warily. I couldn't blame him. Kenneth clearly thought he was humoring us—the feeling was radiating off him so loudly that I didn't have to make any effort at all to know that—and thought all he was going to find when he opened himself to Mark was a monster.

To be honest, I understood why he had that impression. Mark was even more of an aberration than I was, and if you'd asked me a week ago whether I'd be willing to defend a cuckoo's motives, I would have laughed and denied it was even a possibility. Kenneth had never met a cuckoo before. He'd met the Johrlac who traveled with his grandfather, though, and I was sure they wouldn't have had anything nice to say about us.

Kenneth stopped an easy five feet from Mark, raising one hand in a beckoning gesture. I blinked. No one else moved, especially not Mark, who looked at Kenneth like a mouse looks at a cat, radiating fear and wariness. Kenneth held that pose for about twenty seconds before lowering his hand and offering Mark a shallow bow.

"I must apologize," he said. "I find no ill-intent in your feelings, nor desire for revenge or mayhem. You will be free to go with your friends."

"Again, are we prisoners?" asked James, a little louder.

"Not prisoners, but it is unsafe to walk the world alone when the hunters in the dark roam the fields," said Kenneth. "We have driven them back as far as we could, but your mound appeared in the middle of their ceded hunting ground, crushing many of their matriarchs, and they are angry."

I glanced at Greg, who hadn't been angry when he leapt after us, just hungry and defending his territory from intrusion. "I don't think they're angry," I said. "I think they're just animals, and it's not fair to act like them being animals is somehow personal."

"That may be," said Kenneth. "But they are still a danger, and does it matter if the thing which devours you means it personally?"

Even I had to admit that it didn't. Kenneth took a breath.

"You are not prisoners, sorcerer," he said, to James. "You are our guests, until it is safe to return you to your own mound. Will it remain where it now is forever, do you think?"

"No," said James. "We need to go home, and we need to take the campus with us if we possibly can. I'm pretty good at research. Do you have any notes from the travelers who came here before us?"

Kenneth radiated a brief, sharp spike of surprise before nodding and saying gravely. "We do."

The notes were kept in another, smaller room, the ceiling studded with more of those glowing grubs. We had seen them on the walls as we passed, the locals shying away from Greg, even as he followed me placidly, as tame as it was possible for a mind-controlled giant spider to be. I hoped I'd be able to undo the damage I'd done to his mind when the time came for us to go. If not, maybe I could convince Kenneth and the other locals to let Greg live here with them. Not perfect, but what really was.

Annie gasped as we stepped into the room. Two of the walls were lined with bookshelves, laden with clearly homemade books, their spines stitched with silken thread that looked a lot like spider silk. A third wall had been turned into a primitive chalkboard, paneled in slate and covered in mathematical notation. I drifted toward it, enthralled by the little bits I could understand.

This was Johrlac math. Not the damaged, neutered equations they'd allowed to go with the cuckoos when they were banished, but real Johrlac math, the result of a culture built on spending centuries carefully refining their mathematical magic. I caught my breath as Mark stepped over to join me, both of us staring enraptured at the possibilities in front of us.

"I don't even know what that does," he said, gesturing toward a line of numbers and symbols, including several I didn't recognize. They appeared over and over again across the chalkboard, incorporated into multiple problems. "Do you?"

I squinted at it, starting at the solution and working my way backward. "Brief change to the local laws of physics," I said finally. "Run that equation and you can invert gravity for a few seconds."

"So what's the downside?" he asked.

"Get it wrong and you'll liquify your lungs."

"Huh. So probably not the best stupid math trick to start with."

"Nope."

Annie and James descended on the bookshelves like intellectual locusts, pulling down books and flipping through them, beginning to argue about their contents in almost the same breath. I smiled. At least they were happy. Looking over my shoulder to Kenneth, I said, "If you can trust us without an escort, this should keep us busy until morning."

"You truly believe you can return your entire mound to its universe of origin?"

"I don't know," I said honestly. "Bringing it here required more brainpower than we have left, and I might hurt myself very badly trying to shift it again without all those minds to buttress mine. But it's worth the attempt. Your dimension doesn't deserve to have us littering like this, and my dimension deserves to get its children back."

"Children?"

"The, uh, mound is a place we call a university," said James, looking up. "A school for ongoing education. We send our adult children to universities to learn how to be better adults. Some of those children were in the mound when it transitioned to your world."

"Why would any parent allow someone else to have the teaching of their children?" asked Kenneth, sounding confused. "We apprentice only with those we know and trust intimately, and our children do not leave the mound of their parents until they are fully adult and ready for the world. They never need to learn to be 'better.'"

"Chalk it up to cultural differences," said Annie. Unlike James, she didn't look up from the book in her hands, preferring to focus on something she didn't already know. "Do you have any other intelligent species living in this dimension?"

"There are people by the big river on the other side of the uncrossable forest, which was more permeable once, before the hunters in the dark claimed it as their own," said Kenneth. "According to my grandmother, who had been there with her own parents in her youth, they were not like us in form or function, and lived most of their lives below the water in harmony with the great snakes, even as we and the mind-speakers share our lives with the patient ones."

"You mean the mantises?" asked Annie. To get her point across she raised her head and took one hand off the book she was holding, mimicking the stabbing motion of a praying mantis arm.

Kenneth nodded. "My grandfather and his companions called them that as well."

"Okay, well, you know how these river-people had a different way of living than you do? And so did your grandfather and all the people he brought with him? Those are what's called cultural differences. Sometimes, the rules are different for different people. Sometimes, what's rude or cruel or just outright wrong for one person is exactly the way things ought to be done for someone else. And in our dimension, for better or for worse, humans are currently culturally dominant, and we say children who are old enough to be considered adults but have not yet finished learning everything they need to know for successful adult lives should go to school to spend time learning more things, and preparing themselves to become full members of society. Not everyone does it. Some people get by just fine without a university education, or do all their studies remotely, using machines that let them talk across a great distance, or drop out because everyone around them is stupid and they're tired of pretending to be somebody they're not. Legally, the people in our mound are adults, but the people back home still think of them as children, and we're not leaving them behind."

"They're not all adults," I said, still studying the chalkboard. "The cuckoo kids are there, too."

"There are more cuckoos in our dimension than just this one?" Kenneth's thoughts darkened, concern and anger rolling off him like storm clouds.

"Oh, we're here because your grandfather was right," said Annie. "The cuckoos *were* planning to make your dimension their next target, and they *did*, once they finished getting their demonic ducks in a row. It just took longer than his Johrlac friends thought it was going to. I guess they had an overly-optimistic view of how quickly the cuckoos were going to finish sucking our dimension dry. So they forced one of their own through all the instars they needed to make her a queen, and then used the boost that gave her to work the equation they had for travel between dimensions."

"It was nothing near as elegant as these," I commented. "The fact that Earth has such a low magic level compared to this dimension may have been a factor. They needed more oomph before the ritual could even start to work."

These equations had a full field to tap into. They were designed to be scalpels, not hammers, meant to make smooth, clean cuts that would heal without scarring, open without tearing. We could use this math as the foundation for a clean escape. It wouldn't be easy. It wouldn't be painless. And the longer I looked at it, the more I wondered whether it would be something I could survive.

I've always been pretty happy to keep living. I like being alive, and Rose and Mary aren't guarantees for me that existence continues beyond the grave the way they are for everyone else. They represent an afterlife that may not be available to me, and I have things I want to do. I want to solve more unsolvable math problems. I want to find out how long it takes Marvel's narrative inertia to overwhelm Hickman's reboot the way it did Morrison's and return the X-Men to their everlasting status quo.

I want Artie to fall in love with me again. And not in that Disney movie way where he cradles my cooling corpse and confesses that he never really forgot me, he loved me all along, he never wanted to live without me. That's fine if you're already thinking about the inevitable Broadway musical, but that's not my life, and looking at these equations, I could tell my life probably wasn't going to last much longer.

Do you see what I see? asked Mark silently. He didn't gesture at the chalkboard, but he did turn to look at me, adding the weight of his physical gaze to his mental one.

I do, I said. There was no point in lying. He hadn't undergone the royal instar. He couldn't work the math. That didn't mean he couldn't understand it. I cleared my throat, looking back to Kenneth.

"We want to take everything we brought with us back to our own dimension," I said. "*Everything.* That includes the cuckoo children. They're too young to be your enemies, and they're only here because they were forced to be. They miss their homes and their families." The ones who still had families, anyway. Most of them were going home as orphans, and might never recover from the trauma of what they'd experienced.

And all that could be dealt with later. For right now, I just needed to keep Kenneth from thinking the presence of other cuckoos in his dimension was something that he and his hive should be trying to deal with.

He met my eyes, projecting irritation at me. I got the distinct impression that as their patriarch and the eldest living descendant of their nameless Incubus wanderer, he wasn't accustomed to being contradicted. He didn't like it.

Finally, he looked away and said, "We couldn't hunt them now if we chose. Not without facing the hunters in the dark. If the children do not survive to suns' rise, it will not be because of us."

I shot a quick thread of thanks to Greg, who responded by lifting one foot and stroking my hair. His hunger was growing. It would be difficult to stop him from going after the grubs before much longer.

"Understood," I said. "And while I understand that you don't want Greg to eat your grubs, he needs to eat *something.* Can you please find us some creature your larders can spare so my spider can eat before he decides James is extraneous to needs?"

"Leave me out of this," said James.

"Sorry, James," I said. "Just trying to get some Mc-Donalds for my arachnid pal."

James turned to Antimony. "My life was never this weird before you came along," he said accusingly.

Her answer was a beatific smile, accompanied by a radiant smugness that made her expression fully comprehensible. "I know," she said. "Isn't it wonderful?"

James sighed and went back to flipping through the book in his hands.

"I will find you one of the honey-makers," said Kenneth, somewhat sullenly. "Hunters have been known to risk their own lives to take them, so I must assume they are a delicacy to the monsters."

"Thank you," I said.

He turned to go, and Artie followed.

"Hey, where do you think you're going?" demanded Antimony.

Artie looked back at her. "There's nothing for me to do here," he said. "I'm not a math nerd, and you and Jimmy have the magical research sewn up. Without a computer, I'm useless. So I'm going to go learn more about this incubus, and the warnings he left about the cuckoo invasion. I'll be safe." His tone turned as sullen as Kenneth's. "I won't leave the mound or put myself at risk."

"I appreciate that," said Annie. "Your mom would have my ass if I let you get hurt."

"Yeah, well, we wouldn't want that, now would we?"

Kenneth left the room. Artie was only a few steps behind. I sagged, trying to hide it as I turned my eyes back to the keyboard.

"You're not a great liar, you know, which is funny as hell, since cuckoos are normally amazing liars," said Annie. "What's wrong?"

"Nothing," I replied, and pointed to a calculation. "Mark, what do you make of this?"

"I make it utterly incomprehensible. You're the one who gets the weird science magic parts of all this; I have normal math. Tame math. Math that doesn't try to eat me when I do it." Mark sighed. "She's not wrong. You're a terrible liar. Something's bothering you."

I turned to stare at him, annoyed and betrayed in equal measure. He knew what was bothering me. He could read enough of the math for that. But I went for the answer Annie *didn't* already have. "The most important people in my life—the ones who cared enough to follow me through a rift in space in order to keep my biological mother from turning me into a dimension-buster bomb—have *forgotten who I am*. Deciding to believe me doesn't change the fact that they're treating me like I'm someone they just met, because to them, that's exactly what I am."

Mark's eyes flashed briefly white as he dipped below the surface of my thoughts, into territory I would have preferred to keep private. I didn't resist. It wasn't fair that they couldn't keep me out; as long as he wasn't trying to influence me or dig for things I had buried, he deserved as much access to my mind as I had to his.

He pulled back, eyes going blue again. "You love him," he said wonderingly. "And he loved you. You spent your whole life in love with him."

"I really don't want to talk about this."

"But you have to—you're grieving, and that's going to impact the way you work this equation." Mark jabbed a finger at the blackboard. "This is describing an emotional state. The mathematician is supposed to divorce the hive for a week before they do the math, and settle their thoughts on solitude and serenity, to make it possible for them to commune with the universe. If you're not serene when you go into this equation, I don't know what's going to happen."

"I do," I looked back to him. "I'm going to have to fight every step of the way not to let it burn me out, because it's going to want to consume me. But you're right. I've loved him for my entire life. I fell in love with him when we were children, and I never let myself believe anything could come of it, because I'm a fucking *cuckoo*, and if he loved me, it was because I wasn't giving him a choice in the matter. Love you have to compel someone to feel isn't love, it's submission. I didn't want him to submit to me, I wanted him to *love* me. And he did! He did! He loved me for as long as I loved him, and he never said anything because he was afraid that if *I* loved *him*, it would be because of his pheromones forcing me to fall."

"That's impossible," said Annie. "Your biology is too different from ours. Lilu pheromones don't work on Johrlac."

"And Johrlac influence doesn't work on the descendants of Frances Brown," I said. "I couldn't passively make him fall for me any more than he could accidentally make me fall for him. We fell for each other because we were good for each other, and he finally told me he loved me right before I deleted him. The version of Arthur Harrington-Price who loved me is gone, because of something *I* did. He told me to do it, but I'm still the one who pulled the metaphorical trigger. How would you be feeling right now if Sam forgot who you were, hated you for messing with his head, and was never going to love you again? How would you be coping?"

"I sold myself to the crossroads to save his life," said Annie slowly. "I would not be coping very well at all."

"There's no love in this equation." I waved a hand at the blackboard. "There's a lot of emotional involvement with the math; that's part of what's missing in the broken version, like the cuckoos forgot how they were supposed to feel about every step in the process."

I'd wondered how we could be the children of exiles who knew so much about where we'd come from but were missing so many essential pieces—like how to find the way back home. Ingrid had given me a lot of the information I was missing when she'd explained the instars and how Mom had so carefully scooped the packet of embedded history out of me. When you're born knowing everything your mother knew, just waiting for the day that knowledge will spread and blossom like a flower in the corners of your mind, it's hard for things to get lost. And I had unwittingly figured out the rest of the answer, by removing so much essential knowledge from my allies in order to protect them.

"When the Johrlac pushed the criminals who would become the cuckoos out of their dimension, they wrapped their minds up the way I did yours, and they cut out all the things they didn't want them to remember. They cut the dimensional-transit equations, and they cut most of what's been written on this board. They were trying to strand them, and if they couldn't manage that, they were just going to make sure the cuckoos could never fly back home, no matter how much they wanted to. Taking out what they did changed us from Johrlac into what the cuckoos became. But math is in our blood. We're insects, even if we don't look like it, even if we look more like college students. They couldn't take all the math without husking the exiles out the way I did the cuckoos I dragged into my equation. And if you leave a naturally mathematical species with the building blocks for their own salvation, they'll figure it out."

"We just didn't do it very well," said Mark.

"I don't think we ever could have," I said. "I don't know what our ancestors did wrong, but they weren't exiled intact. They were modified by people who had already made up their minds about them, who thought they were criminals who couldn't feel compassion or remorse, and those assumptions impacted what they removed. I thought the equation was going to kill me, and I wanted to reduce the amount of pain I caused in death, so I removed myself from the memories of the people I was trying to protect. Meaning . . ."

"Meaning if the Johrlac thought the proto-cuckoos could never feel for anyone else, they would have guaranteed that became true during the conditioning to expel them from their home dimension," said Mark slowly. "And the nature of the history we get when we're born means we've been getting the echoes of that psychic damage this whole time. We have to scoop the memo-

ries out of those kids. We can't let them go through their
instars the way I did."

"You turned out okay," said Annie.

"Barely," said Mark, and spun to face her. "I spend so
much time trying not to focus on how easy it would be
to kill you all. Or how much easier it would be for me to
find a way home if I just left the fucking campus and all
the people I don't give a damn about behind. I am a
reasonable facsimile of a person who knows how to care
about other people because Cici needs me to be this
man. Everything I am, I am for her, and she's a human
girl who walks in the world humanity made, which
means she's at risk every minute. You can't appreciate
how much effort I'm putting into being calm right now,
and not screaming for you to get me home even if it kills
every single one of you. I don't know what happens
when she's old enough to start dating. I don't know if I
kill the first person she brings home, or if I rewire her
brain so she only wants to be with me—and I don't know
if I'm going to do that while we're both asleep, when
neither of us has a choice about what I'm doing! I. Don't.
Know. I'm not a better man, I'm a slightly less immediately terrible monster, but I have the potential to be so
much worse. We can save these kids from being the kind
of monster I am. We can give them back the choice the
Johrlac took away when they kicked our ancestors out
of their home dimension. This is how we start to heal
the remnants of a species."

"That's a good speech," said James, sounding faintly
stunned. "You come up with that off the top of your
head?"

"I've been thinking about it for a while," admitted
Mark. He turned back to me. "We have to spare them."

Not save, because he really had turned out okay by
the standards we applied to most cuckoos, but spare.
And what is our duty to the children of any species if not
to spare them unnecessary harm? I nodded.

"If we run the numbers right, I think we can make
that part of the ritual that gets everybody home," I said.

"Good." Mark turned back to the blackboard. Annie and James went back to their books. And we all set ourselves silently to our respective areas of study, working toward an end that wasn't going to be soft or easy, but was coming, one way or another, and couldn't be put off much longer.

Fifteen

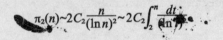

$$\pi_2(n) \sim 2C_2 \frac{n}{(\ln n)^2} \sim 2C_2 \int_2^n \frac{dt}{(\ln t)^2}$$

"The difference between sacrifice and slaughter is consent."

—Alice Healy

Standing in front of a blackboard, looking at the place where it ends

MARK WAS A PHENOMENALLY gifted mathematician, which made sense; all cuckoos are gifted mathematicians compared to the human norm, and most of my study experience has been with humans. He made intuitive leaps that surprised me, skipping from one side of the blackboard to the other with ferocious speed before asking for my interpretation of a symbol or conditional operation.

And even Mark being a phenomenally gifted mathematician couldn't change what the numbers were saying, which was that I wasn't going to survive this second equation. It had been constructed by three Johrlac, all properly trained and experienced in the magic of our species, and their design, while it was cunningly balanced to keep too much of the cognitive load from falling on a single person, had still resulted in one of them burning out and dropping dead before they finished running the numbers.

Mark could help me, but he was just one man. Two is not as many as three, and the basic math of our situation dictated that this equation would have costs. If he'd been at the same instar as me, he might have been able to take the lead on the actual math, and with it, the bulk of the metaphysical weight. But he wasn't. That job was reserved for me, and me alone.

I could look at the numbers and symbols in front of me and see the exact moment I died. It wasn't a pleasant exercise. I guess it would have been even worse if it had been.

There was a thud as Annie snapped a book shut. "Betsy documented the entire process as it was supposed to happen," she said, a note of excitement in her voice. "She couldn't document the actual ritual, but she wrote down the way it was supposed to go."

"She was from Kansas originally," said James. "Do you think there's something that ties our elemental affinities from where we were born? I'm from Maine and I got cold. You're from Oregon, which is in the Ring of Fire, and you got flame. She's from *Kansas* and she got wind."

"Interesting question," said Annie. "Add it to the list."

"The list?" asked Mark blankly.

"Our grandfather is a sorcerer who managed to scrape together enough training by the time he met our grandmother that we don't know what his elemental affinity was," I said. "He's missing. His wife has been convinced for decades that 'missing' doesn't mean 'dead' since he disappeared, and she's been trying to find him. For decades. Annie has a list of questions to harangue the poor man with when he gets home." I glanced over my shoulder at her. "Accurate?"

"I'm going to introduce myself before I start bombarding him with questions," she said. "Otherwise, yeah, accurate. If anyone can help us start filling in the gaps in what we understand about magic, it's going to be Grandpa Thomas."

"Huh," said Mark.

"Do you have enough to help us set this up?" I asked. "Because the math as originally designed is for a doorway large enough to accommodate a small group of people, not an entire college campus, and I don't know that you can help us modify the equations."

"I'm smart. I took calculus."

"Really? Okay." I read off a line of the equation, choosing one that wouldn't immediately vaporize or transform anything in the room. The air still grew thick as cornstarch mixed with water, becoming difficult to breathe, and all sound stopped, save for my voice, which changed timbres, sounding suddenly heavy and portentous. Greg waved his forelegs in the air, distressed. I stopped speaking. The air snapped back to normal as I turned and smiled sweetly at Annie.

"So do you think the exponential of the third modifying function should be double or . . . ?"

Annie put her hands up. "All right, point taken. We won't mess with the math. It's going to take a while, but we should be able to set the boundaries of the ritual to encompass the campus."

"Okay." The original math had been for less than a dozen people and it had still killed one of the mathematicians responsible for enacting it. I might not just be looking at my own death; this could kill Mark, too. "Or we could gather everyone up, take them home through an essentially unmodified version of the original equation, and leave the campus here."

"If we have to, we'll do that," said Annie. "I'd really rather not if there's any way around it. This is massive destruction of property. It's going to be hard enough to keep the Covenant from using this as an excuse to invade North America. Maybe if we put it back where we found it, people will believe this was all a hoax, and stop screaming for blood."

"Does the Covenant have the numbers for that?"

"Not really, but they have the zealotry," said Annie. "The people I met in Penton Hall would be perfectly happy to die if they did it killing cryptids. And while they may not have the numbers for a full purge of North

America, they have more than we do. They could do a lot of damage before we were able to stop them."

I wanted to keep arguing with her. I wanted to point out the specific places in the equation where my organs were going to fail, the twists in the mathematical structure where my bones would shatter and I would collapse. I didn't. We were all being faced with an impossible situation, and she wasn't wrong—putting the campus back where it had come from could be the act that saved thousands of innocent lives.

Mark worked next to me, radiating fierce selfishness that tasted like honey on my tongue. He was by-God going to get home to his sister, he was going to get back to her, he was going to find a way to deal with all the problems he'd described earlier, and then he was never going to have anything to do with our family ever again. I envied him that state of blissful selfishness. It was inherent to the cuckoo condition, and Mom had taken it away from me when I was too young to consent. It had been the right thing to do—I would have been someone else if she hadn't—but sometimes I wished she hadn't left me with so much room to learn how to care about other people.

Maybe if I hadn't been trying so damn hard not to be a monster, I wouldn't have grown up to be a martyr. Too late to know now.

We kept working. Artie stayed gone.

Kenneth didn't return, but three more of the people who owned this mound—I wanted a name to call them so badly, something other than "the strangers" or "the natives," something that acknowledged we were in their space, where they had every right to be, but I didn't have the words—came into the room, carrying their pole-arms and leading something that looked like an aphid the size of a bear. Greg became visibly excited by its arrival, drumming his feet against the floor and dancing in place, never straying from my side. I put a hand on his side to calm him.

"Is that for my spider?" I asked, both aloud and in their heads, where they would hopefully be able to understand me.

They nodded and radiated their affirmative.

"Good. Thank you. He can handle things from here, but you may want to step away."

They took that as their cue to flee the room as they dropped the aphid's lead, leaving it standing placidly in the middle of the room. This was definitely giant insect-as-livestock: the thing was in the presence of a massive predator that wasn't bothering to conceal its hunger, or its intentions, and it wasn't flinching.

"You may not want to watch this if you're feeling squeamish," I said, dropped the stream of calming thoughts I'd been sending to Greg's mind. He leapt instantly, landing on the clear patch of ceiling that had opened above us. The grubs recoiled further, humping their way toward the edges of the walls. He ignored them. I'd been telling him for hours that they weren't food, no matter how much they looked and smelled like other things he'd eaten, and he couldn't have them anyway. Instead, he inched across the ceiling until he was directly above the aphid, which raised its head and made a worried squealing sound, finally appearing to recognize that it might be in danger now that it couldn't see the predator.

It never thought to look up. Greg dropped from the ceiling onto its back, wrapping his legs around it and biting efficiently down on the nape of its neck, shattering the exoskeleton and severing whatever nerves it had in place of a mammalian spine. The aphid squealed more loudly this time, and then went limp, collapsing. Greg remained latched onto its back, driving his fangs into its flesh and beginning to almost spasm, like he was trying to suck an overly-thick milkshake through a straw.

I wrinkled my nose and turned away. Mark kept staring.

"Sarah, your giant spider is *drinking* the big green bug," he said, sounding horrified.

"Yup, and that's why Peter Parker's life is secretly a horror movie," I said.

"What?"

"She's not wrong," said Annie. "Spiders don't chew the way mammals and most herbivorous insects do. They inject their prey with chemicals that liquify the flesh, and then they drink it. If Greg here were a weaving spider, he would have wrapped it in a web before he started to eat it. Since he's a jumping spider, he's more interested in striking fast and eating faster. I wouldn't get near him right now if I were you."

"I wouldn't get near him at all," said James.

"You're not afraid of spiders, are you?"

"Weirdly, yes, I am. I'm just not afraid of this one. It's too big to be real, and so my brain doesn't know how to deal with it. Like, I *know* that it's real, but it doesn't register that way with the fear centers of my mind. So I'm not freaking out."

"Cool." The conversation stopped. The sucking sounds continued. Greg was radiating waves of satisfaction and satiation, happy to be filling his stomach—assuming spiders have stomachs, and he wasn't filling some other organ; anatomy is hard—with liquified aphid. I turned my attention back to the math.

Artie didn't return. The numbers didn't get simpler. Mark and I both made corrections, smoothing out the rough edges of the formulation, pursuing something closer to perfect. Perfect is always the enemy of good, but sometimes we need to chase our enemies. Sometimes we need to pin them down and make sure they understand that we're on their tails, we're not giving up, we're never, ever giving up.

But Artie didn't return. The hours ticked by. Greg finished draining his dinner and returned to my side, folding his legs under himself and becoming a perfect statue of a spider, replete and content and willing to wait with me for as long as I needed to. His mind was too simple for me to mine for coherent memories, but I got the impression that a meal like the aphid wasn't a common thing for him; he normally had to fight off other spiders when he wanted to keep anything he'd managed to catch, and his small size meant he rarely got the first pick of the prey. He was satiated in a way that was very rare, and which only served to solidify his loyalty to me.

In my company, he could travel to forbidden territory and be protected, and now he was well-fed and safe enough to sleep off his meal. Such luxury for a predator was not to be discounted. I stroked the top of his head, wondering if this were proof that spiderlings could be domesticated if they were taken from the nest young enough. Maybe that would be cruel, but it also might make the locals stop hunting them quite so vigorously.

Not that I had any proof of actual hunts, only that they'd fight when their territory was encroached upon. Building a framework on suppositions and incomplete assumptions is just another way to be a monster. I didn't need to tell these people how to live their lives. I needed to get out of here, whether or not that cost me my own.

And Artie didn't return. One by one, the grubs on the ceiling flickered and went out, leaving the room no dimmer than it had been, since the light outside the windows was getting brighter as the suns began to rise. On a pile of pillows and shed exoskeletons, James snored softly, one arm thrown up and over his eyes. Even Annie was beginning to flag, her eyes barely focusing on the page in front of her. Mark and I exchanged a look.

"I think we're done here," he said. "I don't see any way to make this tighter."

"At this point, neither do I." I wanted to find the miracle solution, the single pivot that would change the outcome of the whole equation. "Annie, go ahead and go to sleep. I'm sure we're out of here on our hosts' schedule, whatever that is, and it's not like we're going to get much rest once this all starts moving."

"Oh, thank fuck," she said, and put her book back on the shelf before collapsing next to James, closing her own eyes. In a matter of seconds, her breath had evened out and she had become completely motionless.

Mark blinked. "She's already asleep," he said. "Does she always fall asleep like that?"

"I'm glad you're finally willing to accept that I might know things about my own family." I sat down, putting my back against the base of the blackboard, well below the level of the equations we didn't want to smudge. "Her parents started her combat training when she was six. That's normal for us. We all learn two things well before we reach our teens: sleep when you have the chance to sleep, and eat when you have the chance to eat. Everything else is optional, at least for a while, but if you don't have those things, you're screwed."

"Do you need a nap?"

I turned and wearily smiled at him, dropping my shields enough that he'd be able to feel the intent behind the expression. "I can't have one. I'm a Queen now, remember?"

"Yeah, but what . . ."

"We had to make a shielded room for me at the house when I turned thirteen, because otherwise everyone in range would wind up dreaming my dreams. You want to talk embarrassing? Try falling asleep on the couch when the boy you have a crush on is in the next room." One sex dream and Artie had been too embarrassed to look me in the eye for the better part of the summer. Maybe it wasn't entirely a bad thing that he'd forgotten our childhood together.

Except that a life is made up of every moment, not just the highlights. It's the burned eggs and the mistimed farts and the stupid comments and the little fights. It's the accidentally shared sexual fantasies. Wishing he could only remember the good bits would just poison any chance of finding our way to a new future of shared experiences and mutual memories. Sometimes I hate being the responsible one. Sometimes I hate being aware of the potential consequences of my every action. I groaned and let my head thump back against the blackboard.

"So you can't sleep without an anti-telepathy charm?" asked Mark.

"Right. Wait—where are you going?" He was rising from his place on the floor, walking toward Annie and James.

"Will she wake up if I touch her?" he asked, looking back at me.

"Wake up, and probably break your wrist before she realizes that you're not the enemy."

"Got it," he said, and angled toward James instead, sliding his hand into the other man's pocket. James made a sleepy snuffling noise but didn't move.

"Fun as it is to watch your first forays into pickpocketing, is there a reason you're stealing from a sleeping sorcerer?"

Mark held up his hand, opening his fingers so the anti-telepathy charm he'd taken from James' pocket fell and dangled on the end of its chain. I sat up straighter as he walked toward me, and when he dropped the charm for me to catch, I was already prepared.

"There." He sank back into his original place and closed his eyes. "Now you can sleep."

Except I couldn't, because there was no way the charm was active—they would have used it to shield James from me before I woke up, or in the cafeteria, or . . .

But the glass was intact, and the charm gave off the comforting cooling sensation of an active mental screen. Maybe they'd just . . . forgotten they had the thing for some reason, assuming they'd lost it, the same way I had, while Mark had remembered it. It was the first indication I'd had that maybe they didn't all receive the same memory extraction. For Annie, an anti-telepathy charm was a tool. For Mark, it was a way for his enemies to disappear and target him unseen. It mattered more to him.

This might work.

I wasn't currently exerting active control over Greg. I shifted positions to lean against him, sending out one last wave of comfort and safety before I looped the chain around my neck and the background noise of the world dropped away, replaced by only the sounds I could pick up with my actual ears.

No more thoughts, no more feelings, no more anything but a world turned soft and nonintrusive. I closed my eyes and the world dropped away even more, becoming the misty gray of dreams, and I sank into them, and if time passed, I didn't have to be aware of it anymore.

I woke to someone shaking my shoulder, and I couldn't tell who, or read their thoughts, or tell anything about them except that they were touching me. I opened my eyes, lashes gummy with sleep, and blinked until the room became clear.

The ceiling above me was both free of giant grubs and covered in a beautifully painted mosaic that had been concealed before by the bodies of our mobile light sources. The image showed a tall bearded man, two smaller figures, and three people who could have been painted from pictures of Mark and me—Johrlac apparently haven't experienced any phylogenic drift since they exiled the cuckoos. We would be able to blend perfectly into a crowd if we ever found ourselves in our ancestral home dimension. That was nice to know, even if I was pretty sure our arrival in Johrlar would be immediately followed by the formation of a large, angry mob.

The final figure in the fresco was a tall bear-wolf beast with bows incongruously tied in the fur above its ears. It looked terrible and ridiculous at the same time, like someone had given the artist conflicting notes. I blinked at it.

"That's the last group of travelers through here, isn't it?" I asked, turning toward the person who had woken me.

Annie nodded, pulling her hand away. "I asked Kenneth about it when I woke up, probably about an hour ago."

She turned her face back toward me, expression totally unreadable. "Mark told us he gave you an anti-telepathy charm so you could sleep without worrying about hurting anyone. I'm sorry I didn't think of that earlier. None of us knew James was carrying the thing."

"It's okay." And it was. Even if her memories had been intact, she might not have thought to turn me off like a malfunctioning printer just so I could close my eyes for a little while. I sat up, causing Greg to make an annoyed grunting sound—my giant spider was apparently still content to sleep, and no one was going to be shaking *him* awake any time soon—and stretched. "How long was I out?"

"It's hard to say, since I was asleep when you passed out, but I'm guessing around six hours, probably, based on what Kenneth said and the way people keep coming to the doorway to stare at your spider. He's been here long enough to be less impressive now, while still being something most of them have never seen up close and alive."

"Hear that buddy? You're the circus bear." I lowered my arms and reached for the chain around my neck.

Annie moved, catching my wrist before I could take the charm off. "Wait."

I stopped, blinking at her. "Wait?"

"Yeah, wait."

I blinked again, suddenly realizing that the three of us—me, my cousin, and the giant spider—were alone in the room. "Where are Mark and James?"

"They went to have breakfast with Kenneth and Artie. I wanted to talk to you before I joined them." She shrugged. "You know. While you couldn't read my mind."

I pulled my hand away from her, twisting it out of her grasp and lowering it to my lap. "You know I can't read your mind right now."

"That's sort of the point of you keeping that charm on." I could hear her amusement, even if I couldn't see it in her face.

"You also know I can't read your facial expressions when I can't read your mind."

"Grandma's mentioned that a degree of prosopagnosia comes with being a telepath who can't reach the minds around you," she said. "She's had to learn ways around it. I guess you never did?"

"I can't reliably tell people apart when I can't see their thoughts," I admitted. "Mark and James and Artie are all dark-haired males, and they're basically identical without their minds giving me a hint. I can tell who you are because you're the only bipedal female in this mound who isn't me and doesn't have spots."

"Good to know I'm recognizable by something other than what Sam calls my astonishing breasts," said Annie, again with a trace of amusement. "I can't read your mind either, you know. There are some references to mind-reading in Grandpa Thomas' journals, but I'm nowhere near confident enough to try those rituals yet. I'd probably make someone's head explode."

"Telepathy isn't as much fun in practice as it sounds in theory, anyway."

"So while neither of us can read the other's mind, I wanted to ask you a question." Annie looked at me steadily, and I didn't need to know how to interpret her face to understand that this was a deeply pivotal moment. She wasn't kidding around. "Sarah, that math you and Mark spent all night working on, it's described in the notes kept by the other members of the party. And they all understood, from the moment they realized they were trapped in this dimension unless someone could come up with a miracle, that miracles have costs. The Johrlac they were traveling with were apparently fine with the fact that running any equation they could come up with would result in at least one of them burning out."

"If that's what the books said, then that's what the books said," I said calmly. "I could read them for myself if I wanted to. Is there a question here?"

"Yes. Sarah, is doing the math the way they wrote it going to kill you?"

Mark and I had been staring at that blackboard for hours, silently trading suggestions and stabs at solutions back and forth faster than we could have spoken them aloud, and we hadn't found any mechanism of moving between universes—especially not with an entire college campus in tow—that wasn't going to create more strain than our minds could handle. If I didn't want it to kill us both, I was going to have to dump the whole load onto one person. I wanted to live. I wanted to live more than just about anything. But if I didn't, I had cut the number of people who would mourn for me virtually in half, and if Mark didn't make it home, his sister would wonder where he was for the rest of her life. We both had a choice to make here, but while I'd be choosing survival, he'd be choosing Cici.

I didn't know her, but from what I'd seen in his thoughts of her, I already halfway loved her. She was a terror, and a cuckoo's baby sister, and she deserved to get her brother back. So I did something I would have thought was impossible: I looked my cousin dead in the eye, and I lied.

"If we'd done it exactly as written, yes, but we've made some modifications. The variation we're planning to use should be perfectly safe. You don't need to worry."

Technically, the first part of that was true, but the rest was a blatant lie. Annie laughed, sitting back on her heels as I reached up and finally removed the anti-telepathy charm. Her relief washed over me in a warm wave.

"I'm so glad to hear that," she said. "I know we're all pretty messed up right now, but I don't want Mom to kill me for losing her sister here."

She was being completely sincere. "Why did you make me keep this on?" I asked, holding up the charm.

"It was just a theory. I figured if you couldn't hear the answer I was hoping for in my thoughts, you couldn't just say what I wanted to hear. But you gave me the answer I wanted anyway. I may not remember growing up with you, Sarah, but that just means I have a chance to get to know you, and if you were someone I liked before all this happened, I'm sure you're going to be someone I like now. I'm looking forward to having the chance."

She smiled, the expression reflecting in her thoughts. "Come on, let's get something to eat."

Without the charm, I could feel Greg's thoughts again. He wasn't comfortable being so exposed now that the suns were up, and if I left him alone, he'd go looking for a place to den up until dark. That would probably get him killed. "I think I'll stay with my spider," I said, offering her a smile in return. "He doesn't do well alone, and I'm concerned these people might kill him if they get the chance. Can you bring something back for me?"

"Sure. And now that the suns are up, we can head back to campus and get to work setting up whatever you need to run that equation and get us home." Annie was perky as she bounced to her feet and made for the door. "I'll be back soon, with whatever serves for scrambled eggs around these parts."

"Got it," I said weakly. I managed to keep smiling until she was out of sight. Then the expression crumbled like the façade it was. I slumped against Greg, putting my hands over my face. I'd known they were going to figure out I hadn't been honest about the risks as soon as the ritual got properly underway. I'd known I was going to be taking those risks onto my own shoulders as much as possible, sheltering them from the damage I was preparing to do. I'd known I couldn't use them as storage and extra processing power this time; there was no telling what I might delete. I had to rely on the resources I had, which meant me and Mark, and of the two of us, I was the more expendable.

Was it even reasonable to bring an intact cuckoo queen back to Earth? I'd become something I didn't fully understand, and like Annie with her fiery fingers and James with his frost, I needed training, but that training wasn't available for me the way it was for them. I'd just break everything if I went home.

I might not be Annie's family anymore, but she was mine, and always would be. And I had just done something I'd never done before. I'd lied to her face, as if that were somehow forgivable because of everything else that was going on. As if that could ever be okay.

Greg made a worried grunting sound. I twisted around and buried my face in the fur of his side, hanging on as tightly as I dared without hurting him.

I was a liar, and I was going to die for my sins, and there was nothing I could do about it. So I just sprawled against my giant spider and cried.

Sixteen

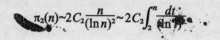

$$\pi_2(n) \sim 2C_2 \frac{n}{(\ln n)^2} \sim 2C_2 \int_2^n \frac{dt}{\ln t}$$

"Death isn't a new beginning or a miracle
transformation. Death is death. It's an end-
ing. What happens after you die isn't life.
That's the whole point."

—Mary Dunlavy

*Crying into a giant spider, which is a really rather
unique experience, all things considered*

IT TOOK A WHILE for me to stop crying, and when I did,
it wasn't so much because I'd finished crying as it was
because I had run out of tears. My mouth felt like a desert as I pushed myself away from Greg, wiping my eyes
with one hand. My backpack was only a few feet away. I
grabbed the strap and pulled it toward myself, unzipping the main flap and producing one of the remaining
bottles of Gatorade. Blue. Not my favorite flavor, but
that was all right; it still tasted like sugared heaven, and
the first sip hit the back of my throat as a benediction. I
chugged about half the bottle without stopping for
breath, then pulled out the bottle of ketchup.

There was no one in the room to tell me how disgusting I was being, and I was grateful for that as I squirted
a healthy amount of ketchup into the blue liquid and
replaced the bottlecap. Shaking the bottle vigorously
mixed the beverage and condiment into a thick, murky
soup that tasted even better than the Gatorade on its
own. I forced myself to sip this more slowly as I got to

my feet, giving Greg one last pat on the head, and turned my attention to the blackboard. That was enough self-pity and despair. Time to get back to work.

The math was as stark as it had been the night before, leaving no real room for negotiation. I'd need so much open storage space to run this equation without killing myself that it would probably destroy the minds of every single person in this mound. I sipped my Gatorade soup, squinting at the variables. There were options to direct things in other ways, but not many. Part of it would depend on how much power James and Annie could pour into the factorials I was going to use to magically define the edges of the campus; the original equation had been running on brute power and had just grabbed everything. We were trying to have slightly more finesse.

We wanted to take everything we'd brought with us back, and not strip the topsoil from the entire valley where we'd landed. We also didn't want to transport home with a whole bucketload of giant spiders. They had lungs and we could all breathe the same air; they might be perfectly fine in our dimension. They would still be giant spiders. If they didn't immediately collapse under their own weight, they would cause a massive panic, and be the ultimate invasive species.

As a member of an invasive species myself, I didn't really need the competition.

The only way Mark was coming out of this with his mind intact was if we were quick, flawless, and incredibly lucky. And none of those conditions were going to be enough to save me, not unless we suddenly found a whole system of untapped processors that I could use to handle the pieces I couldn't contain.

Greg stepped up behind me, putting a foot on my shoulder. I must have been radiating distress. I turned to offer him a wan smile he wouldn't understand, stroking the spot just above his fangs, where the fur was softest.

"I'm okay, buddy," I said. "Just a little worried about the trip home, that's all. You don't need to be concerned. We're not going to make you come with us."

If Kenneth's people didn't want Greg, I'd try my best to undo what I'd done to his mind before returning him to the other spiders. It might not work. It was still worth the effort.

"I'm glad to hear that you're not the kind of girl who keeps pets," said Artie. I whipped around to face the doorway. I was so accustomed to the gentle telepathic hum of his presence that I hadn't noticed it getting louder as he approached.

He was standing there, a bowl of something in one hand, a quizzical expression on his face, radiating vague distaste for the scene in front of him. I dipped deeper into his thoughts, just long enough to reassure myself that his distaste was aimed at Greg and not me, then asked, "Did you need something?"

"Annie asked me to bring up your breakfast," he said, holding up the bowl. His eyes flicked to the Gatorade bottle in my hand. "I probably don't want to ask what you're already drinking, do I?"

"Ketchup and blue Gatorade," I said.

He made an exaggerated gagging noise.

"Hey, it's no worse than grape jelly and tuna fish on raisin bread, which I believe is still your favorite sandwich." I said, stepping toward him to take the bowl. "Do you know what's in this?"

"Kenneth said it was a recipe their Johrlac visitors enjoyed, and Mark's had three bowls already, so there's probably not anything in there that's going to kill you," said Artie. "I think it's some sort of bug meat and local veggies."

It smelled vaguely like shrimp gumbo, which made sense, given the similarity between insect meat and crustaceans. I took the bowl, careful not to brush against his fingers, and asked, "Is there a spoon, or do we just sip it?"

"We just sip it." He grimaced. "They had cutlery when I got to the kitchen, but somehow it all disappeared before we could be served. I think Kenneth doesn't trust us with anything that could be a weapon."

"Have they tried strip-searching Annie? And she still has that fauchard she took from the dead guy! I think this is very uneven enforcement of disarming us."

Artie shrugged. "Hey, I dunno, I'm just the breakfast guy." He pulled a roll out of his pocket and offered it to me. "It goes better with bread."

"Thank you." I let him drop the roll into my stew before I moved to sit down in the pile of shed skins. Greg followed, pedipalps working as he scented my breakfast. I had no real idea what spider senses were like, but he didn't seem too agitated, so I assumed I wasn't about to eat one of his cousins. "What did you and Kenneth talk about?"

"Incubus stuff." He kicked the floor. "His grandfather warned him things might be hard for him because the people native to this dimension were going to be affected by his pheromones. He was a lot more realistic about it than Dad was with me. Unless that's something else that got changed when you rearranged my memories . . . ?"

"I don't think it would have been," I said. "I didn't rearrange your memories, I just . . . pulled myself out of them and then yanked the edges together so you wouldn't have a bunch of bleeding wounds in your psyche. It was less proper surgery and more emergency field medicine, if that makes sense? Your dad was preparing you to live in a world where the dominant species wouldn't always recognize you as part of itself. Kenneth's grandfather was preparing him for a world where he would *be* the dominant biped, if not the local apex predator. I think that honor goes to Greg here." I gave my spider a pat. He waved his pedipalps at me.

"That makes sense. I don't like not knowing my own mind. It's weird and it's scary and it's a little bit annoying."

"I don't like the most important people in my world not knowing who I am, or remembering the things we did together." I fished the roll out of the stew before taking a bite.

Immediately, I understood why Mark was so enthusiastic about the stuff. At least one of the vegetables responsible for the brownish gravy that covered the whole thing shared enough of the chemical makeup of tomatoes to taste like paradise. The rest of the flavors were harder to define.

If that sounds weird, *you* try explaining what a turnip tastes like to someone who's never tasted one. If you can manage anything better than "like a potato, but maybe sort of sweet," you're a culinary genius. Now imagine the person you're talking to has never had a potato either. You have no common points of reference. I could tell I was eating something close to root vegetables, and some kind of herbs, and some kind of fungus, maybe, along with the large chunks of what could almost have been shrimp, and a piece of what was almost but not entirely like bread.

Artie watched me, waiting until I'd swallowed before he said, "Kenneth says you could put yourself back in our heads if you really wanted to."

I hesitated, bread halfway back to my mouth. "Maybe I could if I weren't my mother's daughter," I said. "But she raised me not to play with people's heads that way. I did what I did because I didn't really know what I was doing. I thought I was dying, and I thought you'd be better off without me, and that was enough to do a lot of damage. If I went in and changed things intentionally, I'd be hurting you to help myself. I'd be modifying who you *are*. I know I already did that when I messed with your memories, but . . . I didn't mean to. Maybe that doesn't absolve me, but it lets me live with myself."

"Really? Because Annie seems to think you're getting ready to kill yourself."

Guess I wasn't as good of a liar as I'd believed I was. "Why does she think that?"

"I don't know, maybe because the first time you did dimension-crossing math, you wiped our minds in the process, and now you're too scared of doing it again to let us help you. And maybe because when the people who wrote all this weirdo cuckoo math used it themselves, one of them didn't make it. And maybe because you're still in love with me."

I was suddenly glad I wasn't eating my stew. My mouth went dry. I swallowed hard. "What do you mean?"

"You've been shielding your mind pretty hard since we got here, because when you don't your thoughts leak everywhere, and I get it, I really do, but while I was forgetting everything about you, did you forget that I'm an incubus?" Artie looked at me gravely. "Every time you drop your shields, it's like someone's dousing me in maple syrup and pizza sauce. I don't think those things are supposed to go together. Maybe I can't read minds, but I can read emotions, and I know you're in love with me. You have been for a long time, based on how complex the feeling is. This isn't a crush. Those taste more like gingerbread. Although I've never felt tomato sauce love before. I wasn't quite sure how to read it until I saw you drinking ketchup and felt how happy it made you."

I blinked slowly. Betrayed by my taste buds. "You, uh. You never figured it out before."

"Yeah, well, you coming to my birthday party and reading my mind by mistake was probably part of what made me decide I couldn't be trusted out in the world, you know?" Artie shrugged. "I don't think I'd feel comfortable reading the emotions of someone who was that scared of their own abilities, and even if I did pick them up, I don't think I'd be able to believe them. They'd feel too forced, like I had caused it somehow."

"Biologically, I'm a . . ."

" . . . big, super weird bug, I know. But again, caring about you as a person would get in the way of really *knowing* that, not just knowing it. If you're my cousin, you're a member of the family, and sure we're all kinds of different species, but we're all people. And my pheromones make people fall in love with me. If you're a cuckoo, you're not a person, you're a predator. I'm allowed to use my pheromones on predators. So it's easier to accept that I can't influence you when I don't know anything about you."

This was all starting to give me a headache. It made sense, but that didn't make it easier to hear. "I don't know what you think I'm feeling, but I promise you, one boy not being in love with me anymore isn't a good enough reason to kill myself. I have too many comic books left to read for that."

Artie radiated a brief spike of smugness. "So you admit you're in love with me. And, apparently, I was in love with you before you went and deleted all my save games for this particular visual romance novel."

I stared at him. "I didn't—I mean, I wasn't trying to—I mean, I wouldn't—you know I'm not going to pressure you to change your mind back into something I think it's supposed to be."

"Relax. I know that. If you'd wanted to rewrite us, I guess you would have done it as soon as you woke up and realized we didn't recognize you. You were in my head and you didn't do anything to change the way I felt about you. So I trust you not to mess with our heads. I know you didn't do anything."

I watched him warily for a moment. He continued radiating nothing but calm, and I slowly went back to eating my stew. It felt a little weird to be eating right after he'd dropped that on me, but I needed the calories; my stomach was screaming for more, and not just because of the flavor. None of the scavenged snacks in my backpack were going to be remotely as good for keeping me functional as the contents of this bowl.

This time, Artie waited until my mouth was full before he said, "I know there has to be a way for you to do the math that gets us home without dying in the process. You're a Price. Whether that's your name or not, the mice know you and they love you enough to make up for the rest of us still thinking of you as a virtual stranger. And when we get home, everyone else who loves you will be waiting, and we can begin the archeological digs through our own lives to remember a time when we loved you, too. You were smart enough to get us all here alive and with minimal collateral damage."

I wasn't sure how I felt about him referring to me accidentally deleting parts of his mind as "minimal collateral damage," but I didn't say anything. If I spoke, he might stop. I didn't want him to stop. For the first time since we'd woken up in this stupid dimension, he was talking to me like I was a person rather than a problem, like I might actually be a part of his family, not an inconvenient stranger who existed solely to make his life harder than it had to be. Maybe it was an illusion, and he was just getting better at hiding how much he hated me, but—if so—it was a nice illusion. I liked it. I wanted it to keep going for a while.

"So please, get us home without collateral damage we can't recover from. Don't make us tell our parents—and yours—why we don't remember you enough to mourn you." He scrubbed at his face with one hand. "I don't remember loving you. But if I'm still basically the same person, it could happen again, and I don't meet many girls who don't look at me like I'm some sort of chocolate fudge-Jason Momoa hybrid that I can't possibly live up to. So don't leave before I can figure out whether or not we're going to be friends." He paused. "That's all I wanted to say. Enjoy your breakfast. Kenneth says we'll be able to head back to campus in about half an hour—I mean, that's not what he said, but that's how Antimony interpreted it, and she's probably right. So we're almost done here."

Then he walked out of the room, leaving me alone with Greg and my breakfast. He was definitely right about one thing: one way or another, this was almost done.

I turned my attention back to my stew, which had cooled while we were talking, but was still delicious. It was too bad there was no way I could replicate this at home. Mom would have loved it. I was using the bread to mop up the last of the sauce when someone knocked on the doorframe. I lowered my shields and raised my eyes, feeling vaguely embarrassed that I'd been caught unawares twice in one day.

James looked calmly back at me. "I thought you could use some company," he said, and stepped into the room, approaching the place where Greg and I were sitting, if Greg could really be said to have the anatomy necessary to sit. Where we were resting, I guess. "Plus I wanted a better look at the giant spider now that I've had some sleep. Wow. He's a handsome guy."

"Isn't he?" In the light, Greg was mostly black and white, patterned sort of like a magpie, with a broad stripe across his shoulders. The black shaded toward an almost metallic blue as it moved down his abdomen, creating a shimmering, iridescent effect. "I've seen pretty spiders before, but he's the prettiest."

"May I pet him?"

James kept his distance, waiting for my reply. I held up a hand for him to give us a moment, and reached out to send soothing thoughts to Greg, trying to focus on how comfortable I was with James, how much I liked him, how safe he was to be around. Greg responded by relaxing even further, waving his pedipalps languidly in the air.

"I think it's safe, sure," I said, beckoning for James to come closer. "Just not the head, maybe? He's really fast when he wants to be, and if he decides he doesn't like being petted, he might take your hand off before I can tell him not to."

"Got it," said James, paling slightly as he approached. When he was close enough, he reached out and touched Greg's back, cautiously at first, and then with growing confidence as the massive spider neither attacked him nor pulled away. "He's so soft."

"Like a big Muppet."

"Yeah!" James brightened. "This is what I always thought Sweetums would feel like if he were real. And not, you know, a costume."

I smirked at him. "Just keep telling yourself that."

"You know, my whole life got turned upside down when Antimony and her friends rolled into my hometown. I was working as a barista at this coffeeshop downtown, never got to go to college, the crossroads ate my best friend, and my father treated me like I was still twelve years old and likely to run out into the woods where I'd be eaten by a bear. And then suddenly there's this girl in my cousin's house with her weirdo friends, and when she finds out I can freeze things the same way she sets them on fire, her response is to tell me I'm going to be her family now. She meant it, too. It wasn't just one of those things you say because you want someone to go along with your whacked-out plans. I mean, she wanted me to go along with her whacked-out plan, but she already had a girl who could bend luck, another girl who had a really relaxed relationship with gravity, and a guy who turns into a giant monkey sometimes. She didn't need me. One more sorcerer wasn't going to change much." He sounded faintly amazed, like the idea of someone *wanting* him when they didn't need him was so far outside his experience that he still couldn't believe it.

James and I hadn't really had much time to get to know each other between me coming back to Portland and everything turning messy and weird. Maybe that was why this felt comfortable, not tense like my conversation with Annie or obscurely depressing like my conversation with Artie. I took a sip from my ketchup-and-Gatorade, nodding.

"Annie's the youngest," I said. "By the time she came along, Alex was the smart one and Verity was the pretty one, so she had to figure out who she was going to be if she wanted to stand out, even a little bit. She thinks she went for 'the tough one,' and it's what her siblings think also, but really what she went for was 'the flexible one.' She finds a way to make things work, no matter what's happening, and she makes family everywhere she goes. She takes after our grandmother that way."

"Your mom is her grandmother, right? So you mean Alice."

"I do. You've met her?"

"Yeah, when we were on the way back to Oregon after Annie did her terrifying, insane time travel bullshit with the crossroads. I've watched a lot of *Doctor Who* since she unilaterally adopted me, and I still don't understand how she pulled that off without causing some kind of massive, world-shattering paradox." He shuddered. "Annie's scary as hell."

"She is," I agreed.

"Alice is worse."

"So you really *did* meet her."

"Would anyone lie about that? She's terrifying. And Annie says she regularly carries grenades made decades ago, which means she's also a risk to the safety of everyone around her."

"That's not wrong." I've always found Grandma Alice to be remarkably soothing in her unrelenting dedication to her chosen calling. Most of the family doesn't realize how hard the last forty-some years have been on her, but I can't help it, and the psychic damage she's carrying cuts all the way down to the bone. She's basically a big sack of broken glass and feral cats pressed into the shape of a woman, and for all that, she's got one goal: she wants to find her husband and bring him home to meet his children. She's done all this to herself in the pursuit of a happily ever after that may or may not exist.

Basically, my grandmother is what happens when a Disney princess goes horrifically wrong, and the single-minded nature of her goals and pursuits means that she's always been a nice break from spending time around more complicated people. She may be damaged, but she's not complex, and that makes her easy.

"We told her what Annie did to the crossroads, and that Mary knew the people they'd been taking were still alive somewhere, and she lit up like a mall on Christmas Eve and said she had to go. I guess she's off looking for her husband now, and I really hope she finds him. My friend Sally is probably in the same place."

I paused, trying to sort through the emotions attached to the name. Deep love, trust, and affection; Sally was the most important person in his world, and he felt like he'd failed her by letting the crossroads take her in the first place. I nodded, very slowly. "I'm sorry this isn't the dimension where she ended up."

"That would have been a little *too* convenient, don't you think? I mean, there's things coincidentally going your way, like another sorcerer showing up to break me out of New Gravesend before the crossroads bargain one of my ancestors made could trap me for the rest of my life, and then there's things becoming so ridiculously easy that they don't make sense anymore . . . Sarah? What does that look mean?"

"It means you need to go and tell the others that I'll be here when they are." I pushed myself to my feet and turned toward the chalkboard. "I'm sort of assuming Annie sent you in here to have one more try at convincing me not to kill myself today, and I think you may have just done it."

"I don't know what you're—"

"Here's one of the big rules of being a Price, James: don't lie to the telepath. Here's how it works." I looked over my shoulder and smiled at him as reassuringly as I could. "You start by not lying to the telepath. And then you do what the telepath says, so she can save us all."

James made a confused sound as he turned and walked out of the room, leaving me alone with Greg, the blackboard, and the beginnings of a long-shot plan that would get us all home alive. Pythagoras, please, let this work.

Let me get us home.

Seventeen

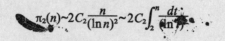

$$\pi_2(n) \sim 2C_2 \frac{n}{(\ln n)^2} \sim 2C_2 \int_2^n \frac{dt}{(\ln t)^2}$$

"Blood gives you hair color and skin color and maybe a few little quirks of biology or personality. It doesn't give you family. Family is something you *build*."

—Evelyn Baker

On the back of a giant spider, heading to Iowa State University, and other new sentences that have never happened before

EVERYONE ELSE WAS COMFORTABLY seated atop one of the massive mantises while I rode on Greg, who leapt with the assurance of a spider being escorted by several predators even larger and more horrifying than he was. With the suns up, it was easier to see just how much distance he could cover with every jump, propelling himself miles with a single push of his legs. The musculature of it all didn't make any sense to me, but I was confident the math would work out if I could just sit down and pick at it for a little while. Math usually does.

Our entire escort from the night before was accompanying us back to the campus, as was Kenneth, who sat in the front saddle of the very largest mantis. I didn't like the way his thoughts kept turning toward Artie, or how covetous they were. His mind was still a convoluted mess compared to the more straightforward, familiar thought forms of my friends and family, but I was con-

cerned that he might try to pull something if not inter-
fered with.

Antimony is basically interference given human form
sometimes. She'd stop him from doing anything we
couldn't recover from, and all I had to do was keep out
of her way long enough to let her do it. I kept hold of that
thought as I clung to the back of my spider, letting him
carry me to our destination.

The land below us was beautiful in the daylight, even
if the visibility made Greg nervous. Giant millipedes cut
channels through the brush, eating everything in their
paths, and centipedes undulated through the sky above
us, cilia waving to keep them aloft. Some of them had
riders, who waved their spears and bellowed incomprehensible calls of greeting across the distance. The forest
in the distance was more visibly draped in a thick, cottony sheet of webbing, concealed by the spiders who
made it their home. I sent Greg a thin arrow of inquiry.

His response was a picture of a spider with longer
legs and a more tapered body, its colors deeper and less
designed for camouflage, hanging suspended in a tree.
He had seen one of the weavers once, when he was a
very small spider, no bigger than a dog, and he had never
forgotten it. The image was accompanied by a wave of
fear, and I realized the webbing next to the spider contained two smaller bundles whose black-and-white fur
showed in patches through the cottony strands.
Greg's . . . siblings? Littermates? I wasn't sure what the
term was with spiders, but given their size and the age of
the memory, they had probably hatched from the same
clutch of eggs, and he'd watched them die after their
infant leaping carried them into the web.

I stroked his head, careful not to let the motion break
my grip on his fur. Falling from this height would not be
fun. "It's okay," I said. "We're not going over there. Don't
worry."

He didn't understand my words, but he was coming
to have a better and better understanding of my tone,
and he relaxed as we kept leaping onward. The up and

down nature of his movement, as opposed to the steady flight path of the mantids, meant the telepathic hum from the others kept dropping in and out of audible range, creating an odd sort of Doppler effect as we pressed onward.

Soon enough, the shape of campus loomed ahead of us, alien against the organic backdrop of the rest of the world, rendered fuzzy in spots by large patches of webbing. We landed in the quad, near the student store, and Greg crouched to let me slide off of his back, standing straight and beginning to clean his eyes with his forelimbs as soon as I was safely off to one side.

"Good boy," I said, patting his thorax. "You are an excellent spider, Greg."

He was an excellent spider who was getting hungry again. Well, based on the fact that I'd eaten the stew and hadn't dropped dead yet, we were compatible enough to eat things from one another's realities, and I was sure a few of the husked-out cuckoos would be available for him to snack on soon enough. In fact, I was counting on it.

The big mantids began touching down around us. Greg backed up and raised his forelimbs and pedipalps in a threat display, trying to look even bigger than he actually was. I knew I had enough of a handle on his mind that he wasn't going to hurt me without warning, but it was still alarming.

"Hey!" I rushed to put myself solidly in front of him, filling his field of vision. "Hey, hey, Greg, hey, calm down, buddy, you're all right. No one's going to hurt you. These are our friends."

Ropes began dropping from the mantids as everyone dismounted and started to slide down. Greg relaxed, putting his legs back on the ground, although his pedipalps remained raised in what I recognized as a signal of high alert. I stroked his head.

"Hey," I said. "You are a very good spider, Greg. Did you know that? Did you know that you were a very good spider?" I accompanied my words with a wave of appreciation and acceptance, trying to get my point across.

Communicating with large, non-sapient arachnids isn't normal, not even for a member of our family, but Greg remained calm as I stroked his head, finally relaxing his pedipalps and shifting positions enough to lean against me, content with the moment. The telepathic hum of my friends getting closer increased. I looked up, smiling at their approach. Their emotional states indicated that at least some of them were smiling back.

"Hey," said Mark. "You decided being a horse girl was too normal for you and what, you'd be a spider-the-size-of-a horse girl instead?"

"It seems to be working out okay so far," I said. "Does everyone know what they're supposed to do?"

The warriors from the mound were still dismounting, moving more slowly due to their polearms—not a limitation that had applied to Antimony, I noted, although she was still holding tightly to her fauchard, and I pitied anyone who tried to take it away from her. Growing up as the youngest child meant Annie's idea of "sharing" was "someone knocks you down and takes your stuff away," and she didn't do it very well.

"I know what you told us to do, but I'm still not sure I like it," she said. "Leaving you alone here seems like a bad plan."

"I won't be alone, I'll have Greg," I said. The spider placed a foot on my shoulder, nearly knocking me over. "If the husked-out cuckoos find me before you get back, he can jump me to safety, and I need all of you at your stations."

"This just seems like a lot of unnecessary splitting of the party," said James.

"People have noticed by now that the campus is missing." I said. "And they'll probably also have noticed the murders all over the world, and the missing kids. We need to get back to Earth as soon as we can."

"How much does this have to do with you not wanting to hang out in a place where only the mice know who you are?" asked Artie.

"Some," I admitted. I was still concerned my extended range might mean I had wiped my existence from the minds of the rest of my family, and I wanted to get home and confirm they remembered me. Call me petty, but it felt important. "Mostly, though, I've just found a bunch of numbers that describe the situation *right now*, and the longer we stay here, the more those numbers are going to change. The number of survivors, the number of mental breakdowns, the number of permanent injuries, that's all going to change. If we'd been the only people on campus when it was transported here, I might be willing to consider a delay. The presence of the other students, and of the cuckoo children, changes things. And if we want the campus, I need as many of the husked-out cuckoos as made it through the night."

Artie made a small sound of assent and moved toward the team of warriors that would be escorting him to the cafeteria. Our divisions were logical ones, given what each of us had to do, even if they did mean splitting the party—something that every horror movie and D&D adventure ever was happy to remind us was a bad idea.

Mark was going to start gathering up the husked-out cuckoos who had managed to survive a night of constant attacks by giant spiders when they didn't have any remaining self-preservation instincts to speak of. They were hungry, not only for calories, but for the mental acuity they'd lost—in this case, the zombies really *did* want to eat brains, they just wanted to eat them on a psychic level rather than a physical one, which would be no more pleasant for their targets than the Romero method. Mark would wander the campus, sending out bursts of nonsense thought and emotion as far as he possibly could, and whenever he managed to attract his targets, he would lead them back to me. They couldn't understand his thoughts, but they could still pick them up if they were loud enough, just like they could still hear people yelling.

Depending on how many cuckoos actually survived

the first ritual, we might have started with hundreds, if not thousands, of the shambling monstrosities. I was hoping he could bring me at least fifty survivors. That would be tight, but it would be enough.

While Mark was doing that, Artie was going to head for the cafeteria, where the survivors we'd already made contact with were holed up, and use his pheromones to convince them to follow him to the quad. Morag and the other girls could help him nudge anyone who was being reluctant, and once they were here, I'd be able to put my proposal in front of them:

We didn't want to leave anyone behind, but for me to run the numbers I needed to get us home, I needed as much storage space as possible. I could take the memory of the last two days away from these people, remove the giant insects and the terrifying isolation, the lies and the trauma, and leave them ready to go back to their lives with no idea of what had happened to them. And for most of them, that offer would probably be a relief. But I couldn't do it without their consent. I mean, I *could*. My ability to reach into their minds and rewrite them to suit myself didn't give a single damn about whether or not they liked me for doing it, but since my goal was getting home without turning myself into a monster, I needed them to give me permission.

And some of them would probably say no. For some of them, the idea of not knowing what had happened to them over the course of these two terrible days would be worse than living with the memory. That was fine. Everyone's different. That's why everybody gets a choice.

Annie was heading for the library, which had the largest concentration of survivors and contained the other cryptids on campus. She stood the best chance of talking them around to coming out, and once she got them to the quad, we'd offer them the same choice we were offering the people from the cafeteria.

There were no other big concentrations of people; Mark's beacon for the husks would also attract the cuckoo kids, like the Pied Piper of Hamelin if he hadn't put such emphasis on the rats, and once he had them, he could bring them back to us. They would have even more processing capacity than the human students, and they all had something big and juicy for me to go in and strip out: their waiting memories of the psychic damage done to their ancestors. Mark was right. The legacy of the cuckoos ended here, under this orange alien sky, far away from the damage they'd done. Far from Earth, and far from Johrlar.

James was heading into the maintenance building, to the room where they kept classroom supplies, to get me as many whiteboards, Sharpies, and dry-erase markers as possible. All of them would be escorted by armed warriors, to help them out if things got unpleasant, and when James got back, I would start doing my math.

It was a convoluted plan. It had too many moving parts, and it depended on too many coincidences, but I had two descendants of Frances Brown with me, which meant I had two people who carried the blood of Kairos, which meant I had two people who thrived on coincidence, whose luck would always bend toward the most ridiculous, improbable outcomes possible. And sure, they were both generations removed from whoever had contributed that specific quirk to their family tree, and sure, I'd seen them both fail horribly when the world didn't line up the way they wanted it to, but if there was ever a time to bank on the Healy family luck, this was it.

"You all know your places," I said firmly. "Now go assume them."

Annie and Mark exchanged a complicated look, the air thickening with the feeling of mental communication that I wasn't privy to, and then they walked away, toward their respective teams.

James didn't follow. Instead, he walked quickly toward me, almost but not quite breaking into a run, and when he was close enough, wrapped his arms around my shoulders and pulled me into a one-sided embrace. I stood frozen, arms at my sides, blinking at him. He wasn't of the blood of Kairos; he had no natural resis-

tance to telepathic influence, and he didn't even have
the potential minimal protection from carrying his own
anti-telepathy charm anymore. I started to recoil.

He didn't let go. "You're not forcing me to hug you,
no matter how much you were thinking you needed a
hug just now," he said. "You're not forcing me to do anything, except go and find you a bunch of Sharpies." He
pulled back, relaxing his grip as he got himself far
enough away to see my face. "I'm a sorcerer, remember?
And I spent years before I met Antimony and the others
studying the journals of all the sorcerers who came before me, trying to find a way out of the situation the
crossroads had put us all into. I research. I study. It's
what I *do*. And I know you're doing your best right now,
and I know if there's any possible way for you to get us
all home safely, you're going to find it, but I read the
notes Betsy made on the first ritual, and all the test runs
they did before they committed to the final version, and
they had a lot more time and a lot more resources than
you do, and one of them still died." His thoughts turned
grave as he looked at me. "They knew it was a risk. They
wrote down that it was a risk. So I believe you know
what you're doing, but I also believe you're risking your
life right now, and I know you're doing it so we can go
home, and I just wanted to make sure you knew how
much we appreciated it. That's all."

James let me go then. He turned and trotted over to
where his smaller detachment of warriors was waiting.
He didn't need as many because he wasn't going as far,
or at least that was the logic, and the mound only had so
many warriors willing to go into the territory of the
hunters in the dark when they didn't absolutely have to.
We were a fun novelty, sure, but as our only incubus
wasn't interested in staying and helping Kenneth lead
the community, they weren't as interested in us as they'd
been when we first met.

Familiarity breeds contempt, I guess. I watched James
go, stroking Greg with one hand, then lowered my
shields, first halfway, and then completely, opening my-

self to the campus. It wasn't hard to find my friends.
They were torches against the dark field of the school,
burning so brightly that I couldn't have missed them if
I'd been trying. I was attuned to them: it was always going to be like this, even after we made it home. I could
never really lose track of any of them again.

Not even Mark. Mark, our proof that cuckoos could
be redeemed, who was hurrying toward the edge of the
campus with urgency and no small amount of fear,
whose own shields were down to make him the most
tempting target possible. I wondered whether he realized that he had more family than just his beloved Cici
now, because there was no way we were getting home
and then letting him just walk away as if none of this had
ever happened. Like James before him, the poor boy
was going to be stuck with us for the rest of his life.

That's how the family survives. We abandoned the
idea that blood was the only thing that mattered a long
time ago.

It felt weird to be standing here waiting with Greg
while everyone else was running around getting things
ready for me to start doing my job. I turned to focus on my
spider, resting my forehead against the spot above his
eyes. Not his "forehead," per se, since he didn't have a
skull and his anatomy didn't really accommodate the idea
of a brainpan, but a spot where I wouldn't brush against
or obstruct any of his eyes. He waved his pedipalps, brushing them against my collarbone. I closed my eyes.

"This has to work, Greg," I said. "If it doesn't, I don't
have a plan B. This is our only shot."

He couldn't understand my words—and only partially understood my tone—but his response was still a
wave of trust and reassurance. He knew I was going to
do the right thing. No matter what else happened here
today, the giant spider trusted me completely.

That was good, since I was standing here in the open,
with the remaining warriors and the mantids to protect
me. And I wasn't exaggerating when I said I didn't have
another way to get us out of here. Even with all my prep-

arations and precautions, there was still a decent chance that performing this ritual would either kill or shatter me, and if I didn't get a stable doorway back to our home dimension before that happened . . .

Well, at least the existence of Kenneth and the other part-Lilu proved this dimension wouldn't kill my people through allergic reaction or misaligned timestreams or anything else ridiculous and *Star Trek*-y. They'd be able to live here until James and Annie could study the written materials in enough detail to let them cobble together some version of the spells Alice used to move between dimensions. There's always another way if you have time and stubbornness on your side.

But not for me. This was my only shot at getting out of here, and I wanted to get out of here more than anything. I wanted to go home. I wanted to find out how much of my own life I'd destroyed. I wanted to fix what could be fixed. And I wanted to see the cuckoo kids settled into whatever waited for them, and given the chance to grow up to be their own people, not broken reflections of the diaspora.

One of the warriors shouted something. I opened my eyes, pulling away from Greg, and turned. A small group of husked-out cuckoos was shambling toward us.

Despite myself, I laughed. "They survived! They survived! Greg, look! Some of them made it through the night!"

The big spider tensed. He wasn't smart, but he knew a predator when he saw one approaching, and he didn't like it. In that regard, he was currently smarter than I was, since I was laughing and clapping my hands as the husks shambled closer.

The four warriors who had been assigned to watch me moved into position in front of me and Greg.

I need them alive, I sent, putting as much urgency into the thought as I could manage. I needed them to understand, despite the language barriers, that I meant it.

One of the warriors nodded. I didn't know whether

that was a gesture native to their culture or something they had picked up from their previous extra-dimensional visitors, and I didn't actually care. They knew what the gesture meant, I knew what the gesture meant, our minimal ability to communicate was bolstered by its mutuality.

They moved forward as a solid line, polearms at the ready, and met the husks in the middle of the quad. The husked-out cuckoos had no fear, no sense of self-preservation, and no weapons. The warriors had polearms, nets, and the strong instruction not to kill. It was not as one-sided a battle as it would have been if they'd been allowed to stab with impunity, but they did their best, netting when they could, and aiming for the legs when the nets were not an option. By the time James and his warriors emerged from the maintenance building with my supplies, all nine of the husks were on the ground, some trying to drag themselves toward me and Greg or the warriors, others writhing helplessly against the nets that held them. Their mouths were still moving, gnashing at the air, and their hands clawed and clutched at everything within reach.

James stopped when he saw the bodies on the ground. "That was fast," he said.

"They must have heard us show up," I said. "Bring those whiteboards over here."

All together, they'd managed to scavenge up six whiteboards and eight big packs of unopened Sharpies. I tore the first pack open and uncapped a marker, inhaling briefly. Huffing markers is bad, even for a cuckoo, but there's nothing wrong with enjoying that first chemical hit of math about to be done.

James watched me, radiating wariness, although it was hard to say whether that was because he thought I was about to shove the Sharpie up my nose or something, or because of the nine functional zombies on the ground not far away. Plus we had the giant insects and arachnids, and the jarringly orange sky, and really, this dimension was an endless cornucopia of things to be

wary of. I lowered the marker and offered him the closest thing I could muster to a reassuring smile.

"None of us were hurt," I said. "The warriors did exactly what they were supposed to do, and now we have
proof that some of the damaged cuckoos survived the
night."

"Is this going to be enough?"

"No. I need at least fifty, preferably more." We had
no way of knowing how many of them would have been
able to get to cover when night fell, or whether they
would have been able to understand on any level that
they needed to; they didn't really have the capacity to
understand anything else. Hiding from giant spiders
wouldn't have occurred to them naturally.

But if they'd been trying to get into the buildings where
the surviving students were holed up, they could have
been in parking garages or under awnings or in other
places the spiders wouldn't necessarily have checked.

I wasn't counting on hundreds of survivors. But given
the number we'd started with, it wasn't so unreasonable of
me to hope for fifty. Especially when we already had nine.

"It's a good start," I said, with all the cheer I could
muster, and recapped the Sharpie so I could start moving the whiteboards into position. "Help me with these,
won't you?"

"Sure." James fell in beside me, and for a few minutes
we were quiet, pushing whiteboards into a circle large
enough to encompass the two of us, plus Greg, and leave
me with the space I needed to move around. James shot
a look at my spider, radiating still more nervousness,
and asked, "When are you going to tell, um, him that he
should leave?"

"I don't know exactly." I moved toward the first whiteboard. It was pristine, the surface glimmering white and
perfect, having never known the touch of ink. I was going
to destroy that, and when this was over, we were going to
destroy *it*, because leaving a bunch of dimension-ripping
math lying around for people to discover isn't just irresponsible, it's *sloppy*. But soon, the work would begin,

and even knowing this might be the last work I ever got the chance to do didn't make me any less eager to get started.

"He can't come back to Earth with us. He'll die."

"No, he won't." I could see the equation glimmering in my mind when I closed my eyes, flawless and crystalline and ready to be written down. It wasn't like the one that had brought us here, which had been large and complex enough to be both alive and hostile; this was an inanimate thing, sculpted by masters, and the doors it opened would be controllable ones. "He has lungs. He's not internally built exactly like the spiders back home, and we've seen nothing to indicate that physics works any differently here. He'd be fine. Except for the not being able to feed him, and him terrifying anyone who gets near him, and him not having any options for mates or colonies of his own kind . . ."

"Okay, okay, I got it," said James.

"But I'll let him know when it's time for him to get off campus." Right now, Greg was happy where he was. He liked being near me; I had led him safely into the territory of his greatest enemies, and had even fed him while he was there. I made him feel safe and powerful in a way the other spiders didn't.

And sure, some of that was psychic manipulation of his little spider mind, but it was nice to have someone around whose thoughts about me weren't conflicted in the slightest, but simple and utterly devoted. I had warped his emotions. I had never implanted or deleted any of his memories, and somehow, that made all the difference.

"You know you can't take him home with you."

I managed not to bristle. "I know."

"Okay." James pushed the last whiteboard into place and stepped out of the circle, joining the combined group of his warriors and my own. "There weren't any more whiteboards in there. Is this going to be enough for what you need?"

"I hope so." Based on the math I already had, the

modifications I'd committed to memory, and the places where I thought it might be necessary to expand the scope or modify the structure of the equation further, depending on how many people were still alive, I would have a whole whiteboard open at the end. I hoped. "Did you get me any dry-erase markers, or just the Sharpies?"

James solemnly held up a pack of dry-erase markers. I beamed at him.

"Good man. Good, good—" A spike of panic lanced through me, bright and bitter as licking a battery. I clutched the sides of my head, barely managing not to fall to my knees in the middle of the quad. Greg picked up my distress, which I was broadcasting on all channels, as it were, and rushed to steady me with his two forelimbs. James was only a few steps behind, which was impressive, given how many more legs Greg had than he did.

I gratefully let the two of them support me. "Get ready," I said. "Mark is on his way back."

"Mark?"

"Mark."

The spike of panic repeated, less fresh but substantially closer. Mark was heading back to us at a dead run, apparently, and while I couldn't quite make out any specific thoughts at this distance, he was radiating panic loudly enough that he was probably freaking out everyone left on campus.

The warriors were starting to shift from one foot to another, looking anxiously around as they picked up on Mark's broadcast. Since it was purely emotional, the language barrier didn't matter as much as it normally would have done. Since they knew they were hanging out with telepaths, they turned toward me, asking a series of sharp, interrogative questions in their own language.

"I understand why they don't all speak English, but don't you think they could have figured out by now that we don't speak whatever it is they *do*?" asked James, sounding flustered.

I took a deep breath, pushing Mark's panic away
from myself, back toward its origin, where it belonged.
To say that I didn't have time for this would have been a
massive understatement. "Shut up and let me try to
calm them down," I said, voice tight.

James didn't say anything, just moved closer to Greg,
like he thought my uneasy, unbalanced spider would
protect him. And maybe he would. Greg had accepted
James as a part of the same colony that I belonged to,
and believed my whole colony was inadequate to defend
ourselves, needing him if we wanted to stay alive for
more than a few more hours. He wouldn't let James
come to any harm.

I took a step toward the warriors. *The fear is coming
from,* and I flashed a picture of Mark, *my companion. It
is not your own. Resist it.*

One of them turned and shook his polearm at me in
a menacing, honestly unnerving fashion. I pushed my
way deeper into his mind, filtering through his thoughts
to try and gauge what he was trying to say. I struggled
for calm. This was a lot harder than it had been yester-
day, when nobody had been panicking and nobody had
been yelling, and there hadn't been another cuckoo
broadcasting incoherently at everybody.

The warrior was demanding to know why I couldn't
make the waves of fear now pushing their way stop, and
when I presented the image of Mark again, the warrior
advanced on me, polearm at the ready. I took a step
back, trying to keep my own alarm from broadcasting.

Greg moved faster than the eye could follow. One
instant he was standing in the quad, and the next, he was
between me and the warrior, forelegs raised in clear
threat. The warrior shouted something, and the rest of
them clustered around him, all of them ready to attack
my poor spider for the crime of defending me.

"All of you, stop this!" I shouted, and pushed myself
between Greg and them. Greg put his forefeet on my
shoulders, effectively pinning me where I was, and
loomed over me, hissing steadily, like a souffle in the

process of deflating. The warriors continued to shout and mutter, stabbing their polearms at us.

It was a bad situation, and it could have gone on for a lot longer, had one of the mantids not noticed the commotion. It turned its head to watch us, slow thoughts forming in its insectile mind. I couldn't fully pull my attention off the scene to focus on its confusion, not without freeing Greg to attack, and maybe I should have, because what the mantis saw was a group of its people, who had been around it since it was a newly-hatched nymph, who smelled like home and safety and domestication, being menaced by one of the hunters in the night.

The domesticated insects still weren't smart by the standards of anyone who worked with mammals, but they had been bred for loyalty and a degree of possessiveness that would have been alien to any Earth insects. I wanted to reject the evidence of its mind as impossible, but I was a bug who felt love; slightly different evolutionary paths could make a huge difference. It looked at us, and it reached its decision.

I heard it decide a split second before it moved, and gathered my thoughts, shoving them at Greg as hard as I possibly could. *RUN, NOW!*

He didn't want to abandon me. His capacity for loyalty and devotion was less than the mantis', but he still had it, and I had inculcated a level of affection for me that should have been impossible given his neurological limitations. My command was too loud for him to ignore, and he leapt before the mantis could strike, but didn't flee as he should have done, instead adhering to the front of the student store and continuing to watch us all warily, fully ready to leap again.

I began to relax now that Greg was at least temporarily out of danger, and the mantis struck.

Like Greg, it moved faster than the eye could follow, stabbing and scything down with its razor-sharp forearms. My size saved me, but didn't spare me; those forearms were designed for hunting prey much closer to its own size. It was like Godzilla trying to target a single person in a crowd. There was no time for me to dodge, and the tip of its left arm slammed into my abdomen. I howled in agony, losing my grasp on Greg's mind.

He moved in an instant, flinging himself across the distance between us and biting at the arm that held me. The mantis was too big for him to battle on his own, and looked at him quizzically for a long moment. Too long: he bit down, and the mantis' pain briefly overwhelmed my own, flaring hot and penetrating in my mind.

The warriors shouted and brought their polearms around. James raised his hands, and the temperature around us plummeted, becoming arctic. The mantis recoiled, leaving its severed striking spike behind. It was a piece of chitin easily eighteen inches long, narrow as the scythe it so resembled, like a natural machete, and it had pierced through the tissues of my gut and into my abdominal cavity, covered in jagged barbs that would effectively disembowel me if someone tried to pull it out. The warriors shouted something else. James took a step forward. The temperature got even lower, and the warriors began to fall back, leaving us alone.

And the whole time Greg, my big, brave spider boy, who had to know all the way to the bottom of his primitive mind that he was about to die, continued to stand guard over me, waving his pedipalps threateningly at the retreating mantis. The cold had to be hurting him, and still he stood, ready to sacrifice himself for the chance to save me.

I lifted one hand and placed it gently on his leg, whispering his name. He turned to look at me, the waving of his pedipalps becoming less frantic and more reassuring. I stroked his leg, trying to project reassurance in return, fighting through the pain. It was dwindling, although it was hard to say whether that was due to shock or cold. "Good boy, Greg," I said. He didn't understand English, but having the words to focus on helped me to amplify my own feeling of being protected and how well he'd done at driving back the mantis. "Good, good boy."

It was still getting colder. Spiders don't shiver, but

Greg's thoughts—such as they were—were slowing in response to the temperature. "James, can you please ease up on the cold? You're hurting Greg."

"Sorry," said James unrepentantly. The air began to warm again. "We need to get that out of you."

"It's going to have to wait until Annie gets back, and one way or another, getting it out is going to do more damage than getting it in did." I grabbed Greg's leg and used it to pull myself to my feet, panting from the effort. The pain in my abdomen wasn't getting worse. Definitely shock, then; good.

Shock can be a useful function if you realize it's happening and know how to exploit it. Was it a good idea for me to be up and moving around while I had a giant bug's leg sticking out of me? No. But where it had hit, it was possible it had missed my internal organs—and that would be a good thing, since the only hospital I know of that has a Caladrius on staff is in New York, and over a thousand miles away from Ames, Iowa.

No one has a lot of experience performing medical procedures on cuckoos. I've probably been to the hospital more often than most of my kind, and I can count the number of times that's happened on the fingers of one hand, with digits left over. Maybe the mantis had pierced whatever served as my liver. Assuming I even *had* a liver, which was a pretty big assumption. Livers filter blood, create bile, and store energy. Well, there are other ways for a body to make energy, my blood isn't like mammalian blood, and I don't know whether my digestive system depends on bile to function. Normal wasps don't have livers. Maybe I didn't either.

Even if no organs were involved, I had muscle and fatty tissue, and they would both be shredded if we pulled the barb out. The waves of panic and fear coming from Mark were still breaking over me, but they were easier to shrug off now, probably due to my own physical trauma.

James took a step back, watching me with anxiety

radiating off of him, then looked past me to the clustered warriors. "What do we want to do about them?"
he asked.

"Keep them back. Freeze them if you have to." I put
one hand under the spike sticking out of my abdomen,
bracing it so gravity wouldn't answer the question of
whether or not we were going to pull it out of me, and
staggered toward the whiteboards. "I need to start
soon."

"You're hurt. Can't you just tell me what to write, and
I'll write it?"

"No. I don't even have words for some of the symbols
from the Johrlac equation. They're totally new to me. I
wouldn't know how to tell you to write them down."
And I needed to modify the starting point of my own
math, to account for the fact that I was injured and
couldn't channel as much of the processing requirement
of the ritual myself as I'd originally intended.

I grabbed a pack of dry-erase markers from the
ground, wincing at the effort of bending over and freeing another cascade of thick, clear hemolymphatic fluid
from the wound in my gut. There still wasn't as much
pain as there should have been, and since the air was
almost back up to normal temperature, I was willing to
chalk that up entirely to shock. Yay for shock. Most
valuable physiological reaction, gold medal for you,
shock. I love shock.

James trailed along behind me, followed by Greg,
who was still waving his pedipalps in dismay. Seeing
your—person? Friend? Adopted child? Whatever I was
to him—get stabbed clearly wasn't very reassuring in his
tiny spider mind. I sent him another wave of reassurance, then looked back at the warriors, most of whom
had returned to their earlier loose formation. A few had
gone to tend the wounded mantis, and were thinking
poisonous thoughts about us. I didn't want to waste the
effort to really dig into their feelings, and as none of the
thoughts I could translate seemed to indicate an inten-

tion to attack us or to stab my spider, it seemed safe enough to leave them alone.

I uncapped the first marker and wrote the series of symbols I had determined would represent me, as an uninjured cuckoo queen guiding the ritual to a successful conclusion. Just looking at it was enough to tell me that it was wrong, even without focusing on the dull ache in my abdomen. I rubbed out a few of the symbols, pausing to consider the math without them, then wrote in their replacements.

The mental effort needed to stay upright with an injury of this severity, plus or minus twenty percent, would reduce my efficiency in the ritual by eighteen percent. I wrote in the new figures, paused, and then revised again, taking it down a full twenty. Better to have too much power at the end than to start on the assumption that not enough would suffice.

"How are you feeling?" asked James.

"Like the geophysicists in *The Core*," I said. His thoughts turned confused. "Oh, come on, you're really going to tell me you've never seen *The Core*? It's one of the best bad science movies ever made. Their physics is so bad that you can cause actual tears by asking physicists what they thought of it." I paused. "I think the screenwriter was either drunk or trying to win a bet. Or maybe both. Anyway, they're trying to use nukes to restart the rotating core of the planet after it accidentally got stopped, and they based all their calculations on a misassumption about the density of the material, so even having way too many nukes for anyone to be comfortable with isn't going to be enough unless they redo everything on the fly. And that's how I feel right now. Like I'm trying to save the world with math done on the back of a napkin."

" . . . oh," said James blankly. My explanation hadn't helped much.

"We'll all watch it together when we get home," I promised. "Annie and Artie love that movie." It would be weird to watch it with them without Artie automatically fixing me a bowl of popcorn the way he knew I liked it, butter and tomato powder and garlic, but I could make my own popcorn. We were going to have the chance to get to know each other again, and I'd get to find out whether or not I had a liver, and all I had to do to get us there was a little bit of math. I love math. I can do math in my sleep.

I could do math while bleeding from a gut wound caused by a giant praying mantis, no problem. Why was that even a question?

As an answer, a twinge of pain lanced through my abdomen, a hint of direr things to come. I shifted my grip on the severed mantis leg, trying to keep it from moving too much while it was still inside me, and waved James away with the hand that held the marker.

"Go," I said. "Shoo. Make sure our hosts don't kill my collection of injured husks. I need those if we want to get out of here. You can't take the bug leg out of me without making it worse, and I can do math without your help."

James wavered, still uncertain. I swallowed a sigh.

"I promise not to drop dead until you get back, and Greg will be right here if anything changes, okay?"

"Okay," said James, and trotted back toward the warriors. He couldn't talk to them and they couldn't talk to him, but we'd been doing decently with hand signals by the time we left the mound, and anything was better than nothing.

Anything that kept them from killing my living processors, anyway.

I tried to shut out Mark's nearing panic and focus on the math in front of me. His situation was going to be a problem for future Sarah. She could deal with it. Right here and right now, present Sarah had some math to do if she wanted to save us all.

It was like I'd finally fallen into a nerd's perfect fantasy in the form of a Tumblr post: you have six whiteboards and seventeen pens and twenty minutes to do the kind of math that literally saves the world. But if you do it, you might die, either because you burn your own brain out or from the gut wound involving an unknown number of your internal organs. What do you do?

The math, of course. You do the math.

I leaned forward and began to write.

Eighteen

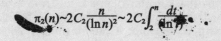

$$\pi_2(n) \sim 2C_2 \frac{n}{(\ln n)^2} \sim 2C_2 \int_2^n \frac{dt}{(\ln t)^2}$$

"Last thing I wanted to do was go. I loved
my husband, my daughter . . . my whole life.
Leaving them was the last thing I wanted to
do. And it's the last thing that I did."
—Frances Brown

On the Iowa State University quad, doing math

MARK'S PANIC REACHED FIRE alarm volume a few seconds before Mark himself came running around the corner of the building, arms pumping, one child hanging off his neck and two more running frantically along beside him. None of them looked like they were more than five, although it was hard to tell exactly how old they were with the way he was running. More children ran scattered around him, old enough to keep up, although one of the girls was carrying a little boy bundled against her hip, his arms locked tight around her torso.

And behind them came a wave of husks, filthy and tattered, some of them visibly injured—one woman looked like she was missing an arm—and shambling along at a steady pace. It was like having our own personal zombie movie delivered right to our doorstep.

"I found them!" yelled Mark, and ran faster. His pace up to that point made sense; he'd both been trying to lag enough to let the kids keep up, and to keep from losing the husks, some of whom were clearly walking on broken ankles by this point. Bodies are not meant to be used by people who don't notice when they get damaged.

Says the woman still standing when she has a giant insect leg sticking out of her abdomen. I put the cap back on my marker and stepped out from around my whiteboard, dropping the few shields I'd been able to construct up to this point. Time for the first tricky part.

In order for me to use the husks as processor banks, I had to catch them. I mentally reached for the mob, grabbing hold, plunging myself into the storm that raged where their core selves should have been.

It was like trying to grab a hurricane. The wind whipping through them whipped through me, blowing my thoughts and feelings in all directions, making it almost impossible to hold onto the part of me that understood rational thought and what it meant to be a person. *Hungry*, said the storm, and *STARVING*, howled the storm, and it was never going to go away, it was never going to end, it was going to consume me if I didn't let it go.

I didn't feel myself hit my knees, but I absolutely felt the piece of mantis move inside my guts, jarred by the fall. It was a bolt of pure agony, severe enough to break through the howling winds for a brief instant. An instant was long enough. I grabbed the pain, working it and amplifying it and finally flinging it out across the husks—both the ones Mark had gathered and the ones we already had—in a thin netting of strands and filaments that felt like the webs I'd seen draped over the distant forest.

The hunger inside them recoiled when the web touched them, and I drew it tighter, focusing on my pain and using it to give them all the suffering they deserved. Gradually, the wind withdrew, until I could focus enough on the reality of my own body and its limitations to push unsteadily back to my feet. Mark was inside my circle of whiteboards, along with the kids—an even dozen of them, ranging in age from what looked like three to thirteen. My eyes tingled as I shifted a tendril of focus to them, scanning for signs that they still had the packets of lurking memory occupying space in their minds.

I brushed against the edge of one of them, and was presented with an image of people who looked exactly like us, walking through some sort of weird, semi-organic shopping plaza, surrounded by butterflies with wings the size of dinner plates. Johrlar. The memory packets were still intact in these children, and would need to be removed. Which would give me extra processing space.

"What a good present," I said, words distant and echoing, like they were coming from terribly far away. "It isn't even my birthday." I didn't know my birthday. No cuckoo did. We'd always celebrated the day I was found—a celebration that was somewhat dimmed by the knowledge that we were celebrating the anniversary of the day after my first set of adoptive parents' funeral.

"Well, they seemed like something you could use," said Mark.

"I could have used a couple more." Even counting the nine who'd come to find us earlier, I was still eleven short of my goal. "Is there any chance you left a few behind?"

Mark shook his head. "This was all of them," he said. "The spiders must have had a field day with the campus last night."

One of the smaller children began to cry, stuffing almost his entire fist into his mouth to stifle the sound. I fought the urge to focus on him. Most of my energy needed to stay on holding the husks where they were. The storm was still raging, only temporarily contained by the weight of my pain.

At least offloading the majority of it meant they couldn't fight me or figure out how to break free. Even after my final instar, I didn't have the psychic strength to hold onto thirty-nine intelligent beings who actually had the strength of mind to push against me. Because the husks were only alive in the most primitive of senses,

I could hold them against all pressures. I didn't have to let them go.

I wasn't going to let them go. "Mark, did you tell the children what I needed to do?" I drifted back toward the whiteboard, numbers and symbols beginning to swim in front of my eyes, like a walking dream—or the start of a hallucination. There were worse things to have as my last vision of the world.

"As much as I could before the zombies showed up," said Mark. "Uh, Sarah? You're, um . . . you're leaking."

"There's a big bug leg sticking out of your stomach," said one of the kids, much more bluntly. That's the nice thing about kids. It doesn't matter what species they are; they don't know how to sugarcoat anything. That knowledge comes later, and at the expense of a lot of innocence.

"That's because I got stabbed by a big bug," I said, and picked up my pen. "We'll deal with it later. Mark, can you tell them, please?"

"All right," said Mark. He clapped his hands, pulling the attention of the children back onto him. "My friend Sarah is doing her best to get us home, where we'll have Internet and pizza and television and all those good things again. But to do that, she's going to need a lot of space, and that space doesn't technically exist."

"How can she need something that isn't real?" asked one of the kids.

"She's going to use the space inside our heads," said Mark. He lowered his voice, like he was confessing a particularly interesting and compelling secret. "There's a lot of room inside a head. It's where your imagination goes when you're not using it. It's where you keep your dreams. And Sarah wants to use that space to do a really, really big math problem that will make it possible for all of us to get home safely."

"How can she do that?" asked another kid.

"Someday you'll be able to do it, too," said Mark. "We're people, because otherwise we wouldn't have to wear shoes."

Several of the kids giggled, the sound a little frayed

around the edges, like they weren't sure whether laughter was allowed.

"But we're not humans."

"That's why my blood isn't red, right?" asked a kid. They didn't sound surprised. "My mom bled red. When the bad men took her to pieces, she bled red everywhere."

It was suddenly easier to hold the husks, throwing my anger into the web of pain that I had wrapped around them.

Mark coughed, his own emotions turning more complicated. He'd been tasked to retrieve the children in part because of Cici. Once we'd stripped out the time bomb of their implanted memories, I wouldn't be surprised if he took several of the children home with him. He could do with a few more siblings. My family can't be the only one that acquires more kids every time we turn around.

"I'm sorry about your mother," he said finally. "It's not right that they did that to you, or to her. But yes, what we are is the reason your blood isn't red, and it may be the reason you can sometimes hear what other people are thinking or feeling."

"There's something you're not telling us," said a child, warily. "What is it?"

"In order for Sarah to use your imagination rooms to do her math and get us all home, she needs to take away a big bunch of information that someone else already put there. It's not something you're using, and it's not something you'll ever need to use. It won't change who you are to take it away."

"Like deleting a junk app," said one of the first kids who'd spoken. They sounded almost bored, which was ridiculous. We were under an orange sky, surrounded by zombies and giant bugs. No one could possibly be bored with all this going on around them. "New phones always come from the store pre-installed with all sorts of stuff you don't need, and then you have to spend an hour stripping it all out before the phone works the way it's supposed to."

Not the metaphor I would have chosen, thought Mark, sounding harried, and I stifled a smile as I kept scrawling numbers on the board. My gut still hurt, but again, the pain was fading, becoming more of a constant, dull ache that I could easily ignore. Aloud, Mark said, "That's just what it will be like. But Sarah is very polite and doesn't like to do things when people tell her not to, so I need all of you to raise your hands if you give permission for her to do math inside your imagination rooms."

There was a pause, presumably while the children were raising their hands, and then Mark said, "They all said yes. You're good to continue, Sarah."

"Thank you." I added the variable representing the processing power of a dozen cuckoo children and the effort of stripping out their prenatal programming to the equation and kept going. The more I turned the world into math, the easier it got to keep doing it—or the easier it seemed to get. It could all be an illusion, the siren song of doing what my species evolved to do making me believe I was on the right track when I was actually stumbling deeper and deeper into the weeds. I didn't think so, but I wouldn't, would I?

One of the kids screamed. The sound was high and shrill and piercing, and I misdrew my symbol, leaving a streak of black against the white. The ritual wasn't activated yet, and so it didn't do anything bad, didn't turn off the gravity or reverse my lungs, but it was still a problem. I wiped it away with a swipe of my finger, saying warningly, "Mark . . ."

"Sorry," he said. "The kids saw some big bad spiders last night, and they just caught sight of Greg."

"Um, Greg?" asked one of the children.

"He belongs to Sarah," said Mark. "He's her friend. She *rides* him."

"Oh. Like She-ra and Swift Wind?"

"Exactly like She-ra and Swift Wind," said Mark.

A wave of admiration washed over me from the children old enough to have seen the cartoon. I kept writing. It was almost time to switch to the Sharpies, to leave behind malleable math for the absolute constants that couldn't be changed without killing us all. I turned.

Mark and the children were still clustered in the center of the circle of whiteboards. The reason it had taken them so long to notice Greg became apparent; he had jumped at some point and was mostly obscured behind several of the whiteboards, only the bottoms of his legs showing through the opening. Exhausted children who believed they could finally stop being hypervigilant could easily have missed him.

I waved my dry-erase marker. "This is what I use for math I might need to wipe out and replace with something else." I pulled a Sharpie out of my pocket and waved that. "Once I start using this, everything I write is permanent, and I can't make any more mistakes."

"So why change pens?" asked a kid.

"Some of the math *has* to be permanent to work the way I want it to," I said. "The equation will recognize my weak spots if I make it all malleable. So I need you all to be very, very quiet, and not do any more screaming, no matter what happens. Mark?"

"I've got them," he said. James was still some distance away, gesticulating at the gathered warriors and occasionally pointing back at the group of us, like he was trying to prove a point. I could have listened in, but I didn't want to take my mental hands off the husks, not even for a second.

Adding the children to my equation made up for three of the missing eleven, not all of them. I still didn't have enough power.

"Good," I said, and turned back to the whiteboard, uncapping my Sharpie. If I didn't have the power I needed, I was going to make it.

$$\textrm{\Large \textbf{\textit{i}}}$$

I was still writing when I heard the familiar hum of Antimony's mind approaching from the direction of the library, accompanied by a cacophony of unfamiliar thoughts and feelings. None of them felt particularly panicked; they weren't being chased by zombie cuckoos. That was probably great for them, but it was pretty lousy for me. I'd been hoping the noise they made would attract a few more husks out of hiding. It was difficult to believe that we'd had hundreds, maybe thousands of them the day before, and been reduced to less than fifty in a single night of giant spider attacks.

Difficult to believe, but not impossible. They had no sense of self-preservation; they wouldn't run, wouldn't flee or hide or attempt to evade when something wanted to eat them. They'd just keep attacking, answering hunger with hunger of their own. It was admirable, in a primitive way. They didn't give up.

I wasn't giving up either. As Annie got closer, I detached enough of my thoughts to send her a harried message: *Did you ask them about their memories of being here?*

Hello to you, too. They're split almost exactly down the middle. Several of them want to remember, while the others want to forget. And I got you a present.

I could use the places I stripped the memories out of for processing space, since they wouldn't have time to fill up with anything else before I could get in there. I added two more processors to my count. I was still six short. Six had never seemed like such a massive number before.

What kind of present? More importantly, you had time to review the notes from when your father dissected that cuckoo in the barn, didn't you?

Antimony's surprise flared along our mental link, briefly brighter than I expected it to be. *Yes,* she replied. *Why?*

Do I have a liver?

Do you have a—you know what, I'm not going to ask why you need to know that. No, you don't have a liver.

I glanced down at the serrated chunk of insect leg protruding from my abdomen. "That's good," I murmured aloud.

"What's that?" asked Mark sharply.

"Nothing," I said. To Annie, I sent, *Going to need you to help me with something when you get here. How far out are you?*

Not far. Her thoughts turned satisfied. *They did pretty well at holding out against the spiders last night. Locked the doors and windows. And I have either five or six more of your missing cuckoo kids, depending on how you want to count.*

That gave us an even twenty kids once I factored in the three from the cafeteria. I was still assuming Artie was going to make it back with them, and that the cafeteria hadn't turned into a slaughterhouse in the night. That might be optimistic of me, but it seemed well past time for luck to break our way, even if it was just once. We only needed things to go right for a little bit longer.

Great, I said. *See you in a minute.*

I returned my focus to the husks and the whiteboard, resuming the slow march of numbers and symbols that would hopefully eventually take us home. James and Greg were approaching from behind me, together, Greg feeling vaguely anxious, James feeling content and pleased with himself. I turned to face them.

James had his hand resting on Greg's back, just behind his head, well out of reach of the great spider's fangs. The children shied away from them as they moved, radiating a mixture of terror and fascination that made absolute sense, given their experiences with the spiders.

"Did you get them to stand down?" I asked.

"For the moment," he said. "I said 'Kenneth' and 'Incubus' and 'no kill' a lot, and they seem to understand that I was telling them to leave your spider alone, but it still seemed like a good idea to move away from them. They're a little upset about one of their mantises being maimed."

"Is that the correct plural?" I asked. "I thought it was 'mantids.'"

"I don't think the correct plural is appropriate for me to use around children."

"Sarah, what the *fuck*?!" shouted Annie, making his careful language for naught. James sighed and put a hand over his face as she came thundering into the circle, a bundle of cloth in her arms and the people from the library trailing along behind her. She pointed at the leg sticking out of my abdomen.

"You're *bleeding*," she said, tone accusatory. "You could have mentioned that you were asking whether you had a liver because you were concerned you'd been *stabbed in it*. Most people would say that part out loud!"

"Hi, Annie, nice to see you, Annie, welcome back, Annie, did you find the people you went looking for, Annie?" The crowd behind her certainly looked large enough to comprise the rest of the people on the campus. I did a quick mental count. There had been twenty-four humans, three more bogeymen, a chupacabra, and a cornwife outside the cafeteria. She was missing two of the bogeymen and six of the humans, in addition to picking up five more of the cuckoo children.

"Most of them," she said, thoughts turning briefly dark. "Got you this, too." She held the bundle out toward me. it made a small hiccupping noise, but didn't quite begin to cry. "Congratulations. You have a baby brother."

I blinked. The mystery of Ingrid's baby had finally, anticlimactically been solved. Well, the baby couldn't give consent yet, but I could still add his processing power to my own. He didn't need those memories.

"Can you hold him?" I asked. "My hands are sort of full right now."

"Sure. Anyway, we'll need to wait for Artie to get back with Crystal to retrieve the two from under the campus."

That made sense. A bogeyman in a dark room is basically invisible; two of them in a steam tunnel would be a horror movie if they didn't want to be found. "And the missing humans?"

One of the survivors started to cry. "The spiders—they came in the dark, and the parking garage door wasn't sealed properly," she said. Then she noticed Greg and screamed, setting off about half of the children in the process.

I was getting really tired of that. "Hello," I said, snapping my fingers. When that didn't work, I hurled a bolt of artificial calm at her mind, extinguishing her panic. "I'm Sarah, I'm the mathematician who's going to be tying my brain into knots to try to get you home in one piece. It's nice to meet you, or it would be under better circumstances. The giant spider behind me is Greg. He's mine. You will not harm him. You will not approach him with aggression. If he seems nervous, it's because the people who live in this dimension normally look a lot like us, and they hunt his kind, for admittedly good reason, so he's trying to figure out whether you're going to attack him. He will not attack you. He *will* defend himself. Got it?"

Confused murmurs answered me. They all spoke English; they just didn't understand why I was defending the giant spider. Well, they would learn, or we'd let Greg eat them.

Probably not, but it was nice to think about. I was exhausted and in pain, and about to do a piece of math so ridiculously improbable that it bordered on becoming actually impossible, and if I wanted to fantasize briefly about letting my fuck-off giant spider eat people who annoyed me, I was going to do it. I shifted my attention to Annie, and the baby.

"We didn't pull it out because I was afraid we'd disembowel me," I said. "Can you come and see whether we can take this thing out of me without killing me instantly?"

"Fuck, Sarah, have you always been this ridiculous, or is this a fun post-amnesia development?" she asked, hurrying over to my side.

"I don't know, would you call ripping a jagged spike out of my own guts a good idea?"

"Not really, no." She bent to study it where it was jammed into me, finally grimacing. "I've only reviewed the notes documenting one dissection. I'm going off what I remember, which probably isn't everything."

"It never is, but I can't imagine being a little bit wrong is worse than leaving this thing inside me indefinitely."

Annie lifted her head to look at me. I couldn't read her expression, but I could feel the gravity rolling off of her, trying to make me understand how serious she was. "Sarah, I don't think you quite get how serious a wound like this can be when we don't have immediate access to a hospital."

"There's a Caladrius on staff at St. Giles' in New York," I said. "Once you get it out, I just have to stay upright long enough to get us home, and then we evac me to the hospital where they have a chance in Hell of stabilizing me."

"If I take it out, I doubt you'll remain stable long enough to get us home," she said. "You might bleed out even if I don't, but at least this way there's a chance you finish your math problem before you do." For the first time, I was glad she didn't remember me. The Antimony I knew would never have agreed to a plan with this high a possibility of killing me, not if she could come up with any other way—and if she couldn't find a way, she'd do her best to make it. Well, this time, there wasn't any other way. This was what we had to do. This was how we got us home.

"James, I need you," she called, and James hurried over, leaving Greg to stand alone.

Annie ignored his discomfort, bending to set the bundled baby on the ground before grabbing his hands and pressing them against my middle, to either side of the spike. "You need to chill her to slow the blood flow, and then you're going to freeze the tissue directly around the spike," she said. "Cuckoos don't get frostbite the way humans do, so you won't hurt her unless you freeze her solid, but we need to stabilize this in place. So you're just going to freeze it exactly where it is for now. If the ice starts to melt, you'll just freeze it again."

"Don't worry about infection," I said, trying to sound

reassuring. I fell pretty far short of the mark, if James' surge of panic was anything to go by. "My blood is a natural antiseptic. Sometimes when other people in the field with me get hurt, I, um, bleed on them to help keep infection at bay."

James stared at me, thoughts a roiling pit of horror. I managed a weak smile.

"Guess I need to work on my bedside manner, huh?"

"Freeze her now," snapped Annie.

A wave of cold washed over me, centered on James' hands, so intense that for a moment it felt like he was actually going to turn me into an ice cube. Annie stroked my hair with one hand. "It's okay, Sarah," she said, and backed up her words with a wave of affection that only felt a little bit forced. "This is how you get us home."

Yes. It was. It always had been, and I knew how the math was going to resolve.

Nineteen

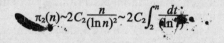

$$\pi_2(n) \sim 2C_2 \frac{n}{(\ln n)^2} \sim 2C_2 \int_2^n \frac{dt}{(\ln t)^2}$$

"Pain passes. Death doesn't."

—Enid Healy

Still on the quad at Iowa State University, in considerably less pain

I LIKED TO TALK about how cuckoos have a certain degree of natural resistance to cold, as one of the few evolutionary adaptations that really helps us out without making us more effective predators. The cold flowing out of James' hands continued to intensify until it was almost painful, and then it cracked, smoothing out into a pleasant numbness, like the sensations I'd picked up from Verity the one time she'd cracked her ankle and needed a cortisol shot.

Then something else felt like it cracked, internally this time, and for a moment my nerves were too overwhelmed to understand what was happening. There was nothing, not even numbness. That was when the pain came roaring back, bigger and brighter than before. James, Annie, and all the other humans echoed my agonized wails, leaving the cuckoo children standing in puzzled silence.

Then Mark was there, throwing himself between something and me. "Sarah, call off your spider!" he yelled.

The words didn't make any sense. I didn't have any spiders. I didn't have any pets. I didn't *want* a spider, I wanted Artie. I wanted—

I wanted—

I wanted to go home. The pain didn't recede as James pulled his hands away, but it recategorized and reassembled itself, becoming something more familiar. I shoved it further back, until it became a distant throb, still big enough to eat the world, absolutely, but manageable, no more than an annoyance. I pushed myself to my feet.

The wound in my gut wasn't bleeding anymore, thanks to being frozen solid and tinged with glacial blue. I didn't look too closely at the rest of the damage or the scope of the wound around the mantis leg still sticking out of my flesh. Knowing what was there wouldn't change it or make it go away. I had to stay standing long enough to finish the math. If I survived that, I could collapse as soon as we were back in our own dimension. Verity and the others had to be in Iowa by now. She'd make sure they got me to St. Giles', and Dr. Morrow would be able to fix me. That was the only thing I had to hold onto now. Dr. Morrow would be able to fix me.

Greg was right behind Mark. No, not behind; partially atop, his fangs buried in the meat of Mark's shoulder. I silently reached out and gathered Mark's pain, adding it to the great, amorphous mass of my own, even as I ordered Greg to let him go.

Greg detached his fangs reluctantly, leaving leaking holes in Mark's shoulder the size of stab wounds. How venomous were jumping spiders, anyway? I didn't know, and even if I'd thought I did, I would have known mostly about the ones back home, not the ones here in this dimension. Mark would be joining me at St. Giles' for medical treatment, obviously. What a treat for them. Two cuckoos on the same day, plus however many of the kids needed to be treated for shock or minor injuries.

There was a shout from the gathered warriors. Annie and Mark's had rejoined the ones left with James and me. I glanced over my shoulder. All of them had their weapons raised and pointed outward—although not, I was relieved to see, at us. They were forming a circle of their own, with themselves on the safe inside and the rest of the world locked out. The mantids, including the one that had injured me, were dancing from foot to foot, arms raised, ready to strike. But at what . . . ?

"Oh, fuck," breathed Mark.

I looked around, then followed his gaze.

The spiders were coming over the roof of the school, following a single human man who was running toward us as fast as his legs could carry him, a look of pure terror on his face. Terrence. Our unlamented little asshole had apparently found the place where the hunters in the dark, or at least some of them, had gone to sleep the day away, and had managed to wake them up. Now they were on their way to the party, driven by instinct to feed and to defend their territory.

Greg pressed up close to me, fangs raised, ready to defend me from his own kind. We'd both die in the attempt, but I appreciated the thought.

Mark, verify consent from the children, now, I commanded, picking up my pen and turning toward the whiteboard. *Annie, there's a gun in my backpack. Give it to James. We need someone to go get Artie, and I need the people who are willing to have their memories stripped to move to my left.*

Telepathy means not meaning to take the time to breathe in the middle of the sentence. "I can't go," said Annie. "You're going to need me chucking fireballs."

"The spiders don't recognize me as edible," said a man with hair the color of corn silk, complete with green undertones. That must be Michael, the cornwife. A dip slightly below the surface of his mind confirmed it. "I can go, if you tell me where this Artie person is."

"Do you know how to get to the cafeteria?" asked Annie.

He nodded. "Everyone knows how to—"

"He's there, getting the rest of the survivors. Go, and try not to get eaten by anything that *does* recognize you as edible." Antimony's voice had taken on that distinctive "I'm the Price, you have to listen to me" snap that members of the family get when they're under stress, and then claim doesn't exist.

It works. Not just on cryptids: I've seen her convince humans to do what she says just by taking that tone. Michael nodded, then turned and ran across the quad, away from us—and thankfully for him, away from the spiders.

Terrence, meanwhile, was still leading his arachnid army in our direction. If they reached us, they'd eat us. If they reached my collection of immobilized husks, they'd eat *those* first, and I couldn't afford to lose the processing power. I also couldn't seize the spiders the way I had Greg. Converting him into an ally had taken all my focus, and that had been one spider, when I was uninjured, not a whole swarm of them when I was freezing and dizzy from blood loss.

This better be all the coincidences, I sent to Mark, a tight needle of thought that caused him to look up from the children for half a beat, glancing over to me. To Annie and James, I said, *Protect the husks. I need them or this isn't going to work without someone's brains coming out of their ears.*

The two sorcerers moved to put themselves between the brainless, immobilized cuckoos and the oncoming spiders. Annie waved the hand that wasn't holding a baby in the air, producing a ball of fire larger than any I'd seen her create before. She bounced it in her palm like it was a hot potato. James made a similarly sized ball of ice, but didn't juggle it, just held it with grim determination, ready to hurl.

I focused on the whiteboard. The numbers were all there, ready for me to make use of them, and as soon as Mark's mental voice said, *All the children have agreed,* I began writing again.

The first step involved chaining all the pain-drenched minds of the cuckoo husks to my own, dumping chunks of equation into the howling void as soon as they were finished and intact. I didn't have time to check my work. I had to trust I was getting everything right on my first try, and I couldn't allow that to slow me down or make me second-guess myself. If I didn't do this correctly, we'd know about it soon enough.

By the time I had filled the second whiteboard, the void inside the husks wasn't howling anymore, wasn't hungry. It wasn't satiated, either, but filled with pieces of equation that connected seamlessly in the emptiness, filling it with secrets that should have been ours all along, if not for the short-sighted punishment inflicted on our ancestors by the people who were supposed to have taken care of them. I had no idea what the crimes of the original cuckoos could possibly have been, but the people of Johrlar should have understood enough about themselves to know they were laying down a punishment that would be inherited, generation unto generation, forever.

Or until we found a way to stop it. More gingerly, I extended a thread of myself toward the children, careful to keep it free of either pain or weariness, and began working it into their inner selves. They were layered with recent trauma and the temptation to remove those memories was strong enough to be almost overwhelming. There was a time when I would have welcomed someone taking away the memory of the accident that killed my original parents.

But I didn't have permission, and until they gave it to me, making that choice for them would be wrong. It's called "formative trauma" for a reason: no child should have to see or experience the things that some of these kids had seen, but those things happened. They had the right to retain their own lives as long as they wanted to, and if they wanted the memories gone later, that could happen.

The packages of hand-me-down memory waiting for the instar that would trigger them were easy to distin-

guish from the minds of the children, even with my attention split between the process, the ongoing effort of
the equation, and keeping hold of the husks. If the children's minds were bright and forming things, these
memories were parasitic sacs, perched atop the surface
of everything those children were and were becoming,
ready to rupture and leak their poison on the pieces of
personality growing around them. In some of the older
children, the sacs had already started to fissure, sending
out runnels of alien cruelty and superiority to infect the
nearby tissue.

Any description of the inside of someone's mind will
be wrong, by definition. A thought is not a thing, any
more than the code that makes up a video game is the
game itself. But the thought is also absolutely and entirely the thing, and much as a non-programmer can't
necessarily look at code and see the game, while the
programmer can, a telepath will build up images around
the ideas, in order to understand them a little bit better.

It's hard for me to wrap my mind around sometimes,
and I'm the telepath. I split the thought fragment of myself into each of the children, approaching the blistering
sac of the poisonous memories over and over again, cautious, all too aware of the threat it represented. I didn't
know whether I could be hurt by those memories if I
contracted them as an adult, with all the experiences
and ideas of adulthood to keep them from taking me
over, but the last thing I wanted to do right now was find
out by killing everyone I cared about.

One by one, I wrapped the memory sacs in filaments
of thought and yanked them loose, leaving gaping holes
where they had been, like extracting rotting teeth from
the gum tissue of the children's minds. Those holes
would heal, given time, filling with all the normal detri-
tus of a lifetime, but for right now, I needed it for my
own purposes. My body was still doing math, out in the
hazy, faintly unreal-feeling world outside their minds,
and as I kept unspooling the equation onto the white-

boards, I began dumping it into the holes I'd opened in
the children, going one by one until the space was gone
and forcing any more into them would have done damage. Reluctantly, I withdrew.

Out in the real world, Annie was hurling fireballs at
giant spiders and James was triggering small but impressive ice storms that pelted them with sleet and hail,
while the warriors stabbed at anyone who came close,
all save the one who was throwing fireballs of her own.
I blinked, my vision clearing long enough for me to
see Terrence taken down by a jumping spider with pat-
terning very similar to Greg's—it was easier for me to
tell the spiders apart on sight than the humans, because
they did me the courtesy of having such clear, bold,
geometric markings—and then I was diving into the
minds of the human and cryptid survivors from the library.

*Do you want the memories of what's happened in this
dimension?* I asked them each in turn.

Almost all of them said no. The ones who didn't had
other traumas in their past, scars that would make the
missing time an unbearable burden for them to carry.
To those, I apologized for even asking the question, and
set them gently outside my forming hive mind as I began
detaching and detangling the events of the last several
days from the minds of the others.

None of them fought me. I wasn't sure they could
have if they'd tried; the equation was riding me hard by
that point, a combination of mathematics and dimensional sorcery that needed more and more power to
keep unspooling itself.

A spider leapt for me. Greg met it in midair, both of
them tumbling away with a terrible keening sound. I
wanted to be afraid for him. I wanted to grieve for what
was surely going to be his demise. The emotional processing power simply wasn't there. I felt numb, detached
from both my own body and the scene around me. All
that mattered was riding this equation to its inevitable

end, making it manifest in the world and giving it the freedom to run.

And I couldn't, not with the space I had available. Even after rooting out every scrap of this dimension from the human students and every trace of the Johrlac cultural memory from the children, dumping as much as I could into the husks and the holes I had created, there was still too much for me to safely hold. If I didn't stop working, I was going to start deleting pieces of myself.

It might seem unfair to target the memories of the people around me while keeping my own intact—and there were certainly things I would have been happy to forget—but I didn't have any good, safe targets like they had. I was already missing the ancestral memories. If I deleted the last several days from my own mind, I would forget what I was doing and why it mattered, and abandoning this equation in the middle wouldn't break it, would just release it to run wild through the world, spraying its stored energy everywhere. I could destroy this reality if I wasn't careful.

I needed more space. I needed more power. I cast frantically around, trying to find anywhere that I could grab and use. There wasn't anything. The warriors were in the middle of a pitched battle against the spiders, and not only did I not have consent to use their minds, but they would die if they lost their focus. The same went for Annie and James. They might be willing to consent, but I couldn't afford to distract them.

Sarah. The voice was Mark's. I looked around. He was bathed in lens flare, like a character from the J.J. Abrams *Star Trek* reboot, and the details of his body were blurred, but he was there. He still existed.

Use me, he said. *Take the memories I inherited from my mother out of me.*

You've had time to absorb the memories, I said. *It would be like pulling the eggs out of a cake after it was baked. I'd destroy the cake. I'd destroy you.*

I can see enough of the math to know that if you don't, it's going to destroy us all. Someone has to make it home. Someone has to take care of Cici. His mental tone turned harsh. *Or are you too much of a coward to risk breaking someone who doesn't think you're a worthless waste of space? Are you really going to put your morals above our* survival? *Did the humans break you that badly? Coward. Stupid useless coward.*

I think I screamed. I was far enough removed from my own body not to know for sure by that point. I dove into Mark's mind, rooting out the black threads from the ruptured memory sac and ripping them free, heedless of the damage I did in the process.

And it wasn't enough. Any space the sac had created when it drained out was long since gone, replaced by memories of his family, his sister, his life. I saw Cici the way he saw her, and she was the most beautiful person who had ever lived, and she deserved more than anything to see her brother again. I rooted out every single scrap of memory, tearing them out of the places where they had dug into his psyche, and who he was going to be when this was over was something I didn't know and had no way of guessing. Mark collapsed, body spasming from the stress.

And it wasn't enough. I still had one whiteboard left to fill, one whole section of the equation left to complete, and I had no more willing storage space, and no room left in the husks. I felt wildly around, testing the minds of the spiders, and found them too small for my purposes.

Annie yelled something. I couldn't understand the words, any more than I could understand the subtleties of a smile. James yelled something in return, and the omnipresent hum of Artie's mind brightened, signaling that he was getting closer to me. I reached for him, finding the rest of the students behind him, along with the girls I'd met before.

They had formed a small hive mind of their own, driven by Morag, who seemed to be using the control to keep Lupe from falling apart completely as they ran. I dove into her thoughts, demanding to know whether I could strip the memory packet out of them.

Sarah? Morag's voice was more quizzical than confused. *You sound upset.*

Everything is upsetting right now, I replied. *Can I do it?*

Yes, but—

There wasn't time to listen to the qualifications. I dove into all three of them, grabbing the ancestral memories and shunting them into the void as fast as I could.

Ava's sac had already started to rupture, worse than any of the others. She'd probably been within a day of starting to murder anyone who looked at her oddly for the crime of not being a cuckoo. The memories hadn't had the time to sink below the level of her conscious mind, but catching and containing them all still took a dismaying amount of effort. I finished mopping up the last terrible traces and slammed as much of the equation as I could into the three of them, moving fast now, too close to the end to stop myself.

Too close to the end to do anything but keep writing, finishing a problem that had killed one of the people who created it, writing a future that I wasn't going to live to see. Because the next thing it would consume was everything that made me who I was, starting from the beginning, from Mama McNally kissing my forehead and telling me the great lie of Santa to Mama Baker telling me not to be silly, of course we didn't have a chimney to Evie cocking her rifle and saying that Santa Claus wasn't a lie, he was a bastard, and if he showed his face in her house again, he'd be sorry. It would wring me out and throw me away, the same way the equation written by the cuckoos had intended to do, and I would let it, because it would get the rest of them home.

Please, get them home, I thought, and stopped fighting to contain the equation.

It leapt free of its confinement, ravenous and frantic. It wasn't hostile the way the equation of the cuckoos had been, but I was coming to understand the Johrlac system of magic a little better: it was alive, every single time, an organism made of thought and pure mathematics that began with the first stroke of the pen and died when its operation was complete. And in the middle, it needed room to run and minds to eat, using the power of thought to sustain itself. I wasn't enough. It needed a whole hive mind to sustain it, not one queen and a bunch of broken husks who couldn't consciously contribute to its well-being. It needed more.

It needed everything I had. The world went white, the lens flare swallowing everything else that was or ever could have been under a veil of burning bioluminescence. I couldn't see the board anymore, but I knew I was still writing, the equation completing itself with the tools I had at hand. It was nibbling around the edges of me, little things disappearing faster than I could remember to mourn them, leaving only itself behind.

The core would go next, the deep memories that mattered to the person I was, and while something might be left when this was over, it wasn't going to be *her*. I took the microsecond before that happened to mourn her.

And someone grabbed my arm.

The equation, which was smart enough, if not to stop feeding, to at least to know that eating the mathematician first wasn't a good idea, surged through that connection, overwhelming the person on the other end. The hand dropped away as its owner collapsed, but it was too late. Skin contact makes cuckoos stronger, makes it easier for us to do the things we do, which is why I've never much liked touching people when I didn't have to.

I wanted to look, to see who I'd just broken, but I couldn't. With the space afforded by an entire unshielded mind, the equation had backed off enough to let me finish my work untroubled. I blinked to clear the last dazzling brightness from my vision and went back to writing as fast as I could, trying to get the numbers and symbols down, out of my head, completed and manifest in the world.

There was a loud whirring sound behind me as the mantids took off, launching themselves into the air, presumably with the warriors on their backs and safely off the campus. As for the spiders, well, Iowa was about to have an exciting new problem, maybe, because I didn't have any way to tell them they needed to leave.

Annie and James were nearby, panting and winded, but uninjured as far as I could tell without actually reaching for them. That wasn't safe yet. Not with as much of the equation as I still needed to write down. So I kept writing.

Artie should have reached us by now, but the hum of his thoughts was gone, removed even from the background of the world. That was odd. Even when he didn't know who I was, Artie was always there.

I think that's when I knew. But knowledge is a burden all its own, and one I didn't currently have the leverage to carry, so I shunted that knowledge to the side, along with everything else I couldn't handle yet, and kept writing.

Annie shouted something. I didn't understand her. In that moment, English was not a language I knew. I kept writing. I was nearing the end of the equation. In a moment, it would be finished, and I could stop.

I wrote the last series of symbols, telling it where we wanted to go and what we wanted to take with us. The pen dropped from my fingers, drained of ink, no longer necessary. The world shuddered, sighing, almost peaceful. I turned, and there was Antimony, on her knees next to Artie, who was staring blankly upward, at a sky that was no longer orange, but the color of badly-washed slate, gray streaked with white. It wasn't a sky I recognized. Maybe it was the sky of Iowa, where I had never been as a conscious being, and maybe it wasn't, and either way, there was nothing I could do about it now.

I hit the ground next to him, neither of us moving, my own vision beginning to blur as my body shut down. I closed my eyes and reached for his hand, but even when I touched his skin, no thoughts answered my presence.

I'm sorry, I thought, and silence answered me, louder than all the screaming in the world.

I'm sorry. I'm so, so sorry.

Twenty

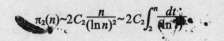

$$\pi_2(n) \sim 2C_2 \frac{n}{(\ln n)^2} \sim 2C_2 \int_2^n \frac{dt}{(\ln t)^2}$$

> "Everyone makes mistakes. It's what you do afterward that makes the difference between good and evil."
>
> —Jane Harrington-Price

Not entirely sure, but not tied to a chair this time, which is probably a good thing

I WOKE UP STRETCHED on what felt like a slab of plywood, with scratchy cotton sheets stretched out over me, and at least—I paused, squinting my eyes tighter shut—two IVs sticking out of my arms. Another discomfort made itself known, and I increased my count of indignities by one catheter. Machines beeped and whirred in the background, steady and soothing.

I opened my eyes. Every patient room ceiling looks essentially the same. They can paint them in different colors, but they're still industrial buildings, designed to be as generic and inoffensive as possible, so they can rotate patients. That was, under the circumstances, reassuring. Another dimension might have a sky the color of ours, might have people who looked like ours, but how many coincidences would have to line up for them to have hospital ceilings that looked like ours?

That reminded me. I still hadn't told Annie what I'd learned from Mark. She'd want to know. We've been arguing for decades about what little extra something Fran may have brought to the family that gave them their resistance to cuckoo influence. Finally having a name would let them start their research, as soon as we got home. As soon as we—

"Artie!" I sat up in the bed, noting as I did that the wound in my abdomen seemed to have healed. At least there was no pain.

The movement gave me my first really clear look at the room itself. It was small, plain, and single, containing me and the bed, the machines that had been monitoring my condition, and a chair. There was no table or TV stand, probably because that space—most of the available space in the room, really—was taken up by the massive black-and-white bulk of a crouching jumping spider.

"Greg," I said, blinking. The spider stood, swiveling until he could see me, then surged forward, pedipalps waving as he reached up to caress my cheek with one foot. He smelled faintly of lemons, and the lice I'd seen before were no longer moving through the hairs on his head. "You're alive. You're *here*. You shouldn't be here. I can't get you back to your own dimension, I don't know how . . ."

Both times I'd performed the crossing, it had been under the influence of something much bigger and more dangerous than I could safely control. Even for Greg, I couldn't do that again.

Greg's simple thoughts were all relief and contentment. I was awake and I was alive, and that was what mattered. He didn't care if he was the only member of his species in this dimension. He didn't care that he'd been hurt. His wounds were healing, he was here, I was here, and while he was hungry, he'd been fed at least once since our arrival. His mind was too simple to tell me much more.

Well, the fact that I could both perceive and touch his mind told me that whatever I'd done to myself this time, it wasn't as bad as that first time in New York, when I'd triggered an instar that had taken me years to recover from.

Not as bad for me, anyway. I didn't know where everyone else was, or even if we were in New York. I hugged Greg around what served as his neck, aware of the ridiculousness of treating a giant spider as a teddy bear, and tried to fight back the tide of panic I could feel rising in my chest. It wasn't a good enough effort, and I was starting to see dark spots around the edges of my vision by the time the door opened and a tall man in surgical scrubs stepped into the room.

He was barefoot, which wasn't the oddest thing about his appearance. No, that honor was reserved for his broad, white-feathered wings, which were half-mantled behind him. "You will *stop* that, Ms. Zellaby!" he snapped. "You are not the only patient in this hospital, and while I am willing to make some allowances for your family and situation, I will not allow you to upset people who need to recover!"

My panic died, replaced by dawning wonder. "Dr. Morrow?" I asked.

The Caladrius doctor snapped his wings shut. "Indeed. I was hoping not to see you again under these circumstances."

I unwound my arms from around Greg and started laughing.

"Or accompanied by such a unique emotional support animal," continued the doctor, before catching himself and blinking at me. "Ms. Zellaby? Are you quite all right?"

"I'm—ha!—I'm fine." It was hard to talk around the laughter. I felt like I was shaking apart at the seams. "I wasn't sure we'd ever—ha *ha*!—make it back to Earth, or that I'd live long enough for them to get me to a hospital, but sure, Greg's my emotional support animal, works for me."

"They weren't kidding?" he asked. "You named the spider *Greg*?"

I stopped laughing as I stared at him. "They who?" I asked.

"The people who brought you here. You arrived with quite the crowd, Ms. Zellaby. I believe the entire Price family is in my waiting room right now, in varying degrees of panic, not to mention all the other . . . what in the world are you doing?"

I had started trying to yank the IVs out of my arms as soon as he said my family was here, but shied away from removing my own catheter. Instead, I looked at him levelly.

"I just crossed dimensions twice and acquired a giant spider for a service animal," I said. "Now get this fucking thing out of my genitals so I can go and see my family."

I was weaker than I'd realized when I was lying flat in a hospital bed, but leaning on Greg and letting Dr. Morrow take my arm, we were able to get me down the hall to the waiting room.

St. Giles' is one of the few cryptid-only hospitals in North America. Staffed and managed entirely by cryptids, they only see human patients under extremely special circumstances. Verity had been treated here, after she was shot by a Covenant field team. Dr. Morrow didn't have to hide his wings because everyone in the hospital knew what he was, and took pride in having an actual Caladrius on their staff.

"HAIL!" shouted the congregation of mice standing on the magazine table. "HAIL THE RISE OF THE CALCULATING PRIESTESS!"

"Sarah!" gasped Mom, passing the baby she'd been cradling to my father before shoving herself out of the chair she'd been crammed into. Human or cryptid, hospitals are all the same.

This waiting room was certainly crowded. Mom and Dad were both there, along with Evie and Kevin, Annie and Sam, Verity and Dominic, Alex and Shelby, and even Drew. Only Uncle Ted and Aunt Jane were missing, along with Artie and Elsie. I don't have a heart.

Literally. My anatomy doesn't work that way. I still felt mine sink.

"Mom?" I managed to squeak, as my mother swept me into an all-encompassing hug. "Mom, where are the Harringtons?"

She let me go, stepping back a bit. "Sweetie, things have been hectic since you and the school reappeared. We were all in Iowa already, looking for you, but we weren't sure—"

"Mom. Where are they?" She looked away, not meeting my eyes. "Mom, where's Artie?"

"He isn't awake yet," said Antimony. She didn't stand, or maybe she couldn't; Sam had his tail wrapped around her waist like he was trying to keep her from floating away, and he didn't look inclined to let her go. "When he grabbed you, it was like he'd put his finger into a light socket. Mark isn't awake yet either."

"But with Mark, we have some idea of what's going on," said Evie. "Dr. Morrow did an MRI, and his brain is contracting and smoothing the way yours did at the start of your metamorphosis. He thinks Mark might be becoming the first known cuckoo king."

"There are so many unknowns when dealing with your species," said Dr. Morrow. "We have to let the process run its course before we'll be able to say anything for sure. As to your cousin . . ."

I turned on him, eyes tingling as they went white. The doctor visibly paled, taking a step backward. "He's breathing on his own," he said. "We can find no signs of higher brain function, but his body is behaving normally. He's alive."

"We just don't know what's happening, sweetheart," said Evie. "His parents and sister are with him."

"We felt it best to minimize visitors until we know more," said Dr. Morrow.

"Take us there," I said. "Now." After a beat, I turned to Evie and said, "And bring the mice."

We more than filled the hospital hallway: two cuckoos, a Revenant, a bogeyman, seven humans, a fūri, a

Caladrius, and a giant jumping spider. Dr. Morrow led the way, stopping outside a door like the one I'd been behind when I woke up.

"He's in here," he said. "Visiting hours are—"

We all turned to look at him. He swallowed hard.

"Are irrelevant," he said. "Stay as long as you like." Then he fled down the hall.

I pushed the door gently open. Aunt Jane and Uncle Ted were sitting next to Artie's bed, while Elsie paced at the back of the room. She jumped at the sound of us stepping into the room, eyes resting on me for only a moment before she recoiled.

"Elsie . . ." I began. The words dried up in my mouth. Annie put her hand on my shoulder.

"We told them what happened," she said. "All of it."

So they knew I'd tampered with Artie's mind at least once before he'd grabbed me and been overloaded by the equation. Was he even in his body anymore? Was there anything left of him to save?

Hesitantly, I approached the bed. Aunt Jane turned to face me, eyed red and puffy in her familiar unfamiliar face.

"Sarah," she said. "You're awake. Can you . . . I hate to ask, but is he . . . ?" She stopped, leaving the anguished hope of her unfinished question hanging in the air.

"I don't know," I said honestly.

She lifted his unresisting arm and held it out toward me, his hand dangling limply. My stomach churned as I reached out and took it, using the skin contact to ease my reach for his mind.

It wasn't there.

Nothing was there, not even the howling void of the husked-out cuckoos; there was only an empty whiteness, a nothing that stretched from one side of infinity to the other. It was like a blank sheet of paper waiting to be inscribed. I gasped, breaking the contact and recoiling.

"What did you see?" demanded Aunt Jane. "Where is my boy?"

I didn't know how to answer her. He was in the bed,

and he wasn't, because Arthur Harrington-Price as we knew him wasn't anywhere anymore. He'd been over-written.

But unlike the cuckoos, he hadn't been *wiped*. They'd been the equivalent of hard drives after exposure to massive electromagnets, warped and distorted, incapable of being rebuilt. He was just blank, a reformatted disk. And we—his family, the only people he had ever trusted to be near him—were all here. In distributed math theory, he was here. In memory, he was here.

"Are any of Artie's clergy with us?" I asked.

Several small voices answered in the affirmative, mice squeaking out their allegiance to the Church of the God of Chosen Isolation. I bit my lip and nodded.

"I need everyone's consent to enter your minds, please," I said softly.

"I don't want you in my head after what you did to my brother," spat Elsie.

"Honey, please," said Uncle Ted. "Of course, Sarah. Whatever you need."

One by one, the others agreed, even Elsie and the mice, until only Greg and the baby remained silent. This was probably a bad idea when I was still exhausted and recovering from severe injury, but I didn't see another choice. It was now, while his body was still functional and his mind was still empty of new experiences, or it was never.

I preferred now.

Closing my eyes, I grabbed Artie's hand again, and reached for the minds around me, all of them, from Aunt Evie down to the youngest member of his clergy. Drew only had a few memories, gathered from awkward encounters at family holidays, while Elsie remembered years piled on top of years. The mice had everything, because the mice never forgot.

Was I building a perfect model? Of course not. Even a telepath doesn't know exactly why someone did the things they did in the manner and order they did them, not unless the person is present for them to ask, but I had an advantage. Over the decades, I had spent more time in Artie's head than anyone else's but my own. I had chat logs and emails and stolen memories and events viewed from a dozen different angles.

I gathered the memories of his entire family and of the mice who worshipped him as a living god, and I built Arthur Harrington-Price anew, from the bottom up. And yes, I built a version of him who knew me, because that was the version almost everyone around me remembered, but I also built in the memories of the nameless dimension where he'd forgotten me—where he had, in a very real sense, died.

It took an instant. It took an infinity. When it was done—when there was nothing left to add, or adjust, or move around—I opened my eyes and wobbled, a wave of dizziness sweeping over me. It was suddenly difficult to keep my feet, and my knees buckled, almost sending me crashing before Evie and Drew caught me, my family keeping me from hitting the floor.

There was so much to deal with, like Greg, and the cuckoo children, and what the lasting ramifications of stealing an entire college campus only to return it littered with inhuman corpses were going to be. The Covenant must have noticed, but would they realize it was us? Or would we be able to dodge this bullet? How long had we been gone? If time ran differently between dimensions, we could have been gone weeks, months . . . even years. Who was Mark going to be when he woke up? *Was* he going to wake up?

And none of that mattered, because Artie's hand was still limp in my own, and I had ruined everything. I dropped his hand, letting Evie and Drew hold me up.

"I want to go back to my room now," I said, voice suddenly very small. "I'm tired."

We started to turn away. Aunt Jane gasped.

I whipped around, knocking my siblings' hands off myself in the process. Artie's eyes were open, and he was blinking quizzically at the ceiling.

"My head hurts," he said, voice weak but clear, cadences distinctly his own. "What happened? Where are we?" He turned, blinking again as he saw me. Then his whole face softened. I didn't have to read his expression to understand the shift in his musculature as he saw me. "Sarah? Are you all right? You look like hell."

I all but flung myself across the room, landing in a heap against his chest. His arms came up, and he held me, and we were both going to make it.

We were both going home.

Read on for
a brand-new InCryptid novella
by Seanan McGuire:

SINGING THE
COMIC-CON BLUES

"You have to love something outside the fight. If you don't, it's going to consume you. Obsession is as dangerous as anything else you might face."

—Alice Price-Healy

A very pleasant, fully furnished basement in Portland, OR, home of the world's most squirrely half-incubus

Approximately nine years ago

THE URGE TO SMOTHER my cousin with a pillow was not a new one. Much to my chagrin, it was an impulse I'd been wrestling with on and off since middle school, and it only got worse as we all grew older and settled more firmly into the people we were going to be as adults. It's one thing to punch someone whose favorite color changes day by day, sending his clergy into an unending tizzy of redesigning their vestments. It's something else to punch them when they've been steady and stable for months. One is consequences. The other is bullying.

And yeah, as we grew out of the mercurial whims of childhood, we'd grown more and more firmly *into* the recognizable adult versions of ourselves. The next generation of Prices, out to protect-slash-save the world from the Covenant of St. George and all the dangers it had come to represent.

Sure would have been nice if we'd *all* received the extra points during character generation that had been doled out to the cryptid members of the family. Mom liked to remind me that humans were useful too, and that she'd struggled with the same feelings when she had been a teenage girl growing up in a house full of cuckoos, bogeymen, and Revenants.

"Just because all the fantasy writers want you to think of humans as the boring generic bipeds, that doesn't mean you need to live like that," she'd said, every time she caught me moping. "Besides, the other options come with problems of their own, and you know any of your cousins would trade with you in an instant if they could."

And I would have taken the trade, then *or* now. I could certainly have done more with Lilu pheromones than Artie did. I glared at the back of his head, willing him to turn around and realize that he was really getting on my nerves.

"You can stare at me as much as you want, it's not going to change my answer," he said, tone almost light, fingers still moving across his keyboard in quick, confident arcs. He knew what he was doing, even if he wasn't letting me in on it.

Sarah, sitting on the other side of the room with her elbows on her knees and an issue of *Spider-Man* in her hands, probably also knew what he was doing. Stupid telepaths.

"I heard that," she said, voice light and relaxed, almost singsong.

"I wasn't trying to keep you out," I countered.

She looked up from her four-color paradise, wrinkling her nose as she stuck her tongue out at me. I resisted the urge to throw a pillow. If I knocked the comic out of her hands, there was no possible way I'd be able to talk Artie around to my point of view. He's a real stickler when it comes to keeping his things nice. Sometimes I think he doesn't even read his own comics, just lets Sarah read them and then shares the memory with her mentally.

It's a weird sort of slow-motion psychic flirtation that I really wish they'd hurry up and get on with. How they can keep insisting that they're not totally hot for each other while they pull this sort of shit is a genuine mystery to me.

But then, most elements of human—or cryptid—sexuality are a mystery to me. Hormones are a waste of time. And how their hormones can even recognize each other is like, double mystery, since he's a human/Lilu hybrid, and she's a giant telepathic wasp who looks like she should be headlining an indie rock act somewhere downtown.

"Very mature," I said. "I bet all the boys at math club love it when you make that face. Artie, will you tell your cousin that no one takes you seriously when you don't know how to put your tongue away?"

Sarah genially flipped me off before closing her comic and setting it safely to one side. "You can throw that pillow now," she said.

"*Thank* you," I said, and threw it. She laughed as she batted it aside. If more cuckoos bothered with combat training, we'd all be even more comprehensively screwed than we are already, since an opponent who can see your blows coming is an opponent who isn't there to hit.

"But seriously." I settled back on the bed, shifting position slightly so that I could look at both of them at once. Sure, in Artie's case, I was just looking at the back of his head, but that was still looking in his general direction. "We have to go."

"I'm not stopping you." Artie kept typing. "You're right; it's our responsibility to look into this, even if we don't do anything else."

"I didn't say *I* had to go. You really want me to roll into this sort of situation without any backup? That's a good way for me to get myself very, very dead."

Sarah shifted positions on the floor, drawing her

knees up toward her chest in what looked like a reflexively defensive motion. That made sense. Maybe it's because she wasn't born a Price, and maybe it's because she's already buried one set of parents, but she gets uncomfortable whenever one of us reminds her that our jobs stand a decent chance of getting us killed one day.

I won't be the first to die. That honor is almost certainly reserved for my sister, who seems to think that looking like our grandmother means emulating her in all things, including a lack of anything resembling a sense of self-preservation. Grandma stays alive through a combination of grenades, stubbornness, and being too scary for even the gods of death to go after. Aunt Mary was her babysitter—Aunt Mary died before Grandma was even born, and that's one of the less confusing things about our family tree—and she says Grandma was always like this, even as a little girl.

Clearly, the only explanation is that she's secretly beloved of some chthonic deity or other, who doesn't want to have to explain her to their spouse before it's absolutely necessary. How else does a woman with a death wish broader than the River Styx wind up eternally youthful, and roaming the dimensional trails with enough ammunition to take out a small army?

But I digress. Verity seems to think Grandma is a role model, and not a cautionary tale, and she's taken the lead in the family "who dies first?" betting pool for the last three years out of four. She's even been known to bet against herself. The only reason she didn't sweep all four years was that we disqualified her when she decided to go off and be a reality television star instead of a good, honest cryptozoologist.

But that's over now. She lost her bid for stardom, and she's back in the real world with the rest of the peons. And anyway, my stupid sister is not the point here. My desire not to go out of state without backup is the point. I glared daggers at the back of Artie's head, daring him to turn around and see the look I was giving him.

He squirmed in his seat, at least aware enough to

know that he wasn't doing much to stay on my good side. And staying on my good side is never a bad idea, especially not for my cousins, who have to live with me, whether they like it or not.

Hi. My name's Antimony, and I have it on good authority from basically everyone I've ever met that I can be really, *really* irritating when I want to be. Call it one of the benefits of being the youngest sibling out of three, and the youngest cousin out of six. Or call it proof that I am evolution's perfect monster, all the obnoxiousness potential of my incredibly aggravating family boiled down into one aggressively geeky body. I am what happens when nerds are allowed to marry nerds and thus produce even *more* nerds, like nerdiness squared, like what happens when Seymour from *Little Shop* is allowed to hook up with Jordan from *Real Genius*. And if you got both those references, odds are good that you're a nerd, too, which would explain why you're following this road trip of the damned.

But I'm getting ahead of myself again. Aunt Mary says it's a natural consequence of being among the living but spending too much time with the dead. Ghosts have a questionable sense of linear time. Comes from being deceased. For them, everything happens in this sort of squishy, unending "now." Makes cause and effect hard on them, and is just one of the many, many reasons that it's not a good idea for dead people to hang out with living ones.

Good thing my family has never put too much focus on prioritizing good ideas.

I picked up another pillow, weighing it thoughtfully in my hand. Sarah raised an eyebrow, watching me. She knew what I was planning—she always knew what I was planning, such are the dangers of spending too much time around an attunement-based telepath—but she didn't seem inclined to warn Artie, which meant she wanted him to go along with this as much as I did.

You'd think that would make things easier on me. You'd be wrong. Sarah's a cuckoo, one of two in the world who actually has some sort of moral center and ethical objection to treating other people like puppets—and since her mother, my grandmother, *can't* treat people like puppets, no matter how much she might sometimes want to, the fact that Sarah *doesn't* really makes her tediously unique. It also makes her remarkably wishy-washy and unhelpful when it comes to things like convincing Artie to leave the house.

Her argument is that she knows exactly what to say to make him go along with what she wants, and so any sort of pressure from her is cheating, like playing a video game after you've purchased the hint book. My argument is that the hint book wouldn't be for sale if they didn't expect people to use it, and if she has the cheat codes, she should damn well be taking advantage of them. Which inevitably leads to her pointing out that I wouldn't want her using the cheat codes on me, and then I have to go and throw knives at the targets in the backyard until I calm down.

Whatever. Screw it. I flung the pillow at the back of Artie's head, scoring a direct hit, as usual, and causing him to turn in his chair and narrow his eyes at me, annoyance warring with amusement for ownership of his expression.

"If you're going to keep throwing my stuff, I'm going to have to ask you to leave," he said, before shooting a wounded look at Sarah. If she'd been able to read human expressions like a normal person, the degree of affronted puppy-dog eye he was giving her would have had her proposing on the spot.

In the books and comics, it's always easier for the telepaths and empaths to get a date. They just know they're meant to be with their true loves forever, and they make it happen, like the big, stupid, fictional people that they are. In the real world, feelings are complicated and people are confusing, and adding new sensory input to the pile just makes things worse, especially when the people in question belong to completely different species.

Sometimes I still wanted to knock their heads together.

"Look, we've been over this," I said sternly. "We know someone, or something—probably a siren, which would put us firmly into 'someone' territory, but I'm open to other interpretations of the data—has been hunting at large media conventions all spring."

"Yes, we know that," said Artie warily.

"And we know that Emerald City Comic Con is happening in Seattle next weekend. Sarah's already said that she can get us into the convention, and get us a hotel room once we arrive—"

"It's unethical, but I'm not morally opposed to defrauding the Hiltons," said Sarah.

"—so there's literally no reason for us not to go and deal with this."

"I never said there was," said Artie.

I raised an eyebrow.

"I just said I wasn't going to go with you."

"You *have* to come with us."

"Oh, really." He crossed his arms. "I have to go with you."

"Yes!"

"I, the incubus, who doesn't like to leave my bedroom, much less my house, have to go with you."

"Yes, you do."

"To a large convention filled with literally thousands of people, many of whom will be sexually attracted to men and thus vulnerable to my pheromones, regardless of whether or not they would actually choose to be sexually attracted to *me* under ordinary circumstances, where we will steal a hotel reservation from someone who has probably planned their entire year around this event, all for the sake of you maybe getting to ruin a siren's day?"

"There were six deaths at the last convention we think she hit," I said calmly. "And that one was just near Lake Michigan. Emerald City has Lake Washington *and* the entire damn Pacific. If a siren is actually targeting these conventions, we could be looking at a lot more than six deaths."

To my surprise, Sarah chimed in: "And if we don't stop this now, we're looking at the possibility of a siren hitting San Diego. That's the biggest of the annual geek media trade shows. It's basically a nerd buffet for someone—or some*thing*—that's decided they would make a good target."

"Don't any of these conventions happen inland?" he demanded, throwing his hands in the air.

"Some do. None of the really big ones, though. Origins is usually inland. Worldcon is sometimes, but it's like, half the size of the Dragoncon writer's track, so I'm not sure it counts," said Sarah. "Mathematically speaking, you'd have to attend almost all the available non-coastal media shows to equal one trip to San Diego. And that includes several large regional anime conventions."

We both turned to look at her flatly. She shrugged, utterly unrepentant.

"What?" she asked. "I like doing my research, when my research involves a lot of numbers, and you're the one who said you thought we might have something using the conventions as a hunting ground."

"Right," I said slowly. "And the fact that only the shows near water have been hit makes me think that it's probably a siren." That, and all the bodies bobbing near the shore of the respective cities to have been targeted. When the Coast Guard has to keep fishing corpses out of the water, "siren" isn't a difficult leap to make.

"And I need to come with you why?" asked Artie. "Before we get so far off the original topic that you start advocating for Aquaman as a solution to our problems."

"Sirens hunt through emotional manipulation," I said. "You're an empath. If there's a siren anywhere near the convention center, you'll pick up on them before they can hurt anyone. We can use you as a dowsing rod."

"Plus I'll be there," said Sarah. "If any of the people who are impacted by your pheromones try to get creepy on you, I can disappear us both."

"Are you sure you're up for making me disappear?" asked Artie dubiously. "Last time you tried, it didn't go as well as you were hoping it would."

Sarah looked abashed, ducking her chin toward her chest and giving off the distinct impression that, had she possessed a mammalian circulatory system, she would have been blushing. Cuckoos don't have red blood cells. It's weird, and according to all my high school biology classes, they shouldn't be able to convey oxygen effectively through their systems, leading to them dying in exciting and unpleasant ways. According to Sarah, the one time I tried to tell her that, biology can fuck right off, since she's doing just fine. I guess a living, non-suffocated cousin is a better argument than Ms. Shindell.

"That was a year ago," said Sarah. "I've been practicing lots. I made Verity disappear twice while she was doing *Dance or Die*, and I made myself disappear lots. I can manage the two of us."

"I still don't think you should have gone to that show with her," said Artie.

Sarah shrugged, chin still tucked down.

"Cryptid" means "unknown to science." We've sort of expanded the meaning locally, using it as a catchall for things that science may *know* about, but has chosen to dismiss as mythological, or illogical, or extinct. Psionic powers, for example, or wasps who look like women, or nonhuman species of primate capable of not only masquerading as humans but hiding among them as if they fully belonged. Technically, half the things we call cryptids aren't. Because science knows people believe in unicorns, science just thinks we're wrong. And science knows that a lot of people say that lake monsters are plesiosaurs of some sort, science just disagrees. But the fact that my family's life work—the work of literal generations, people living and dying for the cryptid world—depends on staying unknown to science means that we tend to keep a pretty low profile.

And then there's the Covenant of St. George, which is *also* unknown to science—and subscribes to a frankly ridiculous interpretation of the Bible, claiming that only creatures explicitly called out as having appeared on Noah's Ark are "real" and have the right to continue existing in our modern world—and would love to kill us all for the crime of not being members of their whackadoo little biological supremacy cult. We used to be members, before my great-great-grandparents figured out that the Covenant was doing more harm than good with their constant attempts to cleanse and conform the world. So yeah, it sucks that we used to play their reindeer games, and there are some cryptids who still hold it rightfully against us—you don't get to erase generations of genocidal behavior by shrugging and saying "whoops, my evil Auntie Agnes' bad"—but we don't do that anymore.

We're conservationists now. For *everybody*, including the humans. If we sat back and let a hungry cryptid slaughter their way through the human population, sure, we'd be feeding one member of a marginalized population, but we'd be really, really risking that "unknown to science" status if we allowed it to happen without stepping in. And losing "unknown to science" would endanger the rest of the population, because if there's one thing the Covenant of St. George has taught us, it's that humans don't like to share.

All this need for secrecy means that we've lived our lives like we were living in a messed-up spy show version of witness protection. I was a cheerleader in high school, taking advantage of the fact that the strength and flexibility training inherent in the sport fed well into hand-to-hand combat and the sort of stealth missions I was best at, and my parents never once attended one of my games. They couldn't safely be seen in my presence, and there was always too much of a chance that a random Covenant observer might spot them in the stands.

Maybe it's being paranoid to assume that a global organization of monster hunters would have someone monitoring a high school football game, but I say that paranoia keeps people breathing. It's better to be safe and intact than sorry and in pieces.

I had to quit cheerleading when I graduated high school, since collegiate cheerleading at a level that would actually challenge me and maintain my skills attracted too much attention. The World Cheer Competitions might be small potatoes so far as sporting events went, but they were still aired on ESPN, albeit at two o'clock in the morning, and if I'd been spotted in my spangled leotard and spanky pants, I could have triggered a purge that would end my entire family. I don't *look* like a Price, in the sense that I actually *do* look like a Price, taking more after my paternal grandfather than the legions of dainty blonde women my ancestors have happily taken as their wives. I was still happier being safe than sorry.

My brother was even more sensible with his choice of extracurricular activities. He joined the Society for Creative Anachronism, playing at being a medieval knight and whacking other people who had the same fantasy with foam-covered swords. Portland, where we grew up, is located in the SCA Kingdom of An Tir, and Alex was one of its staunchest defenders until he turned twenty-two and reached the point where the other knights were hassling him about why he never fought in the Crown Tourney to determine who was going to be the next King. Personally, I like a nerd party where the leader is picked by beating the holy hell out of everyone else who wants the job, but even as relatively innocuous and deep geek as the SCA is, it can—and does—attract media attention. There was too much chance that he'd become King on a slow news week and wind up with his picture in the local paper.

So he quit. He took his existing peerage and his years of experience and his fondness for the community, and he packed them all away with an excuse about needing to leave the state for graduate school. As far as I'm aware, he never approached any other branch of the organization.

And then there's Verity. My older sister, whose chosen extracurricular activity had always been ballroom dance. She'd started competing before I was even in grade school, wearing wigs and colored contacts, concealing her identity behind a series of fake names like it was some sort of shell game, like she was never going to get herself caught. Like the judges didn't move around and see her competing in different cities, different states, different regions. She'd settled on a single legend by the time she turned sixteen, a redheaded tango prodigy named Valerie Pryor who danced with a variety of partners, always toward the front of the mob.

Valerie would have been a worldwide superstar of the ballroom world if only she'd been real. But since she'd been splitting her time between existence and being Verity, she had still been competing on a local level when one of her instructors had come to her with the opportunity to audition for *Dance or Die*, America's most popular dance-themed reality show. Millions of viewers, households across America, and, thanks to the wonders of the Internet, gifs and videos around the world. It was her shot at the big time. It was her opportunity to dance, finally, on a truly global stage.

She couldn't resist. Out of all of us, Verity had always been the one who couldn't stand the fact that no matter how hard she trained, how hard she tried, she would never be allowed to compete on the level she knew she was capable of. The level we all knew that we were capable of; we were smart kids born to a smart family and given endless opportunities at self-improvement, for the sake of making us better at the jobs we'd been born to do. Our parents had always insisted that they wouldn't force any of us to do anything, that if we wanted to move to Ohio and be accountants, we'd be allowed to do it and still be welcome at the family reunions.

But if *you* knew there was a whole secret world of magic and monsters and opportunities to make a difference, would you have been able to walk away from it for the sake of making a run for city council or getting your face on the front of the local paper? The idea that one of us would choose the much-vaunted "ordinary life" had always seemed completely ridiculous, a carrot held out to keep the stick of training from stinging too hard when it smacked us again and again. Until that damn television show.

Verity had gone to our parents with an argument based around her skill with a makeup brush and how the lighting and camera work on the show was unlikely to ever linger on her face. She'd drawn charts of where the necklines tended to fall on her style of dance costume, and she'd put on a performance worthy of the ages. And then, despite spending my entire life telling me that attracting attention would get me and everyone I gave a damn about killed on the spot, our parents had given in. They'd agreed to let her go on television, under a few conditions that were nowhere near strict enough to really keep us safe.

And maybe they were being reasonable, but they were also the ones who'd raised us with the constant fear that even the slightest slip would bring the Covenant crashing down on our heads. It wasn't unreasonable of me to be a little bit pissed that I'd been forced to give up cheerleading out of the concern that someone might freeze-frame a wide shot from a competition I wasn't even guaranteed to qualify for, run my unfamiliar face through facial recognition software, and say, "She has the Price family cheekbones! They must have somehow survived the great Michigan purge! We must hunt them even to the ends of the earth or all our works have been for naught!" All that, and Verity got to go on television. Call it the baby sister blues, but it wasn't fair, and I wouldn't have liked it even if she'd gone alone.

But of course she couldn't go alone, because Prices are functionally pack animals thanks to the way we're raised, and she'd taken Sarah with her, off to Southern California to feed her into the great maw of reality television. To Sarah's credit, we'd watched every episode of the show, sometimes in slow motion, and we'd never spotted her in the audience. Not even in a wide pan shot. Her control had been good enough that the people behind the cameras had managed to convince themselves that she wasn't there to focus on.

Verity, on the other hand, had been front and center for every single episode, right up until the last one, where she'd come in second and come home in a flurry of tears, self-blame, and sequins. The self-blame hadn't lasted long. The tears and the sequins had.

At least getting her back meant getting Sarah back at the same time. Artie had been almost unbearable while she was gone, sulking around the house, refusing to drive me to the comic book store on Wednesday afternoons, and picking fights with his sister Elsie every time she held still in his vicinity. Artie without Sarah was basically like a pumpkin pie without sugar: the texture might be roughly correct, but the flavor was so far off as to become inedible.

And now Verity was talking about fucking off to New York at the end of the summer, and taking Sarah with her for "backup," and I'd be damned before I let that happen without getting in at least one solid family road trip.

"Maybe not," said Sarah. "But I did, and none of us knows how to time travel."

"Can't Sarah just scan for the siren without me doing my empath thing?"

"No," said Sarah promptly. "Too many minds. I'd get overwhelmed and walk into a wall."

"So we're settled," I said, clapping my hands. "Sarah is in control enough to make you disappear if necessary, we're going to load you up on that terrible cologne that makes even your pheromones unbearable, and we're going to a comic book convention, where you will help us find the siren before anyone else gets hurt."

"We're not settled," protested Artie. "I never agreed to this."

"Well, agree fast. You're driving." I got off the bed and started for the door while Sarah was still trying to stifle her smile.

I don't drive. Neither does Sarah. Public transportation is safer and more environmentally friendly, plus it avoids the paper trail of having and maintaining a car. Between the blue slip and the insurance, owning a vehicle would almost double my administrative footprint. No one wanted that.

Sarah can see—cuckoos have eyes, and those eyes work just fine for things like reading comic books and watching television shows—but she's easily distracted by the thoughts of the people around her, and she doesn't recognize faces, which means she won't necessarily know if someone is distracted, or furious, or afraid. It's safer to keep her off the road.

Artie and Elsie, on the other hand, got their licenses the day the state allowed it. I guess when your natural abilities make you a walking consent violation, having your own space winds up feeling a lot more important.

Artie swore softly behind me, but I didn't hear him get up by the time I reached the top of the basement stairs, and I knew I had him. There had never been any real question; Sarah was going, and if Sarah was going, so was he, even if he spent the whole convention hiding in our hotel room.

Love makes people stupid, and unprofessed love seems to make things even worse.

I am never, ever falling in love, with anyone. I know you don't get to decide your sexual or romantic orientation—it's not a choice, it's a function of the way your brain works—but nope. Not for me, thank you. Boys are not better than pizza; girls are not better than ice cream; nonbinary people are not better than being able to do things because you want to, not because the person you're in love with wants it. My parents got themselves the heir, the overly-pampered spare, and me. It's not going to hurt the family's chances of survival if I refuse to play along with the implicit "go forth and multiply" concealed in the "only we can stop the Covenant" instructions passed down from my great-great-grandparents. And can you imagine me as a parent? Please. Even if I could tolerate another person touching me long enough to get pregnant, I'd never be able to put up with *incubating* someone for nine months.

You put in all that work to grow a second skeleton and then someone just takes it without so much as a "by

your leave." The nerve of some people! And as the recipient of one of those stolen skeletons, I can absolutely
say that I'm not planning to make one for anyone else,
or give the one I currently have back. If that's a problem
for my mother, she can take it up with my siblings, both
of whom stole their skeletons first.

We're fun at parties, honest.

I let myself out of the basement, action underscored
by the sound of Artie still swearing behind me, and
Sarah giggling.

My Aunt Jane was in the kitchen, fixing herself a sandwich, while a cluster of Aeslin mice looked raptly on.
They set up a raucous cheer when they saw me, although
the usual cries of "hail" were absent. Aunt Jane's colony
split from the rest of the family when she moved out of
the compound to set up her own household, long before
I was born, and her household mice aren't unified in
whether they recognize my siblings and I as divine.

That used to offend me pretty badly when I was a kid,
since the mice we have back at home absolutely recognize Elsie as a Priestess and Artie as a God, while the
mice who live at their house try to claim that I'm not
divine. Not all of them; the members of Artie and Elsie's personal clergy, who mingle more often with the
home colony, are also more likely to acknowledge my
title. The rest of them are involved in some sort of weird,
slow convocation that involves a lot of arguing about
divinity and its roots and shouts of heresy every time
one mouse says something another mouse doesn't like.

Having Aeslin mice means not needing cable. But it
also means not being able to talk about cartoons with
the other kids at school, so I guess there's a downside to
everything.

"Hey, Auntie Jane," I said, swinging myself into the
kitchen via the classic one-handed-grip-on-the-door-
frame pose, something that had always seemed infi-

nitely cool when I was a kid and in trapeze training for the first time, and which had managed to endure into adulthood through sheer dint of me being too set in my ways to want to find a new way to enter a room. "Making anything consumable by normal people?"

"Why? Are we expecting a visit from the normal people for some reason? I thought I was done with them when Artie graduated and they stopped trying to strong-arm me onto the PTA."

"No, no normal people en route."

"And thank God for that." She waved her jelly-covered knife at me. "You convince that son of mine to go to Seattle with you?"

"Not quite. I convinced him to go to Seattle with Sarah. I think he's accepted me as a necessary complication, but it's hard to be sure when you're not telepathic, and you know Sarah's not going to tell me what he's thinking."

"No, that girl thinks it's unethical to use what her mama gave her."

I raised an eyebrow. "I'm pretty cool with the telepath not pushing her way into people's heads for her own benefit. Sure, it slows things down sometimes, but there are means that don't justify themselves."

"I know, I know, it's just . . ." Aunt Jane sighed and went back to assembling her sandwich. Peanut butter, banana, ham, and maple jelly. "I knew when I married Ted that there was a decent chance any kids would take after him, but he's always been so comfortable with what he is, I thought they'd get that from their father, too. And, instead, I have Artie in the basement, probably for the rest of his life, constantly refusing to go out into the world, and we have someone *right there* who could tell me what he's thinking so I might be able to help, and it's frustrating that she won't."

I squirmed uncomfortably. One major downside of graduating from high school and reaching the age where I'm supposedly a mature adult: the actual adults in the family waffle, hard, on whether I'm a little kid who needs to be coddled and protected, given a juice box and sent outside to play, or another adult who's interested in hearing about their problems. On the whole, I prefer to be thought of as an adult—who doesn't?—but it gets weird when it's my father's sister talking to me like I'm somehow an authority on how to talk to her own kids.

"But you're on her side with this one, and I'm the human lady who married an incubus, so I guess I should leave you out of this." She finished assembling the first sandwich and pushed it toward the mice, saying more sonorously, "The holy ritual of you get one, I get one is now complete."

The mice cheered and fell upon the sandwich like fuzzy piranha, rapidly pulling it into individual mouse-sized pieces and distributing them among themselves. It was an efficient process, practiced within the colony at every meal, and not a single mouse went away empty-pawed.

Aunt Jane watched them for a few seconds before she went back to her second sandwich, spreading peanut butter thickly across the bread. "Did you want lunch?"

"No, I'm taking the bus home. I figure I'll grab a burger before I give up on civilization."

She made a noncommittal noise.

"Hey, Aunt Jane, you know, you're the only one of us who never capitalizes the rituals when you're talking to the mice. Why is that?"

Aeslin mice are hyper-religious. They're born that way. It can happen in humans, too, resulting in people like Joan of Arc, who truly believe that their brains are hot-wired directly into the divine. For us, it's an aberration. For the Aeslin, it's a survival technique. You know the saying, "there are no atheists in foxholes"? Well, when you're small enough that the foxhole in question is probably literal, you can't afford to be an atheist. Religion keeps them connected as a colony, centered around their object of worship, and unwilling to stray. More importantly, it makes them unwilling to schism. A faithful colony is a stable colony, and a stable colony is a surviving colony.

It didn't work out for them as well as evolution possibly intended. As far as anyone knows, the colony that lives with the family—split up as it is between the compound, Aunt Jane and Uncle Ted's house, and Alex's current apartment—is the last one in existence. All the others died out a long time ago, victims of a world built to a much larger, more vicious scale combined with their own overly trusting natures.

It's a hard world for something as small and sweet and essentially pure as an Aeslin mouse. I wouldn't want to live their lives.

Anyway, Aeslin have a funky accent that puts the stress on words in such a way as to make the capital letters on random nouns—mostly, they're really religious but sort of grammar agnostic—and all the words in the title of an established ritual, such as You Get One, I Get One, should be capitalized. We all learn to mimic their accent, not in a mocking way, by the time we finish first grade. Even Mom and Uncle Ted do it, and they didn't grow up with the mice the way the rest of us did.

Aunt Jane thought about it for a second before she shrugged and said, "It never seemed all that important to me. They know what I mean, and it's not like these things are capitalized the first time they happen, so really, I'm just being an Aeslin historical recreationist."

"Huh." As explanations went, it felt like a reach. This wasn't the time to fight about it, especially not with my bus due to roll up the street in under ten minutes. "Anyway, Artie's probably going to be in a mood when he finally comes upstairs, but he's coming with us, and I'll email him the details as soon as I get home. We should be back on Monday."

"Not leaving early if you figure out what's going on?"

"Not planning to. When am I going to get these two to go to another convention?"

Aunt Jane laughed, short and sharp, and dropped her

knife into the sink. "Never, so enjoy this one while you've got it."

"You're sure you're okay with this?"

"My boy needs to get out more, Sarah's heading to New York for who knows how long, and you're willing to put up with being trapped in a car with the pair of them all the way to Seattle. I'm fine with this. This is the best terrible idea you've ever had." She glanced at the clock above the door. "And you're going to miss your bus if you don't hurry. I'm not giving you a ride home today."

"I know." Elsie was going to pick me up from the burger joint. I felt better making the final leg of the journey home in the company of my cousin than I would have in the company of my aunt, who really did want me to take her side in every little family drama or breakdown in communication.

But that's Aunt Jane. I love her, but she never really learned to operate like the rest of us. Her own kids are better at being Prices than she is. Dad says I shouldn't hold it against her; she's the only sister he's got and sisters are important enough not to risk alienating, but he always says it in this pointed sort of way that makes it sound a lot more like a reminder that he wants me to get along with Verity.

I do not *want* to get along with Verity. Verity is selfish and spoiled in a way that none of the rest of us had the opportunity to be. I've spent my whole life trying to figure out why that is, why she gets away with so much more than we can, and the closest I've ever managed to come is that Verity looks just like Mom recast in a younger, slightly taller model—and Very's short enough that her being taller than *anyone* is a big deal. Alex has been using her head as an armrest since high school.

But regardless. I love my sister. I tolerate my sister. I resist the urge to slap my sister every time she opens her mouth and speaks in that squeaky vocal fry voice she's been allowed to think is appealing. Why she can't just talk like *herself* is a mystery that may never be solved. She decided at some point, when we were still kids, that boys would like her better if she sounded like one of the Sailor Scouts, and her voice went up half an octave overnight.

Whatever. Not my problem. I crossed the kitchen, pausing to kiss my aunt on the cheek and wave to the mice, then proceeded through the front room to the door. Outside, it was a matter of three steps down from the porch and I was free, out in the glorious Portland sunshine.

People think we don't have sunny days here in the Pacific Northwest. There's a reason for that. The people who live here know that it's one of the most beautiful, temperate, forgiving places in North America, and we don't want to share. So we only talk about the weather when it's miserable and damp—sort of the opposite of California, where they only talk about the weather when it's beautiful and sunny. California would probably shank Florida in an alley for its nickname—when your whole tourist industry is based on it never raining on Disneyland, "the Sunshine State" sounds a lot better than "the Golden State." Well, we here in Oregon are denizens of "the Beaver State," but really, we'd rather live in the "Go Away and Leave Us The Hell Alone State."

Now there's a motto that's never going to get past the tourism board. Keep Portland weird: keep California out. We are not your quirky hipster theme park, even if we *are* cheaper than Disneyland, but tourists persist in treating us that way. Except instead of roller coasters, we have a guy dressed like Bigfoot playing guitar in front of the Safeway.

That's Danny, and he doesn't *dress* like a Bigfoot, he *is* a Bigfoot, one still young enough to shave himself and pass for a human man about five years older than he actually is. Bigfoot youth hanging out in human cities is sort of like Amish kids going on rumspringa: a chance to go out and see how the cousins live, for long enough to decide that no one with any self-respect would actually want to live that way. More Bigfoot kids go home than Amish kids, meaning that all of human civilization is less appealing than shitting in the woods and a world without cable television.

Now that's something to think about whenever we start feeling too impressive. Everything we've made is not enough to keep some of our closest cousins from running to the woods and not leaving us a forwarding address. If not for the rumspringa kids, we might not know if they ever go extinct. My dad has contacts within the Bigfoot community, but the rest of us have never met them. They don't want humans getting our weird humanity cooties all over their stuff, and honestly, I can't blame them.

I followed the sidewalk to the end of the block, turned, and walked down to the waiting bus stop. There were two seats bolted to the concrete, both filthy with dirt and a reddish substance I really hoped was rust. It was probably rust. People don't usually go around bleeding on the bus stops.

I still decided not to sit, hanging off the bus stop marker by one hand instead, turning the gesture into a sort of one-handed aerial plank. I don't dance pole, mostly because if something has the word "dance" in it, Verity acts like she has the copyright on the activity—the first time someone referred to my trapeze and silk work as "aerial dance" in her hearing, I thought she was going to have a stroke—but I've taken a few classes, and it's amazing for your abs and shoulders. The strength those artists need just to practice their art is ridiculous.

I only had to hang there for about five minutes before the bus pulled up with a hiss of air brakes and opened the door. I bounced into the air-conditioned dimness of the vehicle, showing my pass to the disinterested driver, and moved toward a seat.

This time of day in a residential area, the bus was less than half full, and I had no trouble securing a window for myself, so that I could watch the city roll by. I tucked my backpack into my lap, not being one of those assholes who needs two seats without good cause, and rested my forehead against the glass, unable to suppress my smile.

We were going to Emerald City Comic Con. My stupid cousin was going to leave his basement, and we were going to a real live convention, out in the real live world, where we would solve a real live problem all by ourselves. And it was going to be glorious.

I closed my eyes, smiling to myself. Absolutely glorious.

⊁

"But *Mom*! That isn't *fair*!" My voice peaked on the last word, very nearly cracking. I sounded like a child who'd just been told that dessert was canceled, and I hated myself for it.

My mother looked at me coolly, unmoved. "You have space in the car," she said.

"For a body, maybe. For a body and whatever luggage it wants to drag along with it, not so much!"

"You will not refer to your sister as 'it,'" she said, voice suddenly cold. "This isn't up for debate, Antimony. If you want to go to your convention, you will take your sister. I don't want the three of you running around Seattle unsupervised."

"You mean you don't want to listen to Verity whining that someone else is having an adventure for once!" I snapped. "You think we need supervision? Artie's the same age Very is, and Sarah's probably older! You let Verity go to Los Angeles without a chaperone, and that's a lot farther away!"

"Yes, but Verity gets out more." Mom's face softened. "I wish you would *try* to get along with your sister. It would mean a lot to me if I knew she could trust you at her back."

"Of course she can trust me at her back," I snapped. "The fact that she's a fame-hungry, selfish brat doesn't mean I won't support her in the field!"

"Antimony!" Mom had the audacity to sound shocked.

I managed, through sheer force of will, not to throw my hands up and storm away. It would have been incredibly satisfying, and incredibly immature, and given that I was arguing I was adult enough to go to Seattle without a chaperone—one who was only three years older than me, no less, which had ceased to matter as far as I was concerned on the day I turned eighteen and had to start paying taxes—I didn't want to play into her narrative.

"I'm allowed to have my opinion, and if you want to argue that it's pejorative, I can produce supporting evidence for everything I've just said."

"I'm sure she can produce supportive evidence that you're argumentative, contrary, and irritable," she said. "You're still not going without her, and that's final."

I narrowed my eyes. "How are you going to stop us?"

"I'll call Jane and tell her I want her to ask Artie not to go. I know you talked that boy in a circle to get him to go with you in the first place. He'll be relieved if his mother tells him to stand down." Mom shook her head. "I agree that he needs to get out more. I don't think something like this is the way to start. If he's given an out, he'll take it."

"Sarah—"

"My little sister loves you as a cousin," said Mom, stressing the word "sister" all out of proportion to its importance in the sentence. "She loves me the way sisters are supposed to love each other. She'll take my side."

I wasn't as sure of that as she was. Sarah loved my mom, absolutely. I knew she sometimes wished there was less of an age gap between them, so that she could have been closer to Mom than she was to Mom's kids. As one of those kids, I was pretty content with the way things have shaken out, but people are allowed to wish for a better world if that's what would make them happy.

And none of that changed the fact that Sarah was utterly, ridiculously, stupid in love with Artie, and was about to leave him again, this time without a confirmed return date. She needed this time with him as much as he needed this time with her. Neither one of them was going to go gently if someone tried to interfere.

Artie might feel tricked by the way we'd gone about getting him to sort-of-agree to do this, but now it was an opportunity to spend eight hours in the car with Sarah, plus sharing a hotel room, plus seeing the convention itself. And Sarah had been onboard from the moment I'd told her about the probable siren. I looked at Mom, resisting the urge to huff or roll my eyes or anything else she might take as proof that I was too immature to make these choices on my own.

Mom squirmed, finally looking away. "I really wish you'd work harder to get along with her," she said, quietly.

Guilt is one of the most powerful tools in the arsenal of mothers, especially when trying to make sisters get along. I took a deep breath. "I wish she'd work at all to get along with me," I said.

Mom sighed. "I'll talk to her before you go."

"Thank you."

"But she *is* going with you."

"Mom—"

"I know why you don't want her to. You've been very clear about that. Sarah's a non-combatant, Artie's going to be overwhelmed with all the people, and I don't want you facing off against a siren by yourself."

"Lilu are immune to siren songs." That was part of why I'd wanted Artie along in the first place. We might not have many drivers in the family, but there are buses and trains between Seattle and Portland. Sarah and I could have gone without him if we'd been left with no other choice. From the way Mom was carrying on, that might still be the way we had to do this.

Her desire for family bonding couldn't be more important than the need to stop a siren from preying on the geek community. No matter how much she wanted me to get along with my sister.

Why couldn't she have been passionately invested in the idea of me spending time with Alex? I *liked* Alex.

Sure, he was the kind of nerd whose face basically screamed for punching and whose lunch money would probably have been stolen all the way through school if not for his fondness for dressing up in reproduction armor and whaling the crap out of people in the woods, but listening to him explain the life cycles of various newts had been the background of my childhood, and on nights when I couldn't sleep, sometimes I'd call him up, put him on speaker, and let him lull me into dreamland with lengthy explanations of the axolotl feeding cycle, or the fricken mating requirements, or the rearing of baby garter snakes. Taking Alex to a comic book convention would be fun. It would be a way to add a little recreation to a job.

Maybe that was the answer. I just needed to remember that this was a job before it was anything else. I looked Mom in the eye, keeping my breathing slow and level, waiting for her to speak first.

After almost a full minute, she did. "It doesn't matter if Lilu are immune, since you're taking backup to be able to cover more of what you've described as a fairly large convention," she said, a pleading note in her voice. "You could be alone when you find the siren. I want to know that you'll have the backup you need, or I want to know how you're intending to account for its absence. You have to keep all three of you safe out there. And it's not like you've had that much time in the field without one of us—"

It looks like it's causing her physical pain not to say "without an adult," but she manages it. I sigh, interrupting. "You're right."

"—there to help if something— Wait what, I'm sorry, did you just say I was right?"

"I did. You're right. If part of the point of us going without our parents is proving that we're mature enough to go out into the field by ourselves, fighting with you over who's going to serve as my backup isn't the way to make my case." It was hard to keep the words from twisting and turning sarcastic in my mouth, but I thought of them as if they were Aeslin writ, something to be echoed back exactly as it had been heard originally, and that helped. "I am willing to take Verity with us, providing you are able to provide me with certain assurances."

Mom was smart enough not to leap on the bait. She pursed her lips, interest clearly aroused, and asked, "What would those assurances be, exactly?"

"First, she needs to understand that this is *my* mission, *my* field trial, not hers. She doesn't get to push me out of the way and take credit for any success. As a concession, I will agree not to try to sideline her, order her to stay in the hotel room, or otherwise minimize her opportunities to contribute."

Mom thought about this for a moment, looking for a loophole, before she nodded. "Agreed."

I did not punch the air. It was a near thing.

We would be traveling with a telepath—and Sarah's personal motto is "don't lie to the telepath" for very good reasons—and the Aeslin mice are not only incapable of lying, they remember everything they've ever seen and are absolutely overjoyed by the opportunity to recite it to anyone who'll stand still long enough. If Verity tried to be a jerk about who was in charge, I could demand the Holy Rite of Goddammit, Verity, Mom Said This Was *My* Mission the second we got home.

It wouldn't give me back the mission I'd been planning, but one strength of being the youngest sibling: I have no qualms about running to my parents when my siblings start bullying me. Who cares if snitches get stitches? I can do field medicine as well as anyone else with a lick of training, and snitches also get the satisfaction of seeing their tormentors get grounded. If Mom told Verity to listen to me, she wouldn't have a choice. Either she'd obey, or the mice would rat her out and she'd go down.

"What else?"

"My second condition is that she not decide she's my second-in-command and start trying to give orders to

Sarah and Artie. Sarah and I have a plan, and it depends partially on Artie being as relaxed as he ever gets when there are other people around. Verity is coming as support, not as a new branch of the command structure."

Mom nodded again, more reluctantly. "I'll talk to her," she said.

"Good. My last condition is this: she's joining us for an infiltration mission, not for a safari. These are my people. My nerds, freaks, and geeks. She's not to behave like a townie attending the carnival for the first time. If she wants to come with us, she needs to come *with* us. She needs to be a part of the group, and treat the people she sees there with respect."

Mom frowned. "Verity is respectful of people with different interests."

I scoffed. "Not to argue after we've both won, Mom, but Verity has never in her life been respectful of someone she considers a 'nerd.' She even makes fun of Sarah for reading comic books."

As if reading comics were anything unusual in a world where *Iron Man* is still breaking merchandising and box office records and Marvel Studios looks primed to swing for the moon with an interconnected series of movies focusing on different superhero properties. Age of the geek, baby. It may have taken a little longer than we thought, but it's finally here, and we won.

Now if only we weren't by and large assholes about it.

"Okay, so exactly what do you want me to ask her to do?"

I smiled, aware that the expression would probably look more than half-feral, and unwilling to do anything to change it. "Tell her to blend in."

Mom slumped, and didn't say anything.

As was usually the case, Sarah was the first one out of bed. We don't have a large enough sample size to prove it, but she makes me think that Johrlac probably need less sleep than humans do. Do wasps sleep? They must, everything sleeps, but she's as much a person as she is a pollinator, and she doesn't sleep enough. The telepathic hum of her approaching presence woke me up about thirty seconds before she opened my bedroom door and stuck her head inside, triggering a drowsy cheer from the mice clustered at the foot of my bed. They'd been up as late as I was, and only the most junior clergy were assigned to sleep on the bed, in case something happened in the middle of the night that needed to be added to the scripture.

The life of the mice is not as idyllic as some people would like to believe. I pushed myself up onto one elbow, using my other hand to wipe the bleary ghosts of sleep from my eyes. Sarah was still there, pushing the door further open, carrying a tray that smelled like—

"Coffee." I held out my free hand, opening and closing it in a classic "gimme" motion. When I was a kid, growing up with a telepath *and* an empath, I used to hope that my secret telekinesis would kick in one day and let me Jedi things out of people's hands. It would have been amazing for the times when Verity decided to play keep-away with my toys, or "borrow" my knives.

"Coffee and waffles," said Sarah. She crossed the room to the bed, setting the tray down where I could see it. In addition to the coffee, there were two plates, and one glass of virulently salmon-pink juice which I knew better than to touch. You can get that color, roughly, by blending cranberry and orange juice. That wasn't Sarah's approach. She was drinking orange juice blended with Heinz Ketchup and powdered Tang, and she was going to do it with a smile on her face.

Knowing your family doesn't make them any less disgusting. It just makes them marginally more comprehensible.

The plates each contained a small stack of waffles, a pile of scrambled eggs, and three slices of bacon. It was a veritable feast of breakfast foods, even considering that I would have to share mine with the mice or face their regretful stares. Aeslin mice don't so much do "wrath." Wrath is for bigger creatures.

"The Communion of Bacon is upon us," I rasped, and threw a strip of bacon down the bed to the suddenly much more animated congregation. One strip wouldn't feed the gathered clergy, but it would keep them from rushing the tray while I got some caffeine into me. I picked up the mug of coffee, cupping it in my hands, and relaxing as the warmth of the liquid seeped through the ceramic and into my fingers.

I'm always cold these days. I don't know why. It's not the flu—it's been going on for months. And it's not weight loss destabilizing my own ability to regulate my core temperature, which has happened to me twice, when I first started doing trapeze and then again when I took up roller derby. Some people lose fat in the process of building muscle, and that can make it difficult for your body to tell whether or not it's warm enough. But my weight has been steady for a year, and this wasn't that.

Ugh. I hate mornings. I sipped my coffee and looked at Sarah, frowning.

"Why are you trying to suck up with breakfast in bed?" I asked. "Are we not going to Seattle?"

"Technically, I'm only sucking up with the 'in bed' part," she said. "Verity's downstairs making breakfast. She feels bad about your mom insisting that we take her with us, and she's trying to make sure we get off to a good start."

And a good start always begins with a balanced breakfast. I blinked slowly at Sarah, taking another sip of coffee.

"Verity . . . feels bad?" The idea was alien.

"I mean, she did once I finished telling her she was supposed to."

Ah. That made more sense. I put the mug back on the tray and used my knife to slice the waffle in half. Sarah had fixed it to my preferences, with butter and strawberry jam. I pushed it and half of the eggs to one side of the plate before calling, "Come and get it, but don't touch mine," to the mice.

They cheered and swarmed forward, and when they continued past us, toward the spiral stairway built along the leg of my bedside table, they took exactly half the food with them. That side of the plate was spotlessly clean, not a crumb or dollop of jam left behind. I began cutting the remaining waffle into smaller pieces.

"You know, this is supposed to be a chance for you to spend some time with Artie. I mean, and stop the siren. That's important, too. You can't spend the whole trip riding herd on Verity in order to keep the peace."

Sarah looked abashed. "I just want this to go well."

"It will. You've been practicing your shielding. You can make Artie disappear if you need to. He'll get to experience a convention like an almost normal person, and the two of you can live out the fanfic romance of your little shipper dreams."

She wrinkled her nose and threw her napkin at me, that being the only thing that wouldn't get the bed sticky. "Shush, you. You know he doesn't like me that way."

"I know he *does*. Everyone in the family knows he does. Even Alex knows, and Alex is both a boy and currently in Ohio. Sarah, people who have never met either one of you know he does—they can see it in his forum posts. We just need to get the two of you far enough away from all the local bullshit that you see each other in a new context."

Sarah looked at me, eyes wide and hopeful in their ring of soot-black lashes. That girl has never needed to wear mascara in her life. It's not fair. Cuckoos don't wear a lot of makeup in part because they don't really see faces the way humans do—when you can recognize someone by the feel of their thoughts, you don't need all those little visual cues. But they all have perfect skin, full lashes, and symmetrical features. Sometimes evolution is a *jerk*.

"You really think so?"

"Eat your waffle," I said gruffly. "We need to get moving."

Now that I was awake, the urge to get on the road was starting to make my scalp itch. I shoveled a bite of waffle and eggs into my mouth—Verity can't cook much, but what she can cook, she cooks *well*—and washed it down with a swig of coffee. In just under five hours, we would be in Seattle, ready to roll into our first major pop culture convention. The air felt electric, filled with possibility and potential. We were going to *go somewhere*. We were going to *do something*, and by doing it, we were going to make the world a safer place to be.

And we were going to do it with only Verity for "adult supervision," which made this an event I had been waiting for since I was fifteen and chafing under the expectation that I would somehow be happy to play the merry little foot soldier for the rest of my time at home—a period that seemed likely to continue for the rest of time. Being the youngest comes with a few perks. It also comes with an uncountable amount of "baby of the family," which could keep me sidelined until I was ready for retirement.

This was my chance to show that I could be just as mature, adult, and efficient as any member of the family, regardless of age.

And maybe buy some cheap comic books while I was at it. Win-win scenarios are rare enough that they should be grabbed with both hands when they present themselves.

I swallowed another bite of breakfast before announcing, loudly, "I will be picking up my backpack from its place beside the door in ten—"

"Fifteen, please," interjected Sarah.

"—in fifteen minutes. Any clergy who has been chosen to accompany me should be in the bag at that time." I went back to eating my breakfast. The Aeslin are always in earshot when you're inside the house. Elf on the Shelf never held any horrors for us. What's Santa's private espionage squad when compared to a whole colony of mice who can't lie and believe your parents are literally divine and can hear everything you do? It's a miracle we're not all even more messed up than we are.

"I'm all packed," I said, swinging my attention back to Sarah. "Have been since last night. We couldn't fly with the number of knives I'm carrying, but we can drive."

"Do they not have metal detectors this year?"

"Ceramic knives. A few glass ones in case we hit anything really weird. And my costume will forgive a few beeps and bings."

Sarah nodded. "All right. Did you warn Verity about the metal detectors?"

Verity likes guns a lot more than I do. She usually has at least one somewhere on her person, sometimes as many as four. I smiled slowly, being sure to dwell on the poisoned pleasure in my expression. Sarah sat up straighter, eyes going wide.

"Annie, *no*."

"Mmmm . . . sorry, but I think Annie, yes."

"She'll walk right into them!"

"And that will be a good lesson for her about doing her own legwork. All the info is right there on the convention website. She could have looked it up on her own."

"Why would she, when she's been told that this is your mission and you're going to make sure everything runs as smoothly as possible?" Sarah's eyes went briefly solid white, the color leeching from her irises and pupils as her vitreous humor turned bioluminescent.

I sighed. "Spoilsport."

"Just stopping you from committing an act of self-sabotage." She got off the bed, collecting her plate and over-vibrant juice. "Artie's downstairs, and ready to go."

"Thanks for telling me sooner, brat."

She stuck her tongue out at me as she left the room, and I grinned, turning myself to more fully addressing my breakfast. It only took a few minutes, although my side of the plate was nowhere near as clean as the mice's had been by the time I set it aside. Then I slid out of the bed and made for the door. Time to shower, dress, hide eight or nine ceramic knives on my person, and head downstairs.

We were really going to a proper comic convention, something big and overwhelming and filled with people we didn't know, not just one of the tiny local shows that popped up in community centers and hotel ballrooms. Emerald City was big enough to occupy the entire Seattle Convention Center and sell out all the surrounding hotels months in advance. I kept grinning to myself as I hit the bathroom. Seattle wasn't going to know what hit it.

One nice thing about belonging to a family almost pathologically dedicated to looking from the outside like we don't exist: when Dad decided that he was going to settle in the woods outside Portland, he had called in all the favors he could to get a legion of cryptid architects, construction engineers, plumbers, and electricians to agree to build him the perfect family compound. I don't know if he'd been planning to have a dozen kids before he started meeting us and realized that more than three would be the end of mankind, or if he'd expected Aunt Jane to somehow get over her issues with both him and Grandma Alice and move in, but either way, he'd designed the place to accommodate a small army. Only three of the bedrooms had private bathrooms—and wow is "only" a ridiculous modifier to stick in that sentence—but the rest of us still functionally have private bathrooms, since there are so many that no one needs to share. Why would you, when you could have your own?

I think my parents are hoping that someday we'll do like they did, go out into the field and come home with the perfect spouse, settle down, and make more kids. Dad never wanted to uproot his family again, so he did what he could to guarantee that it was never going to be necessary. It would have been amazing when I was a kid, if we'd ever been allowed to have friends over. Mom and Dad could bring people home from work—I'd shared the kitchen with all manner of humanoid cryptid species before I hit puberty, sometimes with radically incompatible dietary needs—but I couldn't bring home other kids from school.

Nothing that might endanger the family cone of secrecy, that was the rule. Nothing that could ever potentially start a chain of events leading to the Covenant figuring out we existed. I stepped out of the shower, wringing water out of my hair, and suppressed a fully unfair jet of annoyance at my sister. It wasn't her fault our parents had decided the rules were different for her; it wasn't her fault that the thing that made her happy had inevitably brought her to visibility. I flicked my hair back and wrapped a towel around myself. The house is mostly empty most of the time, but that's no excuse for wandering the halls naked.

Of course, if I stopped being mad at Verity for her life choices, I'd have to start being mad at our parents, and that was a much bigger, more complicated kind of anger to carry around. Easier to stay mad at my sister, whose choices had been at odds with my own for as long as I'd been alive.

The mice were back when I stepped into my room, and my plate was spotless. They had clearly swept it for crumbs and jam, one of their more Cinderella-esque attributes. When I was a kid, I used to think things would be easier if we just used the mice in place of the dishwasher. Then I'd learned more about microbiology, and the virtues of soap, but can you really blame an eight-year-old for thinking they've found a way out of doing the dishes?

The mice cheered enthusiastically at the sight of me, waving their paws in the air. "Those who are to Accompany You are in Position," shouted one priest.

I flashed him a thumbs-up.

My backpack cheered.

"Cool. I am invoking the Holy Rite of Getting Dressed." I eased the door shut.

The mice cheered, then dispersed.

Aeslin mice don't do nudity the way humans do, in

the sense that they don't really notice it, and they don't care when they do. They also don't do gender the way humans do—our whole "Gods and Priestesses" structure is their attempt to understand the somewhat confusing instructions given to them by one of my ancestors, who had been happily living as a farmwife somewhere in England and didn't think there would ever be changes in the future to the way people lived their lives. But the fact that they don't recognize those things means they don't know when not to talk about something. If someone forgets to tell the mice they're getting dressed, the mice won't think of keeping quiet on their own.

Their lack of concern for human secondary sexual characteristics means there's no real concern of people using them as crappy second-hand porn dispensers—no one who could get off at hearing a mouse describe someone in the altogether would be welcome in our home more than once—but they *will* tattle when asked about bruises or recent injuries. It only took being woken once by my mother demanding to know whether I needed stitches before I got real, real careful about deactivating the Aeslin surveillance system whenever I needed to change my clothes.

My clothes were waiting on the chair next to my desk where I'd laid them out the night before. I dressed fast, braiding my hair with one hand before tying it off and grabbing my backpack. It squeaked as I slung it over my shoulder, the mice inside objecting to being jostled. "Sorry," I said. More loudly, I added, "Heading out now. See you all after the con!"

The room cheered in response.

Verity had finished cleaning up after her spontaneous breakfast offering, and was waiting by the door with Sarah, one eye on her watch. She looked up at the sound of my feet pounding on the stairs and smirked.

"Told you she'd be early," she said. "And she washed

her hair! How do you shower *and* wash your hair *and* get dressed in less than fifteen minutes?"

"Practice," I said. "Roller derby means some days are four shower days, just to keep the smell from turning physical and starting to shake the fresh meat down for their lunch money."

I reached past her for the handle of my suitcase. Verity blinked.

"Is that all you're taking?"

"Yeah, and it should be about what you're taking, since we need to fit four people in the car, and Sarah and Artie both have suitcases of their own," I said. "One small suitcase and one backpack each, that was what we agreed on for logistical reasons." That would also leave room for souvenirs on the way home. "And the cooler."

"Artie has the cooler," said Sarah, in a chipper, placating tone.

Verity bit her lip.

I raised an eyebrow. "How big's your suitcase?"

"I can consolidate," she said.

I saw red. "Did you not read the email explaining the packing limits?"

"Yes, but this isn't Southwest Airlines! I thought I'd have a little wiggle room!"

I blinked the red away in order to give her a disgusted look. "The trunk doesn't expand because you don't know how to pack," I said, and started for the door.

Verity didn't follow. Sarah did. Artie was parked in the driveway outside, window rolled down and arm resting on the door as he waited for us.

"Before you ask, she only had two suitcases," said Sarah in a meek tone. "We could probably have shoved them in."

"And brought nothing home from the biggest trade show we've ever attended," I snapped. "Plus she agreed to my conditions when Mom gave them to her, which means she's supposed to follow my instructions, which means that when I send an email that dictates how many bags we each get to bring, she's supposed to go along with it. This is where I start asserting my authority. Before we even make it out of the house."

"I told her it wasn't going to work," said Artie, and tossed me the keys. His car is old enough not to have a way to pop the trunk without manually unlocking it.

I sighed. "We all knew she was going to pull something," I said. "At least it was this, and not something way worse."

The trunk was empty save for the spare tire, toolkit, and Artie's old green camping duffle. Sarah and I boosted our respective suitcases into the open space before I nudged her with my elbow.

"Go get shotgun."

"And leave you in the back with your sister? No, thank you. Today's goal is no homicides between here and Seattle."

"Go ride next to Artie for four hours. Keep him from putting on NPR for the whole drive. You know Verity would just try for some horrifying club radio situation, and no one wants that."

Sarah looked at me, clearly torn, then walked away around the car. I heard the door slam a moment later, and managed not to punch the air. Operation Get My Cousins To Hook Up was officially underway, and thanks to biology and adoption, less creepy than it sounded.

Verity came out of the house as I was heading for the backseat, dragging a suitcase that was clearly heavy enough to warrant an oversized baggage fee if we *had* been flying, and easily half again as large as mine or Sarah's. She stopped when she saw me, blowing her fine blonde hair out of her eyes in what could have been a huff.

"This good enough for you?" she asked.

I decided not to interpret her gesture as a huff. It would annoy her more if I went along with her. "That's fine, there's room in the trunk," I said. "Let's get on the road."

Verity didn't argue. She was learning. Instead, she

moved behind the car, where the open trunk beckoned. The whole car settled lower once she finished wrestling her suitcase into it. I buckled my belt, setting my backpack between my feet before leaning forward to ruffle the back of Artie's head.

"Hey!" he objected. "Hands off the hair."

"Yeah, yeah." Several of his mice were on the armrest between the two front seats. They cheered as my own clergy emerged from the backpack, several clutching the Goldfish Crackers I had put in the interior pocket to keep them occupied during the trip. Aeslin mice may not be exactly like ordinary mice, but their ability to sniff out food is just as well-honed.

The door slammed as Verity slung herself into the seat next to mine, dropping her purse between her feet and resting her arm on the cooler between us. The mice cheered again as her clergy began emerging from her purse, scurrying to join the others on the armrest. We were going to make the drive accompanied by the dulcet sounds of an Aeslin mouse rave.

As if on cue, Sarah leaned forward and started the radio, turning the dial to a classic rock station that seemed to be in the middle of a block of hits from the 1950s. The collected mice cheered again, and some of them began to boogie.

"Great, it's a Dreamworks movie," said Verity.

I smiled at her, for once without any ulterior motives or hidden knives. She was my sister, we were going on a road trip with two of my favorite people in the world, and at the other end, we'd have an awesome convention. What could possibly go wrong with this day?

Everything. Everything could possibly go wrong with this day. By the time we reached Seattle and Artie pulled off the highway into the confusing network of one-way streets around the convention center, I was more convinced than ever that Sarah had done things the right way by showing up so much later than her siblings. All three of them were adopted, but she was functionally an only child who also got a brother and a sister out of the deal.

Verity *talked* when she was feeling comfortable. She didn't need anything to talk *about*. She didn't even try to play those stupid road games to pass the time. You know—things like "I spy with my little eye . . ." or "I'm going to the zoo, and I'm bringing . . ." She just talked. About whatever popped into her head. Things she saw out the window (cows were uniquely exciting to her, and likely to spark entire monologues about how big they were, or how black and white they were, or how the majority of cows were just ordinary cows but the really big herds sometimes concealed akabeko or really chill minotaurs or other kinds of cryptid cattle that had managed to survive into the modern era), places she wanted to stop, how badly she needed to pee.

I was no longer sure how she'd survived all those years of dance class, since it seemed like she needed to pee every fifteen minutes. Four hours in a car with her had seemed reasonable at the beginning of our trip. It had only been four hours on paper, with no traffic, no surface streets, and no need to get to Portland from our compound before the journey could officially begin. It had been close to five hours since we left the house, and I was ready to commit a homicide.

"I think I see the hotel!" chirped Sarah, with a sudden, exaggerated excitement that told me she'd been listening to my thoughts again. She pointed, and there was the sign for our hotel. Not that we had a reservation; she was going to take care of that. But it was one of the con hotels, and we'd chosen it for its location and place in a major hotel chain that was unlikely to even notice a little light fraud without a full audit of the location— something that virtually never happened.

Artie continued inching along the road, going as fast as the jammed-in traffic would allow. A convention getting underway didn't constitute a public holiday, and so we had not only the con traffic to deal with, but all the people heading home from work. It was a lot. But we were still moving; we hadn't transitioned to full gridlock yet, and I was willing to take it.

If we stopped, I might wind up getting out of the car and walking the rest of the way. Hopefully, that wouldn't need to happen. Although speaking of things that *did* need to happen . . .

"We're on surface streets, moving slowly enough that people can look into the car if they feel like being nosy fuckers," I said. "All mice, into your respective bags."

The mice, who had stopped dancing after hour two, but had continued to use the front seat armrest as a rodent social club, made disappointed sounds. They didn't argue, turning and running either toward my backpack, Verity's purse, or Artie's backpack and diving inside. I leaned forward to do up the zipper.

Most people, seeing a car with a bunch of mice in it, won't jump straight to "those are endangered cryptid mice with full sentience." But poachers and hunters exist, and tempting fate has never struck me as a terribly good idea.

The sidewalks were packed, even though the show floor wasn't scheduled to open for another hour. Some of the people who passed were wearing capes and corsets, or elaborate cosplay reproductions of characters from all forms of media. I recognized about half of them, which felt impressive enough to say something about my television habits. I scoped up my backpack and hugged it to my chest, trying to suppress the butterflies in my stomach. This was my natural habitat. This was the kingdom of the nerds.

What if they didn't want me here? What if I couldn't fit in among my own people? It had always been an abstract question before, but now it was very real, and surprisingly immediate.

A hand touched my knee. I looked up, expecting to see Sarah, who would be picking up on my anxiety the way she picked up on everything else. But Sarah was staring raptly out the window, pointing out a cosplayer dressed as Marvel Girl to Artie, who looked as pleased as she was by the appearance of the fictional telepath. Verity was the only person looking at me, visibly concerned.

"Hey, you okay?" she asked. "That's the face I always get right before a recital."

My first instinct was to shake her off. I suppressed it. "I'm fine," I said. "I've just been wanting to come to this convention for a long, long time, but never had a good enough reason before."

"It's okay to be nervous."

"I'm not nervous!" I paused. "I'm sorry. I didn't mean to snap. I just mean . . . this is a pretty big deal for me."

"I get it," she said sympathetically. "It's like my first real competition."

Only it wasn't, not really, because unless we got into a massive pitched battle on the show floor, this wasn't going to end with our faces in the local paper—and if we did get into a pitched battle on the show floor, we'd have other things to worry about. I swallowed three replies before I shrugged and looked out the car window.

"I guess."

Verity took her hand off my knee. "Just keep breathing," she said.

Artie turned off the street into the driveway of the hotel. It was a short thing that wound past guest drop-off in the process of making a loop back to the street or depositing drivers down into the parking garage. It was an elegant use of limited space, and I wanted to admire it, except that I didn't want to wait another second to get this mission underway.

"Go," said Artie, pulling up in front of the doors. "Sarah has a picture of my license plate in her phone . . ."

"I'd remember it anyway, it's a pretty number," said Sarah, in the dreamy tone she reserved for math, and for Artie. How could he not see how far gone she was? It was ridiculous.

"And you can text me once we have a room number," continued Artie doggedly.

"Are you sure you'll be okay to walk up to the room alone?" asked Sarah.

"I'll come down and get him," said Verity before Artie could answer.

"Right, let's go." I opened my door, sliding out of the cramped car. The air outside was shockingly fresh after five hours jammed in a car with three other bodies, a colony of mice, and Artie's horrifying cologne, which he practically bathed in as part of his effort to keep his pheromones from manipulating the people around him.

Sarah and Verity were only a beat behind me. Sarah started to turn toward the trunk. Verity grabbed her arm and shook her head.

"I'll get a bell cart when I come back for Artie," she said. "Leave the suitcases. We can get them later."

Sarah frowned but allowed herself to be pulled away. Interesting. What had Verity packed into her bag that she didn't want us to see? Or feel, more likely: that bag had definitely been on the heavy side.

Whatever. Unless she'd smuggled Dad in her suitcase, I didn't really care. I closed the door, smiled at Artie, and said, "We'll see you in a minute," before following the others through the sliding glass doors into the hotel lobby.

Inside, the air was cool, lightly scented with plumeria and rosemary, and filled with voices. People were lined up fifteen deep at most of the desks, waiting to be checked into their rooms. All of them looked as scruffy as we did, not yet having gained access to their rooms to change into their impeccable cosplays; we fit right in, at least until Sarah walked past all the queues to the VIP gold desk, which was conspicuously manned but had no line.

A few people mumbled to each other as they watched her go. A few more smirked, clearly assuming that we were going to be rebuffed by the man in the neatly pressed suit who was standing there at polite attention.

Sarah took the lead, offering him an engaging smile as we approached.

"Hello," she said. "I believe you have a room for us?"

Her eyes flashed white and the telepathic hum that always accompanied her presence got momentarily louder. The man startled, standing straighter as he blinked at her. Then he returned her smile with one of his own, and a solemn nod that might as well have been a bow.

"Miss Zellaby," he said. "Of course."

I made sure to wave at the people who'd been smirking as we followed the concierge across the lobby to the elevators. Mysteriously, none of them waved back.

Oh, well.

"Your room has been kept for you as always, Miss Zellaby," said the man, an almost fawning note in his voice as he opened the door on a hotel room almost as large as the first floor of our house. Sarah entered behind him, a serene smile on her face. This was what nature had designed her to do, after all; bend the world and the wills of the people around her to her own ends. She'd be sorry later, and we'd be right here to calm her down, remind her that she'd done this on our behalf, and she hadn't gone for the man expecting to be given the President's Suite. She'd just wanted one of the rooms they held for visiting executives.

It wasn't her fault the hotel had let out every room that had a price tag in the system in order to accommodate the con-goers. And it wasn't her fault that we were all going to have private bedrooms in our "hotel room," but I was sure happy about not needing to sleep three feet away from my sister, who was *not* one of nature's morning people.

Nor was she with us, having commandeered a bell cart and gone to help Artie with the luggage. It let her keep the secrets of her suitcase a little longer, but since it meant she'd have effectively last choice of beds, I wasn't even annoyed. Sarah was speaking to the man from the hotel, her voice low and her eyes glowing. She touched his hand.

He smiled at her, paternal and familiar, and I knew a switch had just flipped somewhere deep inside his mind that would have him seeing her as family for the rest of his life. Or until she flipped it back, assuming she got the opportunity. We could be leaving here in a serious hurry.

Well, if she couldn't undo what she'd done, it wasn't like it was going to hurt him. Or at least it wasn't going to hurt him much. Narrow edge cases don't provide a lot of opportunity for damage. And if I kept telling myself that, I wouldn't have to think too hard about the ethical implications of using a telepath to get what we wanted.

The man patted Sarah on the shoulder and turned to go, leaving us alone with this deluxe suite that wasn't even listed as available for lease in their computer system. This was the kind of space meant to be used for politicians, celebrities, and visiting hotel chain presidents, who would never experience their own services the way the rest of us normally did. Maybe they would have made some changes if they did.

The door shut. I put my backpack down, announcing, "The coast, as they say in the movies, is clear."

Mice came boiling out, scampering under furniture and up the legs of tables, finding traction with their tiny claws as they began exploring their new space. I decided to do the same, pushing open doors and poking my head into rooms as I determined just how big this hotel sky palace really was.

The first two doors were bedrooms, both bigger than my room at home, both containing two queen-sized beds. I had been expecting Sarah to negotiate us a room the size of one of these, for the four of us to share.

When I saw that one of the rooms had a private bathroom, I declared, "I'm sleeping in here!" and flung myself onto the bed closer to the door.

"Okay!" called Sarah.

The bed was comfortable, thick and plush in that way that only top-end hotel beds ever seem to manage. They don't get used enough to wear down the way a normal person's bed will. I closed my eyes, dimly aware that if I didn't get up, I was going to fall asleep and Verity was going to make fun of me for it. Especially since she wouldn't have to wake me to use the shower.

Get up . . . get up . . . get up. The pillow was exactly firm enough to keep me from rolling off of it. The thought of moving was becoming less appealing by the second.

The main door opened, hard enough that I heard it hit the wall. "Holy *crap*," exclaimed Verity. "This isn't a hotel room. It's a luxury apartment!"

I sat up, shoving my hair out of my eyes.

The baggage cart rattled as they navigated it into the room, and Artie grunted. "Jeez, Very, did you bring a bunch of bricks to the convention, or is this all lead pipes?"

"Which room's mine?"

"I see you're still not answering my question."

"I'll take this one—oh." Verity appeared in the doorway of my chosen room, dragging her suitcase behind her. "Hi, Annie. You cool with me sleeping in here?"

"No." It was impossible to keep the affronted younger sister whine from my voice. "I already called it."

She frowned but didn't argue. "Well, there's enough rooms for us all," she said, in a tone that clearly indicated I had already taken the best one. She vanished from the doorway. I felt a momentary ping of guilt, and squashed it as quickly as I could. Me taking first pick of rooms wasn't going to ruin her life, especially not when she was the one who had insisted on going to the car to get the bags. She was the one who was hiding something, not me.

And I was just making excuses to not be unhappy about telling my sister "no." I sighed and slipped off the bed, once again fully awake as I made my way to the central room to check on the others and retrieve my own bag.

I wasn't worried about Verity sneaking in to steal "my" room while I was out of it. We all learned early not to pull that sort of thing, since Alex always had snakes around and Verity would scream like a banshee if anyone touched her stuff, and I liked setting snares by the time I turned five. We knew to respect one another's space.

Artie and Sarah were still unloading the bell cart, with the "help" of the Aeslin mice, who had swarmed onto the lid of the cooler and were hailing every movement my cousins made. Artie looked flustered. I grimaced sympathetically.

"Lobby bad?"

"Lobby filled with people, Sarah up here with you," he said, in a grim tone. "I am not leaving this room without her until it's time to go home."

"That's completely fair," I said. At least he was still willing to leave the room. "We should all be able to have our own rooms here, and there are three bathrooms according to the map on the back of the door. One of them's en suite to my room, the other two are public."

"I only saw one," said Sarah.

"The third one's off the kitchen, and please no one poop there," reported Verity, emerging from the hall. "This place is *ridiculous*. Makes me wish we were the kind of people who lived our lives on social media."

"I think if we started posting pictures of a hotel room that's not available to the public, the people who own the place would figure out that something was up, and Keith would get in trouble for letting us in here," said Sarah.

It took me a beat to realize that Keith was the man from the VIP desk. It had already been a long day, and it was just getting started. "Anyone need to eat or nap or anything else like that?" I asked. "Because the show floor opens in an hour, and we should get down there to join the queue as soon as we possibly can."

"I need a shower," said Artie. "I can't put on more cologne until I wash off what I'm already wearing, and this stuff has lost most of its stink."

"I assure you, it has not."

"You weren't in the lobby just now."

"Oh, we are going to be the most popular people at this nerd prom," said Verity. "Whatever. We have enough showers that only one of us will have to wait, and it's not going to be me." She waved as she sauntered back down the hall.

Sarah turned to look at me. "Don't start."

"I didn't!"

"You were about to."

I didn't protest a second time. Living with a telepath means knowing when to pick your battles. "Fine," I said. "I'm going to go change."

"Me, too," said Sarah.

Artie shook his head and turned to head for the bathroom.

We scattered.

I emerged from "my" bedroom in khaki and canvas, hair pulled back into a single braid. Full Lara Croft genericism. Was I dressed as the eponymous raider of tombs, or was I an archeologist from some lesser-known franchise? Well, that was anyone's guess, now, wasn't it? It was something I'd been able to put together with pieces I already owned that didn't require me to wear uncomfortable shoes, and that was what really mattered.

Artie, freshly showered and hair still damp, was sitting on the couch. He'd changed his hoodie, T-shirt, and jeans for . . . another hoodie, T-shirt, and jeans. Very fancy. I vaulted the back, thudding down next to him, and stuck my hand out. He raised an eyebrow. I smiled winsomely.

"We're not *all* telepathic, you know," he said, finally relenting and producing my badge from the inside pocket of his hoodie. I beamed as I took it out of his hand.

"That's probably for the best, all things considered," I said. "I don't think we'd all be friends if we could hear what we were thinking about each other. I don't know how Sarah does it."

"She tries not to take things personally unless we say them out loud, and she does her best to be so unassuming that we can't hate her."

"That's sort of sad." The badge was attached to a lanyard that looped over my head, hanging almost to my navel. I wrinkled my nose. "Aren't they afraid these will get caught on things?"

"It's cheap and efficient and people can sell you more expensive fancy lanyards," said Artie. "I think if it seems inconvenient, that's at least intentional."

"Huh." I gave the lanyard another thoughtful look. "You ready?"

"As I'll ever be." He took a deep breath. "If Sarah can't keep me from being swarmed—"

"She'll walk you back over here, and you can text me your shopping list."

"And you won't try to argue."

"I won't, although I'm really hoping we can make this work. If you can spot empathic disruption in the crowd . . ."

"We'll be able to intervene a lot faster than if you have to watch for visible disruptions," finished Artie. "I know. And the faster we do this, the fewer people potentially get hurt. I understand all of that. It doesn't keep me from being nervous about going out around that many strangers. I don't want to deal."

"But you have to deal occasionally. At least this way you're doing it with people to back you up."

Artie lifted an eyebrow as he looked at me. "If your next technique is going to be claiming that this is a controlled situation, you clearly slipped in the shower and smacked your head. This is about as far as it gets from a controlled situation. This is a chaos situation."

"Good thing I like chaos theory," said Sarah, joining us. She was wearing long brown-and-cream robes, belted at the waist.

"You make a lovely Jedi," I informed her.

She beamed. "If I'm going to be Jedi mind-tricking my way through the con, I might as well have fun with it."

"Any sign of Verity?"

Her smile faded into a grimace. "She was out of the shower when I passed," she said.

"Sarah . . ."

"Just give her a minute. It's not like we set an alarm or anything."

"Fine." I leaned back in the couch. "This is a nice room."

They made vague noises of agreement before we settled into a companionable silence that only lasted about five minutes before the clack of heels on the faux wood of the hall alerted us to Verity's approach. I sat up straighter.

Unlike the rest of us, she hadn't gotten the memo about the comfortable shoes. I was reasonably sure that if I even *thought* about wearing heels that high, one of my ankles would spontaneously break. There was also a decent chance that there was more fabric in her shoes than in the rest of her outfit put together. I wasn't sure "mini dress" was the appropriate way to describe it. I wasn't even sure "long shirt" was accurate.

Whatever it was, it managed to be sparkly and covered in fringe at the same time, all of it pristine silver and shaking with the motion of her body. Her eyeshadow and the gel she'd worked into her hair matched. I blinked.

"No," I said, once I found my voice.

Verity raised an eyebrow. "No?" she echoed.

"No."

"Why no? Mom and Dad let me wear less than this

on television, and judging by the sidewalks we passed coming in here, I won't even stand out all that much."

"Those shoes are going to *kill* your feet."

"These? I can dance in these for hours." She looked at me defiantly. "I'll be fine."

At least she couldn't be trying to smuggle too many guns in that dress, which would run out of space after one or two. I sighed and got off the couch. Sarah and Artie followed. "When in doubt, stand next to the target, not in front of it," I said. "Artie, give her her badge."

Verity wrinkled her nose at the lanyard, but slipped it over her head.

"Everyone got their keys and their phones?" I asked. Everyone nodded, except for Sarah, who didn't need a phone to stay in communication. "Great. Let's go." I grabbed my backpack as I levered myself off the couch, confident that it would already contain at least one mouse. They knew what it sounded like when their people were getting ready to move.

We funneled out of the hotel room in an untidy mob more than a group, not quite shoving for position. Verity was as good at walking in her ridiculous heels as she had implied. I didn't understand the physics of it one little bit.

She glanced at me as we walked. "Lara Croft?"

"Generic action movie archeologist. I brought my derby gear for tomorrow, but since it has my name across the back of my jersey, it's not so great for staying anonymous." Sure, the name it had was "Final Girl," and in no way connected to my real name or identity, but it was still an identifier.

"Huh," she said. "And what's Sarah?"

I blinked slowly. "Please tell me you're messing with me right now, and you can recognize a Jedi on sight. From *Star Wars*? You know, one of the biggest media franchises in history?"

We had reached the elevator lobby. The one downside of being in the ultra-special, "you can't touch this" housing: we were at the top of the hotel tower. Even before the con properly got underway, the elevator was moving like molasses. It wasn't going to get better from here.

On the plus side, when the doors finally *did* open, the elevator was empty. Artie was the first one to get on, promptly plastering himself in the farthest corner, back to the wall. Sarah stepped in front of him, blocking him from the rest of the car in a way that would have been comic if he hadn't looked so scared. For the first time, I felt a little bad about insisting he come with us, even though his empathy really was the key to finding our siren before someone else could get hurt.

People aren't tools. Life isn't like putting together a D&D party. You can't just say "we need a cleric" and force somebody to play one. By insisting that Artie leave his basement and come to a place with this many people he didn't already know and trust, I'd been being just as bad as Verity. Thinking of myself and what I needed—to get into the field, to prove to my family that I was ready, and most of all, to do it in a setting that was comfortable and familiar to me, rather than one where I'd have to struggle to understand the social hierarchy and its cues—rather than what my allies needed. I needed Verity to keep a lower profile. Artie needed to be allowed to stay safely home.

There wasn't time to deal with the realization before the elevator doors were sliding closed. I pressed the button for the lobby, watching my reflection as we started to descend.

Sarah touched my wrist. I glanced at her, and she nodded, very slightly. Spending time with a telepath means your epiphanies are never as private as you think they are. But she looked like she approved, and that was better than the alternative. I nodded back, and returned my attention to the doors.

We were almost to the lobby when we slowed and the doors opened again, revealing a small group of comic fans in the allegiance-declaring T-shirts endemic to the breed. They blinked at us. We looked coolly back, not shuffling to the side.

"We'll, uh. We'll take the next one," said the man I assumed was their leader. They stepped back. The doors closed again.

"It worked," said Sarah brightly. I glanced at her. She beamed. "I told them the elevator was full, and they believed me."

"Cool." That fell well within the standard scope of cuckoo abilities. No one ever sits next to Sarah on the bus unless she wants them to. Artie seemed to relax a little, taking this as a sign of things to come. I smiled at my reflection. This was all going to be okay.

Then the elevator doors opened again, revealing a lobby jammed wall to wall with people, most of them in varying degrees of nerd formal, from the graphic T-shirts we'd seen on the comic collectors upstairs to dresses with a slightly more subtle print—one woman was covered in cobwebs and Black Widow logo stamps, while another was blazoned with half a dozen different Harry Potter icons—and finally to full-on cosplay that varied in complexity from our relatively simple efforts to what looked like a functional mecha suit.

"Welcome to nerd heaven," I breathed.

We stepped out of the elevator, Artie sticking close to Sarah's side, and no one gave any of us a second look. Scratch that—several people looked twice at Verity, or more than twice, which made a certain amount of sense, given that she was dressed like a Silver Age pinup, and every strike of her heels against the tiled lobby floor echoed like the cracking of a whip.

"Ignore them," she said, and kept moving with the rest of the group. I blinked. It wasn't like my sister to turn down adulation freely offered. It all started making sense a moment later, when she continued, "There will be a lot more people in the convention center, and some of them will want pictures."

"Nothing that attracts too much attention," I stressed.

Artie laughed. Verity shot him an annoyed look.

"I know how to be unobtrusive," she said.

"Says the woman who's dressed as a disco ball." The hotel doors connected to the sidewalk, and as soon as we were outside, we could see the glassed-in walls of the convention center, and the throng of bodies forming around it. My heart hitched. We were almost there. I had been dreaming of this for so long, and now . . .

We were almost there.

Men in security uniforms stood at the doors to the convention center, checking badges before letting people inside. All of ours passed muster easily, being fully genuine. (Unlike our hotel room, no one had been cheated out of anything. Artie had simply convinced the online registration system that we were supposed to be sent complimentary passes, which he had directed to the comic book store where he and Sarah kept their pull boxes. Our address had never entered the equation, and we hadn't stolen anything from anyone.)

Once inside, we joined the queue to go through the metal detectors. Verity eyed the plain white rectangles, then gave me a baleful look. I shrugged.

"It was all on the website," I said.

"Sure." She turned to Sarah. "Can I borrow part of your backpack?" she asked.

"Sure," Sarah echoed, and slipped her backpack off, holding it open for Verity to divest herself into. Verity reached up under her dress, producing a small handgun and three knives, all of which she dropped into the bag while Sarah's body blocked it from the view of the watching guards. When this was done, Sarah slung the bag over her shoulder as the rest of us joined the line. She didn't. She just looked casually around, then walked in an easy half-loop past the security checkpoint, waiting for us on the other side. No one stopped her, or even appeared to notice that she was there. That was her cuckoo camouflage at work.

Artie was already starting to shift from foot to foot, anxious. It would have looked like codependence in a human couple, but since I knew he was using her for psychic cover, it was easy to understand the source of his tension. I put a hand on his shoulder and squeezed, trying to offer him a little reassurance. He flashed me a quick, tight smile as the line moved forward.

"Could've made sure I saw the thing about the metal detectors," muttered Verity.

"I thought Sarah had told you," I said. "Did she not mention security at all?"

"She said there would be guards on the doors and random badge checks, but I stopped listening after that. This is a bunch of comic nerds all getting together to be nerds in the same place, with sequins. How much security could they really need?"

"Nerds are still people, and people do stupid shit." Like admit that they stopped listening when someone was trying to explain an event's security protocols. "We've had a few people try to smuggle real weapons in, and there's always the cosplayer who thinks that for some reason, the rules about peace bonding don't apply to them."

"Huh," said Verity.

We had been moving forward as we talked, and it was Artie's turn to empty his pockets and walk through the metal detector. He dropped his backpack on the table, following it with his phone, keys, and wallet, before stepping through. Nothing beeped or alarmed, and the guard who poked through his bag rang no warning bells. Artie reclaimed his things and moved to stand next to Sarah.

Two down, two to go. Verity was the next through, and thanks to her little divestment into Sarah's bag, she walked through without a hitch.

When I stepped into the empty doorframe, however, it beeped.

"It's my underwire," I said, trying to sound bored with the whole process. I spread my arms to let the guard wand me. He looked nervous. "Come on, you've encountered bras before, haven't you?"

"Um."

"Sometimes people with larger breasts need more support. When that happens, metal wires are placed inside the structure of our undergarments, and those wires can result in false positives from security systems like this one." People behind me were starting to grumble at the delay. Verity had her hand over her mouth, covering what I was certain was a snicker. I wasn't embarrassed. I was *pissed*.

"Well? Wand me!"

He waved his wand vaguely in the direction of my breasts. As expected, it beeped and whined when it encountered the underwire, which was possibly a little more robust than standard, thanks to the needle-thin lockpicks also tucked into the fabric. He ran the wand over the rest of my body. Nothing else alarmed. The beauty of ceramic knives. Good ones are expensive as hell, but wow do they make up for it with the ability to carry them easily past security checkpoints.

"Sorry, um, miss," he said, lowering his wand. "You're clear to go."

"Thank you." I grabbed my backpack, glad they lacked a proper X-ray machine—the mice knew how to hide from hands digging through the bag, and since these guards were almost certainly not being paid enough to grab for motion if they felt it, there had been no real risk of their discovery, whereas an X-ray would have revealed a bunch of tiny rodent skeletons where none belonged—and marched over to the others. Verity gave me an amused look.

"Your underwire? Really?"

"Puberty was kind to some of us," I said, and started for the escalator that would take us to the second floor.

The trouble with sisters is that we know where all the buttons are and exactly how to push them. I don't think any of us will ever forget Verity's epic meltdown the first time I bought a bra bigger than hers. She'd been convinced that it was somehow like me getting a bigger bedroom or a bigger allowance, not like me having a harder time in hand-to-hand combat due to suddenly coming equipped with a pair of handgrips for anyone who didn't care about being punched in the face immediately afterward.

She huffed and followed me, the four of us merging seamlessly with the surging crowd. I couldn't have named every fandom I saw represented, or even made a decent starting guess at how many of these people were human. Big media conventions are sort of like Halloween: put that much latex and face paint into play and species ceases to matter quite as much. No one knows your skin tone is more gray than would be healthy for a human when you've painted yourself blue, after all. Truly nonhumanoid cryptids were still blocked from public life, but with some of the advancements I'd seen in cosplay props and designs, they wouldn't stay that way much longer.

The walls were festooned with banners advertising various aspects of the convention, all clearly paid for by the highest bidders, and more hung suspended from the ceiling, some of the largest, loudest declarations of geek pride that I'd ever seen. I stopped thinking about arguing with my sister and focused on my surroundings, trying to drink it all in. From the smell of fresh-baked bread drifting out of the Subway near the escalators to the buzz of so many voices that there were no words, just a dull, continuous roar. Occasionally, a laugh or squeal of delight would rise above the rest, but mostly, it was all background.

The queue split at the top of the escalators, half wrapping around past the Subway to head for the open doors of the show floor, the other half heading toward the program rooms.

"Okay," I said, stepping off to the side before the crowd could sweep us away. "This is where we split the party. We can't split up Sarah and Artie—"

"No, you can't," said Artie. He sounded harried but not panicked. Sarah's low-grade "don't notice us, we are not here" field was clearly working. I knew it was still low-grade because her eyes weren't glowing and people weren't trying to walk through us. She was just a cuckoo, doing what a cuckoo did.

Sometimes it's unnerving to be reminded that we could be surrounded by functionally invisible telepathic ambush predators at all times. Other times, it's oddly comforting. As long as there are cuckoos in the world, there's still going to be a need for people like us. Job security doesn't come from a safe world.

"Which means Verity and I will take the front half of the show floor, and you two take the back," I said.

Sarah nodded, looking relieved. "That sounds reasonable," she said, slipping her hand into the crook of Artie's arm, tugging him with her, away from us, toward the mouth of the show floor.

Verity gave me a quizzical look. "I thought you'd never been here before."

"Do you go to a dance competition without looking up everything you can about the venue?" I spread my arms, indicating the convention center around us. "They publish maps online. The show floor here isn't like the one in San Diego, which is basically a giant airplane hangar. This one is more like a sideways capital 'H.' Two floors, supposedly both equal, separated by a skybridge. But all the really big companies, the ones that sell convention exclusives and wind up with huge crowds, are on the front half of the show floor."

"Meaning you just sent them to the less-populated half," said Verity.

"Exactly." I started walking, heading for the open door. "They can dig in the old comic books and look at vintage toys and keep their minds open for signs of our siren. She's probably affiliated with a vendor, if she's not one of the professionals who travels with the convention circuit."

"You don't think she is, do you?"

"No. The incidents are centered around the conventions, meaning the perpetrator has to be moving with the shows, but most cryptids are smart enough to know rule number one." Don't shit where you eat. It's a universal proverb, regardless of species.

Verity nodded. "And you don't think it's an attendee because . . . ?"

"Too consistent. These conventions normally cost *bank*. Ignoring the fact that we're literally staying in a hotel room that money can't buy, all the local hotels put up their rack rates when a con's coming to town. So room alone can set you back two, three thousand dollars. It's like paying for a trip to Lowryland. For someone to be doing this on their own dime and attending even just as many shows as have had a confirmed incident, they'd need to be independently wealthy."

More than a few sirens are what humans would classify as "filthy rich," thanks to having an entire ocean full of shipwrecks ready and waiting for them to loot. But those families who've managed to collect enough filthy lucre to afford something like this have also spent enough time coexisting with humanity to be discreet. Any siren with the funds to do this sort of thing wouldn't do it in the first place, out of fear that their family would make them pay for it.

"So we're looking for someone who gets paid to be here," said Verity. Her tone was thoughtful, and so I didn't reply with anything snarky. We were getting along, if only for a heartbeat. I didn't want to get in the way of this miraculous occasion.

"Uh-huh." I held up my badge, showing it to the guards on the door. They barely looked at it—definitely not long enough to verify that it wasn't counterfeit—before waving us on. Verity paced me, keeping up surprisingly well in her ridiculous heels, and the show floor opened in front of us like Wonka's famed chocolate factory.

Verity blinked, apparently taken aback. "This is . . . this . . ."

"Pretty cool, huh?" The nearest vendor was one I recognized from the smaller Portland cons, selling socks in a variety of nerd colorways. Blue-and-white stripes doesn't mean "geek" the way a Storm Trooper outfit does, but anyone inside the community would easily identify it as a nod to the TARDIS.

"This is *ridiculous*," she declared, spreading her arms. "How is there so *much*? How are we supposed to find one person we don't know how to identify when there's so *much*?"

"Age of the geek," I said, and plunged in.

An hour later, I was starting to understand her point of view.

Two hours later, I was starting to share it.

Sirens can have any hair color found in humans, as well as green, blue, purple, and a variety of shocking oranges and yellows. Thanks to the rise of fashion colors and dyes that don't damage the cuticle, humans can have all those hair colors, too, and while the eyelashes and eyebrows would betray someone whose natural hair color was aquamarine or electric orange or the like, getting close enough to check people's nose hairs wasn't as easy as it sounds. Still, we kept pushing onward, moving methodically through the space, stopping at every vendor to peer at their wares as a cover for seeking our siren.

Two hours had been long enough to bring the skybridge into view. That was good. It was also long enough that some of the booths had started to rotate through their staff, letting people go on well-deserved breaks rather than forcing them to stay on duty forever. That was bad. If we walked this whole show floor only to miss our siren by five minutes, I was going to be . . .

Well. I was going to be blissfully unaware. But if I ever found out, I was going to be *pissed*.

"My feet hurt," said Verity.

"Not my problem."

"It will be if I get blisters and start bleeding."

"Cry me a river. The rest of us wore shoes that didn't chew holes in our feet."

Verity huffed. I looked at her and shrugged.

"I told you to wear comfortable footwear," I said, and kept moving.

Maybe I was hitting the point of petty and a little bit mean, but I was also exhausted, and she was the one who'd insisted on infiltrating my first real shot at field work. This wasn't my fault. This wasn't—

The soft hum of "there is a telepath nearby" got suddenly louder, followed by the sound of Sarah's mental voice declaring, *Artie just tried to grab a girl, I think you need to get over here,* accompanied by the image of one of the lane identification signs.

I glanced at Verity. "Did you get that?"

She nodded grimly.

"Can you run in those shoes?"

She nodded again.

We started moving. Not quite at a run, which could have gotten us booted from the show floor by con security, but at a solid power walk. Verity's heels announced our presence and somehow the sound, sharp and steady, was enough to clear us a reasonably wide path through the crowd. I guess there are benefits to being Ballroom Barbie after all. A few people turned to watch us as we passed, but most just seemed to assume that we were paid cosplayers with someplace to be, and let us go.

The show floor, despite being huge, was clearly labeled, with each aisle marked by a hanging banner that told us exactly where we were. The number Sarah had flashed us was toward the back of the hall, and matched up with the direction of her ongoing telepathic signal. We rushed in that direction.

What came into view was a large secondhand toy vendor, one who seemed devoted to the idea that they could replicate the cramped, claustrophobic vintage shop experience by creating a maze of wire shelves held together with zip ties. It looked like a surprisingly structurally sound place to buy thirdhand Transformers and restored My Little Ponies, and far less hygienic than eBay. Probably more expensive, too. Normally, I'm all about buying local when I can, but it's hard to extend that philosophy to people who want to charge twenty dollars for a vintage Care Bear.

Sarah was standing on the other side of the aisle, eyes blazing, holding onto Artie's arm as he glared daggers at the booth. Good. We had our target, then, and that meant we were almost done with the work part of this trip.

"Hey," I greeted, once we were close enough not to need to shout. "What's good?"

Sarah nodded toward the booth. I followed the direction of the gesture. There were two staffers on duty, their vendor badges clearly distinguishing them from the largely disinterested day one shoppers. When you're on a fixed budget, you wait until later in the weekend to spend it.

One of the staffers was male, brown hair, brown beard. Being male didn't mean he wasn't our siren—it's a gender-neutral term—but the beard did. Dyed beards are always obvious, and his was natural. The other was a young woman, maybe my age, with vibrantly turquoise hair.

Jackpot.

I waited until the two of them had some distance between them, then made my way over to the booth and positioned myself in front of her. She started to smile. "Hello, and welcome to Time's Treasures," she said, clearly a practiced sales pitch.

"Hi," I said cheerfully. "So hey, did you drown all those people on purpose, or are you still not very good at controlling yourself?"

Subtle is for other people.

The siren's eyes went wide, even as her skin went pale and I heard the clack of Verity positioning herself behind me.

Subtle is for other people, but even when faced with my specific brand of blunt-force trauma, some people still try to bluff. "I don't know—I don't know what you're talking about," said the siren.

"Yes, you do," said Sarah, joining Verity at my back.

The siren looked at her and screamed.

It was a panicked, piercing sound, and heads turned all around us. A few people started to move toward the booth. I leaned forward, smiling so as to show every tooth in my head. I have good teeth. Genetics plus early dental care plus fluoride in the water has left me with dentition designed to rip out throats.

"Stop screaming and play it off as a laugh," I said, voice low. "Yes, she's a cuckoo. She's with us. I think you're one of the last people in this building who should be attracting attention right now, don't you?"

The siren stopped screaming. Her laugh was obviously forced, but it was better than nothing. The people who'd been approaching stopped, looking puzzled, before they shook their heads and turned away. So she hadn't been startled enough by the sudden appearance of a cuckoo to avoid putting a hint of compulsion in her scream. I did wonder why I hadn't heard it.

My family has always been oddly resistant to compulsion, whether it be cuckoos rewriting the world or Lilu forcing attraction. That resistance was part of what originally attracted my Uncle Ted to my Aunt Jane, who was the first woman he'd met in a long time who didn't throw herself at him, sighing, the moment he walked into a room. Sometimes, a little resistance can go a long way.

"Who *are* you?" asked the siren, eyeing me.

"My name is less important than why I'm here," I replied. "You've been killing people at these shows. Did you do it on purpose?"

"You should hear the things they say about girls like me." She looked past me, presumably to Verity. "Girls like *us*. When they think we can't hear them, they go to these dark, disgusting places, and they *stay there*."

"Being a creepy fucker doesn't justify drowning someone. I kinda wish it did sometimes, but it doesn't. Believe me, I can relate," said Sarah. "The things people *think* about me make me want to wash until the skin comes off. That doesn't mean I do it. And it doesn't mean I drown anyone."

The siren looked at her with narrowed eyes, and then back to me. "You're hanging out with a cuckoo and— and that's your Lilu over there, isn't it? And you don't look even a little worried. You're Prices, aren't you?"

Sometimes name recognition is annoying. Verity took it in stride, sliding into the gap in the conversation with a blunt, "So what if we are? You're hunting on our turf."

"I'm *working*," snapped the siren. "Not all of us are lucky enough to be the cryptozoological equivalent of the Hiltons. Some of us have to hold down jobs, and I'd like you to let me do mine."

"Ours is getting you to stop drowning people. One way or another." I managed to make that not sound entirely like a threat, even though it sort of was.

The siren frowned at me. "Make them stop being gross."

"Being gross is not punishable with murder," I said. Sirens aren't sarcophages like ghouls, or even predators like waheela. She could live a long and happy life without killing anyone else.

"Says you," said the siren.

"Not a good road to start down," said Sarah. "Since some of us think murdering people is pretty gross."

Since the siren seemed to be deep in conversation with potential customers, her coworker only glanced at us occasionally, otherwise focusing on smiling and trying to attract people to the booth. She looked at him and sighed.

"I can promise not to tell anyone to go and jump in the ocean today," she said.

"Great," I said. "Meet us in the Hilton lobby at six." She looked perplexed. I smiled and shrugged.

"We're having dinner."

We crashed back into our hotel room like a very small, very tired invading army. I made straight for the couch, collapsing across it. Artie was right behind me. Verity paused to kick her shoes off and rub her poor, abused feet one-handed, looking annoyed.

Only Sarah didn't immediately collapse. She beamed, bouncing on her toes in excitement. "It worked!" she squeaked. "We played dowsing rod and we *found* the *siren* and no one bothered Artie, and it worked!"

Artie lifted his head and shot her a weary smile. "It did. It definitely worked."

"And tomorrow, we can do it again! But longer!"

Even I groaned at that, fumbling until I found a throw pillow to throw at her. It hit her in the chest, bouncing off harmlessly. Sarah blinked.

"What did I say?"

Verity staggered, barefoot, over to join us on the couch. "How is shopping this exhausting?" she demanded.

"Nerds are hardcore," said Artie, letting his head flop back against the pillows.

Verity nudged me with her elbow. "You really think just *talking* to a siren will make her stop?"

"We may have to push a little," I admitted. "But if she's been lashing out because she felt threatened by dudes being creepy, there are things that can be done. We can give her other options."

Verity nodded thoughtfully. If the siren wasn't actively malicious, killing her wasn't on the table; yes, she was a killer, but she was also a member of an endangered species. If we could make her stop, that was better than reducing the gene pool any more than it had already been reduced. It was terrible math, incredibly unkind to the families of the men she'd convinced to drown themselves.

It was also a form of paying restitution to the sirens for all their own who had died at Covenant hands, and never threatened anyone. Sometimes there weren't cheap or easy answers.

"Verity." I nudged her with my knee. "Very. You need to go put pants on before dinner."

She grunted and levered herself off the couch, staggering off toward her room.

"And wear better shoes!" I called.

She flipped me off and kept walking.

"Come on, you two." I poked Artie. "Let's go deal with our siren. This way we can enjoy the next three days of the convention."

On the table, the mice cheered.

Sarah hit me with a pillow.

**Price Family Field Guide
to the Cryptids of North America
Updated and Expanded Edition**

Aeslin mice (Apodemus sapiens). Sapient, rodentlike cryptids which present as near-identical to non-cryptid field mice. Aeslin mice crave religion, and will attach themselves to "divine figures" selected virtually at random when a new colony is created. They possess perfect recall; each colony maintains a detailed oral history going back to its inception. Origins unknown.

Basilisk (Procompsognathus basilisk). Venomous, feathered saurians approximately the size of a large chicken. This would be bad enough, but thanks to a quirk of evolution, the gaze of a basilisk causes petrification, turning living flesh to stone. Basilisks are not native to North America, but were imported as game animals. By idiots.

Bogeyman (Vestiarium sapiens). The thing in your closet is probably a very pleasant individual who simply has issues with direct sunlight. Probably. Bogeymen are close relatives of the human race; they just happen to be almost purely nocturnal, with excellent night vision, and a fondness for enclosed spaces. They rarely grab the ankles of small children, unless it's funny.

Chupacabra (Chupacabra sapiens). True to folklore, chupacabra are blood-suckers, with stomachs that do not handle solids well. They are also therianthrope shapeshifters, capable of transforming themselves into human form, which explains why they have never been captured. When cornered, most chupacabra will assume their bipedal shape in self-defense. A surprising number of chupacabra are involved in ballroom dance.

Dragon (Draconem sapiens). Dragons are essentially winged, fire-breathing dinosaurs the size of Greyhound buses. At least, the males are. The females are attractive humanoids who can blend seamlessly in a crowd of supermodels, and outnumber the males twenty to one. Females are capable of parthenogenic reproduction and can sustain their population for centuries without outside help. All dragons, male and female, require gold to live, and collect it constantly.

Ghoul (Herophilus sapiens). The ghoul is an obligate carnivore, incapable of digesting any but the simplest vegetable solids, and prefers humans because of their wide selection of dietary nutrients. Most ghouls are carrion eaters. Ghouls can be easily identified by their teeth, which will be shed and replaced repeatedly over the course of a lifetime.

Hidebehind (Aphanes apokryphos). We don't really know much about the hidebehinds: no one's ever seen them. They're excellent illusionists, and we think they're bipeds, which means they're probably mammals. Probably.

Jackalope (Parcervus antelope). Essentially large jack-rabbits with antelope antlers, the jackalope is a staple of the American West, and stuffed examples can be found in junk shops and kitschy restaurants all across the country. Most of the taxidermy is fake. Some, however, is not. The jackalope was once extremely common, and has been shot, stuffed, and harried to near-extinction. They're relatively harmless, and they taste great.

Johrlac (Johrlac psychidolos). Colloquially known as "cuckoos," the Johrlac are telepathic ambush predators. They appear human, but are internally very different, being cold-blooded and possessing a decentralized circulatory system. This quirk of biology means they can be shot repeatedly in the chest without being killed. Extremely dangerous. All Johrlac are interested in mathematics, sometimes to the point of obsession. Origins unknown; possibly insect in nature.

Laidly worm (Draconem laidly). Very little is known about these close relatives of the dragons. They present similar but presumably not identical sexual dimorphism; no currently living males have been located.

Lamia (Python lamia). Semi-hominid cryptids with the upper bodies of humans and the lower bodies of snakes. Lamia are members of order synapsedia, the mammal-like reptiles, and are considered responsible for many of the "great snake" sightings of legend. The sightings not attributed to actual great snakes, that is.

Lesser gorgon (Gorgos euryale). One of three known subspecies of gorgon, the lesser gorgon's gaze causes short-term paralysis followed by death in anything under five pounds. The bite of the snakes atop their heads will cause paralysis followed by death in anything smaller than an elephant if not treated with the appropriate antivenin. Lesser gorgons tend to be very polite, especially to people who like snakes.

Lilu (Lilu sapiens). Due to the striking dissimilarity of their abilities, male and female Lilu are often treated as two individual species: incubi and succubi. Incubi are empathic; succubi are persuasive telepaths. Both exude strong pheromones inspiring feelings of attraction and lust in the opposite sex. This can be a problem for incubi like our cousin Artie, who mostly wants to be left alone, or succubi like our cousin Elsie, who gets very tired of men hitting on her while she's trying to flirt with their girlfriends.

Madhura (Homo madhurata). Humanoid cryptids with an affinity for sugar in all forms. Vegetarian. Their presence slows the decay of organic matter, and is usually viewed as lucky by everyone except the local dentist. Madhura are very family-oriented, and are rarely found living on their own. Originally from the Indian subcontinent.

Manananggal (Tanggal geminus). If the manananggal is proof of anything, it is that Nature abhors a logical classification system. We're reasonably sure the manananggal are mammals; everything else is anyone's guess. They're hermaphroditic and capable of splitting their upper and lower bodies, although they are a single entity, and killing the lower half kills the upper half as well. They prefer fetal tissue, or the flesh of newborn infants. They are also venomous, as we have recently discovered. Do not engage if you can help it.

Oread (Nymphae silica). Humanoid cryptids with the approximate skin density of granite. Their actual biological composition is unknown, as no one has ever been able to successfully dissect one. Oreads are extremely strong, and can be dangerous when angered. They seem to have evolved independently across the globe; their common name is from the Greek.

Sasquatch (Gigantopithecus sesquac). These massive native denizens of North America have learned to embrace depilatories and mail-order shoe catalogs. A surprising number make their living as Bigfoot hunters (Bigfeet and Sasquatches are close relatives, and enjoy tormenting each other). They are predominantly vegetarian, and enjoy Canadian television.

Tanuki (Nyctereutes sapiens). Therianthrope shape-shifters from Japan, the Tanuki are critically endangered due to the efforts of the Covenant. Despite this, they remain friendly, helpful people, with a naturally gregarious nature which makes it virtually impossible for them to avoid human settlements. Tanuki possess three primary forms—human, raccoon dog, and big-ass scary monster. Pray you never see the third form of the Tanuki.

Ukupani (Ukupani sapiens). Aquatic therianthropes native to the warm waters of the Pacific Islands, the Ukupani were believed for centuries to be an all-male species, until Thomas Price sat down with several local fishermen and determined that the abnormally large Great White sharks that were often found near Ukupani males were, in actuality, Ukupani females. Female Ukupani can't shapeshift, but can eat people. Happily. They are as intelligent as their shapeshifting mates, because smart sharks are exactly what the ocean needed.

Wadjet (Naja wadjet). Once worshipped as gods, the male wadjet resembles an enormous cobra, capable of reaching seventeen feet in length when fully mature, while the female wadjet resembles an attractive human female. Wadjet pair-bond young, and must spend extended amounts of time together before puberty in order to become immune to one another's venom and be able to successfully mate as adults.

Waheela (Waheela sapiens). Therianthrope shapeshifters from the upper portion of North America, the waheela are a solitary race, usually claiming large swaths of territory and defending it to the death from others of their species. Waheela mating season is best described with the term "bloodbath." Waheela transform into something that looks like a dire bear on steroids. They're usually not hostile, but it's best not to push it.

PLAYLIST

"Instar"....... Nancy Kerr & The Sweet Visitor Band
"Waking Up in Vegas" .... Katy Perry
"Hive Mind"................. They Might Be Giants
"I am the One Who Will Remember
Everything" .... Dar Williams
"I'll Stop the World"............... Modern English
"In Another Life" .... Vienna Tang
"Re: Your Brains"................ Jonathan Coulton
"World Burn"......................... *Mean Girls*
"Kiss With a Fist" .... Florence and the Machine
"My Grand Plan"................ *The Lightning Thief*
"Human Voice" .... *Anna and the Apocalypse*
"Scream"............................... Halestorm
"Fight For Me"............... *Heathers: the Musical*
"The Other Side of Hollywood" .... Cheyanne Wright
"We Know the Way"....................... *Moana*
"Tree on the Hill"............... *The Lightning Thief*
"Not Alone" .... Sara Bareilles
"Ode to an Accidental Stabbing" .... *Evil Dead:*
The Musical
"Blood and Brains".................. Monstersongs
"Divide By Zero" .... Jeff and Maya Bohnhoff
"Sycamore Tree" .... Seanan McGuire

ACKNOWLEDGMENTS

You know, I had so much fun the last time we did this—and left you all at such an awkward spot in the story—that I just had to do it again. This is the second half of my sweet Sarah's story. She and Alice were two of the first characters created for this setting, which is part of why it took me so long to get around to them; I not only needed to know that I was good enough to do them justice, I needed to make sure that everyone else would care about them as much as I did. Based on the responses to *Imaginary Numbers*, I achieved that much of my goal: people do care about what happens to Sarah. Now I just have to hope that I did the same with Alice. We'll find out next year, with *Spelunking Through Hell*.

I still live in the Seattle area, but this year, we were blessedly free of extreme snowfall, meaning we didn't shut down over the winter. That's a good thing in any year, but this year it meant that we didn't go straight from shutdown into lockdown as COVID got rolling and the world ground to a halt. This is the longest in my adult life that I've spent in one city, much less one state! I can't say that I've been enjoying it any more than the rest of y'all have. Thanks to all members of the Machete Squad, for keeping me functional and productive during a time no one could have fully predicted. Without them, I would have climbed a lot more walls and written a lot fewer words.

I did manage to jam some travel in before 2020 shut us all down, most especially spending my birthday (January 5th, for the curious) in New York City on what amounted to basically a whim, seeing multiple Broadway shows, including the closing performance of *The Lightning Thief: The Percy Jackson Musical*, and having a wonderful birthday dinner with my publisher at one of my favorite Manhattan restaurants. I have held onto the memory of that weekend for months, as proof that the world will be good again.

Thanks to Chris Mangum, who maintains the code for my website, while Tara O'Shea, who manages the graphics. The words are all on me, which is why the site is so often out of date. Something's gotta give! Thanks to everyone at DAW, the best home my heart could have, and to the wonderful folks in marketing and publicity at Penguin Random House.

I am so glad to be finishing out Sarah's current stretch of adventuring, and giving the poor girl the rest she's so dearly earned, and I'm even more glad to have all of you here with me to see how it ends. I'm glad to have earned your attention and your trust. They are both very precious, very delicate things, and I treasure them.

Cat update (I know you all live for these): Thomas is still doing very well, and still wearing his snazzy sweaters (which he can remove when he no longer wants the one he has on; I think if he could dress himself, I would be entirely extraneous to needs). Megara remains both incredibly soft and incredibly stupid; she is one of the world's perfect angels, floating through life in a cloud of treats and cuddles. Elsie is queen of the castle, and considers me her personal private property. In 2020, both my mother and I got kittens, Tinkerbell for her and Verity for me, to add a little brightness to the household. Nothing like a global pandemic for socializing new members of the clowder!

And now, gratitude in earnest. Thank you to the people who came out to see me at bookstores and conventions, before those shut down for a little while; to Kate, for being one of the rocks that keeps me solidly anchored; to Sari, for price checking every Pony under the sun; to Michelle Dockrey, for existence and random online commentary; to Chris Mangum, for being here even when it's inconvenient; to Mike and Marnie, for Chicago hospitality, warm cars, and cold hands; and to my dearest Amy McNally, for everything. Thanks to Joe Field at Flying Colors Comics and Other Cool Stuff, for believing in me. And to you: thank you, so much, for reading.

Any errors in this book are my own. The errors that aren't here are the ones that all these people helped me fix. I appreciate it so much.

Let's do some math.

Seanan McGuire
The Ghost Roads

"Hitchhiking ghosts, the unquiet dead, the gods of the old American roads—McGuire enters the company of Lindskold and Gaiman with this book, creating a wistful, funny, fascinating new mythology of diners, corn fields, and proms in this all-in-one-sitting read."　　　　　　　　　　　　　　—Tamora Pierce

SPARROW HILL ROAD
978-0-7564-1440-5

THE GIRL IN THE GREEN SILK GOWN
978-0-7564-1380-4

ANGEL OF THE OVERPASS
978-0-7564-1689-8

"In McGuire's beautifully written second story featuring hitchhiking ghost Rose Marshall, set in the same world as the InCryptid series, Rose must confront her most dangerous foe: Bobby Cross, the immortal who ran her down when she was only 16. . . . This stunning, richly imagined story of love and destiny features an irresistible heroine and is one of the accomplished McGuire's best yet."　　　　—*Publishers Weekly*

To Order Call: 1-800-788-6262
www.dawbooks.com

DAW 144

Seanan McGuire
The October Daye Novels

"A compelling heroine in a secret folklore-filled world that still feels fresh and dangerous after all this time."　　　*—Publishers Weekly*

ROSEMARY AND RUE	978-0-7564-0571-7
A LOCAL HABITATION	978-0-7564-0596-0
AN ARTIFICIAL NIGHT	978-0-7564-0626-4
LATE ECLIPSES	978-0-7564-0666-0
ONE SALT SEA	978-0-7564-0683-7
ASHES OF HONOR	978-0-7564-0749-0
CHIMES AT MIDNIGHT	978-0-7564-0814-5
THE WINTER LONG	978-0-7564-0808-4
A RED-ROSE CHAIN	978-0-7564-0809-1
ONCE BROKEN FAITH	978-0-7564-0810-7
THE BRIGHTEST FELL	978-0-7564-0949-4
NIGHT AND SILENCE	978-0-7564-1038-4
THE UNKINDEST TIDE	978-0-7564-1254-8
A KILLING FROST	978-0-7564-1508-2

To Order Call: 1-800-788-6262
www.dawbooks.com

Tanya Huff

"The Gales are an amazing family, the aunts will strike fear into your heart, and the characters Allie meets are both charming and terrifying."
—#1 *New York Times* bestselling author
Charlaine Harris

"Thoughtful and leisurely, this fresh urban fantasy from Canadian author Huff features an ensemble cast of nuanced characters in Calgary, Alberta.... Fantasy buffs will find plenty of humor, thrills and original mythology to chew on, along with refreshingly three-dimensional women in an original, fully realized world." —*Publishers Weekly*

The Enchantment Emporium
978-0-7564-0605-9

The Wild Ways
978-0-7564-0763-6

The Future Falls
978-0-7564-0754-4

To Order Call: 1-800-788-6262
www.dawbooks.com

DAW 200